HIGH TIME

HANNAH ROTHSCHILD

BLOOMSBURY PUBLISHING

LONDON · OXFORD · NEW YORK · NEW DELHI · SYDNEY

BLOOMSBURY PUBLISHING
Bloomsbury Publishing Plc
50 Bedford Square, London, WC1B 3DP, UK
29 Earlsfort Terrace, Dublin 2, Ireland

BLOOMSBURY, BLOOMSBURY PUBLISHING and the Diana logo
are trademarks of Bloomsbury Publishing Plc

First published in Great Britain, 2023

A catalogue record for this book is available from the British Library

ISBN: HB: 978-1-5266-5685-8; TPB: 978-1-5266-5684-1;
EBOOK: 978-1-5266-5681-0; EPDF: 978-1-5266-5686-5

2 4 6 8 10 9 7 5 3 1

Typeset by Integra Software Services Pvt. Ltd.
Printed and bound in Great Britain by CPI Group (UK) Ltd, Croydon CR0 4YY

To find out more about our authors and books visit www.bloomsbury.com
and sign up for our newsletters.

HIGH TIME

To the treasured sisterhood:

Emmy
Fi
Hen
Lisa
Rosie
&
Milly

January 2016

The men were dumbstruck: coming towards them at great speed was a cartwheeling girl. With each rotation, her golden cowboy boots refracted light from the overhead chandeliers, creating an animated halo around her slender body. Her long limbs were perfectly straight and her hair fanned in an arc around her head. On her last turn, the girl did a flick-flack, landing lightly on both feet in front of them. She was the loveliest either had ever encountered. She had unconventional looks: a heart-shaped face and large tawny eyes fringed by thick lashes. Her skin, the colour of milk, had an inner luminosity and a blush lay like two pale rose petals, spread over slanted cheekbones. Her mouth was a little too luscious; her nose, sprinkled lightly with freckles, was slightly too pronounced. Her hair, the colour of polished conkers, fell below her shoulders in wild curls. It was cold outside, but the apparition wore shorts, a cropped stripy jumper and a chunky golden belt that matched her boots.

'Who are you?' Her voice was soft and husky. Later the men would debate if there'd been a trace of an Irish accent (it was an Indian lilt).

'We're from Plymouth Council and we've come to inspect the new tanks – part of regulation 7685.' He was interrupted by a child who came tearing around the corner, her feet slapping on the wide oak floorboards.

'You did it, you did it!' the little girl shouted.

The cartwheeler laughed.

'Again, again!'

'Maybe after breakfast.' Turning back to the inspectors, the young woman asked, 'Can I help?'

'Yes, can we help?' the little girl mimicked.

'We're looking for Sir Thomlinson and Lady Ayesha Sleet,' said the one in the brown suit. Then, looking the cartwheeler up and down, he added, 'Is your mother around?'

'I am Lady Sleet.'

The men, chastened, shuffled from foot to foot. Ayesha, embarrassed for not knowing where the boilers were housed, smiled apologetically and texted the house manager.

'The front door was unlocked,' Brown Suit said defensively.

'We couldn't find a bell,' the other chipped in.

'The key hasn't been seen for nearly three hundred years,' Ayesha explained. 'One of my forebears went to fight in the American War of Independence and took it with him. It appears he lost it and his head on the battlefield.'

The men looked at each other, unsure if she was joking. She was not.

Taking the little girl's hand, Ayesha smiled and disappeared down the grand staircase. Reaching the ground floor, mother and daughter skipped all the way along the north corridor, through the Jacobean hall, and entered the Carolinian dining room, where a large breakfast was laid out on the side table. She lifted the heavy silver-lidded containers one by one. Ayesha considered the scrambled eggs, mushrooms, sausages, fried bread, tomatoes and kedgeree. Everything looked and smelled delicious, but knowing the value of a perfect figure, she resisted.

Two uniformed footmen waited in the corner. They'd been trained to serve but not stare; their gazes were neutral and averted. Away from the family, behind the green baize door, the subject of Lady Sleet's beauty and her husband's oafish behaviour was a constant topic of conversation. In the couple's presence, no one spoke until spoken to.

The footmen, working in unison, slid the chairs away from the table, poised for when Ayesha and her daughter sat down.

'We'll both have boiled eggs, wholewheat soldiers and freshly squeezed orange juice. Please can I also have a home-made yoghurt with blueberries and a green tea.' She looked at her daughter's hopeful face. 'Stella will also have a bowl of chocolate Krispies.'

'Yes, My Lady.'

Ayesha tied a napkin around Stella's neck and tucked an errant curl behind her ear. Next to one place was a child's guide to ponies and by the other was a daily folder. Mother and daughter opened both with great solemnity. Prepared by a junior secretary, Ayesha's contained her future appointments and recent press clippings; photographs of herself at various parties and mentions in gossip columns. Newspaper editors and photographers loved her: Lady Sleet personified glamour. She was ravishing, exquisitely groomed, consistently chic, wonderfully wealthy and titled. Even better, she was a beauty with a backstory: the daughter of the Earl of Trelawney raised in an Indian palace by her stepfather, a maharaja. The press's only disappointment was the lack of scandal. So far. Everyone knew it was a matter of time; muck follows brass and what goes up eventually falls. She was Sir Thomlinson's fourth wife. The previous ones had lasted less than five years. This one had done eight. The Sleets' union was an accident waiting to happen.

No one believed she'd married for love: they were correct. Sleet, then forty to her eighteen-year-old self, had been a solution to a problem which was partly money (or lack of) but mainly Ayesha's longing for security. Orphaned at seventeen, she was evicted by one family and disowned by the other. Sleet offered an instant, wildly indulgent prepackaged life, complete with private aeroplanes, yachts, more clothes than she could wear, drawers of jewels and, best of all, for their wedding present he bought and gave her Trelawney Castle: home to her father's family for eight hundred years. She loved, too, that he'd known her mother, Anastasia, and she was happy to hear story after story about their time at Oxford University.

Like a child trying on a grown-up's pair of high-heeled shoes, she struggled to find balance and slipped around in a world better suited to someone else. To give her life more substance and her marriage more gravitas, Ayesha created a narrative in which she was the heroine and her husband the misunderstood hero. They were, so her story went, injured people healed by mutual love. Both were illegitimate and were told their births had ruined other people's lives. She explained his flashes of cruelty and vulgarity as by-products of childhood wounds and mistook his need to control for caring, and his grandiosity for generosity.

In the early years of her marriage, Ayesha had nothing to do but wait for her husband to come home. For a man stimulated by the unobtainable, her availability bored him. Ayesha spent her days shopping, buying clothes which the chauffeur carried from the store to the car and into the house for the maids to hang in colour-coordinated obsolescence in her wardrobe. She had forty-eight pairs of red shoes, each with a slightly different detail. There were ninety camel-coloured cashmere sweaters, eighty unworn. She fussed over shades of lipstick and read parts of glossy magazines and romantic novels. The birth of Stella and her enrolment at the Courtauld Institute, where she took a first-class BA and was now studying for an MA, were transformative; she was still lonely, but her days had intellectual content.

Flicking through the pages of her folder, Ayesha smiled to see her image on the front cover of *Hi!* magazine and skimmed through an article entitled 'Lady Sleet, London's most glamorous wife?' The pictures were flattering but she was irritated to be described as a 'socialite' – no one took her studies seriously. She made a note to employ a PR agency to work on changing her descriptive pronoun to 'art historian'.

Stella pulled at her mother's shorts. 'Bored.'

Ayesha stood up, her napkin falling to the floor. She bent to pick it up. A footman got there first. She smiled at him apologetically. It was his job, but she hadn't got used to playing 'the grande dame'. Taking Stella's hand, she led her daughter along several passages to the greenhouses where, amongst the banks of houseplants, her husband had commissioned a painting studio complete with easels and massive reserves of paint and brushes. Stella's were stubby, while Ayesha's brushes were made of the finest hair. Because his wife had been born and grew up in India, Sleet decided that Indian painting would be her hobby.

'I'm going to hang your first work in my office,' he said. Ayesha had a great aptitude for studying art but little talent for making it. Each year she bought a Mughal flower drawing from a dealer close to the British Museum, signed it 'AS' and gave it to Sleet. He, in turn, re-gifted it to a member of staff.

The studio's glass windows overlooked the formal gardens that ran down to the estuary. Stella, tired of painting, played with a toy pony on the floor. Ayesha was distracted by an ever-changing sky. Life in Cornwall was a meteorological festival; weather conditions changed several times an hour. There was nothing faint-hearted about nature in these parts; it belted, pelted, blasted, bored, poured, whipped,

4

slammed, burned and blustered all in one day. From the shelter of the studio, she saw a squall approaching from the west. The horizon darkened; streaks of rain like heavy lines of pencil smudged and slashed across the sky. The eye of the storm was probably ten miles away. In the meantime, the sun played hide and seek in a fast-moving cloudscape, and flurries of snow fell but didn't settle.

'An artist called Turner tied himself to the mast of a tall ship in a stormy sea. He wanted to experience really bad weather so he could paint better,' she told Stella who, used to her mother's musings, went on playing. A snowflake landed on the warm window. Ayesha traced its progress down the glass as it turned from a perfectly shaped crystal into a dribble of water. She had secured everything she'd ever dreamed of: why did her life feel so hollow? Her loneliness was a permanent shape-shifting organ. Mostly, it sat like a small rock wedged between her heart and ribcage, until with no warning it became an all-pervasive beast, gnawing her being from the tips of her fingers to the bottom of her toes. An article she'd read suggested naming and visualising negative emotions: 'Make friends with your demons' the strapline said. Ayesha christened her loneliness 'Declan Malregard' in the hope that a silly moniker would diminish its power. She painted images of a hideous purple-faced gremlin. Unfortunately, anthropomorphising her emotion didn't diminish its power – instead she embarked on another dysfunctional relationship.

'Let's go outside and feel the weather,' she suggested to Stella, hoping that the cold air would mollify Declan who, at that moment, was storming around her head and heart.

'We don't have our coats!' The little girl was shocked.

'Race you to the fountain.' Ayesha wrenched open the door. A blast of air nearly knocked them over.

Stella set off, a tiny figure braced against the gusts, slipping in the wet grass. Ayesha's hair whipped around her face. Brushing it out of her eyes, she looked with pride and wonder at the beautifully tended garden. The Castle that she and her husband bought eight years earlier had been in an advanced state of dilapidation inside and out; the roof had collapsed in places and the garden was choked with weeds and ivies. Cornwall was beyond Donna's domain. Here Ayesha had some autonomy. Under her direction, the garden was restored. Even in January there were tiny splashes of colour emerging: early camellia, crocus, cyclamen and hellebores. Each season brought a different mood, a distinct horticultural phantasmagoria.

There was one area where no horticulturalist or gardener could persuade anything to grow. Named Guto's Gulley after a nineteenth-century forebear, it was a wide scar of land, about sixty foot long, running all the way from the burial ground to the sea. The experts had tried to plant everything, from trees to weeds, all to no avail. Nothing would take. Finally, she had the inspired idea to commission the land artist Andy Goldsworthy to transform it from an eyesore into an artwork by laying pieces of slate over the barren area. A pale winter sun broke through the snow and Ayesha watched transfixed as it shone on the wet stones, making the half-mile-long piece look like a vast snake slithering its way from the high hills down to the sea below.

'Mummy, I'm cold,' Stella said.

Picking her up, Ayesha blew gusts of hot air on to her daughter's neck. 'I am a hungry fiery dragon and I'm going to eat your ear.' Ayesha nipped at the tiny pink pearl-like lobe.

Stella squealed and wriggled in delight. 'Tickles.'

'I love you more than anything in the whole universe.'

'I know that,' Stella said.

'Don't ever take love for granted,' Ayesha said, squeezing a little too hard.

'Ouch. You're hurting me.' Stella tried to wriggle out of the iron grip.

Ayesha shifted Stella on to her back and, pretending to be a horse, cantered towards the house. Stella laughed and clung on to her mother's neck. Feeling her squirming body, Ayesha's heart contracted; she was with the person she loved most in the place she loved best.

The little girl's nanny, Janet, was waiting by the door with towels and a fluffy blanket in which she wrapped Stella.

'Thanks, Jan. You go ahead. I'm waiting for Tony and Barty and will join you for lunch.'

Ayesha walked across the Elizabethan ballroom and down the north corridor, her cowboy boots clicking on the oak floor. Stopping by a small, nondescript door, she held her breath before opening it. She'd been in the room many times over the last two years but never without workmen or scaffolding. It contained one of the greatest masterpieces of the seventeenth century by the Dutch master carver

Grinling Gibbons. The Trelawneys had been the first British family to commission the artist, transporting him from relative obscurity in Holland to the depths of Cornwall. From there his reputation grew, and within four years he was working for Charles II. He remained in royal service through the reigns of James II, William III, Queen Anne and George I.

Like the rest of the castle, the room had been left to rot and decay, and for centuries was eaten by woodworm and soaked by Cornish rain (the ceiling had fallen in). Pushing open the door, she gasped in wonder at the intricacy of the restoration. The patina of the oak was once again revealed, polished to look like burnished gold. The centre-piece was an enormous carved oak tree, twenty-four feet high, whose roots spread from the skirting board across the floor and whose crown covered the wall. Eight majestic branches wrapped themselves around the ceiling and peeked into neighbouring rooms. The workmen had done a spectacular job. It looked fresh and seamless. If only her mother could see what she'd achieved – Anastasia never thought Ayesha would amount to much; she'd have been astonished that her daughter had married well and was now the chatelaine of Trelawney, the place where she'd spent so many formative years.

The only unrestored part of the masterpiece were the three initials, each roughly carved into the base of the oak: 'AK' (Anastasia Kabakov), 'BS' (Blaze Scott) and 'JB' (Jane Brown). One of the few photographs Ayesha had of her mother was taken in this room. The colour had faded but the emotions were palpable. Three young women were having a candlelit picnic. There was a striped rug on the floor, a bottle of wine and a couple of roughly cut sandwiches. The camera was on a short self-timer and, to make it into the picture, Anastasia, Blaze and Jane, each about fifteen, had fallen into a laughing heap on top of each other, limbs and hair entangled. Ayesha felt a longing for this kind of familiarity. Declan shimmied up and down her spine, sending sparks of misery to prick the backs of her eyes. Blinking hard, she turned the photograph over to look at the date: 1987. Her fingers touched the tiny amulet on a gold chain that Anastasia used to wear: it was beautiful, hard and cold; just like her.

Her phone beeped, a message from her husband's PA Donna. Suppressing her irritation, Ayesha read: *Dinner at the Solos'. 8 p.m. Smart casual. Helicopter can't take off in snow. Car will leave house at 2.20. Hairdresser and make-up artist booked for 6.30. Notes on guests and subject matters will be in car. Sir T has chosen your dress and accessories.* Sleet deferred all domestic decisions to Donna, who, much of the time, behaved as if she were Lady Sleet and Ayesha a mere detail in her husband's life. Donna was so efficient and indispensable that Ayesha felt surplus to normal uxorial requirements. Occasionally, Ayesha would suggest doing things differently. Why, for example, didn't the family spend a few nights at the Cap Hotel in Antibes – she'd read it was lovely. Donna shook her head: Sir Thom went there with Wife Two; it hadn't been a success. One Christmas Ayesha hand-embroidered some slippers for her husband. Donna smiled condescendingly. 'Might I suggest that you have them lined in kid? Sir Thom has an allergy to wool.' Cocooned by Sleet and his staff, suspended in the aspic of privilege, Ayesha barely matured.

Business dinners made her nervous. She could identify the brush-stroke of many Old Master painters, but financial facts and figures rarely stuck. Her husband found her lack of interest irritating but when she did offer an opinion it was batted away. To shine tonight she'd need to read the crib sheet and google the guest list. Instead, she succumbed to temptation and decided to finish reading a new biography of the Italian baroque painter Artemisia Gentileschi. Two steps at once, she ran up the back stairs to her private study. Unlike the rest of the castle, this room was a jumble of books, mainly on art or museums; a tangle of reproductions, academic journals. It was the one place no one else was allowed to clean; even Stella was discouraged from entering. To an outsider it looked a total mess; for Ayesha, it was her refuge.

*

Ayesha's husband, Sir Thomlinson Sleet, personified material success. A renowned financier, his office occupied the penthouse of one of the City's most prestigious buildings. There were no paintings, just Sleet's favourite quotes blown up and framed like works of art. '*Money is a terrible master but an excellent servant –* P. T. Barnum.' '*Courage is being scared to death but saddling up anyway* – John Wayne.' These mantras, along with Sleet's personal bon mots, were repeated at the beginning and end of all meetings to encourage a 'Kerkyra Capital' culture. The company's speciality was short-selling, a high-risk strategy of making a profit on a falling share price. Often associated with disinformation, market abuse and corporate failure, short sellers had, at the best of times, lacklustre reputations. Barbs and criticisms bounced off Sleet. Once asked by a journalist to define his morals, he had replied, 'Missing any opportunity to make money is a deadly sin.'

His net worth, according to the *Sunday Times Rich List*, was £9 billion. His pronouncements and actions could move the financial markets. Few realised that Sleet was dogged by a fear of failure, which followed and taunted him relentlessly. Each setback, however small, eviscerated all other achievements. He wasn't hungry for success: he was ravenous. But goals reached were always superseded by challenges; his need to win was a bottomless pit, impossible to fill.

A man with greater compassion or imagination, less isolated by wealth, might have found comfort in a hinterland or sought redemption in spirituality. Sleet surrounded himself with people on his own payroll or those enthralled by his money. It was not in their interest to criticise or question. The few who did were expelled or frozen out. He controlled the agenda and the timetable, moving around like a whale surrounded by a fleet of sucker fish. Three associates came on his honeymoon with Ayesha. She didn't complain – her husband was not conversationally gifted.

In the room were four colleagues. His long-standing PA, Donna Mac; Brian and Tracey from the Private Equity department; and his loyal chief operating officer, Rodita Della Cruz. Everyone was quiet – nobody spoke before the boss.

Sleet stood at the window, looking out at the snow falling on to ant-sized people below. Some had umbrellas; others pulled their coats around their necks or held bags over their heads.

'What do you think when you see snow?' he asked his colleagues.

'I don't have time to look out of the window. My eyes are glued to my computer,' Rodita said.

'Christmas with my family,' Tracey said, smiling at the memory.

'Snowball fights with my girlfriend,' Brian said.

Sleet shook his head in disbelief. 'You guys are such losers. I'm kicking myself that we don't sell umbrellas in the lobby. We could bulk-buy in China, mark them up by 150 per cent.'

He walked across the room. He was tall and broad, with larger limbs, features, and a bigger appetite than most. Overweight, as if someone had poured his flesh into his clothes but forgotten to stop at full; with frizzy ginger hair and an unfortunate pink skin tone – it was Donna, not his wife, who made sure that he looked his best. She had his hair relaxed and cut short once a week. She bought ointments to soothe his complexion, upgraded his tailor and built workouts into his daily schedule. Sleet under Donna's management was a better, if not the best, version of himself. He was forty-eight years old and on a good day could pass for forty-five.

'TLG update?' Sleet said.

'TLG's market cap is £350 million, but in recent weeks the valuation marked it down 9 per cent,' Tracey said.

'So we've lost over £33 million?' His voice rose and, putting his face close to Tracey's, he shouted, 'Why did we buy this piece of crap? People give us money to make money.'

Tracey flushed red. 'It was your idea. You read about it in the *FT*.'

'What did it say?'

'TLG is one of the three best suppliers of aeronautical products in the world. Based in Taiwan, they have a low-cost base, a skilled work-force and access to the latest technology. Ren Tenako, their Japanese CEO, is exceptional. I am confident this is a good holding …' She hesitated. 'Long term.'

Sleet circled her, shaking his head. 'Why aren't we number one?'

'They won three out of seven contracts this year,' Tracey said.

'Any less than seven out of seven is shit. S and H and I and T.' Sleet felt his heart picking up pace. He put his hand on the back of a chair and tried to breathe slowly. 'Who's whipping our ass?'

Brian cleared his throat. 'Our competitors are a UK company, Whaley Precision Engineering. Third-gen family business based in Buckinghamshire with 120 employees. Owner is Sir John Whaley. He won the *FT*'s best employer three years in a row.'

'What's their edge?'

Brian chose his words carefully. 'Companies trust them. They've been in blades since Amelia Earhart crossed the Atlantic. Their products and manufacturing have evolved slowly and steadily. They are more expensive than other companies, but most accept that safety comes with a premium. There's been no history of accidents. Whaley does one thing and does it well.'

'They've been working with graphite and are about to launch a new, lighter blade,' Tracey said.

'So copy it.'

'It's patented.'

'So steal it.' Sleet couldn't believe his team. Legality was an opinion, a mere shade in the colour spectrum between right and wrong. Even a top judge would argue that the law was open for interpretation and no one should take it literally.

Brian and Tracey shifted in their seats. 'We don't have time to compete against them for the new Dreamliner contract. Bids close in six weeks.'

'What's that contract worth?'

'About £650 million over five years.'

Sleet paced the room. 'Has it been tested?'

'Stringently,' Brian said.

'Is Whaley publicly traded?'

'There's rumour of an IPO in July with an initial valuation of £400 million, but many think it could go as high as £500 or £600 million.'

'Suppose there was some bad news at Whaley?' Sleet said.

Rodita smiled. She and Sleet had worked together for twenty years and knew enough about the other's malpractices to bind them together for another century. Devoid of imagination or entrepreneurial spirit, Rodita's skill was finding technical solutions to impossible scenarios while staying within the law or at least away from legal detection.

'We can create something to frighten investors,' she echoed. Spreading false rumours was a well-honed Kerkyra Capital technique.

'Not enough – there needs to be a slam-dunk reason not to award the company the contract,' Sleet said. 'We could put about rumours of a crack in the prop. Tell everyone that the new technology isn't as safe as they all thought?'

'They've been through all the necessary rounds of testing,' Tracey said.

'So create another round,' Sleet barked. 'Or bribe someone who works there. Offer a disgruntled worker a new car or a house for falsifying info. Send in some big busty chick to find the chink in his halo?' Sleet ruminated. 'Start a fire in the factory. Burn the inventory.'

Rodita laughed. She loved having a debenture seat on one man's undiluted malevolence. Tracey and Brian looked at each other nervously. Sleet intercepted their glances.

'You're withholding something.'

Tracey coughed, trying to clear an invisible lump in her throat.

'We're too late. Bids have gone in,' she said, looking at the floor as if hoping it might swallow her up.

'We can't lose!' Sleet's heart began to thump. Beads of sweat prickled behind his hairline. The edges of the room were fuzzing up. The only thing worse than having a panic attack was having witnesses; only his inner circle knew of the psychological flaws in Sleet's otherwise impermeable armour; for him, any display of weakness was mortifying.

'Get out,' he screamed at Tracey and Brian.

'Pencils, pencils!' he called. Donna placed a large box in front of him. She and Rodita stayed in the room. His doctor insisted someone remain present in case Sleet hit his head or swallowed his tongue. Donna remained at a discreet distance. Rodita looked at her phone. Sleet fell to all fours and, panting loudly, snapped several pencils in two and then in three. It was a trick suggested by a psychiatrist, a way of trying to break the fits of terror that Sleet had endured since his days at Oxford. Donna ordered hundreds of boxes at a time. Engraved on each in gold letters were Sleet's personal bon mots: 'I am number one' or 'I am the best.' Donna surreptitiously checked her watch. It was only 9 a.m. and she suspected it would be a four-box day. Within minutes broken pencils lay like spillikins scattered on the floor.

Sleet's breathing calmed. Donna handed him a glass of water. He drained it in one gulp. She passed him a towel and he wiped the sweat from his face and neck.

'Can anyone link me to the Taiwanese company?' he asked.

Rodita pursed her lips. 'Your name isn't on any of the mastheads. It's held through companies registered in Panama and the Cayman Islands via a parent company registered at an anonymous address in Harley Street. The board of directors is 90 per cent fictitious and their accounts are registered to non-existent shell structures.'

'So if anything were to happen at Whaley, no one could trace it back to me?'

Rodita nodded.

Sleet let out a belly laugh. 'This is the best bloody country in the universe. You can do anything here and no one bats an eyelid.' He sat down on his chair and closed his eyes. 'I'm going to destroy Whaley and take the business over.'

Donna brought a clean shirt and jacket into Sleet's office and, opening a door in the corner, turned on the shower and made sure that there was a towel. Like Rodita, she'd worked for Sleet since Kerkyra Capital was founded nearly two decades earlier. They had all started in a single rented room on the outskirts of the city. Year by year, entirely due to Sleet's acumen, the offices and profits had grown. Donna's devotion was a source of confusion for other employees. They were only partially correct that Donna was a little in love with her boss. She also took pride in knowing that she played a small but crucial part in his success – without her ballast, Sleet would capsize. She had outlasted three Lady Sleets and was confident that she'd see out the fourth.

'Shower,' she said, pointing.

He obeyed, stripping off his sweaty shirt and leaving it where it fell.

'Will you tell Ayesha we're meeting the Solos' at eight.'

'She has your instructions. Do you want to speak to her?' Donna was, as usual, ahead of the question.

Sleet snorted. 'She's my wife, not my mistress! Who talks to their wife unless they absolutely must?'

*

A little after 10 a.m., on Platform 9 at Paddington Station, two elderly gentlemen advanced towards each other with arms outstretched. Only two evenings had passed since their last meeting, but with so many of their generation indisposed or dying, reunions were always a relief.

'Ahoy there!' the Honourable Anthony Scott called out.

'Hail fellow well met,' Barty St George shouted back.

Shuffling forwards, they stood a few feet apart and air-kissed on proffered cheeks. In their time, both had had many affairs but never with each other: fleeting passion was a poor substitute for enduring friendship. Tony, perennially elegant, wore a blue cashmere coat and a berry-red scarf. Barty, forever flamboyant, was in a three-piece tweed suit with a white silk cravat secured with a small gold tie pin. Draped around his shoulders was a sable coat.

'What have you got on?' Tony asked.

'You must remember! This is a garment of great provenance and distinction, a gift from Greta Garbo.' The coat was one of Barty's prize possessions. 'She wore it to three Oscars, the de Beistegui Ball in Venice and the Derby.' As he brushed the fur with his fingertips, he saw with sadness that the sable was looking tired; he knew exactly how it felt. 'On the wireless, they said snow is forecast in Cornwall. I thought the spirit of the great actress might keep us warm.'

'Has it got moths?' Tony eyed the coat nervously.

'I keep it in the deep freeze.'

Tony wasn't convinced. 'Moths and fat terrify me. One destroys clothes, the other one's confidence.'

'Man-made fibres are all the rage.'

'What is a man-made fibre?' Tony asked.

'Material made from recycled bottles.'

Tony raised his hands in despair. 'Darling Barty, I give up – clothes are not made from plastic. Whatever fantasy will you think of next?'

Their train rolled in to the platform, sucking a cold January wind and flurries of snow in its wake. Tony shivered extravagantly and, seeing his friend's discomfort, Barty unscrewed the silver top of his walking stick and handed it over. 'This will warm your cockles.'

'Voddie?' Tony sniffed the contents.

'Single malt.'

Tony took a long swig. Then a second. Two patches of pink appeared on his cheeks. Feeling much better, he looked up and down the train for the carriage marked 'A'. Working for Sir Thomlinson Sleet and his wife Ayesha came with an expense account that included first-class travel, London taxis and dining cars – luxuries which neither Tony nor Barty had enjoyed for many years. In their prime, both had been sought after as interior decorators and also as spare men. As the decades passed, work and invitations waned. They had gone from being 'must haves' to 'ought to asks' and were limited to a life of toast and baked beans with the occasional treat of a pot of Gentleman's Relish. Tony, a member of the Trelawney family, had been born at the castle in the 1920s when the tradition was to send all younger sons to the army or church: Tony hadn't fancied either. He tried many careers, from cowboy to gigolo, but none stuck. Gradually, his small inheritance ran out and the roofs over his head shrank in size. For the last ten years home had been a rented studio in Earls Court. This long run of financial bad luck and penury was broken when Ayesha Sleet hired Tony (who employed Barty as his assistant) to do up Trelawney Castle. Seventy years after Tony had been sent away from the castle on a bicycle, he returned in a Mercedes.

Linking arms, the old friends went in search of their carriage. Scaling the three steep steps from the platform up to the train took so much effort, heaving, grunting and panting that a fellow passenger asked if they needed medical assistance.

'I have scaled much higher heights than the 10.05 to Penzance,' Tony said indignantly.

'He was trying to be kind,' Barty chided.

'Kindness, like having children, is overrated.'

The first-class restaurant car was the only part of Great Western Rail that was unchanged in half a century. There were white table-cloths, silver cutlery and leatherette menus. The windows were framed with blue pleated curtains and the headrests were covered with freshly laundered monogrammed slips. The attendant, Bob, had been in service for nearly three decades and knew both men well. He helped them settle into their seats.

'Morning, Mr Scott, Mr St George. The usual coming up.' Within minutes he placed a steaming silver coffee pot, a jug of warm milk and two cups on the white starched tablecloth. Knowing that their old hands weren't strong enough to lift and pour, he filled their cups.

Tony and Barty sipped their coffee and discussed furnishings. They were two years into redecorating Trelawney and, with 219 out of 365 rooms left to complete, both suspected their souls would depart long before the job was finished. Half an hour later, as promised, Bob brought their eggs and toast with extra butter and marmalade. By the third slice, conversation drifted, as it always did, to the Trelawney family.

'Ayesha seems lonelier than ever.' Tony was fond of his great-niece (the only member of the family who was). 'If only she could become a full-time art historian.'

Barty threw his hands into the air. 'Much more fun to have fishnet than blue stockings.'

'Her life is such a waste; too much money and too little purpose. Imagine being that well-off, beautiful and young, and living like a prematurely middle-aged woman trapped in the migratory pattern of the super-rich, moving from event to party, lunch to dinner, cruising in private jets and planes from the South of France to the Caribbean to the Alps.'

'Sounds like perfect heaven to me,' Barty said. 'What she needs is an affair.'

Tony hesitated. 'I am hoping that her study of art will help her see beyond her present circumstances to another existence. Did you hear she got a first for her extended essay on women in the Dutch Golden Age?'

Barty had left school at sixteen and never saw the point of education. 'You can't honestly believe that staring at an ugly, warted Rembrandt face will make her think "I can do better" and leave her husband?'

'Shall we play a game?' he suggested. 'What about A and B?'

Tony smiled wanly. 'You start.'

'Would you rather: A – drop Clarissa from a great height into boiling oil, or B—'

Tony didn't let him finish. 'A, A and A.'

'I didn't say what B involved.'

'A is good enough for me. She's beyond dreadful.'

Barty had a weakness for celebrities; Clarissa, Tony's sister-in-law, had 1 million Twitter followers and her own television series, *The Last of the Trelawneys*, so he was prepared to overlook her appalling behaviour.

'Your turn.' Barty sank back into his seat.

'I can't think of anything,' Tony said.

The two men fell into companionable silence, watching out of the window as the train rattled through the suburbs of Reading, past rows of identical red-brick houses and neat gardens.

By the time the train reached Newbury, half an hour later, they were slumped, fast asleep. Bob knew from experience that they'd spend the next two hours in a comatose state. He'd wake them half an hour before Trelawney Station, the last stop on the line.

Two hours later, helped by Bob, Tony and Barty unfurled their stiff limbs and alighted at their destination. The chauffeur was there to drive them the short distance to the castle. It started to snow hard, big fat flakes dancing and twirling. Through the windscreen wipers

Tony could see the crenellations looming above the horizon. His spirits rose as he caught sight of his beloved family home. These days the driveway was as spick and span as a Home Counties golf course; not a blade of grass or box hedge out of place. Tony missed the wild, untamed Trelawney of his youth. Try as he might, he could never remember another human or object that moved him so much as his childhood home.

The two men made their way slowly through the Great Hall and up the stairs into the first ballroom. From the second ballroom there came a hobbling, rustling sound.

'Anyone there?' the shrill tones of Clarissa, Dowager Countess of Trelawney, rang out. 'Yoo-hoo!'

Tony gasped at the apparition. Clarissa was dressed in an electric-pink wig, yellow pop socks and a rubber minidress. Her 87-year-old legs were encased in lurex tights and she wore black lipstick. 'What is one wearing?'

'I'm doing a shoot for Japanese *Vogue*.'

'Halloween issue, or Fright Night?'

'Very funny,' Clarissa snapped. 'You wouldn't know haute couture if it bit you.'

'I hope you had a rabies shot.'

Anxious to avoid an escalation of tension, Barty stepped between them. 'Clarissa, can I borrow the outfit after you?' he asked, imagining his own legs poking out of a black rubber minidress.

Tony looked up and down the corridor. 'Ayesha's around. Does she know you're here?'

'Do I need permission to be in my own house?' Clarissa refused to accept that Trelawney no longer belonged to her. Enacting her rights as a sitting tenant, she'd refused to vacate her old apartment known as the Mistresses' Wing. The moment the Sleets left for London, Clarissa moved back into the main house, making full use of the cellars, kitchens and staff.

'Does anyone know if the Vulgarian is going to be around this week? Or his …' she hesitated '… concubine?' She still couldn't refer to Ayesha or Sleet by their first names.

'Are you entertaining a film crew or a VIP?' Barty clapped his hands together. 'Too thrilling.'

Clarissa drew a small circle on the floor with her toe.

'I'm entertaining *à deux* tomorrow night. I would be grateful if you and the rest of the family could make yourself scarce. Completely scarce.'

'It depends on who's coming. If it's a murderer I will give him a wide berth and permission to do his worst to you,' Tony said. 'If it's someone nice, I'll wait and warn him what's in store.'

To both men's astonishment, Clarissa blushed.

'You've got a beau?' Tony said. In the seventy years that he'd known her, Clarissa had never exhibited a smidgeon of romantic interest, even in the first flush of her marriage to his lascivious brother; she'd married for the title and the position.

'It's never too late,' she said.

'You're eighty-seven!'

'Who is he?' Barty asked.

'A bit of local rough?' Tony said. 'I wouldn't put out the silver. He might nick it.'

'He is a duke!' Clarissa said.

'I know most of their graces,' Barty said, flicking through his mental Rolodex of twenty-four noble lords.

'An Italian duke.' Clarissa failed to keep the smile off her face.

'They're two a penny,' Tony said.

'I once had the Duke of Amalfi – Alessandro. He was gorgeous,' Barty said, a broad grin making his face crumple like a paper bag.

'I've had enough of this ribaldry.' Clarissa turned to go.

'Are you going to wear that?' Barty asked, eyeing the minidress. Clarissa pursed her lips.

'What happens if the snow settles? He won't make it up the drive.'

'He will hire a sleigh. Nothing will keep us apart,' Clarissa said.

Tony's mouth fell open.

'Nothing so exciting has happened to me for yonks.' Barty's lower lip trembled.

Clarissa had had enough. Turning around, she straightened her shoulders and, with as much decorum as was possible to muster in a tight rubber minidress, she walked towards the door and back to her apartment.

Tony began immediately to telephone all their relations to share the news of her romance. The reactions were in keeping with their respective characters. Jane Trelawney, the present Countess who had moved to Florence, was disinterested.

'How lovely,' she said, making it clear that she wanted to return to work.

Jane's estranged husband Kitto, the Earl of Trelawney, was walking along the Cornish coast.

'Your mother has an admirer.'

Kitto had other distractions. 'There's a beautiful sea eagle with a damaged wing. Who should I call?'

Exasperated, Tony hung up. He tried and failed to reach Kitto and Jane's children, Toby and Arabella. Finally, he got through to Blaze, his niece; Clarissa's daughter.

'Tony! Is everything OK?' Blaze asked in a fake bright voice.

'I have delicious gossip. Not just any chatter, but grade-A, gold-plated gossip. You're going to love this. Are you sitting down?'

Blaze looked at the blank page on her computer which she'd been staring at for the last two hours. 'I have a presentation tomorrow.'

'A prize? You are clever.'

'A business presentation. I am trying to get five VCs to invest in my green cement company.'

'Green cement? Why not pink or purple? Imagine how pretty buildings would look if they weren't that horrid grey.'

'Not green as in the colour, Tony!' Blaze said, wishing she hadn't answered the call. 'It's the way it's made. The building trade is the world's second-largest polluter, and the technology and processes that our company are pioneering will dramatically cut these emissions without compromising safety standards. It's a game changer.'

Tony held the phone away from his ears and rolled his eyes. In his opinion, the only thing more boring than business was talking about business.

'Why did you ring?'

Tony cleared his throat. 'It's about your mother.'

'My mother? What's happened now?' Blaze's heart lifted. Maybe the old witch was finally dead. She felt instantly guilty.

'She has an admirer. He's a duke.'

Blaze groaned. 'Isn't there enough drama? It's a publicity stunt.'

'He's coming tomorrow. Why don't you come and meet him?'

Looking out of her window, Blaze caught sight of her husband, Joshua, his head covered by an oilskin, his beloved craggy face spattered with flakes of snow. He opened the door to her office, letting in a gust of wind. Blaze checked her watch. It was already 2.15 p.m.

'I have to go, Tony. Time for the school run.'

Blaze hung up the phone and went to hug Joshua, wondering if her heart might burst with gratitude. Finding love so late in life had been totally unexpected.

Joshua kissed her on the forehead. 'Done the presentation?'

Blaze groaned.

'I'll help you later.' He got her coat from the peg inside the door and handed it to her. Like Blaze, he'd stepped away from managing money to investing in sustainable start-ups. Both were determined to make the world a kinder, fairer place for their daughter, Perrin. Their intentions were pure, but the returns were poor by comparison to those enjoyed by their nemesis, Sir Thomlinson Sleet.

Outside, snow was falling, covering the trees in a fine dust. The river running along the middle of the valley cut a dark snaking shape in the white landscape. They walked hand in hand to their battered old Land Rover, the only car capable of making it up the rough, icy track. Joshua turned on a blow heater which puffed ineffectually at a steamed-up window. Taking an old towel from the back seat, Blaze wiped the condensation away. Their frozen breath made cloud-like shapes. She shivered and pulled her coat around her body.

'Let's hope today was better.' Joshua looked tired. His face, normally animated by an easy smile, was forlorn, making him look older. His merry heart was hiding. He put the car into first gear and set off.

'The teachers say that a settling-in period is normal.' Blaze repeated a phrase they'd been told many times.

'It's been four months! I don't know how many more days I can take,' Joshua said, thinking of their daughter's pinched and anxious features. The windscreen wipers squeaked in sympathy.

Blaze's silence echoed his thoughts.

'Let's give it to the end of next week,' she said, trying to sound confident. As older parents, both had anticipated many challenges; but neither foresaw the misery of having a child who hated school. 'There is some positive news. The Whaleys have asked us all to lunch.' Joshua let out a whoop. In most circumstances he ran a mile from social life, but Sir John and Lady Susan Whaley were the parents of Lily, Perrin's only friend, and if it made an iota of difference to his daughter's happiness then Joshua would spend every evening at their house. Stopping the car, he put on the handbrake and, leaning over, kissed his wife passionately on the mouth. Blaze responded, throwing her arms around his neck and pulling his handsome face to hers. Married for eight years, they were still giddy for each other.

'Let's go or we'll be late.' Blaze smiled broadly, smoothing her hair.

'Make up for it later,' Joshua said, crinkling his eyes at her.

2

February 2016

'I thought this was an exclusive event,' Sleet grumbled, looking at the queue of cars stretched from the Mall to the entrance to Buckingham Palace. On the seat next to him, Ayesha pulled her cashmere wrap around her shoulders, hoping her husband would remain calm. Five minutes and three yards later, Sleet slammed his hand on the back of the seat. 'Jump the line,' he instructed his chauffeur.

Sanjay Tnang was used to Sleet's outlandish demands. Overall, he complied. Previous requests (all met) included transporting a box of Maltesers to Italy to satisfy a sudden craving; searching Gascony for a certain kind of cheese; and turning a blind eye to various 'indiscretions' committed by his boss. A generous pay packet and an onerous Non-Disclosure Agreement kept Sanjay's mouth shut. As a Buddhist, he found further consolation in the knowledge that in his next life, Sleet would be reincarnated as a cockroach.

'I wouldn't advise it, sir,' Sanjay said. 'The police have to check under the bonnet and in the boot of every car. They operate a shoot-to-kill policy near royalty.'

'Tell them I know Prince Andrew,' Sleet said. 'That should do it.'

'I'd keep that quiet,' Ayesha said. Sanjay caught her eye in the rear-view mirror and suppressed a smile.

'What did you say?' Sleet asked.

'Nothing.'

Sleet slumped back into the soft cowhide of the Maybach's rear seat. 'Next time we'll bring the chopper.' Then he opened a side pocket and, taking out a packet of M&M's, poured the contents into his mouth.

'Did you know that the "in thing" is label-less labels?' Sleet asked his wife.

'What does that mean?' Ayesha asked.

'According to *Taste and Refinement* magazine, it's uncool to have any indication of the brand – on clothes, objects, even on wine.' He shook his head. 'Everything you drive, eat and wear should be anonymous.' Sleet shuffled forward and ran his fingers over the logo on the back of the car seat.

'What's worrying you?' Ayesha asked, seeing that her husband was in a state of discomfort.

'If it doesn't have a label then how do you know?' Sleet asked. 'And how do others know that you know?'

'Does it matter?'

'I want people to look at me and see more than a pile of cash. I want them to think, "Hey, that guy is something."'

Self-contempt wrapped itself around Sleet's shoulders; he wasn't and never would be good enough.

'I think you're something.'

Rather than calm, her words inflamed. 'You come from a family that's had eight hundred years of aristocratic breeding. People look at me and think I am common.'

'Darling, it's not true,' she said, suspecting it was.

'One of the reasons I married you was to get class, but your own family doesn't talk to you. The neighbours don't ask us over. I have to pay to go to events like tonight.'

Ayesha fought back tears. Sleet cared about the social slight, she about the lack of friends. Her hoped-for life in Cornwall, full of picnics and bracing walks with like-minded people, was yet to materialise.

'Do you think we'll meet the Queen?' she asked, changing the subject.

'Tonight is the Prince of Wales's evening.'

'At least her collection will be on display,' Ayesha said, her voice rising in excitement. 'Maybe we'll see Romano's portrait of Isabella d'Este.'

'Isabella who?'

Ayesha swallowed her disappointment; she'd told her husband so many times. 'The subject of my dissertation.'

'Oh yeah,' Sleet said. 'Who was she again?'

'One of the greatest patrons of art in history. Mostly it's men who are remembered and celebrated – think of the Medici or Pope Julius

II. Women get notoriety for their bad behaviour – Lucrezia Borgia or Mata Hari – but Isabella d'Este was …'

Looking sideways at Sleet, she saw he wasn't listening so didn't finish her sentence. The car inched forward in the queue.

'I thought you grew up in a palace?' Sleet asked. 'Weren't there fancy parties?'

'I was never asked.' Ayesha stared out of the window, wishing she could forget those evenings. As the illegitimate daughter of the Maharaja's third wife, she was never included or invited to any grand dinners. Her life was confined to servants' quarters. Sometimes she was allowed to watch her mother or her stepsisters get ready, but only if she remained out of sight. She never guessed that the Balakphur women were scared by her beauty. Closing her eyes, she recalled the smell of scented powder and incense and the serving girls carrying the finest saris to drape around their well-born mistresses. She could still hear the jingle and clink of the golden, jewel-encrusted headdresses, the rustle of silk, the chatter and laughter of the women. She remembered the misery of exclusion and the humiliation of not being good enough.

When the parties were held in the Great Hall, Ayesha crawled on her stomach along the narrow ducts in the ceiling from which huge fans hung. Before the advent of electricity, servants were ordered to lie in these mini-tunnels and operate the overhead fans by hand. Lack of maintenance and a rickety ceiling meant that several punkah wallahs crashed to their deaths. Ayesha would peer over the edge of those gaping holes to watch guests below moving and dancing like animated rainbows. Spying was dangerous: the access tunnels had become home to snakes and poisonous spiders. It was a risk worth taking; she couldn't bear being left out. Even now she could taste the disappointment – a flat, metallic furry feeling on the back of her tongue.

'What did you do all day?' Sleet asked.

'I read fairy stories and romantic novels for hours and hours every day.' She felt a rush of gratitude towards her husband. He had rescued her from an uncertain future. She was going to the Palace as a guest. She, her husband and daughter were going to live happily ever after. Waves of wishful thinking covered over the cracks.

'Thank you, darling,' she said.

He looked confused. 'For what?'

'For our life.'

Sleet marvelled at her beauty. He wished he wanted her more, but like everything he owned, once possessed, it lost its sheen. Staring out of the window at the line of grand cars in front and behind him, he felt a familiar knot of fear; would his wife love him as much, would his children keep in touch, would people return his calls if they knew that he was worth a fraction of the number listed in the *Sunday Times Rich List*? There, his fortune was listed as £9 billion. If only. He was worth about a tenth of that. His interest payments were £6 million a month. His outgoings, including maintenance payments to ex-wives and children, were another £15 million per annum. Every dollar made was leveraged seven or eight times over. It was an exhausting churn. To prove you were a captain of the universe, there were obscure rules and elusive trophies: the right boat, a certain vintage of wine, the best table in a restaurant. Was his wife more beautiful, his plane bigger, the thread count of his sheets higher? One false move and it was over. Everything was a matrix, a calculation and measurable.

'Now that the house is habitable, why don't we spend more time in Cornwall? Stella could go to the local school,' Ayesha suggested.

He shivered, unable to imagine the horror of such obsolescence. Occasionally he'd hear about a colleague who retired, stepped off the merry-go-round and chose a different kind of life. How could anyone subject themselves to a life of has-beenism or the ignominy of anonymity? Of being a nobody. Who could bear a life of such utter irrelevance? Like a former tennis star or Formula One driver sitting in the stands, their life was one of reminiscences.

'I am trying to make Trelawney the best version of itself. Somewhere where our grandchildren will play and eventually inherit.' Ayesha hesitated. 'It's our investment.'

'It's an investment, all right, and a pretty little one too,' Sleet laughed, a short bark.

Hearing his tone, Ayesha felt a flicker of fear.

The car reached the front of the queue. With the necessary checks completed, they were waved through the gates and under an arch into the Palace's inner courtyard.

'Nearly as big as our house,' Sleet said, looking at the walls of windows.

'Neither as big nor as beautiful,' Ayesha replied. And then started to recite a poem. '"*Oh to once more lay my lonely head on Trelawney's mossy breast/to feel her misty breath on my cheek,*"' she said out loud.

'What's that?'

'It's the beginning of a famous lament written in the trenches by the First World War poet Owen Florence about Trelawney.'

'Oh to have the time to learn poetry,' Sleet said, thinking about the relentlessness of his day.

The car pulled up under a large, enclosed portico and a footman dressed in red with gold livery stepped forward to open the door.

Ayesha smiled at the young man; her face was so pretty, her figure so entrancing, her hair so buoyant that the footman froze. There was an uncomfortable moment where the guests and their greeter were struck dumb and blocking the entrance, the Sleets not sure whether to walk around him or wait until he recovered. It was not the first time something like this had happened; it used to delight Sleet, but now he found it irritating.

'Are you going to show us where to go?' he asked.

The young man blushed a deep red. 'Apologies. Please leave anything, including mobile telephones, in the cloakroom. It's just up the steps and straight in front.'

Sleet held out his arm and Ayesha took it. Together they walked up the red carpet.

'It looks a bit like the Hilton in Delhi,' Sleet said, looking at the attendants in their frock coats and the cavernous lobby with its red damask walls and gold detailing along the cornices.

'Think about all the heads of states, royalty and VIPs who've walked up these steps,' Ayesha said, feeling the weight of history settle around her. 'The Shahs of Persia, Emperors of Austria, Nelson Mandela probably.'

'I wonder what Julius Caesar would have made of it?' Sleet asked. 'It was built before his time!' he added, qualifying his joke. 'Bet you didn't know that.'

Ayesha grimaced.

They stood behind a couple and Sleet watched horrified as other guests gave up their mobiles. Reaching the coat check, a man held out his hand.

'You want my phone?' Sleet asked.

'It will be kept in an individually locked safe box,' the attendant explained.

'The thing is,' Sleet said in a low voice, 'this phone to me is like a guide dog to a blind man or a pacemaker to someone with a dicky heart. I have to be plugged into the financial markets at all times. Without it my lungs might stop functioning. I might get a panic attack. I haven't been without my phone since ...' He couldn't remember. 'If I call my doctor – he could verify.'

The attendant smiled kindly but continued to hold out the box for Sleet's phone.

'I bet you don't make the Pope or the Dalai Lama hand in their phones?' Sleet said nastily.

'I don't believe they own one,' the attendant replied.

'What about Angela Merkel or Warren Buffett?'

'Sir, there are a group of people behind you and I'd be grateful if you could comply with regulations.'

Sleet shuddered. What if the markets crashed or he missed a good tip? He looked at his wife for a reaction – nothing – and then at the attendant; neither looked interested. He handed over the phone reluctantly. 'If I miss out on a deal, I'll sue.' The Sleets walked up a curved staircase to the first of what appeared to be a series of interconnecting chambers decorated with coloured damasks, all largely empty. One carpet ran from room to room, a deep red with a crown motif. On the walls there were portraits of men in uniform staring stiffly out from highly ornate frames. Ayesha stifled a feeling of disappointment: where were the great masterpieces?

Then she froze, spotting two familiar figures walking towards them: Ajay, the Maharaja of Balakphur, her former stepfather's eldest son and heir; and his wife Tinky. Both were splendidly dressed in the finest silks and jewels; nothing could hide their astonishment at the sight of Ayesha, also bejewelled, in the heart of Buckingham Palace.

'Ayesha? Is that you?' Tinky Balakphur asked. One of the most beautiful women during her youth, age and fine living had not been kind to the Maharani or her husband, who was known (though no one could remember why) as Scullypoo. Like wax versions of themselves left in the sun too long, their faces had become misshapen and distended.

'You are so glamorous,' Tinky said, looking Ayesha up and down, noting the designer dress, the poised figure, the diamonds around her neck and on her finger.

Ayesha was lost for words. The sight of her former tormentors catapulted her back to a miserable childhood. Scullypoo saw her discomfort and smiled. This, he knew, was the way of things. Seeing his superior expression, Ayesha's insecurity was superseded by another memory – the morning of her stepfather's death, Scullypoo evicted her and her dying mother from the palace. A flash of anger overcame her. She wanted to remind them that her mother had died on the floor of a cottage hospital, without drugs or proper medical attention. She wanted to scream at him; but before she could formulate the words, Sleet cleared his throat.

'Do we know you?'

Ayesha introduced the Balakphurs. Sleet looked at his wife knowingly – he'd heard the stories.

'We gotta go.'

For once Ayesha was glad of his rudeness.

As they walked away, Sleet commented, 'You've gone a strange colour.'

'They bring back unhappy memories.'

'At least they saw you in a palace with an important person.'

Husband and wife wandered through rooms, each splendid, mostly empty of furniture apart from rather stiff gilded seats with notices saying, 'Do not sit.' Ayesha recognised a few other couples but hoped Sleet wouldn't stop: she was keen to reach the picture gallery.

'What's the hurry?' Sleet asked.

'I want to see Vermeer and Rembrandt.'

'Have I met them?'

'You're so funny, darling.'

'I heard Steve Schwarchdorf and Barry Trinket were going to be here.' He looked around for the two CEOs of Goldfarb and Hendel-Dunne-Fox.

'Hey, there's Steve. He's a legend.' He headed towards a dapper man standing next to a tall, beautiful blonde. 'Steve. Thomlinson Sleet.' He held his hand out. Schwarchdorf shook it and said, 'My wife Christy.'

Sleet nodded disinterestedly in her direction. Unable to manage small talk, he addressed the titan. 'Tell me your thoughts on gold futures?'

Schwarchdorf ignored the question and stepped forward to introduce himself and his wife to Ayesha.

'I'm thinking of taking a position in Canadian miners,' Sleet continued. 'Most are piling into ETFs, but why not go straight to the source? If major governments keep printing money, gold and precious metals will be our only haven.'

'What do you think about Cameron and his Brexit pledge?' Schwarchdorf asked.

'It was something to keep the right wing of his party quiet. There'll be a vote and a lot of loose talk. Great Britain is a country where nothing ever happens.' Looking at Schwarchdorf, Sleet saw that the other man, though a decade older, was in astonishingly good shape. His shirt, made of the thinnest cotton, clung to a toned six-pack … Sleet pulled in his own belly and squared his shoulders.

Ayesha, wanting to show her husband that she could participate in business conversations, took the momentary lull in conversation to add her own comment. 'In the West Country, where we have a place, many are longing to get out of Europe,' she said. 'Now that Boris has declared for Brexit, I think there's a chance we'll crash out of the Union.'

Sleet grimaced. 'My wife thinks she's an expert!'

'I talk to farmers, shopkeepers and suppliers. It's Londoners who live in a bubble,' Ayesha said.

'If she's right, we should short the pound,' Schwarchdorf said.

'I don't listen to women's talk,' Sleet said.

'I defer to my wife on everything. Never met a wiser person,' the other man replied.

Christy smiled at the younger woman. 'I've heard nice things about you.'

'Thank you,' Ayesha said, flattered that anyone talked about her. She was about to answer when she caught a glimpse through the open door of a self-portrait by Artemisia Gentileschi, one of the painters she most admired. She made an excuse and slipped away. The picture was slightly larger than lifesize and showed Artemisia reaching up towards a canvas with a paintbrush in her hand. Her body weight was supported by her left arm. Her green silk dress was low-cut, showing a full breast, but she seemed simultaneously feminine and masculine. Her arm was strong, her gaze clear and she held the brush with determination and precision. The background was nearly black, making the figure even more lifelike.

Christy had followed Ayesha. 'She looks fierce,' Christy said.

'"You will find the spirit of Caesar in this soul of a woman,"' Ayesha quoted Artemesia. 'She had to fight for every single brushstroke. There were hardly any women painters at that time. While she was apprenticed to her father, a well-known Baroque painter, she was raped by one of his assistants. She took the rapist to court. The judges didn't believe her until they put thumbscrews on her fingers, and even through the intense pain, while her joints were splintering, she was able to scream, "It's true, it's true, it's true."'

'What a horrible story.'

'The saddest aspect is that once it was over and and she'd won the case, all Artemisia wanted was to marry him.'

'After all that happened?'

Ayesha shook her head. 'Better a raped wife than an unmarried soiled outcast.'

The two women stood side by side looking at the portrait.

'I like the intensity of her gaze,' Christy agreed, mesmerised by the painter glaring at her own canvas, willing her brushstroke towards its target.

'Can you imagine how unusual it was to see a woman painter pursuing a passion or a creative career? Normally they are bent over a stove or caring for a child. Here Artemisia is laying claim to an internal life and painting women as people not fantasies – fleshy, human, with cellulite, physically imperfect, humorous, brave.' Turning to the older woman, Ayesha asked,

'Is it true you're a doctor?'

'An oncologist.'

Ayesha looked at her closely. 'How do you manage to work and travel and be the wife these men expect?'

'Work is my saviour, my ballast, my outlet. Make it yours.' Christy smiled. 'Now teach me how to look at art.'

'My teacher at the Courtauld says you have to pace around an artwork to make it come alive. Otherwise it's two-dimensional.' The two women moved backwards and forwards in front of the painting. 'Look at it from a low angle and then from the side.'

Onlookers watched bemused as the two women snaked around and bobbed up and down.

'It's so different from seeing it in a book!' Christy exclaimed. 'You can hardly pace about in front of a reproduction.'

'My Uncle Tony says you must spend at least twenty hours with a work of art. Real appreciation takes time.'

'Why do you like this painter?' Christy said, squatting down and staring up at Artemesia's strong arm.

Ayesha thought for a few moments. 'Because she's both strong and intensely vulnerable. And you feel that in all her pictures.'

'You strike me as that kind of woman. Strong and vulnerable,' Christy said.

A lump rose in Ayesha's throat. It was a lovely compliment. She was about to say thank you when a large hand thumped on her shoulder.

'There you are,' Sleet said. 'I'm glad you kept Mrs S engaged.' He turned to Christy. 'Your husband had to talk to someone else.'

'Your wife has made my evening,' Christy said, smiling at Ayesha. 'You are a lucky man.'

'Tell that to my accountant.' He nodded at her curtly and then, with one hand on Ayesha's back, steered her away.

'Those people think they're better than us,' Sleet said.

'I thought she was nice.' Ayesha wondered what had happened.

'I hate these events,' Sleet said. While his wife looked at more paintings, Sleet examined other men's physiques and realised that the more successful a person, the better their body. How did these guys have the time to make money and abs? Was physical perfection the outward manifestation of material achievement? He understood having a great-looking wife was part of the package, but did it extend to himself? Casting his eyes downwards, he saw that his own tummy obscured his shoes. Flickery shots of panic pulsed up and down his neck. Not now, he begged. With no pencils to snap, he went over to Ayesha and pinched her shoulder hard. 'Just remember that we were both outcasts.'

'You're hurting me,' Ayesha cried out, knowing that his fingers would leave a red mark, possibly a bruise, on her naked shoulder. Her pain soothed Sleet and his heart slowed.

A horn sounded and then a gong. A uniformed servant asked guests to take their seats. Sleet headed towards the dining room. Ayesha stayed for as long as she could in the gallery, marvelling at the Queen's paintings.

Sleet did not have a good placement. He was at least thirty-five guests away from the Prince of Wales – if not quite Siberia then certainly Northern Canada. On his left was an ageing minor royal, Princess Amelia, and on his right the editor of a women's magazine. Sleet checked his watch. It was 8 p.m. and on the invitation it said carriages at 10.30. Two and a half hours in the company of post-menopausal trouts. He wondered if he could invent a personal emergency or, better still, have his PA call Scotland Yard with a hoax bomb threat to the Palace? Then he remembered that he didn't have his phone.

His thoughts were interrupted by the sound of two buglers. The room rose and stood to attention. Their Royal Highnesses had arrived. Sleet looked down the table and saw to his astonishment that Ayesha was seated on Prince Charles's right. The guest of honour. Typical! He'd given £50,000 and his wife got the top spot. His resentment hovered in the air. At least she bore his name. That was some small consolation.

The Prince and his Duchess took their seats and everyone else followed. Waiters filled their glasses with white wine and a plated first course arrived quickly. Sleet said hello to the Princess. The conversation got off to a flying start.

'Where do you stand on political correctness?' she asked.

'As far away as possible,' Sleet replied.

The Princess let out a shout of laughter and knocked back her wine in two large gulps. 'We'll get on, then.' Waving her empty glass at a waiter, she called for some more. 'You must ask them to fill every empty vessel: red, white, champagne and port. It's such a treat being treated.'

'Have mine while you wait,' Sleet said. Used to the finest wines, he found the Chardonnay undrinkable, thin and acidic. She swapped glasses just as the waiter appeared. 'My friend here is thirsty. Fill him up, please.' Princess Amelia took a gulp and wiped her lips on the back of her hand.

'What do you do?' she asked.

'Finance.'

'God, how dull.' She downed her drinks, then leaned over and took Sleet's refilled untouched glass. She waved at a passing waiter. 'More, please. Pronto.'

'What about you?' Sleet asked.

'I was put out to grass years ago. Couldn't keep my tongue in check. I kept faux pas-ing everywhere. Final straw was an encounter with an African ambassador. I called him something non-U.'

'Non-U?' Sleet asked.

'You must have read Nancy Mitford?'

Sleet was nonplussed. 'I grew up in America.'

'Ghastly place.'

'I agree with you.'

'Where do you live now?'

Sleet hesitated. If he gave his London address, the Little Boltons, the Princess would disparage it and he couldn't face any more criticism. So he said Cornwall – not giving a damn what anyone thought of there.

'I have a total pash for Cornwall,' the Princess said. 'Used to hunt and party there. Proper country. One of the last bits of unwrecked England.'

'That's because it's so far away,' Sleet said, thinking about the four-hour drive. It was quicker to get to Paris or Rome and both were, in his opinion, much nicer. Cornwall was a dump – it rained, there was nothing to do, no one to see.

'My last public engagement was there – I opened a once-magnificent stately home to the public in 2009. Frightfully sad. Had been in the same family for eight hundred years – hard times came to them along with everyone else. Stupid heir thought he could be clever in the stock market. Whoopsie. He lost the whole lot.'

Princess Amelia took a hunting flask out of her bag and poured a large shot into her water glass. 'Want some?'

'What is it?' Sleet asked.

'Vodka. Makes the evening go quicker.'

'Sure.'

She filled his glass to the rim.

'Then what happened?' Sleet asked. He knew the end of the story. He could write a damn book on useless British aristocrats – most of them were bankrupt spiritually and monetarily. All they had left were airs and graces.

'It became an absolute tragedy.'

'How so?'

'It's been bought by a vulgarian – a hedge trimmer or whatever those people are called.'

'A Bulgarian?' Sleet thought for a minute that she'd been talking about him, but he was from America not Bulgaria. The old dear must have her stately homes mixed up.

'He has the prettiest wife. Poor her. One shudders to think of her under such an unattractive, overweight man.'

Sleet pulled his stomach in defensively. 'Pretty wives are easy to come by,' he said. 'I am on number four.'

'Isn't that a little careless?' she asked. 'My day we put up with one person and had fun on the edges. It was an arrangement. Much less costly and disruptive. Staff hate change.'

Sleet, unused to personal questions or self-reflection, shuffled in his chair. 'I guess I get hung up on the idea of Miss Right,' he said, thinking about all four Lady Sleets. 'I'm a romantic.' He smiled at this description: it made him feel noble.

'Or a fantasist,' the Princess countered. 'You think the women the problem.'

'Of course they are,' he said, taking a large sip of her vodka. 'The first one nagged. The second spent. The third shagged a chef. And the last –' he hesitated as a small wave of emotion broke over his defence barriers '– I'm not sure she ever cared about me.'

Princess Amelia looked at him sharply. 'Poor me, poor me, pour me another.' She topped up her glass.

'This morning, when I left for work, neither my wife nor my daughter bothered to say goodbye.' He loosened his black tie. 'Tell me about the Bulgarian's wife.'

'She's got excellent taste in fabrics and paintings.'

Sleet made a mental note to introduce himself to the Bulgarian – they had a lot in common and could commiserate.

The Princess was momentarily interrupted by the arrival of the first course: a floppy bit of smoked salmon and half a quail's egg. Sleet was glad he'd eaten earlier. Princess Amelia fell upon the plate with gusto.

'My cook retired and I've been living off baked beans and Rice Krispies,' she explained.

'When did she go?'

'Ten years ago.'

Sleet pushed his plate towards her. 'I'm not hungry.' He felt selfless; giving his food would count as his good deed for the year: he might tell Rodita about it. He consoled himself with the thought that the Princess, though a member of the royal family, had no idea about taste or refinement. There was hope for him.

'Tell me more about the Bulgarian.'

'What Bulgarian?'

'The one with the pretty wife.' He drained the vodka.

'Pass your glass and I'll fill you up,' she said, gesturing with her flask. Sleet complied. He was enjoying the very pleasant first stages of inebriation: the room and conversation were a little fuzzy.

'He's one of those types that thinks that wealth buys freedom but is so paralysed by being seen to do the "wrong thing" that he can't get off the money-go-round.'

Sleet was pleased she wasn't referring to him. He knew where to go: St Barts at Christmas; Aspen for skiing; Antibes in the summer, broken by a quick visit to Mykonos. Now all he had to do was get the coolest guides and the best bookings at the right restaurants.

'How do you know so much about all this?' Sleet didn't think Princess Amelia could be stuffed away in a cottage in Surrey. She was too well informed.

The Princess looked left and right to make sure she wasn't being overheard. 'I'm an avid reader of something called *Taste and Refinement*.'

'I live by that magazine,' Sleet agreed.

'It's even funnier than P. G. Wodehouse. As if you can teach class!'

Sleet's spirits fell. 'Tell me more about the Bulgarian's wife?' he said, changing the subject.

'The queer thing is that she's the illegitimate daughter of the Earl of Trelawney.'

Sleet sat up. The old woman *had* been talking about him.

'I thought you said he was from Bulgaria?'

'I never mentioned Bulgaria. I said he was vulgar. A vulgarian. That's what the whole household, even the staff, call him.'

Sleet loosened his collar. 'And the wife too?'

'Not sure, but she did marry him for the money and castle.'

'No man can be so gullible,' Sleet remonstrated, feeling distinctly nauseous.

'Have you seen the girl?' She tapped Sleet on the arm and pointed down the table. 'She's working her magic on Charles as we speak. No wonder Camilla is looking so thundery.' Following her gaze, Sleet saw his wife wrap one of her auburn curls around her finger and lean in towards a mesmerised prince.

'Her mother was just the same. Anastasia something,' the Princess continued. 'She could stop traffic, you know. I remember the Duke of Maddingly blubbering when he saw her. One evening, at Chatsworth, she walked into the drawing room and everyone fell into amazed silence.'

'I scaled the wall of an Oxford college to give her a rose,' Sleet said.

'You knew her?' Amelia looked at him in amazement.

'I was twenty-one, sitting on a bench outside the library. She wore a pheasant's feather tucked into a trilby, a long skirt and a shirt tied under her breasts.' He remembered the moment as vividly as the day it happened. 'I followed her back to her college, like a child following the Pied Piper.'

'Was she aware?' The Princess supposed that this large, ginger-haired man must have been conspicuous.

'She was used to the adoration. She closed her door in my face. Two nights later, I climbed the drainpipe outside her room. The window was open and I managed to squeeze myself and the red roses I was carrying inside.' Sleet didn't add that he'd landed with an unceremonious flop at her feet or that Anastasia had been with two girlfriends, Blaze Scott and Jane Brown.

'Was she thrilled?'

Sleet shifted uncomfortably. 'Surprised.' He omitted the three girls' reaction: they had laughed and mocked him, holding their sides in unified hysteria. It still seemed as if his life had been divided into two sections, BA and AA – before Anastasia and afterwards. Until the age he'd seen her, his life lacked purpose: he'd done well at school, fought his way out of penury, won a Rhodes scholarship to Oxford, been the first in his adopted family to go abroad; but these efforts were fuelled by a hatred of his hometown. From that moment on he focused only on being the best in all areas. What he lacked in class or breeding he was going to make up for in wealth.

The Princess, seeing that she had lost his attention, tapped Sleet on the arm. 'The moment the Vulgarian leaves the castle, the old

Countess sneaks back into the house, uses his cellar and his staff. He never notices – the stinking rich are good at avoiding bad smells.'

'Maybe he never realises the depths people can sink to?' Sleet undid his black tie and the top button of his shirt. Now he thought of it, his accountant had mentioned an extraordinary quantity of oysters, foie gras and red burgundy consumed during December while he and Ayesha had been on the boat in the Caribbean. He had been distracted by an unexpected blip in the stock market – £2,000's worth of shellfish was nothing to a run on the yen – and had forgotten to raise the subject again.

'So what do people say about the financier?' Sleet asked, dreading the reply.

'He's what's known as a snollygoster.'

'A *what*?'

'Someone who's driven by personal gain not principles.'

'Where did principles ever get anyone?'

Princess Amelia looked at the man out of the corner of her eye. Something was not quite right.

'What did you say your name was?' she asked.

'Sir Thomlinson Sleet.'

The Princess spluttered and then fought for breath. She was sitting next to the Vulgarian himself. It was almost as bad as the incident with the Ambassador. How perfectly ghastly and wildly embarrassing. Drawing herself up and trying to maintain her decorum, she nodded at Sleet.

'I have to turn now and talk to the man on my other side.'

The magazine editor was talking to the man on her right. Sleet sat in dejected self-piteous silence.

Thirty-five seats away, Ayesha and the Prince were deep in conversation. Convention dictated that he should turn after the second course and talk to the Maharani of Balakphur, who was on his left, but HRH couldn't tear himself away from the captivating young woman.

'I can't believe your great-aunt is Tuffy Scott. She is my absolute heroine,' the Prince said. 'Her theses on climate change have informed my entire life. I read her work when I was at Cambridge and it made total sense. For years I was ridiculed for my beliefs, but thanks to Tuffy the world is catching up.' He grimaced. 'Let's hope it's not too late.'

'Do you like her work on fleas too?' Ayesha asked.

38

The Prince laughed. 'Of course. People assume that they are jumpy biting things, but a study of the flea, its changing environments and hosts offers a window onto our world. Destroying natural habitats will lead to wild animals living in more confined areas, which will enable mutations of viruses often carried by fleas. We'll see a major pandemic in my lifetime, probably several in yours.'

Their conversation moved seamlessly from global warming to art and then to Cornwall. 'I haven't had such an interesting dinner for a long time,' she told him truthfully. She wanted to kiss his royal cheek and thank him for making her feel so intelligent and charming – something she rarely experienced around her husband or his acquaintances. As delightful for Ayesha were the furious faces of the Balakphurs, who felt slighted by the British royals and upstaged by the young woman who in their eyes would always be a Little Miss Nobody.

Draining the last of his vodka, Sleet got to his feet. It was bad form to leave before the royals and even worse to abandon a dinner before the end of the main course – he was torn between wanting to leave and maintaining his dignity. The former won. He walked down the table, keeping the Prince and Ayesha in his cross hairs. Spotting the interloper, the royal bodyguards stepped forward. Sleet pushed them out of the way.

'I am looking for my wife.'

Assuming he was not an assassin, the security guards flanked Sleet for the last few steps, ready to take him down. Leaning over, he whispered into Ayesha's ear. 'We're going home. Now.'

'I'm not ready,' Ayesha, flushing with embarrassment, replied in a low voice.

'Your wife is so charming,' HRH said.

'So I'm told,' Sleet said. 'Something has come up and we need to leave.' He looked at his wife expectantly.

Ayesha didn't get up. She guessed correctly that Sleet wasn't happy with his placement. 'Sit down, darling. Let's not make a scene,' she whispered. Out of the corner of her eye, she saw the Balakphurs exchanging delighted glances. The Prince, wanting to avert an incident, decided, finally, to turn and talk to the Maharani. Ayesha rose to follow her husband.

Sleet, angry that she hadn't reacted more quickly, pushed her back into her chair. 'Don't bother coming home.'

Ayesha watched him walk to the door, flanked by nervous security guards. Trying to compose herself, she turned to the man on her right. 'There's an incident at work,' she said loudly, hoping that the Balakphurs would overhear. 'My poor husband had no choice.'

Her neighbour, unconvinced, scribbled a name on the back of his place card. 'Raymond Mishra. Dry as a crust, sharp as a rapier. Best divorce lawyer in town. I should know; he represented my last wife.'

Ayesha laughed. 'It isn't that bad – just an off day.' She took the card and put it into her evening bag.

Sleet went to retrieve his telephone.

'Are you all right, sir?' the attendant asked.

'No,' Sleet said. 'But there's damn all you can do about it.' Leaving the portico, he walked into the courtyard and banged on the window of his car to wake the napping Sanjay.

Settling into the Maybach's soft leather upholstery, he burned with humiliation, imagining not just his wife and her relations mocking and belittling him. This ribaldry had spread through society as far as the royal family. He shrank into his seat imagining British high society roaring with merriment about 'the Vulgarian'. His heart started to thump; beads of sweat broke out on his hairline.

'Pencils, pencils.' He felt the onset of a panic attack.

'There are four boxes in the armrest next to you, sir.' Sanjay glanced in the rear-view mirror apprehensively. An eighteen-stone man in the full throes of a panic attack in the back of a car was difficult to control.

Sleet started snapping pencils. Within twenty snaps, confusion was superseded by fury and, with each breath, fury transmogrified into a vindictive, venom-soaked anger. What had the Trelawneys done apart from being born? They hadn't added to the economy or made a name for themselves. They were blood-sucking spongers, and his wife was one of them.

When the car passed Sloane Square, he felt calm enough to call his PA. Although it was ten o'clock, his team was always on duty. 'Donna, first thing tomorrow I want you to engage a team of personal trainers and masseuses twenty-four seven. We are starting Operation Six–pack,' he said, thinking of the Princess's stinging comments and Schwarchdorf's abs.

'Certainly, sir.' Donna had been given the same instructions in the past: the diets never lasted long.

'I am moving all my operations to Trelawney for the foreseeable future.'

There was a lengthy pause on the other end of the line. Donna thought the idea of living in Cornwall in winter was hellish. Her husband wouldn't be best pleased, either.

'Where will everyone stay?'

'It's got three hundred and sixty-five rooms. If there aren't enough, book out the local hotels.'

'What shall I tell the Trelawneys?' Like others, she knew that Clarissa used the castle when the Sleets were absent.

'Don't tell them anything – it'll be a nice surprise.' He paused. 'Get Rodita on the phone.'

'Sir, it's 10 p.m.,' she said. Everyone knew that Rodita went to bed at nine and woke up at six.

'Am I speaking Cantonese? Get her.'

A few minutes later, a sleepy Rodita answered. 'An emergency?'

'Yeah. That bitch and her fucking family.'

Rodita ran her fingers through her long hair. Next to her Wilfredo turned over, groaning slightly. 'Can we deal with this in the morning?'

Sleet ignored her. 'What assets are in Ayesha's name and what provisions have we made following a divorce?'

Rodita wasn't shocked by the request: she'd managed the last three break-ups.

'The castle is held in a trust.'

'Sell it.'

'Really?'

'Get rid of it.'

'It shouldn't be too hard. Lady Sleet has turned a crumbling old asset into a highly desirable object; you might even make a profit from this marriage.'

'That'll be a first,' Sleet said. 'What else does she get?'

'Some jewellery. Custody of the child and alimony up to her eighteenth birthday. Usual package – education, the odd holiday, clothes allowance, rent on a mid-size house.'

'Don't tell anyone she's on the way out. Make sure the sale goes through first.'

41

'Is there anything else?' Rodita was longing to go back to sleep.

'I want full custody of the child.'

Suddenly wide awake, Rodita sat up in bed. 'What?' She'd never seen Sleet show interest in any of his offspring.

'No child of mine will be brought up by the Trelawney family. Stella's a Sleet. She'll be proud of it.'

'Let's talk about this in the morning,' Rodita reasoned. She wasn't a fan of the fourth Lady Sleet, who she considered a spoilt dilettante, but Ayesha had a reputation as a devoted mother.

'I told you what I want. Get it.' He hung up the telephone.

Rodita slipped out of bed and went through the flat to the kitchen. She flicked on the kettle and sat at the table. Thirty years earlier, she and her husband Wilfredo had emigrated to London from the Philippines, leaving behind their three children and intending to make enough money to give the next generation a better chance. Her whole life had been about providing for and protecting her offspring. They came first, even if she was absent from home.

Arriving in London with nothing, an extensive church network helped Rodita and Wilfredo perfect their English and find jobs. Wilfredo started in catering; Rodita worked as a hospital cleaner and attended night school, studying law. Within five years she was top of her cohort. Two years later, she graduated from the LSE with the highest MBA in finance. Joining Kerkyra Capital as a junior paralegal, her succinct analysis caught Sleet's eye and she worked her way up through the ranks to become his chief operating officer. Wilfredo now owned a catering business. Every spare penny of their salaries was sent home. They had fifteen grandchildren, were the largest landowners in their district and had built eleven houses for members of their extended family.

Wilfredo came into the kitchen and put his hands on her shoulders.

'I'm sorry I woke you,' she said, leaning her head against his stomach.

'What does he want this time?' Night-time calls were rare but never straightforward.

Rodita shrugged. 'Another divorce.'

'As long as it's not contagious.' He kissed the top of his wife's head and gently massaged her knotted shoulders.

'Do you think about going home? To the island?' Rodita asked.

Wilfredo let go of her shoulders and sat down next to his wife. 'Are you ready to fish all day and harvest rice?' It was the answer he always gave.

Rodita smiled. 'Nearly, but not yet.'

Wilfredo looked at the clock on the wall. Then he stood up and held out his hand, quoting a favourite passage from the Bible. '"Good and bad do not belong together. Light and darkness cannot share."'

3

March 2016

Blaze and Joshua sat side by side on one of Sir John and Lady Susan Whaley's overstuffed sofas, drinking tea from dainty bone-china cups. It was Perrin's third play date with Lily Whaley. Blaze looked out at the garden where swathes of brilliant-yellow daffodils were gently buffeted by a breeze. Her thoughts predictably returned to Trelawney and she remembered the long driveway, from the gates to the front door, lined with thousands of bobbing yellow heads. Her mother, Clarissa, used to call them the curtsey flowers, imagining that they were bowing their heads in deference to the returning Countess.

'I'll be mother,' Susan Whaley said, topping up their cups. 'John loves Earl Grey. This one is grown in the Himalayas.' She pronounced each syllable with care.

Sir John looked at his wife with pride. 'Terrific woman, my Susan.' He stood in front of a fireplace that wasn't lit: the room had under-floor heating and the temperature was kept to a steady twenty-one degrees.

'Tell me the story of how your business got started?' Joshua asked.

'I don't want to bore you,' John said. 'Or the ladies.'

'I'd love to hear,' Blaze said. 'I'm in awe of families who can make multigenerational businesses work.'

'Your lot have been around for centuries,' John countered. 'We're only just getting started.'

'For the last four out of eight hundred, our only skill has been spending, not making money.'

John and Susan laughed, thinking Blaze was making a joke. She wasn't.

'My family's greatest skill had been switching sides at opportune moments. One minute they were Roundheads, the next Cavaliers. In the Wars of the Roses, they realigned several times between the Yorks and the Lancasters. Ennobled in the fifteenth century for military valour, their prize was an earldom and great swathes of Cornwall. They bought land widely and prodigiously and by the end of the eighteenth century could walk on their own fields from the south-west coast to the Bristol Channel. There is literally nothing left.'

'You have made a great success of your life,' John said. 'People are always talking up Mr and Mrs Wolfe – examples of investors who make money responsibly.'

Joshua smiled. 'Thank you, but neither of us have ever built a business.' He hesitated. 'Whaley Precision Engineering was started by your grandfather, wasn't it?'

John nodded. 'In 1928. My father changed the name to make it sound grand.'

'It's ever so grand, John.' Susan handed round the cups.

'Grandpa was a handy chap. He worked as a fitter in an automobile shop in South Wales. Nothing much happened in that part of the world until a certain Miss Earhart landed there on June 17th 1928.' He pointed to a framed photograph on a side table. Written across the famous aviator's face were words. Blaze got up and read them aloud. '"For John, my saviour. Love Amelia."'

Sir John beamed. 'It was an unscheduled stop. Bit of engine trouble. Not many in that area had ever seen a plane or serviced one. Old John, as we still call him, was called in to have a look at it. He didn't even look at Amelia; he was fascinated by the propeller, unable to believe that something so delicate and yet so strong could have got her and her co-pilot over the Atlantic in only twenty hours.'

Blaze and Joshua nodded. From the next room came sounds of two little girls playing happily: this was all they wanted to hear. Perrin had a friend. As peals of laughter echoed from next door, Joshua squeezed his wife's hand.

'Miss Earhart knew a good thing when she saw one. She took my grandfather back to the States and made him head mechanic. But John had bigger dreams.'

Blaze dug her fingers into Joshua's leg. He pushed his shoulder against hers.

'Would you like more tea?' Susan asked and, without waiting for an answer, filled both of their cups. She rang a small bell on the table and a maid appeared with a plate of perfectly cut cucumber sandwiches, crusts removed. 'Lily is gluten intolerant,' Susan explained. 'So I have arranged for her and Perrin to have carrot sticks and hummus.'

John smiled benevolently at his wife. 'She frets a lot about Lily's health.'

'It took us fifteen years to conceive a child, so you'll forgive us being a little bit protective,' Susan explained.

John put his hand on his wife's arm. 'You and Lily are my world.' He hesitated. 'Where was I?'

'Old John's about to go solo,' Susan prompted.

'Ah, yes. Returning to home turf, he couldn't face small-town Wales so settled near here and set up a propeller business. Everyone laughed at him. What was a garage mechanic doing setting up a factory? But John had a vision. Slowly but surely, he brought his designs to market. The first propeller he made was for Rolls-Royce. Not a bad start. Did you know it was Old John who invented the metal-bladed props for Rolls-Royce, including the Hawker Siddeley 740 and the Fokker F27?'

'Fokking hell,' Joshua said.

Susan was unamused. 'Please don't use that kind of language near the children.'

Whatever their pretensions, Blaze felt immense respect for the Whaleys and their family. Growing a business from scratch was impressive; keeping it going for generations was rare.

'My John inherited a small business and transformed it,' Susan said proudly. 'Whaley's the largest employer in the area. He invented a prop whose airfoil systems generated higher efficiencies – increased take-off and climb performance, reduced noise and vibration levels – as well as high-speed, four- and six-bladed composite prop engines with 2,000 to 6,000 shaft horsepower ratings.'

'Susan knows as much about the business as I do.'

'You were about to tell us about your new invention,' Joshua said.

John beamed. 'If I told you, I'd have to kill you.'

Joshua made a mock-horror expression. 'Then I'd rather not know.' He put his arms out as if to shield Blaze from the attack. She took the opportunity to bury her face in his shoulder, inhaling his delicious smell. 'I love you so much,' she said silently. 'My wonderful husband, the man who's made my life so much better.'

'Stop making out, you two!' Susan said. 'Those of us who've been married for more than ten years can't cope with public displays of affection.'

Joshua smiled at her and put his arm around his wife. 'We're in year seven – you'll have to forgive us.'

John leaned forward and whispered, 'Graphite. We have made the world's lightest and strongest propeller. It's passed all the tests. We're waiting for the final patent. And next month Boeing are putting out an order for their whole fleet.' He hesitated. 'We're going public in July. An IPO.'

'Sounds like an embarrassing procedure, doesn't it?' Susan joked.

'Why are you doing it?' Blaze asked.

'Partly to realise some cash, and I want to raise £200 million to build a new factory. It'll create three hundred and fifty new jobs in the area.'

'It'll make us.' Susan patted her husband's arm proudly.

'You look quite "made" already,' Blaze said.

'We do nicely, thank you, but this will be serious money.'

'I want Old John to look down from heaven and see that his tinkering led to our blades being in every new plane in the world,' John said, his chest puffing up like a pigeon. 'The bankers think the company could be worth as much as £500 million. Old John went to the States in a third-class cabin with five other people. Susan and I will take the Royal Suite in the QE2.'

'Right, that's enough business – shall we go for a walk?' Susan suggested, standing up. 'The daffodils are at their best. I do love a daff, don't you?'

'I never know if they mean the end of winter or the beginning of spring,' Blaze said.

'Snowdrops are spring for me,' Susan said.

Blaze took Joshua's hand and they followed their hosts into the garden. Perrin and Lily rushed past them, chattering and tumbling over each other.

'How are you?' Blaze asked when they were out of the Whaleys' earshot.

Looking at his daughter's glowing face, Joshua laughed. 'Propellery happy!'

*

48

Walking under the arches of Somerset House always made Ayesha smile. She loved the columns framing the grand facade, the merry waterscape in summer, the ice rink in winter. For her, Chambers's building was the best of eighteenth-century British architecture. She also felt a sense of personal achievement. She had won the top first in her undergraduate year and a place on the coveted MA course on her own merits: it had nothing to do with her husband's wealth or her father's title. Determined to prove her critics wrong, she worked harder than any of her contemporaries, reading while suckling her newborn daughter, setting her alarm for 5 a.m. each day to have uninterrupted study time, and carving out daytime hours to finish essays. When anyone asked how she managed to juggle marriage, motherhood and academia, her answer was simple: I treat my work like a love affair. If you really want to make time for something, it's possible.

Her friendship with fellow student Yasmin Palavi started when a tutor put them in a study pair. Theirs was an unlikely alliance: the daughter of Iranian refugees who worked part-time as a paralegal and the wife of a city financier. They both felt like outsiders, ship-wrecks from another life, and were also bound by competitiveness and a love of their subject. The two best students of their cohort, they fought amicably for the top prizes. Their beauty combined with their academic achievements made them celebrities amongst their fellow students.

Built in the late eighteenth century, the Courtauld Institute, housed in Somerset House, contained state rooms with one of the finest collections of impressionist art. By contrast, the students' subter-ranean lecture theatres are low-ceilinged and airless. Nevertheless, many crammed in to hear the distinguished lecturer Dr Sheles Treves talk about 'The Role of Women in Art'. Ayesha and Yasmin shared a chair and just had room to balance their notebooks on the corner of a desk; many sat on the floor or leaned against the walls.

Twenty minutes into the lecture, Treves reached the nub of her argument. 'In AD 79, Pliny the Elder wrote that painting was invented by a woman, Kora of Sicyon, in 650 BCE. Twenty-seven centuries later there are fewer than twenty paintings by women, less than one per cent, in a collection of more than 2,300 in the National Gallery of London.' In her right hand she clicked through some examples: Rosa Bonheur, Rachel Ruysch and Vigée Le Brun. 'Most are not even on display, considered poor seconds to the main event: paintings by men. There is not even one work by Artemisia Gentileschi.'

Dr Treves paused. 'You will, of course, find scores of naked, servile and married women hanging on the walls.' As she spun through hundreds of examples, there was a rustle of indignation in the lecture hall.

'Shocking statistic, isn't it?' Yasmin wrote on a piece of paper and passed it to her friend.

Ayesha, confused, looked at her and wrote a question mark. The lecturer's words seemed to meander around her consciousness like uncatchable autumn leaves. All she could think about was her husband's cruel behaviour. Since the dinner at Buckingham Palace, Sleet had ignored her. She was no longer invited to dinners. Now that the couple lived at Trelawney, and inhabited different wings of the castle, it was possible to go days without meeting. She'd tried everything she could think of to talk and even to ingratiate herself – only to be met with indifference. Then there had been the trickle of newspaper articles. The first in the *Mail*, raking over the story of Ayesha's real parentage: her father had not, as she and most thought, been Kitto Trelawney but his father Enyon. The paper delighted in the facts. Anastasia had been eighteen at the time, the older man over seventy. Ayesha knew it all but seeing the story in black and white compounded her sense of abandonment. The second article was about absent mothers who put their careers before childcare. Most of the examples were women from history but, to Ayesha's astonishment, she was mentioned as a contemporary who parked her child in the country with a devoted father while she worked as an art consultant in London.

'Are you listening to a word?' Yasmin scribbled.

Ayesha responded with a sad smiley face.

Treves continued her lecture. 'As the great Linda Nochlin said in her essay of 1971, "Why aren't there more women artists?", the fault lies not in our stars, our hormones, our menstrual cycles, or our empty internal spaces, but in our institutions and our education – education understood to include everything that happens to us from the moment we enter this world of meaningful symbols, signs and signals.'

A smattering of applause broke out in the room, mainly from female students but also a few men wanting to show solidarity.

'Nochlin argued that women must conceive of themselves as potentially, if not actually, equal subjects, and must be willing to look the facts of their situation full in the face, without self-pity, or cop-outs; at the same time they must view their situation with that high degree of emotional and intellectual commitment necessary to create a world in which equal achievement will be not only made possible but actively encouraged by social institutions.'

Ayesha winced, remembering how, after Sleet left Buckingham Palace, few including her dinner companions talked to her. The invitation of a private tour evaporated. With no money for a cab or public transport, she'd walked home in the rain, tottering through puddles in high heels.

'I am equal, I am deserving, I must face the next step with courage and determination,' Ayesha told herself, not believing a word. From the inner depths of her body, Declan shape-shifted to cover her heart and lungs.

Later, as they walked out of the Courtauld, through the large grey portico on to the Strand, Yasmin cross-questioned Ayesha.

'What's up? You were miles away.'

'Can we talk? I could come over later?'

Yasmin linked her arm through her friend's. 'I have a date!'

Ayesha felt a tinge of jealousy; both women were the same age but Yasmin's life was appropriate to a 24-year-old student – studying, dating, living with friends in the East End, staying up too late, dancing and getting into scrapes. Three years ago, when Sleet was on a business trip, Ayesha went clubbing with Yasmin and some of her friends in Dalston. They'd gone on the Tube (also a novelty for Ayesha) to a club in the basement of an old warehouse. The walls were decorated with graffiti and the carcasses of old light machinery were piled in corners. A technobeat thud bounced off the walls and pulsated through every cell in Ayesha's body. She danced without a break until 5 a.m. The following morning she'd woken late; muscles in her body ached, her toes were blistered, and her throat burned from laughter and shouting; her eyes were dry from dehydration. Glugging down glass after glass of water, she could barely remember ever feeling so alive and well. After much cajoling, she persuaded Sleet to go to a nightclub. He chose Annabel's, a suitable location for wealthy men with younger consorts. They danced to ABBA and the

Rolling Stones, Sleet stamping and gyrating in the middle of the floor. 'I'm Nureyev,' he shouted, prancing from one large foot to another. Halfway through 'Lady in Red', their slow dance, he got bored and they went home. After that Ayesha refused all Yasmin's invitations. She didn't dare; next time she might not make it home.

Pushing those memories out of her mind, she asked her friend, 'Who's the lucky guy?'

'His name's Ali – I met him at a family event.'

'The one you didn't want to go to?' Ayesha laughed, remembering how cross Yasmin had been the week before her Cousin Jamshid's wedding.

'Our eyes met over a *khoresh-e fesenjan*. We both agreed we hated the traditional stew.'

'Can we meet tomorrow? I don't have to be back in Cornwall until the evening.'

'Are you going to see the lawyer?' Yasmin asked. For several weeks she'd urged her friend to seek professional advice.

'It feels treacherous.' Ayesha looked up and down the road as if someone could overhear their conversation. 'After everything he's done for me.'

Yasmin took her arm firmly. 'Husbands don't move out of bedrooms and stop talking to their wives without a reason. If you don't do it for yourself, think about your daughter's future.'

Ayesha bit her lip and nodded. 'I'm going tomorrow.'

Yasmin leaned over and kissed her friend on the cheek. 'And eat something – you're too skinny.'

Neither saw the photographer snapping the two young women as they embraced.

Ayesha hailed a taxi, making sure that Yasmin and the other students didn't see (most lived on less per week than the cost of a single cab journey between the Strand and Chelsea). Arriving at their white stucco pillared house in the Boltons, she didn't need to find a key – the staff were expecting her. One took her coat, another brought a cup of her favourite green tea, all without asking. The house and the Sleets' life had been curated by a team of advisers. Marrying at eighteen, hotfoot from a life on the other side of the world, she'd had no idea how to run, let alone decorate a house; nor, apparently, did her husband. She shadowed the teams of experts and researched her new role with the same assiduous energy and meticulous attention to detail that she'd later expend on her prize-winning work at the Courtauld. She bought books on manners and interiors; she combed magazines and employed specialists in etiquette. Her best guide was Uncle Tony, who showed the newly married Lady Sleet how to hold a knife or eat an artichoke; how to address a duke or a butler. 'Anyone can buy lifestyle; it takes class to live well,' he told her.

Ayesha walked around their large home and smiled, knowing that she'd got most of it right. The carefully designed spaces were in perfect harmony. There were fine modern British works and a few minor impressionist paintings (bought before Ayesha learned about art). Her garden was a symphony of green and white. Running her fingers over surfaces, Ayesha knew there wouldn't be one speck of dust. The cushions were plumped and arranged in perfect formations. Sleet's boxes of pencils were placed in neat rows on tabletops. There were professional flower arrangements in strategic places, some framed by windows or at the end of long passages. The latest magazines were neatly fanned on side tables. The fridge was restocked with favourite foods. Unopened bottles of water with polished glasses waited by their bedside.

Deciding to skip supper, Ayesha dismissed the staff, then settling into a pristine white sofa, a glass of wine at the ready, she resumed work on her Isabella d'Este dissertation. Employing two researchers in Mantua, she'd had copies made of all the patron's letters, invoices and other sundry correspondence – some 50,000 in total. Slowly but surely, she was working her way through them, building up a hitherto unknown portrait of her subject's character and courtly life. Visiting Isabella's marital home, the palace in Mantua, Ayesha had been shocked to see that the Marquesa had been expunged from its history. There wasn't a single reference to their former ruler and greatest collector. Looking at the frescoes and art that did remain, she noticed that the only female role models on view for Isabella or the other women at court were either slaves or objects of desire. How, she wondered, did a sixteen-year-old girl from another part of Italy learn statecraft and about art? What, Ayesha mused, could she learn from Isabella's example?

She worked without stopping until 11 p.m., when hunger rather than boredom forced her to pause. She thought about ordering a delivery pizza but couldn't remember the codes for the front-door alarms. She rang down to the kitchen but there was no answer. Then she texted Donna. It was far too late to call but, Ayesha reasoned, if Donna wanted to control every aspect of the Sleets' life, she could order her a pizza and a can of Coke. The PA answered, her voice foggy with sleep. Ayesha proceeded with her order – the most complicated pizza she could think of, piled with lots of toppings. Hanging up, she smiled: it was time, Ayesha thought, to show who was boss.

The following morning Ayesha woke at seven. She showered while the chef prepared her breakfast which she ate chased down by two wheatgrass shots. With time still to kill and a head to clear, she decided to walk to her appointment at the Temple to meet the lawyer, Raymond Mishra. Sleet liked their chauffeur to shadow his wife when she set off alone; he said it was keeping her safe, while she suspected it was keeping tabs. This morning she was adamant that no one should follow. It was a clear, crisp day. With Stevie Wonder singing through her headphones, she meandered towards her destination, turning down roads with the best display of cherry blossom and admiring the daffodils and crocuses in well-tended front gardens. Two laughing women, dressed in Lycra and clutching their yoga mats, came out of a gym. Ayesha followed them for a block, looking at the ease and familiarity of their gestures, listening to their laughter and shared jokes. She would join when they were back in London. The Sleets' peripatetic lifestyle made friendship challenging; dates were hard to keep when locations changed, often several times a week.

Workmen on construction sites stopped to throw lascivious glances in her direction. A young man had opened a telephone exchange and sat cross-legged before a brightly coloured tangle of wires. A traffic warden hid in a doorway, eyeing up an illegally parked Porsche. She passed a flower stall with gorgeous, wildly expensive, out-of-season blooms; past the trendy shops promising transformation of feet and legs and bodies; the restaurants with perfectly pressed white tablecloths and perfectly dressed, coiffed coffee drinkers raising glasses to neon-toothed smiles. She imagined sitting there with her newfound 'yoga' friends and smiled in anticipation.

She walked from Chelsea to Knightsbridge, on through Berkeley Square and Belgravia. The grand wide streets were deserted except for chauffeurs polishing cars and dog walkers heading for the park. On the corner of Chesham Place, a black Rolls-Royce pulled over and a chauffeur leapt out to open the door for a woman about Ayesha's age. She walked on tottery heels to a door which was opened by a maid in uniform. The chauffeur followed, carrying top-brand shopping bags. Ayesha took a note of the address and decided to drop a note in the following day. The woman, her doppelgänger, could be a new friend. She imagined sharing shopping trips and make-up tips. Her spirits rose with each step. She was about to start a new chapter: a renewed effort in all areas. Why was she visiting a lawyer? There was no need. Imagining Yasmin's disapproving face, she continued; it would be useful if only to dismiss her friend's concerns.

At Hyde Park Corner the atmosphere changed. Gone were the eerily silent boulevards and instead it was jostling locals, aggressive cyclists and hapless tourists holding their maps like compasses, turning them around, looking hither and thither for landmarks or clues. It reminded her of Balakphur and the cacophony of noises, the smells, the colours and thrum of movement. To escape she cut into Green Park, past the front of Buckingham Palace and into St James's. Tracing the lake from one end to the other, she looked at the pelicans and black swans preening by the banks. At the exit, she was just in time to catch the Prime Minister, his forehead shiny, his expression self-satisfied, as he swept out of Downing Street flanked by motorbike outriders. Her feet, in flat leather brogues, crunched across the parade ground, empty save for a few guardsmen. The entrance to Admiralty Arch was guarded by two soldiers astride horses standing patiently as tourists took selfies and children tried to touch their velvet muzzles. Taxis and buses were nose to tail by the Cenotaph, surrounded by halos of violet-tinted diesel fumes.

Looking at her watch, she saw that her appointment was in half an hour. She hailed a cab and arrived at the Temple with minutes to spare. Finding the doorway, she was ushered into a dark-panelled office where a large desk was piled with stacks of bound paper at least two foot high. From behind the mounds rose a man as tall and thin as a stork. He wore a pinstripe suit, several sizes too big, round gold glasses, a white shirt, and a knitted tie which had been through the tumble dryer too many times.

'Lady Sleet. Will you take a seat?' he said, pointing to a leather chair. 'How can I help you?' Mishra could hardly believe that the person before him, who looked so delicate, was married and a mother; she reminded him of a granddaughter.

Ayesha sat in the chair, capacious enough for a baby elephant and slippery. 'I'm not here to get a divorce,' she explained, putting both hands on the armrests to stop herself from sliding off. 'I just want some reassurance. Things are a bit tricky right now.' Above the solicitor's head, hanging on the wall, there was a portrait of an elderly judge. Ayesha wondered if it was a relation of his or if the firm bought random paintings of bewigged men.

Mishra looked at her sympathetically. 'You sent some copies of documents in advance. Are you sure they were the correct ones?'

Nodding, she lifted her briefcase from the floor. 'Here are the originals.' She handed them to him.

Mishra read through them. He tapped his fingers on the documents and then looked at her, his expression one of concern. 'Are you aware that these don't give you any security?'

Ayesha knew it was a mistake coming here. She could recite the papers blindfold; she didn't need a lawyer to translate what they meant.

'Lady Sleet, these documents are of no use. They are fakes: you don't own the castle.'

'Of course I do. It was a wedding present from my husband.' Ayesha laughed, aware that it sounded rather tinkly. She tapped the property's title deeds with a sugar-pink fingernail. 'It's here in black and white.'

Mishra shifted in his chair. He wanted to please this beautiful young woman, offer her words of reassurance, but it was impossible. 'These are not legally binding.'

'They were signed in the presence of a solicitor with three witnesses.' A knot of panic rose in Ayesha's chest. 'I was there.'

Mishra rested the tips of his two index fingers together to make a steeple and then threaded his remaining fingers between each other. 'Lady Sleet, I took the precaution of checking the Land Registry details. The castle is held and owned by an offshore trust for the beneficiary of the settlor. There are so many companies between the original and the subsidiaries that it's impossible to work out who the actual owner might be. The notary was a Mrs Rodita Della Cruz on behalf of an unnamed settlor who is the beneficiary of the trust.'

'And that person could be me?' Ayesha's spirits lifted.

'Have you had any papers relating to a Panamanian trust?'

Ayesha shook her head. Her breath became laboured. Was it her imagination or did the painted judge wink at her?

Mishra steepled his fingers again. 'Land Registry documents take precedence over all other deeds.' He cleared his throat with a short, high-pitched cough, 'The aforementioned solicitor, Ms Della Cruz, who ratified your deeds, works for a company called Kerkyra Capital Inc. where her services are listed as Chief Operating Officer.'

'Kerkyra Capital is my husband's company.' Ayesha's voice came out as a whisper.

Mishra paused. 'Can you think of any reason why your husband might have falsified these documents?'

Ayesha looked up at the solicitor, her eyes swimming with tears.

Loath as he was to deliver more bad news, it was his duty to clarify recent developments. 'In the last few weeks, a property called Trelawney Castle in Cornwall has been put on the market.'

'For sale?' Ayesha thought she might pass out. Clutching the arms of the chair, she took sips of breath.

Mishra hadn't finished. 'They are asking £145 million. The deal includes the house, the park and one thousand acres of farmland, woods, river frontage, gardens and the burial grounds.'

Blood whooshing around her head was making her hot and dizzy. She pulled at her dress, trying to get more air into her lungs. 'Did you say 145 million?' She began to sob.

Mishra was used to crying women; in his desk he kept boxes of tissues. He wondered how many he'd use today.

'Might I see a copy of your wedding certificate?' he asked.

'I don't have one. We got married on a boat, my husband's boat, by his captain.'

'Was the wedding ratified in a registry office?'

Ayesha squirmed in her chair. 'I thought a ship's captain had the authority.'

'A common misapprehension. It's only legally binding if the captain is also a judge, a JP, minister or public notary.'

'If I am not married, does my prenup hold?' Ayesha felt beads of sweat forming on her brow and between her shoulder blades.

Mishra's news was about to get worse. 'Next time get married in an official place in Scotland or the US.'

In his business, Mishra witnessed the lowest form of human behaviour: Sleet and his ilk were not unusual. Money often became the battleground, the proxy war in divorce. It was easier to focus on financial balance sheets than emotional tallying. The stronger side nearly always won. He hoped the girl had supportive parents and siblings.

'I thought we made a good couple. That we both met the other's needs.'

Mishra nodded understandingly. Sweat was now coursing down Ayesha's back. The room had got much smaller. 'What rights does a common-law wife have?'

'Very few. Common-law marriage has no legal validity in the United Kingdom. Moving in together doesn't give you automatic rights to each other's property, no matter how long you cohabit.'

Scenes from her favourite childhood books flooded her mind. Sleeping Beauty, Cinderella, the Little Match Girl: all ended happily ever after. She had stumbled into the wrong story – there must be a way out, back to the right narrative. Looking up at Mishra, she said, 'He rescued me. I was no one. He gave me a life. I gave him mine. We have a child. How could he do this?'

'Can you think of a logical reason why your husband might have falsified these documents?' Mishra asked.

Ayesha shook her head. 'What will become of me?'

'You will of course get child and personal maintenance until your daughter is eighteen. I can build a case for a generous allowance. You are young – lots of time to rebuild a life.' He hesitated. 'Will your husband agree to shared custody of your daughter?'

Shock reverberated through her body. It had never occurred to her that Sleet would want access to their daughter – he hardly saw her; and his other children, three in all, got Christmas gifts chosen and sent by Donna. 'He's never shown any interest. He wasn't even there for the birth.' It had been the day of a stock-market rally and Sleet's personal priorities were elsewhere.

Mishra decided not to tell her that children were often used as pawns between couples. He'd seen cases where an absent parent suddenly rekindled a passion for their offspring if they thought it would strengthen their case. He steepled his fingers again and leaned over his desk. 'Lady Sleet. Might I give you a word of advice? Stay in the relationship. Make it work. It'll give you a better outcome materially. Maybe you can persuade him not to sell the castle.'

Ayesha had slipped further down the chair. She gripped the armrests firmly to try and wriggle her way back up. Her feet dangled above the floor. 'People find it hard to believe, but it's not all about money.' She hesitated, not knowing what to call the man who, until half an hour ago, had been her husband. 'He can be clever and generous.' She hesitated. 'We both had rotten childhoods. We need each other.' Repeating her narrative made her feel better. 'Is it enough not to want to separate?' she added in a small voice. 'I've never cheated or taken one penny for myself.'

'I'm assuming you don't have many resources?'

'Twenty-seven thousand pounds.'

Mishra didn't have the heart to tell her that if the case went to court, this amount would not cover his fees. 'I'd advise you being focused and unemotional.'

Ayesha wondered what that meant.

Mishra arranged his features sympathetically. 'Lady Sleet, you have very few cards in your hand, but you have a lot to lose or gain. Even if the marriage comes right, and I hope for your sake that it does, my strong advice is to try and gather as much information as possible.'

'What would I do with it?'

Mishra wondered how she'd remained so naive. 'If things got difficult, it might be helpful to have some firepower, some arsenal you could deploy.'

Ayesha looked bemused.

'For some, reputational capital has enormous value. It's something easily lost and hard to regain. Most are prepared to pay a lot of money to keep their images clean.'

'My husband doesn't care what people think. He's in the short-selling business where you can destroy other people's lives to make a quick buck. He has a thick skin.'

Mishra straightened the edges of some papers on his desk and looked at the young woman. 'Why do people put money with him?'

'To make money.'

'What if they thought he couldn't? What if something leads them to believe he'd lost his touch?'

'Like what?' Ayesha asked.

'That his judgement was off?' He tapped his fingers on his desk, wanting her to listen carefully. 'You need to help me build a case of neglect and cruelty. I want you to note down every single detrimental thing that he does to you, your child or any member of your household. If possible, back it up with evidence. Emails, text messages, conversations. Record every single meeting you have. If you must needle or goad him on, do it. Try and inveigle or persuade friends or employees to help. Dirt is ammunition. If this goes to court, the judge and jury must be in no doubt what and who we are dealing with.'

Ayesha nodded.

'If we can put together enough damaging material, evidence that would impact on his business or the esteem his clients hold him in, we might be able to negotiate.' Mishra hesitated and then wrote a name and number on a page of his notebook, tore it and handed it to Ayesha. 'Lawrence Digby is a former police officer turned private detective. He is good at "unearthing" information. I would give him a call.'

'I don't like spying on people,' Ayesha said, putting the piece of paper in her pocket.

'Needs must,' the solicitor said. Then he looked at the clock on the far wall and got to his feet. 'Lady Sleet. I am here at your service. Please reflect on this conversation and see if I can offer any help.'

'Thank you.' She rose and held out a hand.

'My fees are £750 per hour, but in this case I could make an adjustment. Not everything is about money,' he added.

Ayesha left his office in a daze. In less than one hour her life, her future and her sense of security had been shattered. She had entered the lawyer's office as a wife, a lady, a chatelaine and a person of consequence. The man who she'd loved to the best of her ability for eight years had duped her from the start, knowing that one day he'd tire and needed the easiest and least expensive exit. And she had never, even for one minute, imagined this scenario. She passed a jeweller's repair shop which had a notice in the window advertising 'on-the-spot valuations'. On impulse she went inside. In the far corner, behind a thick glass partition reinforced with metal, sat a man bent over a workbench.

He looked up and, seeing her, called to the back. Another assistant appeared; punching numbers into a keypad, he released the door.

'How can I help?' the first man asked. He had a long thin face, sparse grey hair and a lugubrious expression. Around his neck, on a chain, was a small magnifying glass.

Ayesha put out her left hand to display her engagement ring. It was a diamond the size of a plover's egg set on a platinum-gold band. The shop owner did a second take.

'That looks fine,' he said slowly, wiping spidery fingers on a velvet cloth.

'Would you value it for me?' Ayesha asked, reassured that the jeweller couldn't take his eyes off her ring.

'It would be a pleasure to hold it.'

Ayesha wriggled the ring off her finger and handed it to him. The man took his magnifying glass from its chain and a small torch from the desk. Placing the ring on a velvet cushion, he shone the torch on the diamond and examined it from different angles. After less than a minute he passed it back to Ayesha.

'A very pretty piece of glass,' he said, looking at the clock above his desk.

'It has a name, the Bangalore diamond,' Ayesha said.

'It's a fake. A good fake but a fake nonetheless.'

'Don't you need to check with that?' Ayesha pointed to the microscope at his side.

'I've been at this for over half a century,' the man said. 'From a long line of diamond merchants. I don't need to.' He shrugged. 'Can I help you with anything else?'

Ayesha put the ring back on her finger and, with as much grace as she could manage, walked out of the shop. In the street, she was hit by a walloping wall of anger; the ring had been both a 21st-birthday present and a gift to celebrate the birth of their daughter – so their combined value to Sleet was a worthless piece of glass? Fury was followed by fear: there was no plan B. She had become infantalised; every aspect of her life – her money, her homes, her schedule – was entirely dictated, owned and controlled by her husband. She didn't know how to buy a car, how to get a job. She stopped in the middle of Waterloo Bridge. The wind whipped her hair around her face. She leaned against the balustrade and stared into the depths of the River

Thames. Suddenly her mother's face appeared like a mirage on the surface. 'What do I do?' Ayesha shouted at her.

Anastasia just laughed, a hard, mean cackle, and then her image dissolved in the murky water.

*

Sleet was tiring of life at Trelawney. The house was comfortable but disconnected from the City and he worried that deals and opportunities were out of his reach. There were a lot of people around, but not 'the right people'. He decided to give being a landed gentleman one last try. In the Great Hall there was a full-length swagger portrait of a former earl with a massive Irish wolfhound. Sleet told Donna to get him an identical animal and, while she was at it, find a portrait painter to immortalise this master and his dog. 'Wolfie' arrived on a Tuesday and a painter from the Royal Academy trailing a giant canvas came the following afternoon. The painter, unfortunately, feared dogs. Wolfie saw the easel (and most other surfaces) as a useful urinal and liked the game of chasing a screaming disappearing man. On Thursday the dog and painter were dismissed (destinations unclear but certainly different).

Following the advice in *Taste and Refinement*, Sleet told Donna to find a jeweller who could take all the labels and logos off his cars and other possessions. When no one gave his prize Aston Martin a second glance, he recalled the craftsmen from London to reattach the names. Bored to distraction, he started sleeping with one of his trainers, a Croatian woman who made him sweat in unpredictable ways. Sleet preferred these kinds of arrangements: people didn't understand that it's not the sex you pay for, it's the ease of getting the other person to leave.

Donna put together a list of people for Sleet to meet. These fell into different categories, including science, art, business, love and other opportunities. To his delight, Sleet discovered that, for many, the offer of a free return helicopter ride, a visit to a castle and an excellent bottle of wine was enough to lure people all the way to Cornwall. In the three weeks since his arrival at Trelawney, he'd met a Nobel-winning scientist (impossibly dull); three supermodels (none as pretty as the incumbent Lady Sleet); an award-winning novelist (with an ego the

62

size of the Ritz); two tech start-up wizards (incomprehensible) and a captain of industry (beyond gloomy). To his surprise, the person he thought would be the easiest to lure, Nigel Farage, leader of the Leave party, was playing hard to get. Given the perilous state of the opinion polling and party's finances, Sleet found this vaguely titillating. He agreed to meet Leave's campaign manager Tahira Khan, but only for lunch in the local pub.

After his morning workout, Sleet made his way to the dining room where his three chefs prepared his daily power shake. Calling for his daughter and her nanny, he had a conversation with Stella about her pony, Mickey, insisting that the chefs stayed within earshot. He'd employed a photographer to capture the father–daughter moment.

Then he took a briefing from his heads of departments, took a short position on a large tech company whose results had been disappointing and read the Lex column of the *Financial Times*. It was only eleven o'clock. For reasons he couldn't fathom, time passed more slowly in the country. He walked down the drive to the converted stable block where he kept his collection of cars. Conservatively valued at £50 million, they included a McLaren F1 and a vintage Ferrari 275 GTS. Today he chose his Mercedes-AMG G63, a car that *Taste and Refinement* called 'A-class understated chic', and left the property with a screech of tyres. A few days earlier he'd killed two sheep on a hairpin bend: it had been the most exciting thing that had happened all month.

Providing he went to pubs several miles away from Trelawney, no one knew or cared who he was. He liked the anonymity of sitting at the bar, stuffing his mouth with crisps and downing pints of local ale. His favourite hostelry was in a village called Watersmeet. The entrance was so low that Sleet bent down to get through the front door. The walls were covered with vintage black and white photographs taken between seventy and twenty years earlier: little had changed. The beams were still blackened, the wallpaper grubby and fire-scorched. An assortment of men leaned against the bar. An old boy and his dog sat in the far corner. Each time the door opened, notices for the weekly quiz or the bus timetable flapped in the draught. Over the last weeks, Sleet had become an aficionado of a local dish known as the pasty, a highly calorific combination of fat, potato, pastry, butter and beef – enough to give his London-based nutritionist cause for serious concern. Sleet ordered four at a time. His favourite was a Cornish Yarg pasty with extra sorrel, potato and cheese, fashioned into the size of a thick paperback and deliciously greasy.

Arriving at the pub one hour before his guest, Sleet reckoned he could put away two or three pasties in advance. He took his seat at the end of the bar where he could overhear the chat and during these forays he discovered that his wife had been correct about the Cornish stance on Brexit: by and large, the locals felt abandoned by their government and blamed the Europeans. To their minds, the Brussels bureaucrats were dictating every aspect of their lives – from the shapes of their bananas to the taxes they paid.

'That twat Cameron is planning to let in all those foreigners,' his neighbour said. 'What do you think of that?'

'Disgraceful,' Sleet replied, keen to stoke the fires of disgruntlement. It was a fun sport getting the old boys' blood pressure to rise. He hoped it might bring on a heart attack one day. He'd yet to see a man die.

'Brussels is going to bail out the Greeks. A cool £86 billion. Guess where that's coming from?'

'Where?'

'Our pockets.'

'My pockets are already empty,' one said.

'My daughter went to Santorini on her holiday last year,' another chipped in. 'She said they were all lazy. Took thirty minutes to get a cocktail even when the bar was empty.'

'They're getting our money while we're being laid off.'

'Was it Greece where they gunned all those holidaymakers to death?'

'No, Tunisia.'

'One of them owns Arsenal.'

'He's a Russian.'

'Wish he'd buy our local club – it's shit.'

When Tahira Khan entered the pub there was a sudden hush. Wearing narrow black trousers and platform shoes, long glossy hair falling over a cropped cashmere polo neck, she returned their gazes with an efficient smile. Sleet rose to his feet and offered her a chair.

'Find a corner table,' she suggested. 'I'll get myself a drink. Want one?'

'A pint of Skinner's.'

The two old boys exchanged knowing looks.

'I wish,' Sleet said to them. 'I wish.'

He found a table where they couldn't be overheard and watched her order the drinks. It was a novelty being bought a drink, particularly by a woman. She returned and set the sparkling water and beer carefully on the table.

'How was the chopper?' Sleet asked, raising a glass.

'We flew along the A303 – it was packed and it's a drizzly Wednesday in March. Imagine what it'll be like on a Friday.'

Sleet had never taken the A303 or any other main road. His preferred mode of transport was either his jet or helicopter. Occasionally he took the train but hated to pass so many hours in the company of others. One of the advantages of immense wealth was never having to share your oxygen with anyone else.

'Why did you come?' he asked.

'Curiosity. To see if you were as awful as the press makes out.'

Sleet laughed. 'Luckily I don't care.'

Tahira shook her head. 'Can't be good for business to be known as a ruthless shit who'll destroy anyone to make a buck.'

'I have £48 billion under management. My reputation doesn't seem to worry anyone.'

'If it was better, you might get more. People loathe short sellers.'

Sleet looked at her. 'We aerate the market. We're the detectives that find and expose weaknesses and bad managers. Think of me as the Viagra of the financial world, pumping a bit of hardness into flabby areas.'

Tahira gave a tight smile.

'How's your boss?' Sleet changed the subject. He'd seen an interview with the UKIP leader on television the night before and was impressed. While the Old Etonian Cameron couldn't resist showing off his polished erudition, Farage peddled one line repeatedly and it was beginning to stick in the public's consciousness. His party was polling at 3 per cent but many were beginning to take his impact seriously.

'Unstoppable,' Tahira said. 'We're going to win the referendum.'

Sleet waved his arm around. 'You can count on this lot's support but the polls are against you.'

She nodded. 'We will win by 52 per cent to 48 per cent.'

Sleet laughed. 'Are you a fortune teller? Have you got a little crystal ball in your bag?'

Taking a sip of her water, Tahira leaned back in her chair. 'It'll be won by a tiny percentage of voters – possibly as little as a 5 per cent swing. We're concentrating on them. We won't bother with campaigning or doorstepping. We're not going to take out ads or do any lobbying.' She looked around to check if anyone was listening. 'I don't work for Leave. I work for its biggest donor, Aaron Flanks, and a company called Alabaster Analytics – we're a political consultancy firm which specialises in deep data mining. We use military intelligence, AI and algorithms to identify those who might be "persuadable" to join our cause and then we target them ruthlessly.'

'Mailshots? Phone calls?' Sleet asked.

'That's so last century,' she said dismissively. 'We work online, via Facebook, Instagram and other social media platforms. We start by sowing seeds of mistrust and offer alternatives. In the morning we tell them that the Germans are going to take their jobs. In the afternoon it'll be the Poles and Bulgarians. We only need to convince 5 per cent to the cause.'

Sleet looked unconvinced.

'We do other things too. I can tell you more about yourself than even you know.'

'I'm not on Facebook or Instagram.'

Tahira smiled and took a piece of paper from her pocket. She started to read from a list. 'You buy history and economic books on a Kindle but only get to page twelve before boredom sets in. You spend an average of £468 a bottle on red wine, £230 on white. Your favourite websites are Bloomberg, CNN, Fox, about thirty porn sites and Reuters. You spent over £1 million last year on fuel for your boat and plane. Your top search words are "prostitutes", "billionaire" and "private jet".'

Sleet's face froze. How had she got this information and from whom? He would fire Donna that afternoon.

'Your fantasy woman is a tall, slim, Slavic-looking blonde with pale blue eyes.'

There was no way, Sleet reasoned, that Donna could know this.

'You go to Chelsea football matches only because they have the most high-net-worth supporters. You were adopted by trailer trash, had a traumatic childhood and suffered rejection and humiliation which has led to difficulty maintaining steady relationships and multiple marriages. You have very few friends. You believe you're better than most, if not all people.'

Sleet was appalled; her assumptions were uncannily accurate.

'Your cash balance is £75 million spread over eighteen accounts. You claim to have a net worth of £9 billion and a number of credit facilities in various territories including accounts in Panama, the Channel Islands and the BVI. You're planning to divorce your wife.'

Sleet got to his feet. 'I'm going to fucking sue you.'

'Sit down,' Tahira said. She folded the paper and handed it over.

'How did you find out this stuff?' Sleet asked.

'The net is the least policed place in the stratosphere. Anyone who has an online presence is vulnerable to spying. We buy information directly from social media sites.'

'They sell personal information?' It took quite a lot to shock Sleet.

'That's how they make money: advertising and data.'

'Are you trying to blackmail me?'

She laughed, throwing her head back to reveal two white rows of teeth. 'I am trying to help you get even more wealthy.'

It was the last reply he expected. 'Why?'

'The more money you have, the more useful you'll be.' She smiled. 'We have the technical know-how but without the financial muscle, it's wasted.'

Sleet looked at her but his thoughts were elsewhere: calculating how much money he could make betting on a Brexit result and where else he could use her algorithms. If this woman was correct and the so-called cognoscenti didn't foresee the result, betting against the pound might be lucrative.

She made no attempt at small talk or to ingratiate herself. Even the Nobel scientist had tried a little bit.

'Who are you?' Sleet asked.

'Daughter of first-generation Pakistani immigrants – a bus driver and teacher. Born in Sheffield. Went to Glasgow University. Joined the Communist party. Got disillusioned. Joined the Tories. Couldn't bear their sexism. Like others of my ilk, think the country is going to the dogs. Loathe immigrants.'

'You loathe immigrants!' Sleet spluttered his pint.

'And those who are endemically, pathologically racist.' She looked at him coolly.

Sleet held up his hands in mock self-defence.

'Is he giving you a hard time, love?' an old man called out from the bar. 'Let us know and we'll look after you.' A group of men laughed. Tahira didn't. They turned back to their pints.

'I need another drink.' Sleet took out his wallet. 'You want something?'

'Water, sparkling.'

He returned with her drink, a pint of Skinner's and two pasties. He offered her one and wasn't surprised or disappointed when she refused.

'I'll give the Leave campaign £10k,' he said.

'Oh please!' Tahira made a dismissive gesture with her hand.

'Why so blasé? Everyone knows you need donations.'

Tahira traced drops of condensation from the rim of her glass to the table with a red manicured fingernail. Then she fixed her dark eyes on his. 'We can help each other make a lot of money.'

Sleet smiled, unsure what kind of proposition she was making. 'I'm listening.'

'We have the best data – intel on over 75 million people. We work with another country with the best hackers – they can bust any computer.'

'Russians? North Koreans?'

Tahira looked out of the window.

'This can't be legit?'

'Getting information is legal and there's no legislation about how you use it.'

Tahira looked from side to side to make sure no one was listening. 'You're in the business of shorting companies. Now, you must rely on paying journalists, bribing officials, setting up elaborate stings to erode confidence. What if you could target the weak links? Reach the CFO directly and discreetly through his Facebook account? Get a little message to the personal inbox of the largest shareholder? Drip-feed misinformation to the top ten clients?'

Sleet felt the salt and fat of the pasty coagulate in his mouth as he used the momentary pause in conversation to consider her proposal. That morning he and Rodita had discussed how to destabilise Whaley. It would cost at least £150,000 in bribes to unscrupulous journalists and their editors. It was a dangerous (he could be traced) and inexact method. Could this woman be offering a direct targeted link to key people without any fingerprints?

Tahira passed him a napkin and Sleet balled the gunk into it.

'I think we can save you between 50 and 75 per cent and guarantee maximum engagement with the necessary parties.'

Sleet nodded wanly. It could be useful. 'What do you get?' he asked.

She didn't hesitate. 'We propose 5 per cent commission on top of our expenses; 3 per cent of anything you make from our information.'

Sleet laughed. 'You have a nerve.'

Tahira smiled. 'And there's another sweetener.'

'It'll have to be very delicious.'

'An introduction to the next Lady Sleet.'

Sleet looked unimpressed. 'Pretty girls are two a penny. I'm going to give commitment a rest.'

Tahira yawned. 'Men like you are so predictable.'

'What about an afternoon with you?'

'I don't bat for your team,' Tahira said.

'Meaning?' Sleet was confused.

'I'm a lesbian.'

'What a waste.' Sleet couldn't hide his disappointment. 'Do you have a girlfriend?'

Tahira licked her lips. 'We don't triangulate, if that's your next question.'

Sleet had had enough. It had been an entertaining meeting and he made a note to congratulate Donna.

'Wait.' Tahira took her phone out of her pocket and tapped in a name.

'I have Sir Thomlinson on the line.' She passed it over. A live video came up. Sleet saw a figure in the distance climbing out of the sea and up on to the deck of a large yacht. She walked towards him. An attendant handed her a towel and he saw her rubbing her blonde hair dry. She wore a tiny white bikini which showed off her long legs and small waist.

'Is this some kind of porn site?' he asked Tahira. 'I'd like the details – she's hot.'

The woman stopped a few feet short of the phone and slowly dried her limbs and her belly. Then she took the phone.

'Hello.' She spoke with a heavy accent that Sleet couldn't place. She was strikingly his type – more like Anastasia than her own daughter, with sculpted cheekbones, white-blonde hair, icy blue eyes.

'Hi, Sir T,' the woman said huskily.

Sleet saw that her boat dwarfed the others in the bay behind it. He tried to recognise the location – it reminded him of St Barts but he wasn't sure.

'Where are you?' he asked.

'Caribbean today. Who knows tomorrow.'

'Have a good time.' He handed the telephone to Tahira, hoping that the sweat on his back wasn't visible.

Tahira ended the call.

'Who is she?' Sleet tried to sound casual.

'Her name is Zamora Lala. She's a cryptocurrency billionaire.'

'What the fuck's cryptocurrency?'

'It's the future, and if you don't have a seat at the table now, you'll regret it for the rest of your life.'

Sleet laughed. 'I only just met you and you're trying to manage my love life and fix my business?' He found the combination exciting. 'Is this some strange prank or reality TV show?'

Tahira stood up, smiled at him and left the pub. Sleet sat there for a while longer. Outside, he was surprised to see his pilot.

'Where's the woman?' Sleet asked.

'She had her own driver and car. An Audi.'

It was the first time anyone had turned down a ride.

On the way home Sleet could think only of Zamora Lala and her currency. Pulling the car over, he scrolled through every photograph and scrap of information he could find online about this new money. Just the word 'cryptocurrency' made him feel excited: it implied intelligence, secrecy and subterfuge. Her brand was called Queen of Coins, QOC for short. The name showed she had class and aspired, like he did, for the finer things in life. The combination of her beauty and the newness of this field was intoxicating. Sitting in a roadside lay-by he entertained a flight of imagination and was transformed from a short-fund manager into a swaggering cowboy galloping over new frontiers. Riding by his side was Zamora. His pulse quickened with excitement. By the time he'd finished, it was dark; and by the time he turned into the castle's driveway, a fantasy – for that's all it could be – had taken hold.

4

April 2016

The announcement appeared in *The Times* and was picked up by every major newspaper and most of the television networks. Clarissa, the Dowager Countess of Trelawney, was to marry Rodolfo, Duke of Prugnole. Who is he? most asked. The *Daily Tittle Tattle* dispatched journalists to check out his credentials. The news spawned a plethora of talk shows, articles and television programmes: was there an age limit on love? Clarissa was eighty-seven and her swain was in his seventies. What about sex? The nation divided into those who thought it 'revolting' and others who found it 'romantic'. Agony aunts opined; gossip columnists dug up tasty morsels (there were many) from Rodolfo's and Enyon Trelawney's pasts; new potions and creams (for all parts of the body) were rushed to market; there were style and honeymoon suggestions. Lawyers presented templates for prenups, and nurses offered tips on emergency resuscitation.

The Sleets granted Clarissa permission to hold her wedding at Trelawney Castle on condition that she signed a legal document guaranteeing that, following the ceremony, she would never return and waived any rights to occupancy. Kitto, her eldest son, agreed to walk his mother down the aisle. Arabella, Kitto and Jane's daughter, consented to be her maid of honour with Perrin and Stella as her bridesmaids. Her brother-in-law Tony and his friend Barty oversaw decorations. *Hi!* magazine and Clarissa's production company split the cost of the celebrations. Her personal producer Damian Dobbs, deviser of the original series of *The Last of the Trelawneys*, was recording every detail.

One of the first segments Dobbs captured was Tony and Barty setting up the backdrop for the bridal photograph. The two elderly gentlemen spent nearly an hour choosing material for an ormolu sofa.

'It's only April; the wedding's not for four months – hope she makes it,' Barty said.

'How's her health?' Dobbs asked.

'She'll outlive all of us. Tough old broiler.' Tony sniffed. Publicly, he disparaged television but was secretly enjoying the experience of performing for the camera. He draped some gold brocade over the back of a chair.

'Why gold?' Damian asked.

'Gold is the most flattering colour for the face. It reflects and refracts light,' Barty said, making a turban out of the material and dancing in circles.

'Careful, darling, you'll do yourself an injury,' Tony warned.

'What do you think of the bridegroom?' Damian asked.

Tony and Barty exchanged looks. 'We only met him once. Clarissa has kept him strictly under wraps.'

'Do you find this kind of secrecy odd?'

'In this family?' Tony laughed. 'It's the norm. It's easier to divide and rule with lack of information.'

'What have you heard about the Count of Prugnole?'

'Duke, darling! He is a duke,' Tony said.

'We know as little and as much as everyone else – nothing,' Barty said, and then, clearly enunciating each letter, he repeated: 'N O T H I N G.'

'Have you tried to google him?'

'To what him?' Tony asked.

'I keep telling you about the search engine on the internet,' Barty said.

'He's not in *Who's Who*, that's for sure. I checked,' Tony said.

Damian pounced on this remark. 'Are you suggesting that the Duke of Prugnole might not be who he claims?'

Tony and Barty stared at the floor.

'Why's there such an unseemly rush to get up the aisle?' Tony said. 'They have managed to live apart for eighty-seven and seventy-two years respectively. Had she asked my advice, which she didn't, I'd have told her to wait a year.'

'She should visit the marital home before committing,' Barty said.

'She's giving up one home in return for an unknown.'

'When I spoke to the Duke, His Grace, yesterday,' Damian said, 'he seemed to think they'd be living here.'

Tony and Barty didn't comment.

'I asked to film the Duke's residence for the programme but he said it's "*non possibile*",' Damian said. 'I searched for it on Google Earth and the only record of a Castello Prugnole is a hotel near Pienza.'

'What's your point?' Tony asked, a bubble of fear rising in his scraggy old throat. Though he loathed Clarissa, he did not wish penury and disappointment on anyone.

'If she were my mother or sister-in-law, I would be a little anxious,' Damian said, trying to stoke the fire of concern.

'She is a grown-up,' Barty said. 'It's her life, her decision.' He was looking forward to the Dowager Countess's comeuppance. Only this morning she'd called him 'common'. How dare she? He might not have been born into wealth, but he was not riffraff.

'What's going on here? What are you filming? What are they saying?' Clarissa's imperious tones rang out from three ballrooms away. When she appeared, all three men admitted she looked radiant. Dressed in a Chanel tweed suit, her grey hair freshly coiffed, she had a slight pink blush and wore a pale lipstick with a hint of tangerine.

'Why are you filming these mischief-makers?' she asked her producer. 'Don't you dare make fun of me or my big day,' she told Barty and Tony. Turning back to Damian, she said in a stage whisper, 'They're jealous.' Damian caught the whole exchange on camera; his heart gave a little skip as he imagined the spike in ratings.

'Come with me,' Clarissa said. 'I want you to film my morning call with my beloved fiancé.'

'I'm surprised you let him more than four feet away,' Barty said. 'Where is he?'

'I don't ask where he is,' Clarissa said. 'I trust him. He's a king amongst men.'

Barty and Tony giggled.

Clarissa drew herself up. 'You tragic old queens. You'll never know love. Real love.'

After she'd left the room, the two men continued draping the gold fabric behind the chair and discussed whether on the big day they should put candles on small tables and muslin across the windows to keep out midday glare. Both were consumed with their own memories.

'Has true love ever called you?' Barty asked.

'It had the wrong number.'

Tony sat down on the window seat and gazed at the park. The sun broke through clouds casting shadows across verdant landscape. His face in repose was like a walnut; his once merry blue eyes had faded to tepid pools; his hands, mottled and liver-spotted, shook slightly on his lap.

Looking up at his friend, Tony knew that he'd never loved anyone more, but it wasn't done to make sudden declarations, particularly at their age and in an undecorated family ballroom.

Instead, he turned the subject back to Clarissa. 'It isn't going to end well, is it?'

Barty, relieved not to be dwelling on his own issues, recovered his humour and clapped his hands together. 'It's going to be a catastrophe. I can't wait.'

'That's not kind,' Tony remonstrated.

'I'm much too old to bother about kindness,' Barty said. 'Staying alive is a full-time job. I don't have the capacity for compassion.'

*

The weeks following Ayesha's visit to the lawyer passed in a blur punctuated by tears. Declan roamed across her heart like a restless elephant. Too proud to talk in any depth to Yasmin or Tony, she projected different scenarios on to her future. One of her main fears was the loss of identity: Lady Thomlinson Sleet would revert to Ms Ayesha Scott. The invitations would cease, and the paparazzi would ignore her. There'd be an initial ripple of interest, but the waters of indifference would soon close over her head and she'd be another pretty girl trying to get noticed, a former somebody demoted to a nobody. As she went about her day, Ayesha tried to think of a plan B. An obvious solution was to find another wealthy husband, but it was a buyer's market and she'd be evaluated like a stock, share or chattel. The ultra-high-net-worth men were used to having the pick of all. Ayesha was still young, world-class beautiful, clever and sophisticated, but in those echelons, a divorcee was soiled goods: she could hear the whispers. Why couldn't she hang on to her husband? What was her problem? She'd married for money the first time around – wasn't insanity making the same mistakes and expecting different results?

Then there was Stella: the presence of a five-year-old daughter in tow was akin to adding twenty years and fifteen kilos to her eligibility. She'd never give up custody of her daughter but knew that few, if any, would take on both. Alongside these thoughts was a deep feeling of shame: she couldn't manage alone or wasn't brave enough to try. Other people made independent lives for themselves and their families; she was pathetic – hoping that someone else would rescue her, whatever the cost or compromise.

Worst of all was the thought of condemning Stella to a broken family life. Looking at her daughter's innocent, happy face, Ayesha knew she'd do anything to avoid inflicting unnecessary or avoidable pain on the little girl. There was only one decent option. She would throw herself into making the marriage work. If she did a good enough job, she might persuade Sleet to actually marry her and it was this tendril of hope that kept her going.

In preparation of their eighth 'anniversary' at the end of the month, she put all other work to one side and spent hours compiling a photograph album which she called 'Our Wonderful Moments': photographs of exotic holidays, Stella's early years and some of the two of them looking happy. The last category was harder to find. Scrutinising the many hundreds of pictures, she saw that most of the time her husband was on the phone or giving instructions; she was the only one smiling into the camera. The intimate shots, it turned out, were etched in her memory, not caught on celluloid. She began to question how much of their relationship was built on her fantasy and not reality.

Since they bought Trelawney from Kitto's son, Ambrose, Sleet had complained that they were, to the Cornish aristocracy, social outcasts.

'I thought getting this place and marrying you was the way in,' he complained. 'Turns out you have no clout.' Ayesha suspected the locals had closed ranks with the evicted Trelawneys and saw her and her husband as usurpers. Using every ounce of her charm (and promises to contribute to their respective charities), she managed to persuade local grandees, including the elusive Marquis of Scaramanga and the glamorous Lady Minniver (rumoured to be a mistress of a royal personage), to come for dinner. The dining room had never looked so lovely. The table groaned with important pieces bought at auction or at the Maastricht art fair; a set of Hanoverian silver and china commissioned and used by Marie Antoinette in Paris. Huge silver candlesticks from the collection of George III marched down the centre. The flowers were all grown in Trelawney glasshouses and Ayesha personally oversaw their picking and arrangements. The dress code was black tie – unusual in 2016, even in aristocratic circles. The invitations, hand-engraved in London, read: *Lady Sleet at home for her husband Sir Thomlinson. Dinner 8 p.m. for 8.30 p.m. Carriages at 11 p.m.* The guests arrived promptly at 8 p.m. At nine there was still no sign of Thomlinson. Ayesha excused herself and ran through the castle looking for him; no one had seen him (a few knew exactly where he was but were not saying). The champagne flowed but the guests checked their watches. At nine thirty Ayesha suggested they eat. Lady Minniver was so tipsy that she slipped off her chair. Lord Norton-Ferrars, the Lord Lieutenant of Cornwall, and his wife Diana wondered if the police should be told about the missing person. At 10 p.m. Sleet, dressed in jeans and a T-shirt, strode into the room followed by his rather sheepish-looking Croatian trainer. His hair, recently relaxed, was longer than usual and the faint outlines of a six-pack suited him. Only a few months earlier he'd have been delighted to see the local dignitary assembled in his dining room, but his obsession with Zamora and the sale of Trelawney had shifted his goals. Looking around, he saw the collection of aristocrats as they were: rather dowdy middle-aged people in paste jewellery and tired taffeta. Amongst them, he decided Zamora would look like a swan who'd strayed into a pond of mallards or a thoroughbred racing horse against ponies. He liked his analogy and grinned broadly at the assembled guests.

'Hope you're all enjoying my food, my wine, my table!' he said, feeling magnanimous – they were yesterday's people; might as well throw them a bone of generosity.

The guests looked at each other, embarrassed.

Ayesha jumped to her feet. 'Darling, here's your place, head of the table, next to Her Grace the Duchess of Trebethin, and Lady Minniver.'

Sleet looked at the two middle-aged ladies. 'There's a good match on the TV.' Then, going to the sideboard, he piled a plate high with food and left the room.

Ayesha did her best to explain his behaviour. 'A long day. A difficult deal. Just got back from the US. Under a lot of pressure.'

After that the room fell into silence. The second the pudding plates
were cleared, the Marquis of Scaramanga stood up and thanked his
hostess.

'What about coffee or tea or port?' Ayesha suggested. Not one
person accepted. Within ten minutes all the guests left. Ayesha walked
them to the front door. It was her first and last county dinner and a
dismal failure.

The following night, the anniversary itself, she tried a different
approach and gave the cook and staff the afternoon and evening off
and spent four hours preparing Sleet's favourite dinner: soufflé Suisse
followed by Wagyu beef and finishing with Chocolate Nemesis. As a
child in Balakphur she'd learned to make Indian food and could still
remember how to crush herbs and spices for marinades; how to boil
rice so it stayed fluffy and light; how long to knead dough to make
the perfect naan; and the correct consistency and ratio of cucumber
and yoghurt to make raita. She had never, however, tried European
cuisine. Assembling the ingredients on the large marble work surface,
she printed out the three recipes. It couldn't be that hard, could it?

The first instruction was to make a roux; an unknown recipe. There
were no cookery books in the kitchen, and she skimmed through pages
of the internet to decide what combination and which order to whisk
the milk, flour and butter. The first attempt was lumpy, the second a
little better and the third a perfect creamy consistency. Looking at the
clock, she saw that it was 5 p.m. Sleet liked to eat at eight sharp. She
put the mixture to one side and whisked the egg white. The recipe
called for firm but not stiff peaks, a bewildering definition. Sticking
a spoon into the middle, she deliberated on what constituted firm.
Her hands and brow were sweaty – not from exertion but nerves.
She folded a third of the eggs in, and then the rest. It looked pleas-
antly foamy. Then she buttered some tartlet moulds. The recipe said
to spoon the mixture into these and bake for three minutes. This she
did before realising that she should have folded the roux into the eggs.
Turning back to the roux, she saw that it had developed a thick skin
across the surface. She placed her hands on the marble top, lowered
her forehead on to its cool surface and breathed deeply. There was
nothing for it but to start all over again. Once she was happy with the

small semi-baked soufflés, she prepared the cream sauce and put it to one side. It was 6.15 p.m.

The recipe for cooking Wagyu steak was supposed to take three minutes on a hot grill. Ayesha had spent hours researching the best side of meat and had had long discussions with butchers on whether to buy Kobe Wagyu or American Tajima Wagyu. She'd settled on the last as it was the most expensive. This was followed by another decision, how thick to make the steaks – knowing Sleet, the larger the better. She'd bought a new plancha or cast-iron skillet and as a backup a hibachi or grill to sit over the pan. The Japanese recommended two ounces of meat per person; Ayesha decided ten would suit Sleet. He hated salads and green vegetables, so she made an heirloom tomato salad and left the meat, sprinkled with salt, on the side table.

Nemesis was the dish that defined the best aspects of their relationship: silky, chocolatey, melt-in-your-mouth pudding perfection. They'd eaten it on their first date at the River Café in London and, when things had been good between them, returned on every important event and birthday. Sleet once asked for Nemesis to start, Nemesis as a main course and Nemesis for pudding. The waitress didn't bat an eyelid: it wasn't the first time. Hoping to titillate memory and senses, Ayesha started beating the eggs and sugar together until the mixture expanded fourfold. Then she made a light syrup by dissolving sugar in water and boiling it for two minutes. Separately she melted the chocolate and butter in a bain-marie and lined it with foil. By now she was feeling confident. Next the recipe said to mix the ingredients together and pour into a cake tin, wrap that in a piece of foil and then put a folded tea towel into the bottom of a deep-sided oven dish. Her nerve wobbled. There weren't many more eggs, so she had to get this right. It was six forty-five and she hadn't changed. The next instruction was to pour hot water around the cake and bake for fifty minutes until set. She boiled a kettle and then filled the bowl. She carried the steaming dish so carefully, shuffling rather than walking, and manoeuvred it into the dark recesses of the preheated oven. Once the door was closed, she slid to the floor overcome with a sense of relief. She set an alarm on her phone for fifty minutes later. Then she laid the table using good Minton china. In the centre was the lovingly assembled photograph album, wrapped in gold paper, and a card which read: *To the love of my life. Thank you for eight glorious years.*

At 7 p.m., checking and rechecking that everything was perfect, she ran upstairs and jumped into the shower. She chose the red silk sheath dress she'd worn to her engagement party. There wasn't enough time to dry her hair properly so she towel-dried it and pinned it into a ponytail. Then she quickly applied blusher to her cheeks and put on bright red lipstick. She grabbed a pair of stiletto heels, spritzed her neck with his favourite scent and headed back downstairs.

'Mummy,' a distraught voice called out. 'Where are you?'

Ayesha's heart tugged. 'Not now, darling,' she thought.

'I'm frightened,' Stella wailed. 'I was sick.'

Ayesha turned on her heels and pelted back upstairs, taking two at a time. She found her daughter in the corridor. Her face was hot, and her tiny curls stuck to her forehead. Ayesha picked her up and carried her back to her room. The smell hit her when she opened the door; vomit covered all the surfaces. She held Stella close, there was another retching and Ayesha's front was covered by warm, foul-smelling bile. She placed her daughter on her bed and stripped the sheets and blankets off the other. Then she rang the bell for help. Nanny Janet and a housekeeper arrived quickly but Stella clung to her mother. Ayesha bathed and soothed her daughter, picking pieces of sick out of her hair, laying cold flannels across her forehead to bring down her temperature. Stella fell asleep close to nine o'clock. Ayesha showered and changed and ran downstairs. She tried in vain to find her husband, searching in the dining room, games room, his bedroom, office and state rooms. She returned to the kitchen. The food was untouched. She took the charred Nemesis out of the oven and sank a knife into the centre. It was rock solid. She cleared away the rest of dinner and unset the table. Then she went upstairs to wait. Just after midnight she heard the front door open and close, the sound of laughter and then Sleet's familiar heavy tread on the main staircase.

Knowing his preferences, Ayesha put on some red lacy underwear and crept along the corridor to the room where Sleet slept, determined that even if dinner hadn't happened, tonight was the night to reignite marital passion. It had been months since they'd touched. Pushing open the bedroom door, she saw he was awake and reading his tablet. Hearing her enter, he looked up.

'What do you want?' His tone wasn't friendly. Hardly a good start, but Ayesha continued with her routine and, letting her black silk dressing gown slip to the floor, she shimmied towards the bed, flicking her long hair over her shoulders, caressing her limbs with her fingers, her face fixed with an inviting smile.

Sleet gave her a cursory glance and returned to the tablet. Ayesha refused to be put off. She got on to the bed and crawled towards him, swinging her hips to the left and right. Then she straddled her husband, removed the computer, and let her breasts brush against his face. It was a move he used to like, and she watched his face anxiously for a sign of arousal. She was met with a blank stare.

'Go back to your room,' he said dismissively. 'I'm not interested.'

Stung, Ayesha pulled a pillow over herself. 'I don't understand. What's happened?'

Sleet got up and walked across the room to pick up her discarded dressing gown. He held it out to her. 'Take this and close the door behind you.'

She made one last attempt. 'Why don't we make love?'

Sleet opened the door and waited for Ayesha to get off the bed. Then he handed her the gown. 'I don't want you.'

Ayesha crept to the door. On a whim, she turned and asked, 'Have you ever loved me?'

Sleet looked at her and showed a momentary interest. Perhaps she did care for him? He'd assumed that she, like most of the other people in his life, was just after his money. 'You were sweet, naive, desperate.' He hesitated. 'I thought I could make something of you.' He stopped and looked almost wistful. 'You were just like all the rest.'

'You don't mean that,' Ayesha said taking his hand and kissing it. 'We have to make this work, for our sake and for Stella.'

Sleet looked down at her hand and pulled away.

'I've only loved one woman my whole life,' he said. 'I would have killed for her. With her I'd have conquered the world. My shrink says I've been trying to find her substitute ever since. Next to her, women are disappointments with convenient holes.'

Ayesha was horrified, both by the derogatory remark and by the revelation. 'Who is this perfect person?' she asked.

'You don't know?' Sleet laughed.

'No, you've never spoken about her.'

Sleet rolled his eyes. 'I speak about her a lot, including to you.'

Ayesha scurried back through her imagination. Who was he talking about?

'Anastasia.'

'My mother was the love of your life?' Ayesha stepped backwards towards the door. 'I knew you knew her but never had any idea there was anything between you.'

'Anastasia 22.5.72.'

'Her birthday?' Ayesha could hardly believe what she was hearing.

'Engraved on my heart.' His voice, for once, was low and soft.

Ayesha scanned his face, hoping to see signs of humour. It had to be a joke. 'Why don't you replace it with Anastasia 16.10.2008? The year of her death,' she shouted.

Taking Ayesha by the shoulders, he shook her hard and held her face close to his. 'She will never die. Never.' He pushed her into the corridor and shut the door.

Ayesha crept along the passage, hugging the walls of the corridors in case anyone was up and caught sight of her. She went to her bedroom first, ripped off her underwear and stuffed it into the bin. Then she put on a pair of pyjamas and went to sit in the window seat overlooking the park. Moonlight had turned the long drive into a silvery ribbon stretching from the house all the way to the main road. In the distance the soft coo of a hunting owl rang out over the trees. Her thoughts fragmented. She tried everything not to think about Sleet and her mother; his revelation was even more distressing than fake certificates, valueless rings, the smirk of the Croatian trainer, the session with Mishra or the disastrous dinner. She'd spent eight years in a relationship that was nothing more than a sham. She was just another employee, the beautiful adornment, less useful than his PA Donna and soon to be expended. Worse still, he'd married her hoping for an Anastasia substitute and she had been found wanting. Perhaps the only thing she and Sleet had ever shared was a longing to be loved by the same woman. Neither succeeded.

Climbing into her bed, she pulled the covers over her head, hoping that the enveloping darkness and silence would be calming. Instead, she felt a rising panic. *Stop it, stop it*, she scolded. Forcing her breath to slow, she tried to think of a plan B or a role model.

She got up and went to her study and sat in the middle of the room, cross-legged on the floor. Being cocooned in her own research, amongst her books, was soothing. Her eyes fixed on the cover page of her dissertation: Isabella d'Este. What would she have done? Scenes from the Marquesa of Mantua's life flicked past at great speed. She too had had a philandering husband who left her for long periods of time while he was fighting off marauding neighbours. Francesco fell in love and had a child with Isabella's sister-in-law, Lucrezia Borgia – Ayesha grimaced, knowing how painful it was to be cuckolded by a close relation.

Isabella had enlisted the help of her contemporary, Machiavelli, to help guide her through the quagmire of local politics. The philosopher taught the Marquesa to value pragmatism over emotion, strategy over sensibility. Ayesha knew she had to do the same – strip feelings out of her issues and concentrate on outcomes. She needed allies. Taking a piece of paper from her desk, she started to scribble down names. The list was short and slightly pathetic – Yasmin, Tony and Barty. Then she included, without hope, Blaze and Joshua. She also needed a war chest. Her £27,000 wouldn't last long. She returned to Isabella, looking for similarities rather than differences between their situations. The kingdom of d'Este was not wealthy. Isabella had used art and artists as collateral and bargaining chips. Could Ayesha do the same and monetise her newfound knowledge? Many made a living buying and selling paintings but she needed to make money, a fortune, and quickly. She was determined not to let Thomlinson sell her home and that meant raising the asking price: £145 million. It was an unlikely goal but the consequences of failure were far worse than the loss of a roof over her head: the Trelawneys would never forgive her and her longing to be accepted as part of the family would remain an implacable dream.

5

May 2016

Blaze, Joshua and Perrin, along with Blaze's Aunt Tuffy and her niece Arabella, were in the Wolfes' kitchen. Blaze was making a picnic. The bluebells were out in force, and they planned to walk through the farm to a far wood and enjoy the spring weather on a carpet of iridescent purple, cobalt and indigo flowers. Persuading Tuffy to leave her Oxford lab was something of a triumph. The old lady, now ninety years old, was in a race against time, determined to finish her life's work on the effect of climate change on insects. Arabella had only managed to persuade her aunt to come because the Wolfes' farm had never had a drop of pesticide or fertiliser. After lunch they'd collect specimens to take back to the labs to study.

While Blaze cut hunks of bread and Joshua buttered, Tuffy and Arabella delighted Perrin with a box of caterpillars.

'Why are some blue, some green?' Perrin asked.

'That is very perceptive, young lady,' Tuffy said. 'We might have another scientist in the family.'

Perrin beamed with pleasure. Thanks to her friendship with Lily Whaley, she was finally enjoying school and gaining in confidence. She and Lily had several play dates a week and Blaze and Joshua were working with John Whaley to create a more environmentally sustainable profile and working practices for his company.

'We've found out that the colour of a caterpillar's skin changes according to what they eat,' said Arabella. 'The green ones are on a traditional diet of cabbage, and we've used natural food dyes to alter the colour for the blue lot.'

'If I eat blue food, will I look like them?' Perrin asked, looking nervous.

'In theory, yes. It's why people who eat too many carrots can get yellow fingers,' Arabella explained.

'She's emailed again,' Joshua said quietly to his wife.

'Ayesha?' Blaze put down the knife and turned to face her husband.

'She's begging us to meet her.'

Arabella overheard the name. 'What does she want? Bound to be an evil, manipulative request. Maybe he's leaving her and she'll be thrown out of our home,' she said, tossing her auburn curls over her shoulder.

Tuffy smiled. 'The history of our family is littered with those trying to get in or out of the castle.'

'She got us out!' Arabella flushed with anger. 'Evicted her own father and siblings.'

Tuffy stabbed a gnarled old finger in the air. 'You should thank her. She set you all free. It's just a lump of bricks.'

Arabella looked at her great-aunt in amazement. 'Trelawney is much more than that. It's a place, a home, an inspiration, our heart.' Her voice rose by an octave to a high quaver of emotion.

Tuffy rolled her eyes. 'Arabella, I thought you were a scientist, not a fantasist!'

Arabella blushed – she cared more about Tuffy's endorsement than her own resentment.

'The secret of a happy life, Arabella, is to live in the present, concentrate on the job in hand, and if your mind strays make it look forward but never succumb to the past; sentimentality and reflection are a waste of time.'

'Who's Ayesha?' Perrin interrupted.

'She's my half-sister,' Blaze said.

'You have a sister?' Perrin looked at her mother in amazement. 'Where is she? Why don't you see her?' The little girl's eyes filled with tears. 'I'd like a sister.'

The stark simplicity of Perrin's words filled Blaze with remorse. She, like the rest of her family, had ostracised Ayesha since her marriage to Sleet. They held her responsible for the Trelawneys' financial demise even though rationally they all knew it had started many centuries earlier. Ayesha was a convenient vessel to contain all their failures.

'She lives far away,' Blaze said quickly.

'Let's ask her to stay,' Perrin said. 'We have a spare room.'

'We've lost touch,' Blaze said, hoping to explain it away simply.

'How can you lose a sister?' Perrin shook her head: it didn't make sense. Sometimes she lost one of her toys, but it never took that long to find it.

'We're a careless family,' Tuffy chipped in. 'Lost all sorts of things – the Wars of the Roses, huge estates and our reputation.'

Perrin's grey eyes widened with concern. Grown-ups could be so confusing.

'Ayesha has a daughter about the same age as you,' Tuffy added. Blaze squirmed with embarrassment. Even Arabella, so utterly set in her vilification of Ayesha, was unsettled by Perrin's attitude.

Perrin's hands flew into the air. 'A daughter, like me?'

Joshua stepped in. 'Will you and Lily play with her?'

Perrin pushed her chair away from the table. 'We will look after her,' she announced seriously. Then she scrambled down and on to the floor. With her hands on her hips, she announced, 'I am going to make a list of games right now.' Turning to her mother, she asked, 'What is her name?'

Blaze's mind went blank. What was the daughter called?

Tuffy saved the day. 'She's called Stella, after a star in the sky.'

'Stella the star,' Perrin said. 'I am going to make her a drawing.' She ran to the next-door room where her pencils and paints were kept.

'That's settled that, then!' Tuffy said.

Joshua kissed his wife's wrinkled brow, guessing how confused and guilty she was feeling. 'It'll be fine.'

Blaze hoped he was right.

*

Four hundred miles away, Sleet insisted on taking Stella up in his helicopter. Ayesha was torn between wanting to keep her daughter safe and knowing how much her father's attention meant to the little girl. She watched Sleet with bombastic enthusiasm thrilling their daughter as it had once delighted her. She watched him pick her up and plant kisses on her neck, hold her hand and carefully strap her into the front seat next to him, remembering similar treatment. When the blades started to rotate, Ayesha raced upstairs to the first-floor ballroom to see Sleet climb in next to Stella, settle her teddy bear, between them and put headphones on both. The photographer, Jamie, captured every angle, crouching down to avoid the whirring blades and holding his camera steady against the wind. Then he got into the back seat and clicked away.

'Please keep her safe,' Ayesha prayed. 'I'll do anything.'

The helicopter took off from one of the long terraces to the west of the house and circled the estate a few times. Then it headed towards the castle, lowered, and hovered level with where Ayesha was standing. Stella waved excitedly from the front seat. Ayesha saw her curls bouncing and her tiny face turned pink with excitement. All Ayesha could think about were her flowers, and she tried to wave them away, shouting unheard through the panes of glass. Sleet made a hand movement and the pilot dropped; Ayesha watched as the blades created a tornado of wind that tore the petals from her roses, delphiniums and aquilegias. Sleet looked down at the vortex of petals and pointed left. The pilot guided the helicopter along the beautifully planted borders and sent leaves, petals and buds whirling like a trail of confetti in its wake. Then, to make the point it had been deliberate, the chopper returned to Ayesha's eyeline and Sleet held up a single finger.

When the helicopter landed, Ayesha, unable to face the gardeners or her husband, sent the nanny to pick up Stella and stood out of view inside the front door. Stella came running in.

'Mummy, I flew in a bird. Did you see me?'

Fighting back her tears, Ayesha hugged her.

'Daddy is going to take me again, lots.' Then Stella stood back and looked up at her. 'Why are you shaking, Mummy?'

'It's so exciting, darling,' Ayesha said, attempting to keep her voice level. 'Now let's go and have a snack.' She used every piece of self-control to appear positive. She must not let their marital problems infect her daughter's mood. 'I'm going to London today. Jan is going to take you riding.' Leaving her daughter with her nanny in the kitchen, she grabbed her handbag and ran for the train.

*

Sleet flew on from Trelawney to Battersea heliport where he met Tahira in his Riva speedboat for the final leg of their journey to the O2 Centre. He'd read that one of his heroes, Nos Megantons, did it that way. Wanting to make the right impression for his meeting with Zamora Lala, he wore a blue blazer, dark slacks and Aviators, a must-have according to *Taste and Refinement*. Tahira, waiting on the dock, was sure that the same journey taken by train and then Tube would have been far less stressful. The captain helped her on to the boat and, with a nod from Sleet, put the throttle down. There was a roar of engine, the bow lifted out of the water and the boat shot along the Thames. Tahira tucked her bag under her arm and turned her back to the wind. The water churned, leaving a frothy white wake.

Shouting above the noise, Sleet gave a monologue on the necessity for a man of his importance to travel well and fast. 'The conspicuous purchase of time and privacy is as important as owning a great work of art or house.'

'To put it another way,' Tahira said, holding on to her long black hair, 'the super-rich have to be transported in discreet and expensive style, to minimise contact with the general public while maximising their feelings of self-importance.'

Ignoring her, Sleet extolled the virtues of his boat. 'This is a Riva Domino 88. It has a top speed of thirty-eight knots.'

'Nice leather.'

Sleet beamed with pleasure. Tahira had, inadvertently, touched on one of his favourite topics. 'I chose the cow myself. It was a young Blonde d'Aquitaine, a virgin.'

'How did you know?'

'I got a certificate.'

The deflection lasted a few moments.

'I'd like you to run your fingers along the rosewood interiors downstairs,' he continued. 'There is a wonderful master cabin.'

'I get claustrophobic in small spaces.' Tahira found his innuendoes tiresome.

Ignoring the Thames's strict speed limit, the boat bounced in the wash of a passing barge. Tahira held on to a rail to steady herself. Two houseboat owners, rocked by the Riva's wake, shouted expletives after them.

'How often do you use it?'

'A few times a year.'

'An expensive plaything.'

Sleet shrugged. 'Real quality never loses its value. I look at this as a class A investment and it's more fun than holding some Microsoft shares.'

'Zamora will love it,' Tahira said.

'Will we meet her today?'

'If she feels like it.' Tahira didn't disclose that she and Zamora had spent time strategising how the Queen of Coins should treat Sleet on this first meeting. They'd decided on polite indifference. Both knew from his extensive internet searches on Zamora that his obsession was growing.

Seeing her mind had wandered, Sleet started on another tack. 'Not long until the referendum,' he said. 'Still confident?'

'Of course,' she said. 'The question is not that we'll win, it's by how much.'

'Not everyone is so sure.'

'Alabaster Analytics has superfast broadband, giving us split-second trading advantages. If Leave wins, the pound will collapse. Suppose you bet against the pound, went short. How much money could you make?' Tahira asked.

'I don't need you to make that bet.'

'Certainty would make you braver. We can predict the results hours ahead of the count. We have people in all the major pollsters' offices. We cross-correlate their findings with our online research. Do you remember I told you the final result would be 52 per cent versus 48 per cent in favour of Leave?'

Sleet nodded.

'We're on course. None of our predictions have deviated.'

Sleet didn't say anything. If she was right, then he should make a major bet against the pound.

'Zamora finds men with courage really attractive.'

The remark landed.

The boat passed under Tower Bridge. Tourists waved. Someone shouted out: 'James Bond.'

'I like my women stirred not shaken,' Sleet said, winking at Tahira who longed for the journey to be over.

Alighting from the speedboat, Sleet looked around in amazement at the hordes of people pouring out of the Underground station and walking towards the O2 Centre.

Seeing the look of surprise on Sleet's face, Tahira explained, 'Zamora draws huge crowds.' She led the way towards the VIP entrance where a row of black-suited, earpiece-wearing guards stood with their arms crossed.

Tahira, followed by Sleet, walked over to the central door where she surrendered her coat and bag to an X-ray machine.

'Like, who is this dame?' Sleet had read every word he could find on the cryptoqueen, but although there was loads of information on her cryptocurrency and public appearances, there was little about her personal life, dependants, husbands or even her age. Tahira ignored the question.

They waited at the bottom of a private staircase until two striking-looking blondes in tight-fitting black dresses and stiletto heels appeared from a side door.

'Miss Khan? Sir Thomlinson?' one said and, without waiting for an answer, turned and walked back where she'd come from. Following her, Sleet heard the strains of loud music.

'Are you sure this isn't a rock concert?' he asked.

Tahira smiled condescendingly.

The lift rose to the sixth floor and opened directly into a small suite of rooms. On the side tables there was a selection of drinks – champagne, premium vodka and tequila. Sleet spotted a favourite red burgundy, Domaine Romanée-Conti. There were rows of perfectly presented sushi and an extra-large pot of caviar.

'Are we expecting anyone else?' he asked.

'This is an appetiser, just for you,' a silky voice said. 'I know what you like.'

Sleet spun around and came face to face with Zamora Lala. She was draped in a floor-length red dress which managed simultaneously to be elegant and provocative. Her white-blonde hair hung around her shoulders and her eyes were as blue as the large single sapphire adorning her neck. Her skin was lightly bronzed, broken only by a painted scarlet mouth. For the second time in his life, Sleet was struck dumb by the sight of a woman. He could not think of what to say.

'Do you have everything you need?' Zamora asked.

Sleet shook his head.

'Forgive me, but I need to get ready.' Without smiling, she turned and left the room, flanked by two bodyguards. Minutes later, Tahira and Sleet were led into a private box overlooking the stage. Below them, on the arena floor, every seat was full. ABBA's 'Dancing Queen' boomed. The atmosphere was tense.

'I've never been to a shareholder presentation like this,' Sleet said, looking at the disco balls and laser lights shining over the crowd. Everything went dark, there was a drum roll and from the centre of the stage a huge pyramid emerged. The lasers turned and spotlit a small door in the middle that opened slowly to reveal Zamora, back-lit, so that only her silhouette showed. She raised her arms and, as she did, a silver staircase extended from the pyramid and she walked gracefully down to the stage.

'Hello, fellow investors,' she shouted. 'Hello, partners. Hello, my family. Welcome to the Queen of Coins presentation.' At the end of every pronouncement the crowd roared.

'I am Zamora Lala, your leader, your champion.' The audience were on their feet, stamping their approval.

'Why are we here?' Zamora asked. Then she dropped her voice to a whisper. 'Why are we here?'

The stadium was eerily quiet.

'We are here for two reasons. Together we form the Queen of Coin family.' She hesitated and then, raising her voice from near-silent to a clarion call, she continued, 'And together we are going to get very, very, very rich.'

The audience hollered. Sleet stood up, swept away by the excitement and the sentiment. He didn't know or care about the cryptocoin; he adored money and this event was a front seat at the Temple of Mammon. The combination of this extraordinarily beautiful woman, the light and staging, their shared interests in the pursuit of power and wealth, went to his head. Gazing at Zamora, he was powerless to resist. It was a feeling he'd felt only once before, with Anastasia, and this time it would have the right outcome.

One man stood up and started to shout; he had brought a small portable megaphone and his voice, though tinny, could be heard widely. 'You're a thief and a liar. You took my money. Queen of Coins is a con.' He turned to the crowd. 'Don't be fooled. Don't do it.' Sleet looked at him closely. The man was in his fifties, well-spoken and dressed in a smart blue blazer and old school tie. He held up a briefcase to the audience. 'These are the court papers; I will get you.

Listen to me, everyone; please listen. There are no Queen of Coins, no cryptocurrency. This is fraud on a massive scale.'

A hush went around the auditorium, eyes switching from Zamora, whose face remained impassive, to the man.

From the sides four large security men worked their way down the aisle towards the heckler. Reaching their target, they scooped him up by his limbs and rough-handled him down the row. One stamped on his megaphone. Still shouting, 'Thief, liar, fraudster,' he was dragged out of the auditorium.

Zamora's expression didn't change. She waited until the room fell silent.

'Every session a competitor sends someone like that to try and derail your dreams. He was paid to come by evil central bankers. Our success, our new way of doing things, this disruption of old financial markets, terrifies others.'

The crowd were reassured. One or two whistled and stamped their feet.

'You know what I'd say if that guy begged me to invest?' Zamora raised her voice. 'I'd tell him: "I don't want your fucking money!"' Throwing back her head, she laughed.

The crowd roared their approval. There was widespread yelling and shouting. Sleet jumped up. She spoke his kind of language.

Fanning her arms, Zamora entreated the audience to be quiet and sit down again.

'I have an admission,' she started. 'In 2009, I was offered a deal to buy a load of something called bitcoins. A mere £100 then would have made me a multimillionaire. I was such a fool and so arrogant.' Members of the audience shook their heads in disbelief. 'I knew better, or so I thought. I was an Oxford graduate, a Doctor of Psychology, and I'd worked at McKinsey. At Goldman's. I was a regular at Davos. I was on speed-dial to the rich and powerful. What, I asked, is this bitcoin? To me it sounded like the emperor's new clothes. Fantasy money. I wanted my money tagged to real things: gold, governments and central banks.' She hit her head with the back of her hand. 'Sure, I had a few questions: How does it work? How do we know that one of these coins exists and can be traded? I was told the same answer: all money is a figment of the imagination. The only guarantee is words on the notes, a promise to pay the bearer. Bitcoins are the future. Bitcoin

93

owners police each other, record all transactions – unlike traditional banks where we have no control and no idea what's happening. Central banks can, on a whim, print more money, thus devaluing your stake. They don't have to ask your permission; they don't even have to tell you.' She hesitated. 'What happened in 2008? The traditional banks failed us. They took our money. They embezzled it, and even worse? Our own governments used our money to cover up their mistakes. The ordinary person on the street was screwed. Not once but twice.'

Sleet hadn't ever considered how the financial crisis had appeared to the average person. It didn't make him feel compassion or indeed regret (he was one of those who'd profited from the bailouts). Instead, he realised the power of harnessing discontent – this woman was a genius.

'So are we going to let this happen again?' Zamora raised her arms once more.

'No!' the crowd bellowed.

'I can't hear you. Are we going to let this happen again?' she repeated.

Everyone was on their feet yelling.

'Repeat after me: Queen of Coins, Queen of Coins, Queen of Coins.' Zamora punched her right fist in the air.

The audience shouted, 'Queen of Coins, Queen of Coins, Queen of Coins.'

Sleet joined in: 'Queen of Coins, Queen of Coins, Queen of Coins, Queen of Coins, Queen of Coins.' He couldn't remember ever feeling so alive.

'Ladies and gentlemen. Don't hesitate. On your way out you'll find forms and people to guide you through your investment. Welcome to our collective future. To great riches. To being part of one family. I love you. Till we meet again.' With that, Zamora turned and walked up the crystal steps towards the glowing pyramid. Reaching the top, she gave a final wave to her audience and then the doors closed. The music started up. This time it was 'We Are Family'. Sleet looked down to see several thousand people dancing and laughing.

Wiping sweat from his forehead, Sleet announced 'I can't wait to see her again. Let's go backstage.'

Tahira looked surprised. 'Zamora never sees anyone after a presentation.'

'What do you mean? We came all the way here.' Sleet couldn't hide his disappointment.

'Thomlinson, you met and heard her. The only people who are allowed second viewings are major investors.' She looked at her watch. 'See you soon.'

'Where are you going? How will you get there?'

'The Underground,' she said. 'It's much faster.'

*

After Sleet flew off, Ayesha took the train to London and a cab to Earls Court. It was the first time she had been to Tony's flat, a one-room studio with high ceilings overlooking the busy Brompton Road. Not expecting guests, Tony and Barty had been playing chess with a half-bottle of whisky and two shot glasses. There was nothing to suggest a link between the elegant, pared-back interior of Tony's home and the elegant, extravagantly decorated interiors he'd created for the Sleets and other clients. He had few possessions, but all were excellent. A museum-quality Isfahan carpet straddled the room. A chesterfield sofa upholstered in green velvet was wedged between two armchairs. To one side there was a kitchenette and opposite that the door to the bathroom. A thick pair of curtains cut the studio in half and, through a chink, Ayesha saw a single bed, neatly made, covered with a pink satin eiderdown.

'Dear girl, what brings you to these nether regions?' Tony took her coat and steered her towards a sofa. His great-niece, normally so effortlessly chic and radiating youth, looked crumpled. Her beautiful face was stained with ribbons of mascara and her complexion was blotchy. Her limbs folded in on one another.

'I must have a third glass somewhere,' Tony said, peering up at a shelf. On the draining board there were two plates, two cups, two knives and two forks: for the last twenty years, Barty had been his only visitor.

'I don't mind a mug.'

Tony felt a dash of concern. 'Are things that bad?'

Ayesha nodded. 'Worse.'

The two men exchanged wary glances. With little experience of distraught females, they were unsure whether to give her a hug or a wide berth.

95

'She looks frozen,' Barty said. He was standing behind a chair as if he needed protection from the waves of despair coming from the young woman.

'How about a bath?' Tony suggested, remembering that Nanny Conrad thought baths the panacea for all bad things. He hoped that Ayesha wouldn't burden them with too much information: there was only so much reality an 85-year-old could manage. He'd stopped watching the news or taking a paper a decade before. A little bit of Radio 3 on a Sunday morning was his limit.

While Tony ran the bath, Ayesha sat mute by the fire: the tsunami of feelings had abated into a void. She watched the glowing red embers and held her hands out to warm them. In the background she heard a kettle filled, a tap turned on, and felt someone placing a heavy fur coat over her shoulders.

'I've run you a nice hot bath,' Tony said, touching her arm.

Ayesha looked up at him gratefully.

'You can manage to …' Tony said, trying to hide his nerves. The thought of helping to undress a woman was horrifying.

Nodding, Ayesha got to her feet and went to the bathroom, closing the door behind her.

The two men resumed their position in front of the fire.

'This is too exciting,' Barty whispered. 'What's the Vulgarian done this time?' He rubbed his hands together in anticipation. 'There's nothing like a good drama to get the old juices flowing.'

'Everybody except the poor girl knows that he's tired of her. There's talk of some Albanian.'

'Don't forget the Croatian trainer!'

'She's not important.'

'Do you think we should have told her?'

They both looked guiltily at the floor.

After a few minutes, Barty recovered his humour. 'There's a woman in your bath!' he teased. 'Must be the first time ever.'

'I'll say,' Tony replied. 'I keep expecting David Attenborough to come out of the bedroom and explain what's going on. "The female species in times of extreme distress resort to taking off their clothes and sinking into gallons of hot bubble bath.' He checked his watch. Ayesha had been locked in the bathroom for nearly an hour.

Another ten minutes passed.

'Is she alive?' Tony paced up and down the room. It was ten to six and he wanted to put on his supper. Thanks to his generous salary, baked beans on toast had been upgraded to caviar on baked potato and there was only enough for two. There'd be no bath tonight: Ayesha had used all the water. He went to the door and knocked. 'Are you still there, dear girl?'

'Yes,' a small voice came back. The bathwater had gone cool and she sat shaking, holding her knees close to her chest.

'May I open the door two inches?' Tony asked. 'I won't look, promise.' Without waiting for an answer, he turned the handle, which to both men's relief was not locked. They stood side by side, facing away from the bathroom.

Barty effected his sternest voice. 'Crying will get you nowhere. What you need is a plan and to have a plan you must define your purpose.'

'You know?' Ayesha said and, realising that everyone knew except for her, dissolved into fresh tears.

Tony stood up tall. 'You need to banish sentimentality. Play his game – be a cynic and a pragmatist devoid of any ethical considerations.'

'You sound like Machiavelli.' Ayesha smiled and then shivered. 'Do you have a towel? I'm cold.'

'Oh, poor dear girl. I forgot about that.' As he turned towards the airing cupboard, Ayesha rose from the bath. She reminded him of a Botticelli Venus, her long hair streaming around her shoulders, perfectly shaped honey-coloured limbs, round breasts. It was the first time he'd seen a fully naked three-dimensional woman.

Tony averted his eyes and, feeling for the wall, worked his way around the room to the cupboard where he pulled out a clean towel. With one hand over his eyes, he passed it to her and then backed out of the door.

Twenty minutes later, Ayesha was wrapped in Greta Garbo's fur coat on the sofa with a mug of whisky. Tony and Barty sat opposite her. 'I tried to come up with a plan, but I don't know where to start,' she said.

'We'll help you.' Tony went to his cabinet and found a piece of paper and a pencil. He laid these on the table in front of her. For Ayesha the blankness was overwhelming. Her eyes flitted between the two elderly men.

'What do you want most?' Tony asked.

Ayesha picked up the pencil and wrote: 'Stella.'

'Step one. Good.' Barty drained his glass and poured another tipple.

'Steady on!' Tony reprimanded.

'He won't try and take her, will he?' Ayesha pulled the fur coat more closely around her shoulders.

'He couldn't spot her in an identity parade of four-year-olds,' Tony said reassuringly.

The second word she wrote was 'Trelawney'.

The two men exchanged glances, wondering if she knew the castle was the main attraction in *Country Life*'s 'For Sale' section.

'The first two are rather predictable. What about love? Do you want to meet a nice man?' Barty asked.

Ayesha shivered extravagantly. 'Never,' she said vehemently. 'I am absolutely over romance.'

Barty suspected it wouldn't be long: women as beautiful as Ayesha were rarely alone. He tapped the piece of paper with his finger. 'You need to channel your motivation. It's the only thing that will get you out of bed on dark mornings.'

'Have you been reading that tosh in free magazines again?' Tony asked his friend.

Ayesha sat back on the sofa. A few months ago, her life had seemed set, clear. Declan wallowed around inside her and tweaked the backs of her eyes.

'Do you want the Vulgarian to walk all over you?' Tony asked. 'I thought more of you.'

Coy about speaking out loud, she wrote 'MONEY' on the paper in capital letters.

Barty sniffed, unimpressed. 'How much money? Are we talking one million? Or one hundred million?'

Ayesha shrugged.

'Now is not the time to play shrinking violet,' Barty said. 'No more upper-class flimflam or "I am too grand to think about pennies." Concentrate your mind!'

Ayesha thought about what it took to heat and light the castle – and then the repairs and improvements. She totted up the staff bills – gardeners, cooks, cleaners – and then added a personal clothes allowance, travel and some money to buy art. Overcome with embarrassment, she found it hard to voice the total.

'I need an income of three million a year.'

Tony's face fell. 'We won't be buying many Old Masters then.'

'Or damask,' said Barty. 'Forget about you. We need a lot more.'

'We?'

Tony and Barty nodded. 'You've got to consider us girls. We're not getting any younger.'

'I don't think I can cope with another round of poverty,' Tony agreed.

Ayesha smiled. 'It's more fun being a group. The Three Musketeers.'

'My friend, Jenny Aga Khan, said that a decent nest egg is fifty million pounds,' offered Barty.

'Lady Carmen de Roula got a hundred and twenty million,' added Tony.

Ayesha wriggled in the coat. The fur smelled strangely delicious – moth balls, baby powder and decay. 'Mishra said he might get me a hundred thousand in maintenance for Stella but nothing for myself.'

'According to the *Times Rich List*, Sleet is worth nine billion, give or take a few hundred.' Barty changed tack.

'Go for four hundred million and settle for half.'

Ayesha blushed, thinking of the beggars outside Balakphur Palace asking for a few rupees. 'Mishra gave me the name of a private detective.'

Barty sat up. 'I'm seeing the craggy type. Who played Philip Marlowe?'

'Dear, dear Humphrey,' Tony said, remembering a night in Hollywood with Bogart and Bacall.

'Can I meet him? I promise to dress normally.'

'Call him first thing tomorrow.' Tony looked at his watch. It was nearly 7.30 p.m. and his tummy was rumbling.

Ayesha smiled at her two accomplices. 'In future we will put a 25 per cent mark-up on everything.'

'What is a mark-up?' Tony asked.

Barty understood her perfectly. 'Oh dear.'

'Every picture, every piece of material, every stick of furniture.' Then, seeing her uncle's dubious expression, she asked, 'Are we or aren't we a team?'

Tony nodded. 'The last train to Cornwall leaves in half an hour,' he added, wanting her to leave before agreeing to anything else.

Ayesha jumped to her feet. The coat fell to the floor and she walked naked to the bathroom.

'If I were a younger man …' Barty said, looking at her.

'Don't be so utterly ridiculous,' Tony chided.

6

June 2016

Each time Ayesha met Lawrence Digby, she loathed him more; nevertheless, with little progress so far in 'Operation Sleet', she hoped that the private detective might yet unearth a useful piece of information. Digby had an anvil-shaped face with blubbery lips which he smacked together when making a point. He was tall but must have had a desk job for most of his life: his shoulders rounded into a belly that rose from his navel to his chin. A sandy, receding hairline was combed over the top of his balding pate but left long enough at the back to cover his shirt. He was proud of his burner phones and the precautions taken for meetings – this, their third encounter, was in a pub in Islington. Digby sat with his back to the wall ('a trick learned from a colleague in Mossad') and drank directly from a bottle ('advice from a mate in the FBI'). Although smoking had long been banned, the room smelled of nicotine and stale beer. As per their arrangement, Digby wouldn't speak until Ayesha handed over an envelope with £2,000 cash in 'pink grannies' (£50 notes) which he counted under the table. Satisfied with his payment, he leaned towards her.

'Let's do a stocktake of "Operation Banana".' He had a nasal twang and a slow delivery. He'd chosen the code name and insisted on referring to Sleet as Mr Yellow. Ayesha detested herself for getting embroiled with this sleazy character but had few other options.

'Did you install the app?' he asked.

Ayesha nodded. As Digby promised, downloading MySpy onto Sleet's phone had been easy. One morning while her husband was in the shower, Ayesha took his mobile, downloaded the app, created a passcode, and synced it to her account. Then she hid the app from his view, ran back to her room and repeated the same process on her own handset. From that moment on she'd had total visibility of every call, text, internet search and email Sleet sent or received.

'You've made notes of every number and registered the names?' Digby asked, smacking his lips together.

'I can't say I understand a lot of it,' she said. Much of it was financial speak. When she first read the expressions 'open the kimono', 'spread' and 'golden handcuffs', she assumed they were sexual references, only to find out, after a lot of googling, that they were slang for various types of financial transaction. Over the last few weeks her vocabulary had grown to include other acronyms and expressions. Her office cork board, once a cornucopia of dates and articles relating to her dissertation, was now covered in sticky notes with words and definitions including 'waterfall', 'poison pill', 'leverage, risk synergy', 'EBITDA' and 'IRR'. After learning the phrases, she didn't understand how to decipher their meanings and thread them together into something intelligible. In one conversation she wrote down: 'Don't dump holdings of peripheral Asian government bonds – these can be unwound by a run-off.' Financial language, she saw, was a way of excluding others. She was tempted to give up a few times but, with stakes so high, she blundered on until she had an epiphany. It wasn't only about words, phrases or their meanings; it was about sounding good. Financial speak, like art lingo, was just a shorthand known only to insiders.

'I can see everything he's doing. How can this software be legal?' she asked Digby.

'There are many interpretations of the law,' he said, opening a packet of crisps, tipping his head back and pouring them into his mouth. Catching sight of his red, glistening oesophagus, Ayesha looked away.

'I thought phone hacking was illegal?'

'It should be but the government wimped out. A few people have been given sentences and fines but nothing's changed. Journalists and the police have got more sophisticated. The authorities' eyes are blinder.'

'I'm shocked.'

Digby laughed. 'Why? You give away all your personal information for free every time you turn on your phone, check your Facebook, buy something online, walk down a street, turn on your fancy car, open a webpage. We're totally compromised, wide open.

It's a trade-off between expediency and privacy and our generation is so lazy they'd rather give Google their every dark secret than walk up the road to a public library.'

'It's sad that the invention of a system that was supposed to set us all free, guarantee equality of information and access, has ended up being exactly the opposite.'

Digby wasn't interested in her musings. 'What you got on Mr Yellow?' he asked, crunching away on his crisps.

Ayesha stifled feelings of nausea – his lips were covered in salt which he occasionally licked, lizard-like, with a long dark-red tongue. 'There's a lot of activity. A few common themes are appearing. There are frequent mentions of Panama, aeroplane blades, LighterYou, crude oil, sterling.'

'UK companies?' Digby wiped his lips with the heel of his hand, tipped his head back once more and, rustling the bag, poured another avalanche of crisps into his open mouth.

Ayesha hesitated, not wanting to appear stupid or admit that little of what she'd been reading made sense.

'Some of his operations are registered in Panama, others in the Channel Islands, Switzerland and Liechtenstein, but Panama comes up more frequently than the others.'

'Do you know what kind of companies?' Digby said, spraying small pieces of crisp in her direction.

'Mostly trusts and holding companies.'

'It's hard to get someone on that stuff. Even the Queen and the Prime Minister hold assets in those vehicles. Turkeys aren't going to vote for Christmas, are they?'

'Surely it's illegal?' Ayesha said.

'Tax evasion versus tax avoidance? You tell me.'

'How can people get away with it? Why should the poor subsidise the roads those kind of people drive on, the hospitals they frequent?'

Digby looked at her with a condescending smile. 'Do you want to nail your old man or fight some cause? I can help you with the former, but if it's the latter, go and cosy up to some cunt at the *Guardian*.' He folded the empty crisp packet into four and looked ready to leave.

'Hang on,' Ayesha said. 'I've made hundreds of notes but nothing makes sense. There's a lot of mentions of a company called Whaley Precision Engineering but no reason why. He's going long oil, whatever that means, and is doing a lot of work on the referendum vote.' She hesitated. 'I don't know what I'm looking for.' Ayesha didn't add that, rather than empowering her, spying on her husband made her feel stupid and slightly grubby.

'That's detective work for you. Lots of sitting around waiting for a break.'

Ayesha nodded, thinking of the hours she'd spent wading through the letters of Isabella d'Este in the hope of discovering a new insight or piece of information missed by previous generations of art historians.

'What have you found out?' she asked, her heart leaping with expectation.

Digby made a show of taking a small notebook out of his top pocket. 'Your old man likes a pub. The locals say he can eat six Cornish pasties in one sitting. No wonder the weight isn't shifting. Chauffeur's having an affair with the Croatian trainer. '

'Sanjay?' Ayesha tried to remember which trainer was the Croatian, which the Brazilian. She wondered if her husband knew that he was sharing his mistress with his driver.

Digby shifted in his seat. 'Tell me about the Whaley business.'

'I looked them up. A family-owned company which makes aeroplane parts.'

'Why's he interested in that?'

'One email mentioned a Thai company registered in Panama that works in the same space. I can't yet make any connection.'

'Maybe it's for his jet.'

'Don't think so.'

'Do you know anyone who understands business?' Digby asked.

Ayesha had made several overtures by email to Blaze and Joshua. The day before, Blaze had replied suggesting breakfast in a few weeks' time.

'Did you find anything else?' Digby asked.

Ayesha went through her list. 'He's teamed up with someone called Willy Perkins to short the stock of something called LighterYou.'

'My missus does that. Loses ten pounds in a week and puts it back on at the weekend. Fucking waste of money. My money,' Digby said. 'What does it mean, short the stock?'

'When an investor borrows shares at a certain price from a lender and sells them on immediately in the hope that the price will fall; then, when the day of reckoning comes and the value falls, they buy back shares worth a fraction of the original price.' Ayesha was pleased with her description – it had taken her a long time to understand the principle.

'So they make money on the difference?'

'Basically. It can go either way. In this case they've doubled their money.'

Digby let out a low whistle. 'Why don't you copy what your husband does? If he's so good at making money, use his expertise.'

Ayesha's mouth fell open. Why hadn't she thought of that? Thanks to Tony and Barty's mark-ups on all things bought for Trelawney, she was growing her nest egg. It now stood at £40,000 ... With Sleet's inadvertent help, maybe she could double her money.

Digby leaned over the table. 'Why leave, Lady Sleet? Why not lie back, think of England, the private jet, the fabulous holidays, and let him do what he wants with the trainer?'

Ayesha couldn't admit to the odious man that the timetable wasn't in her hands. Donna, along with Rodita Della Cruz and most of the household, knew she was on the way out. Hers was a race against time: to get money from and insinuating evidence against Sleet. Looking up at the clock on the wall, she saw it was midday. If she hurried, she could catch a train back to Cornwall in time to put Stella to bed. 'So what can you do for me?'

Digby clicked his fingers one by one while he thought this through. 'Mr Yellow is a challenging case.' (Ayesha wanted to say: 'Try living with him.') Digby went on after a long pause. 'He spends most of his days at a desk, so I can't follow him. When he does go out, it's to a pub. His office pays his bills. He doesn't seem to have a particular mistress' – Ayesha winced – 'and when he does go away it's on a PJ, so I can hardly be on his tail.'

'So you're saying you can't help.'

'I can make things a bit uncomfortable. Send in a SWAT team to check for drugs. Have him stopped in the car by the local force. Scare him a bit with a petrol budgie.' Seeing Ayesha's sceptical look, he added, 'Policemen don't earn much. A little bit of extra cash for "surveillance" and "interruption" comes in handy.'

'I don't want my daughter frightened,' Ayesha said, imagining Stella's face when twenty armed officers stormed Trelawney. She got to her feet. 'Goodbye, Mr Digby.'

Digby cleared his throat. 'Whatever you need, I can source. Class As. Fake passports. Security.' He tapped the side of his nose.

Ayesha gave him a chilly smile.

'Leave by the back door, Mrs Yellow, and leave by different entrances. First rule of good policing.'

Ayesha walked out of the main door to prove a point – which point she wasn't quite sure. Walking down Angel Street, looking over her shoulder for a taxi, she reflected on the hopelessness of her situation. She must raise over £144 million as quickly as possible to buy Trelawney. In her fight against Sleet, she had few insights, no incriminating information or leads to help build a case of neglect or illegal activity. And recently a new foe had entered the fray: a woman. When Ayesha first googled Zamora Lala, she looked so extraordinarily like her deceased mother that she thought it must be a sophisticated joke and that Sleet, having uncovered her spyware, was trying to teach her a lesson. But no computer-generated imagery could have put Anastasia in a tiny bikini on the back of a boat in France only last week or at an opening of a new club in Monaco two days earlier. As concerning as the Albanian's looks were her achievements; she was phenomenally successful. Ayesha was a few months off submitting her first dissertation; Zamora was about to reach $1 billion of sales of her new currency. Of course Sleet would fall for her: he'd see her as an equal. Ayesha felt her self-esteem drip away. Then she stopped herself. There were bigger battles to fight than one with her own self-confidence.

*

JUNE 20TH

It was 7.30 a.m. and already hot. John Whaley paced around his home office waiting for the stock market to open. In half an hour, the last tranche of shares in Whaley Precision Engineering would be placed. John was keeping a controlling stake of 51 per cent. Over the last few weeks, banks had presold 20 per cent of the stock at £50 per share. Providing demand matched supply, the company's value would be over £500 million, making it one of the FTSE top 500: not bad for a business which started in a tool shed.

John, who hadn't slept well, stared into the depths of the tank which housed his collection of rare tropical fish. When he sprinkled a tiny amount of organic matter on to the water, scores of fish rose expectantly to the surface. It was his daily aquatic firework display: swirling fins and tails of every imaginable colour flicked and flashed before his eyes, beauties of all breeds. It was even more poignant for him as the first fish to reach the falling flakes was a nondescript-looking guppy. John identified most with this creature: not flashy, easy to take care of and a good breeder. It did the boring jobs like eating the algae off the corners of the tank; a chore that the gloriously coloured betta fish, rainbow fish and ram cichlids would never stoop to. Nor were guppies dull: they were so territorial they'd eat their own young. John found their amorality fascinating – he'd never killed anything, even taking care to lift trapped spiders out of the bathtub. Overall, he thought the best of people too; the nasty ones, he believed, were rare aberrations, driven no doubt by extreme poverty or hardship.

In anticipation of their newfound riches, John and Susan intended to set aside £50 million to create the Whaley Charitable Trust and donate a significant amount each year for the benefit of local children. Aylesbury, their largest local town, had one of the highest numbers of families living below the poverty line. The foundation would create after-school clubs for needy children and provide an extra meal a day; their money could lift the very ordinary from a life of penury. Charity, John decided, sprinkling a little bit more food on the water, was as satisfying as personal wealth.

At 7.55, Susan came through the door carrying a pot of tea and a bone-china cup on a paper doily. Next to it on a matching patterned plate were two digestive biscuits.

'Try and eat one, darling.'

John tried to speak but only a croak came out. When he looked up, she saw he was crying. Susan took a small white handkerchief from her pocket and dabbed at his eyes.

'John Whaley, you are the most wonderful, talented, best man I know. There's nothing to be frightened of. The stock will sell and, if it doesn't, we still have each other and Lily. Do you hear me?'

John nodded.

'Now blow your nose.'

The phone on the desk rang. John and Susan looked at each other.

'Answer it,' she said.

John pressed the speakerphone button. 'John Whaley here.'

'John,' his broker said. 'The share price has opened at £63 and is rising fast – demand is outstripping supply.'

'Keep me posted. Toodle-pip,' John said. He stepped towards his wife and, taking her hands in his, kissed them. 'Where would I be without you, darling?'

'Eat your biscuits.' Susan smiled. 'I'm taking Lily to school.'

He watched her leave the room and felt waves of love for his steadfast wife. Susan had always wanted a convertible Audi. He would call the local garage and order one.

Going to his desk, John sat down and dunked a biscuit into the warm tea. Sucking on the corner, he felt the sugar and butter dissolve on his tongue. His eyes wandered over his desk to the framed photographs. He looked at Old John and remembered a day when his grandfather had shown him how to whittle and plane a piece of wood. He could still smell the resin floating in the air and picture Old John's hands clamped over his own tiny fingers, guiding the lathe backwards and forwards. His parents had been hard taskmasters. No breakfast before chores even on a school-day. There was a rota on the fridge and each task was checked and ticked off by 7 a.m. John's day started with feeding the chickens, while his sisters made the beds and cleaned the bathrooms. He'd felt sorrier for them: if their hospital corners weren't perfect, if the mirrors didn't shine, they had to redo everything. Susan was the first woman to spoil John. No chores for my husband, she said on day one of their marriage, and she meant it. She brought him tea every morning and prepared a two-course dinner at night. Nor did she miss a moment to tell John how proud she was of him and how much she loved him. Like water falling on a seed, her dogged belief turned him from a scared and nervous young man into a leader. Her affirmation gave him the strength to transform the family's small workshop into a successful factory. Every milestone the business reached, John thanked his wife with a piece of jewellery. 'Soon I'll look like a Christmas tree,' Susan said as she fixed the latest brooch on her jacket or pearls around her neck. 'Forget a tree, darling,' he'd reply. 'I want you to sparkle like Oxford Street in December. I want the whole world to see you twinkling.'

*

Voting to decide if Britain should leave or stay in the European Union started early that morning. Tahira called to confirm their predictions were strong. Sleet called George Osborne to try and gauge the Chancellor's mood – he was reassuringly gloomy. Mud was flying; none of it was sticking to the Brexiteers. Boris was denounced as 'squalid' and 'deceitful' by an ex-Prime Minister, but few cared. Cameron had fudged an immigration pledge and the UK lost its AAA rating. Sleet sat in his office at Trelawney. He'd chosen the Carolinian ballroom partly because it was the grandest. Opposite his desk there were four television screens, each tuned to a different station. If the country voted to leave Europe, the pound was bound to crash. Advised by Alabaster Analytics, Sleet had placed a huge bet against the pound and the FTSE – depending on the result, he stood to lose or gain a significant sum of money, as much as £400 million. That morning, sterling had hit a high of £1.5 against the dollar and the FTSE had climbed to a height of 6338. The market and press still thought Remain would pip Leave to the post. Sleet nearly lost his nerve. Tahira swore that Alabaster's predictions were correct. Farage, a currency trader, agreed. Their advice was to take a bigger punt and extend it to the US market. Predicting that a Brexit vote would affect the world, Sleet shorted the Dow Jones. Knowing that investors looked for safe havens in times of trouble, he bolstered his holdings of gold by 20 per cent and shifted a large proportion of his currency allocation into yen. Now all he had to do was wait.

Watching her husband's activity on her spyware, Ayesha was amazed to see Sleet putting a bet of tens of millions on the pound falling – ironic given his public dismissal of her opinion about Brexit at Buckingham Palace. Her fingers hovered over the keyboard. Should she follow his lead? Her nest egg had risen to £175,000, the dramatic upturn due to a large mark-up she'd secretly charged Sleet on a new painting by Howard Hodgkin bought for their London home. She'd learned from Sleet that making money wasn't about having a good idea; it was about conviction. Holding her breath, she followed his lead and bet more than half her net worth: £100,000. The stab of fear was so acute that she ran to the bathroom and threw up, retching until the contents of her stomach were empty. Then she sat on the floor, her throbbing head in her hands. How, she wondered, did anyone have the nerve to work in finance? Her first foray and she was a wreck. She washed her face, brushed her teeth, and went to find Stella.

Since Sleet had moved out of the marital bedroom, Ayesha and Stella were sharing. It eased the loneliness of Ayesha's situation and delighted her daughter. Together they'd transformed a spare room into a magic fairy den and draped the walls with lights and pink gauze. Every evening they'd put on paper wings, paint their faces and enact stories.

In another part of the castle, Sleet paced backwards and forwards across his office. The referendum votes were cast and countdown to the results had begun. He instructed his chefs to bring him a bucket of chocolate ice cream with whipped double cream and four giant bars of Toblerone. Tonight wasn't a calorie-counting evening. His sommelier had chosen a bottle of Romanée-Conti 1961 to wash the sugar down. Using the world's most expensive burgundy to accompany ice cream was an affront; he did it because he could and because Zamora had served the same wine at her event. Since their meeting and her presentation, Sleet's obsession had grown, stoked by her indifference.

Nigel Farage addressed the nation. 'Dare to dream that the dawn is breaking on an independent United Kingdom!' Sleet raised a glass at his friend Nigel and downed it in one. On another channel, he saw a confident-looking David Cameron invoking Churchill's memory: 'He wouldn't have quit.' Next up were Gordon Brown and Tony Blair. Sleet began to feel nervous. He rang Tahira. 'Are you sure?'

She laughed at him. 'Turn on the BBC now.'

To Sleet's horror, he saw a chastened Farage conceding that Remain had won by a narrow margin.

Sleet thought he might faint. The pound shot up; gold went down. 'Are you trying to ruin me?' he asked.

'Don't be so wet,' she said. 'Increase your shorts. Zamora has.'

At the mention of his inamorata Sleet made an even bigger bet that the value of sterling would fall, leveraging his own net worth by 200 per cent.

Rodita, normally unemotional, raised her voice. 'There's only so much I can do to keep you afloat.' Sleet had borrowed so much money that there wasn't enough projected income to cover the margin calls.

'Just do what you're told,' Sleet shouted at his associate.

Rodita hung up and executed the instruction.

Over the next six hours, husband and wife sat in their different wings waiting for the final results. Sleet finished off two more bottles of Romanée-Conti, half a bottle of brandy, four litres of ice cream and seven slabs of chocolate. At 4.39 a.m. the results were announced. It was 52 per cent to 48 per cent in Leave's favour, exactly as Alabaster Analytics had predicted. From both of their rooms, Sleet and Ayesha, like many around the world, watched in amazement. Ayesha ran downstairs to her office. Pinned to the wall of her study were her financial projections. She'd made money, £50,000 in one evening, but the gap between what she needed and what she had, a total of £225,000, was gigantic. Worse still, it felt like ill-gotten gains; from a cause she despised with a tip from a man she loathed.

Sleet shouted with relief and jubilation. He tried to call his friend Michael Gove, only to be told that he'd gone to bed at ten thirty. Boris's number was engaged. Nigel was as drunk as Sleet and neither man could understand what the other was saying. Sleet felt extremely pleased with himself. In a few more hours markets would respond to the news that the Leave party had triumphed. The pound would fall. The stock market was bound to follow suit; Sleet reckoned he'd made at least £400 million, possibly more. The thought of all that extra money made him feel sexually aroused. His mind turned to Zamora. In the meantime, he'd make do with his wife. Swaying slightly, Sleet made his way slowly up the grand staircase to their bedroom. He was glad none of the staff were around to see him bang and crash into the banisters and fall twice. He didn't remember what happened next.

The following day, Sleet didn't wake until the early afternoon. His head throbbed and his throat was dry; he tried to remember how much wine he'd drunk. He decided to spend a couple of hours in his steam room followed by a massage to dispel the toxins. He reached for his phone to check the time. It was nearly 4 p.m. Out of habit he turned to the Bloomberg financial pages. His heart contracted so hard he wondered if he was having an attack. He rubbed his eyes, hardly believing what he was seeing. Sterling had fallen to £1.37, a 31-year low. The FTSE had gone down by nearly five hundred points to 5806. The Dow was in free fall. Meanwhile the yen and gold were shooting up. He grabbed a piece of paper and a pencil from his bedside table and jotted down some numbers. Then, using his phone's calculator, he began to do the sums. He had made nearly £800 million.

His hangover forgotten, Sleet went to the shower and turned it on full blast to cold. At first the freezing water made him feel faint but his body quickly adjusted and he played his favourite game, Let's Count My Money. He'd made a killing in the 2008 crash, betting against the banks and shorting the market. Since then, his fund was up but every dollar he made, he leveraged. Most people would put £10 in a bank and collect interest. For Sleet, that same money should be multiplied by whatever a bank or individual would lend. He'd made a billion in 2008 and borrowed a further seven against it. He used that money to bet against companies, buy and asset-strip others or invest in stocks or privates. On paper he was now a billionaire nine times over. His sense of triumph was mitigated by sadness. He had no one to share his success with. Ayesha had never shown any interest in his work. His thoughts turned to Zamora: she'd get it. She'd understand how exciting a moment this was. He dialled her number and was bitterly disappointed when it went to voicemail. His follow-up email was greeted with an 'Out of Office'. That week's *Taste and Refinement* had a piece on philanthrocapitalism. The 'in thing' for rich people was to practise widespread unexpected micro-generosity. He composed an email to Rodita instructing her to give every member of staff £10,000. Totting that up it came to £1 million. Sleet sat back in his chair. According to the article, he was about to feel a rush of energy and warm feelings inspired by his own generosity. He hesitated. Maybe £10,000 wasn't a meaningful amount. He decided instead to give ten people £100,000. His top traders' bonuses were many multiples of that figure, so it would mean little to them, but there was a risk that the ones who deserved it, like his driver Sanjay or PA Donna, might be tempted to retire on that kind of uplift which would be a bore. He scratched his head – none of them were worth it anyway. He pressed Delete.

*

When Ayesha woke up, she clicked open her phone and logged into MySpy. Her heart sank. There were fifty new calls and thirty messages from Sleet to Zamora Lala. They started out playful and soon turned to irritated and then cross. Zamora returned one in fifty of his calls. Her texts were blunt. Panic gripped Ayesha. What if Sleet left her before she secured her future? *Call me. I'll fly anywhere, any time zone, I need to see you*, he wrote. When Zamora didn't reply, he wrote again. *Zamora, together we can make music and money. Call me*. Another hour passed. *Where are you?* No response. *What the hell does a guy have to do to get you to call him back?* Only then did Zamora reply. *I only meet Queen of Coin investors – no bother with time wasters.* Sleet wrote back within seconds. *Let's discuss sizeable investment on my yacht.* To this Zamora had written, *Boats are so last summer.*

Ayesha watched their 'affair' play out in real time before her eyes. She couldn't believe Sleet's naivety. Eventually, Zamora agreed to breakfast if the financier invested £1 million in her cryptocurrency. If he added a nought, then she'd consent to dinner. Ayesha expected Sleet to laugh contemptuously; his typical reaction if she asked for anything, even a new dress. She watched his phone in astonishment as Sleet replied to Zamora's offer: *£5 million. Harry's Bar, Monday at 8 p.m., TS.* Ayesha leaned back in her chair, winded. She reread the text several times, imagining what she could do with that kind of money.

Not for the first time, Ayesha's thoughts turned to murder. What if her 'husband' met an unfortunate end? Maybe not death but absolute paralysis and loss of speech. How would she do this? Sugar in the helicopter's petrol tank, snipping the brake cords of the Maserati? Could Digby help? Send some of his goons? Tempting as it was, she couldn't do it, for Stella's sake. Ayesha knew what 'fatherless' felt like and would do everything possible to keep Sleet in her daughter's life. She tamed her inclination but not her fantasy. Each time the doorbell rang or a siren whined, she imagined a policeman at the door, a face arranged in sympathy, the news broken, crocodile tears, and her sudden guilt-free redemption from this awful mess. Lying awake, unable to sleep, she planned her funeral outfit (a black suit and a Jackie O hat), the message to staff and his other children. She planned a grand funeral but knew she'd never, under any circumstances, let his body rot and decay at her beloved Trelawney.

Her thoughts flicked to her mother, Anastasia. A mixture of pride and dread stopped her from asking Sleet about the nature of their relationship. It was enough to know that the man with whom she'd shared a bed and with whom she'd had a child held her own mother as his ideal, his ultimate fantasy. In life Anastasia had been a ghostly presence; now she haunted every crevice of her daughter's being. Sleet's revelation magnified her impact. Ayesha saw traces of her mother everywhere – in her daughter Stella's face; in her mannerisms, dreams and in her own behaviour. Anastasia had turned from flesh and blood to an all-pervading vapour.

Minute by minute, Ayesha's desolation increased. Like atmospheric pressure forcing the reading on a barometer, she both longed for and dreaded a storm breaking. 'Go away, Declan,' she shouted but the gremlin was on a rampage. Unable to contain herself, she began to pull books from shelves. Each thud and eddy of dust brought a tiny relief. Then she ripped out the files, sending a storm of paper around the room. Ten, fifteen, twenty minutes passed, and she was so out of breath that she paused to catch her breath. Raising her head, she looked at the debris; it was an act of self-sabotage not relief.

She boiled a kettle and took a cup of the tea to the window seat, resting her swollen face against the cool panes of glass. The gardens were still bereft of flowers, and it would be months before they recovered from the vortex of air created by the helicopter's blades. At least Trelawney's wilder parkland was unscathed. The sun was already setting, bringing insects and chasing after them a swoop of swifts wheeling in the currents. The tide was out, and the mud was as dark and shiny as patent leather. Guto's Gulley shimmered. A lone oystercatcher, long-legged and red-beaked with a tawny plumed body, picked its way across the centre, stopping occasionally to peck out a marooned grub. The sense of continuum, knowing that her forebears had sat with the same view, watching generations of flora and fauna, calmed her. This was more than a home; it was part of her identity.

Ayesha pushed the hair off her face and caught a glimpse of her nails. They were bitten and the varnish was chipped. Turning to look at herself in the pane of glass she saw an unkempt reflection. She'd been banking rather than spending her maintenance allowance. Little wonder that Sleet, who liked glossy new objects, had looked at her so strangely in recent weeks. Ayesha had never felt the absence of family or lack of friends so keenly. She had no idea who or where to turn to. Even beloved Uncle Tony, normally sympathetic, was annoyed with her for not spending more time on her dissertation, but when she sat at her desk, other concerns were overwhelming. Every spare minute was needed to secure her and Stella's future.

A hawk hovered over the park, its wings barely moving, like a cross pinned against a grey sky. Suddenly it plummeted to the ground and, moments later, took off again with nothing in its beak or talons. Ayesha watched it wheel in the breeze, all the time looking downwards for more unsuspecting prey. She must be more hawk-like, watch and wait. She had to be patient.

She took her phone from her pocket and dialled Yasmin's number.

'All good?' her friend asked after a few rings. In the background there were voices and loud music. Ayesha checked her watch. 'Are you at a party?'

Yasmin laughed. 'We haven't been to bed! My friend had a gathering. We danced till the sun came up and haven't stopped.'

'How great,' Ayesha said. Declan came back and sat with a thump on her heart. She fought for breath; the weight of loneliness was almost unbearable.

'It was so much fun,' Yasmin continued. 'There'll be another soon. You gotta come.' She squealed. 'Get off!'

Ayesha heard a friendly tussle and muffled sighs at the other end of the phone. Declan shifted positions and lay on her stomach.

'Gotta go. Call you later.' There was a shuffling and heavy breathing and then Yasmin's phone clicked off.

Ayesha wondered if she wanted Yasmin's life, to be free, to stay up all night, behave badly, and yet she had a duty to her daughter and to Trelawney, this place called home. And after years of cosseted infantilisation, could she walk like Persephone from her husband's underworld back into the light? Was Yasmin's world even one she wanted?

The hawk returned, hovering above the same spot in the park. Ayesha willed him on. Suddenly he fell like a dart. Crouched on the ground, his head swivelled. She caught a flash of yellow beak and watched as he took off, dragging his feet. His beak was empty. No success again. Her heart sank. Let it not be an omen.

She forced herself to concentrate on her MySpy notes and make connections. She started with Tahira Khan and her company Alabaster Analytics. Clicking on 'About', she saw that AA claimed to have 'positively affected' election results in Tobago and Africa by arranging direct communications with disaffected voters. What did that mean? A lead shareholder and chair were Aaron Flanks, who was connected to the Leave party. Could AA be playing a part in the UK referendum?

Sitting back in her chair, she let her mind wander. It was the same technique she used researching her dissertation – read as many facts as possible and then allow the brain to free fall. Often not trying was as productive as hours spent looking at a computer or sifting through endless books. An idea started to form. Short sellers often manipulated market confidence by spreading negative information. What if Sleet with Alabaster's help could reach customers directly through their email or Facebook accounts? Swivelling her chair away from her desk she reached down and looked at her cork board where she'd pinned random notes, cuttings and words. The name that came up again and again on MySpy was Whaley Precision Engineering. Back at her computer, she typed the name into the search engine. WPE had recently floated. It had an amazing record, and the share price was 25 per cent higher today than at the IPO. If that was the case, how would Sleet and Alabaster make money? If they'd bought a block of the company when it floated, then they needed the price to rise. If they'd shorted the stock, then it had to collapse. She sat back in her chair, knowing that there must be a link but unable to work out what. Blaze and Joshua had finally agreed to meet in a few days' time – perhaps they could help her make sense of the information.

There was a knock on the door. Ayesha gathered up her papers and hid them beneath a sofa cushion. She couldn't trust anyone in the house. Their first loyalty was to their employer not his wife. She suspected that most knew his intentions; openly sleeping with a fellow member of staff didn't bode well for the lady of the house. She opened the door to their head chef, Madame Grabel, who wanted to discuss menus for the next three days. The cook looked around in consternation.

'What happened?'

'Nothing, nothing,' Ayesha said, following her gaze to the mounds of books and magazines. 'I am having a tidy-up. Things always look worse before they look better.'

Madame Grabel raised her eyebrows. How long the present Lady Sleet would last was a staple of below stairs gossip.

Moments after the chef left, the head gardener, Mr Kettle, arrived to discuss how they'd restore the borders in time for Clarissa's wedding. If he noticed the mess, he didn't mention it.

Once the gardener was dispatched, Ayesha put the books back on to the shelves. Stella was having a riding lesson and, as it was her nanny's day to make supper, Ayesha had an hour before putting her daughter to bed. Her research into 50,000 pieces of correspondence and other detritus regarding d'Este had taught her how to be systematic. She needed to apply the same rigour and concentration to finding out about Zamora. Perhaps there was a detail that could be used against her or at least something she could use to dampen Sleet's ardour.

Bizarrely, there was little information on the Cryptoqueen. After an hour and a half all Ayesha had ascertained was that her nemesis was Albanian with a law degree from the University of Bologna and a doctorate from Oxford. There was a PDF of a cover of *The Economist* with an article entitled 'The Future of Money?' And a reference in the *Tatler* to a star-infested party, showing photographs of Zamora with minor politicians, pop stars and society types. The reporter gushed about the young woman's beauty: lots of fluff but scant substance.

Mrs Lauder, the head housekeeper, knocked on the door at 5.30 p.m., hoping to run through some issues. This time Ayesha refused, saying she was too busy. Between 6 p.m. and seven she gave Stella supper, a bath and put her to bed. For the next six hours until 2 a.m., without interruption, even for food, she combed every available record on the Albanian. No detail was too small to click on. Eventually, her eyes burning with pain, she turned off her computer. The lack of information about Zamora was more surprising than a surfeit: most people leave stains. Even in a pre-internet and digitised age, there are records of birth, death or marriages. The unsuspecting are caught in national censuses or creep into public accounts. Only those determined not to be found, with something to hide, expunge their histories. Ayesha needed to unearth those secrets.

7

Early July 2016

The meeting place was a café near Paddington Station.

'To think it took a seven-year-old to bring us back together,' Blaze said to Joshua as they emerged from the Underground and walked across the concourse and up Praed Street.

'Our daughter is a forceful person,' Joshua laughed. 'I wonder where she gets it from?'

Blaze pushed him playfully. 'You, obviously.'

Joshua rolled his eyes.

'Where is this café?' Blaze asked, looking along the row of tatty shops, most selling touristy stuff: masks of Princess Diana, miniature double-decker buses and plastic Union Jack flags.

Joshua squinted at his phone. 'It's called Romeo.'

'"Wherefore art thou Romeo"?' Blaze asked. They walked up and down until they saw it, a sliver of a sandwich bar with a stainless-steel counter and a few tables at the back. Ayesha was already tucked at a corner table. The lighting was low but she wore dark glasses, jeans and a white shirt.

'Thank you for agreeing to meet me,' she said.

Joshua leaned forward and kissed her on the cheek. Blaze hung back.

Joshua waved to the waiter. 'Are you eating?'

'A small green salad,' Ayesha said.

'I'll have the prawn cocktail,' Blaze said, taking in random details. She noticed the large diamond on Ayesha's left hand and, looking closer, saw that her nails were bitten to the quick and the polish was chipped. She'd lost a lot of weight and her chest seemed almost concave. Blaze wondered if she'd succumbed to 'New York thin', a strange aspiration that she'd noticed in East Coast Americans, where perfectly lovely women starved themselves to resemble prepubescent girls.

Ayesha took off her glasses, revealing red-rimmed eyes. Seeing Blaze's critical stare, she explained, 'I've been up for four days and four nights finishing my dissertation. I handed it in this morning.'

'Congratulations,' Blaze said, hoping it sounded more sincere than she felt.

Joshua decided on a BLT and a sullen young waitress took their order.

'How's Stella?' Joshua asked. Small talk was never his strong point, but he wanted to make the meeting easier for his wife.

Ayesha's face lit up. 'Divine. She's in love with a small hairy pony called Mickey.'

'We've been too scared to let Perrin ride,' Blaze said. 'Luckily, her best friend Lily is allergic to horses so we have a bit of time.'

There followed an uncomfortable silence. Ayesha spoke first. Later she'd realise that her conversational muscles were out of practice: she should have eased her way into the discussion, allowed more preamble, re-get-to-know-you stuff, but desperation made her socially inept.

'I've come across some financial statistics and information that I don't really understand.' She hesitated, caught between wanting to tell her half-sister everything and being too proud to admit the sordid mess. 'My husband has a stake in a Taiwanese engineering company, TLG.'

Blaze felt irritated. Was this a reason to meet? She'd hoped that Ayesha might for once be honest about what was happening in her life. She was as secretive as her mother had been. Ayesha hadn't told anyone about her marriage to Sleet or that they'd bought the castle from Ambrose Trelawney. The reveal made at Ambrose's eighteenth birthday party and its consequences had been shocking. Kitto, Jane and their children were immediately evicted. Only Clarissa refused to leave.

Sensing his wife's restlessness, Joshua placed his hand over hers.

'TLG makes aeronautical parts. Blades, propeller casings, specialist fixture and fittings for 747 and Dreamliners,' Ayesha continued. 'It was runner-up a few times in recent years to a company called Whaley Precision Engineering.' She knew from Sleet's emails that the Wolfe and Whaley children went to the same school and hoped this would pique their interest.

Blaze and Joshua exchanged glances – why would Ayesha be interested in their friend's company? As far as Blaze was concerned, Ayesha was a pampered housewife, not someone who cared about business. 'Whaley's are a fantastic company. Best safety record in the UK,' Blaze said.

Opening her handbag, Ayesha took out a piece of paper and pushed it across the table. 'TLG is owned by another company registered in Panama.'

Joshua shrugged. 'Nothing unusual there. Thousands of companies are owned by shell structures.'

Ayesha hesitated. 'I think Thomlinson is planning a takeover of Whaley.'

'It's just floated – the price is high. Sleet doesn't like paying inflated market price,' Blaze said.

'He can build up his position in the company by buying more shares, like anyone else,' Joshua added.

'If it was that simple, then why do it through Kerkyra Capital, not an anonymous holding?' Ayesha asked. 'He has a shell company called Austell. The nearest town to Trelawney.'

'Still doesn't prove anything,' Blaze said, wishing she had never agreed to meet. Seeing Ayesha, thinking about Sleet, took her back to a dark episode in her life.

'It has one company director. Her name is Rodita Della Cruz,' Ayesha continued.

This time Joshua's face contorted. 'She's a killer,' he said, remembering dealings with Sleet's chief operating officer.

Ayesha looked around to make sure that she wasn't being overheard.

'I think he's planning some kind of an attack on Whaley Precision Engineering. There's a big contract in the offing.'

'You don't understand business!' Joshua was irritated by her conspiracy theory. She was trying to entice them by making obscure connections between his nemesis, Sleet, and a company he cared about. 'Whaley has a peerless record. It's just gone public and has a lot of new shareholders with vested interests in keeping the business upright. Even if Sleet were trying to discredit it, investors will look at its track record and reputation. They won't be put off by a few negative pieces in the press.'

Ayesha took a deep breath. 'I've read emails which imply Sleet and Della Cruz are spreading false rumours about Whaley's new technology.'

'It's too far-fetched.' Blaze checked her watch. In half an hour she was meeting her brother Kitto, another encounter she was dreading.

The conversation was interrupted by the waitress bringing their food which she plonked on the table with an uneremonious thump. The three picked without enthusiasm at the dishes. The awkward silence was broken this time by Blaze.

'We haven't met for eight years and all you want to do is talk about an aeronautical company?'

Ayesha squirmed. Pride stopped her from revealing what was going on at home. Instead, she said, 'I need your help exposing Sleet.'

Two spots of anger rose on Blaze's cheeks. 'I have a life, Ayesha. Can I suggest that you try and get one too? You drove a wedge in your own family and now want to do the same with your husband! If you don't love him, divorce him, get your payout and get on with it. Anything else?'

Ayesha realised she couldn't hide the truth for much longer. Unable to look at either Blaze or Joshua, she told them, 'We are not legally married. There is no prenup. I don't own or have the right to live in Trelawney.'

Blaze nearly laughed. The irony. Serves her right, she thought. Stupid young woman, thinking she was being so clever marrying a rich man, taking away their home, only to find out, eight years and one child later, that the dreaded Sleet was one step ahead.

Joshua said nothing. Privately he thought that not living at Trelawney was a blessing – that castle brought nothing but misery to its inhabitants.

Ayesha leaned across the table. 'I stand to lose everything. My husband and Ms Della Cruz have neutered my future.'

'Surely the courts will see you right?' Joshua thought about the innocent young woman he'd met eight years earlier when Ayesha had arrived from India with nothing but a few suitcases of clothes. She'd been spoilt, gauche and quite charming.

'Why do you need us?' Blaze asked. Much as she longed to see Sleet ruined, she had no wish to get involved in a revenge plot or someone else's divorce.

'You hate him too.'

Blaze and Joshua looked at each other, remembering how Sleet had tried to destroy Blaze.

'I need someone who can help prove my theories. How, for example, does one trace an offshore company?'

'With the greatest respect, Ayesha, we are out of that world. We've set up environmental-impact-based companies.'

'We have zero interest in Sleet or his dealings,' Blaze added.

'How's your history of art degree?' Joshua asked, changing the subject. He finished his sandwich in three short bites.

Ayesha looked at him coolly. Another man fobbing her off, treating her like a brainless child? Anger made her brave. 'What if I'm right, Joshua? What if he does manage to damage Whaley and you could have done something about it?'

'Are you threatening us?' Blaze asked.

Ayesha knew she'd misplayed her hand and antagonised her half-sister and her husband. 'I just thought we could do this together,' she said, trying to get the conversation back on a less contentious footing. 'I want to save Trelawney. For all of us.'

Blaze shook her head in amazement. The absolute gall of the woman, trying to pretend that this was about anything or anyone other than herself. Joshua put a steadying hand on his wife's arm. She looked at him and he smiled gently. *Not now*, he seemed to be saying. *Keep calm*. She trusted him implicitly. Taking two deep breaths, she turned to Ayesha.

'I'm sorry that things haven't worked out for you. You're so young – there'll be plenty of other opportunities,' she said and got to her feet. Joshua rose with her and put £20 on the table.

'Lunch is on me,' Ayesha said.

'Thank you but not our style,' Joshua replied. He held out his hand to Blaze and they left the café and walked in silence up the road.

'Did you believe a word she said?' Blaze asked after a while.

'She's frightened; her hands shook the whole time.'

'But to use our friendship with the Whaleys, to invent some subterfuge with their company and Sleet to inveigle herself back into our lives. That's disgusting.'

'Misplaced, certainly.' He put his arm around his wife's shoulder and kissed her on the cheek. 'Are you sure you can face meeting Kitto?'

Blaze groaned and looked at her watch. Her brother's train was due in ten minutes' time. 'Might as well get all the batshit relatives done in one day.' She glanced at her husband. 'Are you smirking, Mr Wolfe?'

'Being a sibling-less orphan has some merits.' Joshua took his wife in his arms. 'I love you, Mrs Wolfe.'

Blaze lifted her face and rubbed her mouth against his. 'Meeting you was the best thing that ever happened to me.'

*

Blaze hadn't seen her brother for some time and was shocked by the transformation – in only a few months he'd aged. When young, he'd been famously handsome, regularly appearing in the 'best dressed' columns of society magazines. The man before her had a straggly beard and lank hair hanging over his collar. His clothes were unironed and there were old food stains on his shirt. Looking down at his shoes, she saw odd laces: one black, one brown. Since his estranged wife Jane had gone to Italy, Kitto had been left to fend for himself and one look at her brother convinced Blaze that he wasn't managing. Worst of all was his demeanour – the once swaggering public-schoolboy, the Earl of Trelawney, Old Etonian and Oxonian, had been replaced by a person with a tentative and nervous disposition. Blaze watched as he searched his pockets for his ticket.

'I don't seem to be able to find anything these days,' Kitto said, rummaging around for something but forgetting what he was looking for and smiling at her sweetly. 'Awful thing getting old, you know. The memory goes.'

'Kitto, you're only fifty-one – two years older than me.'

'Am I? I feel one hundred.' He gazed at his sister. 'You, on the other hand, have never looked better. Where is your handsome husband?' He glanced around for Joshua.

'He's doing meetings – sends his best.'

'One of the finest of men.'

'I agree.'

Looking at the pathetic figure in front of her, Blaze felt a wave of compassion. 'Are you taking care of yourself?'

124

'I miss Jane. Will she ever come back? Bit damaging for the old ego when your wife prefers a woman.' He burst into tears and stood with his chin on his chest and his arms hanging by his sides.

Since Jane had left, Blaze had received a few texts but that was it. Nor would her sister-in-law respond to questions about when she was returning. She felt desperately sorry for her brother but couldn't begrudge Jane her newfound freedom in Italy or her love affair.

'Are you hungry?'

'I'm a bit strapped for cash, old girl. You might have to pay. That train ticket was £68 – sadly I don't qualify for a Senior Railcard for a few more years.'

They walked out of the station and back down Praed Street. Luckily Ayesha had vacated Romeo and, steering Kitto to the same table, Blaze waved to the sullen waitress. He ordered a panini which he demolished in a few minutes, eating too quickly to speak.

'Would you like another?' Blaze asked.

'I wouldn't say no,' Kitto said, picking up the crumbs off his plate with the pad of his index finger.

'When did you last eat?'

'Maybe yesterday or the day before.'

After the second one, Kitto wiped his mouth and sat back in his chair. A bit of colour had returned to his cheeks. 'Where are we going now, darling girl?'

Blaze fought the urge to snap at her brother. It had been his idea, not hers, to join the demonstration outside Parliament. 'I thought you wanted to show support for the new laws governing environmental protection.'

'Remind me what that is, dear girl?'

Blaze counted to three, hoping that by the time she opened her mouth, her irritation would be less palpable. Even Perrin was more worldly.

'To make landlords responsible for cleaning up their land and not dumping toxic waste into the ground or our rivers.'

'That sounds like a very sensible idea,' Kitto said.

Blaze got up and held out her hand. 'Let's walk across the park to the Houses of Parliament. It would be nice to get some air.'

Brother and sister walked side by side. There were a lot of cyclists and runners, and each time someone passed them Kitto flinched.

'I don't know how anyone lives in London,' he said. 'It's so frightening.'

Blaze, wondering what had happened to the debonair young man, the most eligible bachelor of his generation, steered him off the tarmac path and into the grass. Like a photograph left in the sun too long, the man before her had faded away: his hair grey and thinning; his eyebrows like dejected sashes over his now watery blue eyes; his figure, once erect and proud, was stooped. He looked more like a beaten dog than lord of a castle.

It had rained hard the night before and the ground was soggy. Soon both their shoes were wet. Kitto, whose soles were made of leather, slithered about. He found this funny and pretended to skate, pushing one long leg in front of the other and flaying his arms backwards and forwards.

'Come on, Blaze – it's such fun. Do you remember we used to do this on the estuary at Trelawney? You were the best.'

Blaze remembered her father trying to get Kitto to go first but she was always the bravest. Brought up to believe that girls were inferior in almost every way, she was determined to do better than Kitto where possible. It was she who tried out the new ponies or climbed the highest trees. On the lake, they'd tied a rope around her waist in case the ice broke (it did once or twice) and sent her out to test the thickness. If she gave the all-clear, they organised mini battles and pageants using chairs as pretend horses and bulrushes for swords.

'It was fun, wasn't it?' Kitto said. 'Our lovely home.' Then he stopped and burst into tears again. 'I lost it, Blaze. It was all my fault. I ruined our life, your life. Stupid me, thinking I could make money on the stock market but not knowing the first thing about it.'

'You were trying to do the right thing by all of us. Lots of people lost money – you weren't the only one.'

'I didn't know what a CDO was. Or a subprime mortgage. I bet the house and lost. Silly old fool.'

Taking her brother's hand, Blaze pulled him towards her. 'We're OK. No one died.'

'I destroyed the family. Tore it apart.' He was wailing now. 'We don't have a home any more. Ambrose, my own eldest son, double-crossed us. Toby's joined a sect. Our mother is about to marry a foreigner. The ignominy, the infamy, and it's all my fault.' His voice rose an octave.

Blaze tried to remember how Jane used to deal with Kitto's self-pitying outbursts. She was tempted to run away or hide behind a tree.

'You've had a good cry, now pull yourself together,' she said.

Kitto looked surprised and then rather relieved. 'You're just like Jane.'

Blaze turned and walked away so he wouldn't see her expression. Kitto ran to catch up with her.

'Tell me about your life.'

Blaze's face lit up. 'I feel so blessed by Joshua and Perrin; I wake up every morning unable to believe my good fortune.'

'If anyone deserved it, you did,' Kitto said. 'You suffered so much. I am so sorry for the part I played.'

Please don't make this about you, Blaze thought. And of course, he did.

Kitto chatted most of the way to Parliament. He told her about the badgers' sett up the hill from the house. In his opinion the number of seagulls was slightly down from last year, but this year he'd spent hours counting them so he could make a more systematic study. He told her that Lidl had better deals than Morrisons, including a buy-one-red-wine-get-another-one-free. He started to quote his favourite Wordsworth poem but couldn't remember much after the first two lines.

'*I wandered lonely as a cloud*
'*That floats on high o'er vales and hills ...*

'Oh, it's so frustrating,' he said, hitting the side of his head repeatedly with his hand.

Anger whooshed around Blaze's body – this was all Ayesha's fault. If she hadn't got involved with Sleet, if they hadn't forced Kitto out of the castle, maybe he'd still be living with Jane. Damn her.

Kitto appeared to read her thoughts. 'The other day, I was thinking how long it'd been since I'd tasted a decent wine, long before 2008. Come to think of it, I remember Jane and I cracking open our last good bottle when I bought into that ridiculous fund.' He stood by the Serpentine and looked at a pair of swans gliding towards them. 'I never thought about loss back then, thought I could depend on Trelawney and a decent claret.'

127

'Why don't you get a job?' she asked.

Kitto looked at her, astonished. 'I am a bankrupt. Who'd have me?'

'You don't have to work in the City. You could work in a bookshop.'

'That's a rum idea. What would Clarissa say?'

By the time they reached Westminster, Blaze was exhausted. Looking after Perrin felt easy compared to a walk in the park with her brother. There was a sizeable group in Parliament Square; those opposing the agreement vastly outnumbered the supporters.

'We must show solidarity and convert the heathens,' Kitto said, making his way towards a burly and angry man carrying a placard saying 'Save Lives Not Mice'.

Kitto was considerably smaller than his opponent but undeterred by his size or persuasion.

'Mice are just as important as humans,' he told him. 'Some, like field mice or voles, are more endangered.'

The man looked down at Kitto in amazement – who was this raggedy person telling him what to think? 'They don't have brains or consciences.'

'That's why we have to think and protect them.'

Now irritated, the man took a step towards Kitto. 'It's entitled pricks like you that destroy society.' He had a scar running from his temple to his chin and hands the size of dinner plates.

'You have to learn how to farm without pesticides and other noxious chemicals.' Kitto smiled.

The man's face turned red. 'I'll give you noxious pesticide and a rich punch.'

Blaze stepped between the two men, smiled apologetically at one and took the other firmly by the arm.

'You posh fuckwits can afford to have principles,' the man shouted after them. 'Not an option for the rest of us.'

'Come on,' Blaze said, finally on the verge of losing her temper with her brother.

'Honestly, darling. We were having a most interesting conversation. I was bringing him round to our way of thinking. Only needed a few more minutes.'

Blaze saw a taxi with an orange light and held up her hand. There were trains only a few times a day that went as far as Trelawney. Looking at her watch, she saw there was one in twenty minutes.

'Paddington Station. Please can you be as quick as possible?' she asked the driver.

'What's the hurry? I thought we might have a spot of lunch and then supper. It's been so long.'

Blaze sat back in her seat and watched the buildings whizzing past.

Kitto tapped on the driver's window. 'What do you think about field mice?'

Blaze closed her eyes; she didn't care if he missed the train, she was taking the first one back to Buckinghamshire. Her father used to say that the problem with families is that you couldn't live with or without them. What utter rot.

8

Late July 2016

'Operation Whaley' was taking shape. Since the flotation in June, Sleet had shorted Whaley's stock, hiding his actions behind several Panamanian shell companies. It was a dangerous bet. The shares were trading at £75, £25 higher than offered at the IPO. If they continued to rise, Sleet could lose a lot of money and suffer margin calls, but if the share price went below £50, he would make a significant profit.

John Whaley had taken out a loan to pay for a new factory secured against a high share price. If this dipped, then his carefully constructed scheme would face challenges. Sleet's aim was to destabilise confidence against the company through a smear campaign, force the share price down and then swoop in and buy Whaley Precision Engineering and merge it with his own Taiwanese business, TLG. Sleet suspected that Whaley's graphite technology could be adapted across different spheres of manufacturing and saw synergies between cheaper Taiwanese labour costs and Whaley's skills. Rodita researched other companies they could acquire, including makers of jet parts or fuselage. Put together, they could create the leading and profitable aeronautical conglomerate. Then Sleet would sell it for a multiple of all their parts.

He and Rodita ran through the details several times a day.

'What could go wrong?' he asked.

Rodita didn't hesitate. 'The Alabaster Analytics smear campaign doesn't work and the share price continues to rise.'

'What else?'

'You don't like running companies, and merging two disparate businesses – one based in the UK, another in Taiwan – will be complicated.'

Rodita was right. Sleet was a big-picture man; the thought of annual board meetings, shareholders' conventions, P and Ls and all the other detritus of building a business bored him.

'Is there any chance we'll fail?' A sliver of fear lodged in his brain.

'We could.'

'What's our downside?' Sleet asked. Reaching for a box of pencils, he fought for breath.

'So far, about a hundred and fifty million,' Rodita said.

'We can't lose – do you hear me? We can't fucking lose,' Sleet said, snapping pencils. Sweat bubbled on his brow; the armpits of his cotton shirt turned dark.

Rodita knew the signs of an impending anxiety attack.

'Why does Whaley mean so much to you?' Sleet had got less exercised on many larger deals.

Sleet snapped pencil after pencil. 'Did you read the private detective's report on the owner?'

Rodita thought hard. As far as she could remember, Sir John and his wife were pillars of the community and unlikely to be the types that Sleet ran into. 'What did I miss?'

'Did you see where his kids go to school?'

Rodita shook her head.

'Haddenham Primary.'

'And?'

'Same place that Wolfe and his wife's brat attends. They are best friends.'

'I don't get it? They're kids.'

'Imagine the disruption to the local community if the single biggest employer goes down?'

Rodita winced. She'd underestimated the animosity felt by Sleet towards Ayesha and her family. There were no limits to his desire for revenge – as far as he was concerned, every Trelawney man, woman and even their offspring should suffer.

'You know, Sleet, all marriages are a compromise. Why not stick with her?' Rodita asked. She didn't know or care about Ayesha but wanted, in a rare moment of intimacy, to tell her boss about her own life: how she had grown to love her husband Wilfredo more with each year; familiarity didn't breed contempt, it fostered content in all meanings of the word. They were a team, united against a hostile world and clear about their purpose.

'The reason that you'll always be a number two and I'll always be top dog is that one of us won't settle for anything less than perfect.' Sleet put down the box of pencils and wiped his brow. 'I am number one. I deserve the best.'

Rodita wondered if he was reading the inscriptions on his pencils or if he believed these slogans. 'Did you know that there was a man called Lucifer who became Satan?' she said, remembering the warnings of Isaiah who predicted the fall of a beautiful archangel undone by hubris and false pride.

'Oh fuck off with your Bible,' Sleet said and pointed to the door.

On the morning of July 25th Sleet and Tahira activated 'Operation Whaley'. Alabaster Analytics began targeting Whaley's shareholders, particularly their Chief Investment Officers, with inference and innuendo. Fifteen men and women received an email asking if they had heard about a technical fault with Whaley's new graphite blade. Seven of the fifteen put the mail straight into their junk folders – either because they hadn't heard of the sender or because they were concentrating on other things. Four people read it and flipped it on to other members of their team to check out. Another four picked up the phone and called a friend in another company.

The next spread of disinformation took place the same day. A lengthy, extremely technical report labelled 'Top Secret' was sent to two of the major independent non-institutional investors. One of them, Josh Graham, put the folder in the bin – it was his daughter's school play that night and he had a stinking cold. But the other, Jane Aubyn of Scimiter Shacter and Glenn (SSG) which held 7 per cent of the newly floated Whaley Precision Engineering, opened the document and, having read the headline data, gave the order to liquidate her company's position.

News of the loss of confidence spread quickly. Sleet, sitting with Tahira in his office, watched in real time as the price of Whaley's shares started to drop. SSG was the first company to sell but by midday on Tuesday others had copied and the share price had fallen from £75 to £68. At this point Alabaster sent out another safety warning, apparently from Boeing, raising doubts about the blades following a second testing. The report landed on the desk of a paid associate of Alabaster, a journalist at a leading paper. On Thursday morning an article appeared in a national newspaper with the headline 'Does Whaley deserve the term "Precision"?' By midday the share price had dropped £20 to £48 and by 4 p.m. there was widespread contagion.

'Jesus Christ, this is so easy,' Sleet said, watching as the shares tumbled and calculating how much money he was making.

'What are you plotting?' he asked, seeing Tahira's smile.

'I think you should run in the next election.'

'Election for what?'

'Parliament.'

'Fuck off.'

'I'm serious,' Tahira said.

'Seriously batshit crazy.'

Tahira ignored his protestations.

'What about a safe seat in Cornwall?' she asked.

'Who wants to go into politics? It's a shit game.'

'Not if you use it properly. Knowledge is power. Access is lucrative. Clever politicians know how to monetise their position.' She paused. 'Your castle is on the market; think how much more it'll fetch with planning permission for ten thousand houses.'

'It's listed – the local council would never agree.' He smiled at the thought of the Trelawney family's horror.

'If you're the MP, you can override.'

'That's a swing of several hundred million.' Sleet looked interested.

'You want more than money; you crave power,' Tahira said. 'This is the way forward.'

'You only won one seat last time; why's this time any different?'

'People want change. They want to take back control.' Tahira repeated Trump's mantra.

'You're running ahead of yourself, Ms Khan. First you disrupt my business modus operandi, then my love life; now you're trying to turn me into a politician.'

Tahira smiled. 'Admit it, you've had a lot more fun and profit since you met me.'

Sleet didn't deny it.

'For all your wealth and opportunities, despite a beautiful wife and homes, you are a lost and lonely man dogged by the fear of failure and abandonment. Be part of our club, Sleet – we'll take over the world.' She leaned in; her kohl-rimmed eyes fixing on his, she let her hand lightly brush his fingers. 'You haven't reached anything near your full potential.'

Sleet let her words swish around his head. He did deserve more. He could achieve more. There was something about this woman and her friend Zamora which empowered him. They made him taller, braver, and surer.

'What's the constituency called?' he asked.

*

July 28th

In Haddenham, Sir John Whaley hadn't eaten for three days. Unable to tear himself away from his computer and the carnage unfolding in front of his eyes, he couldn't understand what was causing his company's share price to collapse. He read and reread all the safety records, went through the testing schedules and the certificates of excellence. Unable to find a single fault, he opened the first bottle of whisky and wept. Susan, normally a pillar of strength and rationality, was in pieces, distraught at the loss of the family's standing in the community and the threat it posed to their charitable foundation. Most of all, knowing how fragile her John was, she feared for his sanity.

By Thursday evening, Whaley's share price had fallen to £16. Boeing delayed awarding the contract. At the beginning of the week, the business had been making enough to cover all the repayments on the new factory. Now the same banker who'd thrown money at them to cover R&D and a new factory floor was screaming at John: he wanted their house, their cars, their boat, their holiday home on the Costa del Sol.

When he wasn't talking to investors or bank managers, John fielded calls from his employees, all desperate for information and surety. He knew each of them individually; many were second or third generation. Their pain and confusion was more debilitating than his own. The local community was in shock – their foundations were crumbling and all for a reason none quite understood and in a timeframe none could fathom. Most assumed that John was responsible; he must be involved in subterfuge and wrongdoing.

On the morning of Monday August 1st, when John and Susan took their daughter Lily to school, the only people to acknowledge them were Joshua and Blaze. Everyone else turned their backs – there were no friendly greetings at the gates, no quick chats or bonhomie; they were social lepers. After the school run, Joshua and Blaze drove straight to the Whaleys' home but no one answered the bell. Blaze saw a white-faced Susan at the upstairs window who looked down at the Wolfes and then drew the curtains. That afternoon John Whaley called a town-hall meeting for all employees and struggled to get heard above the hurls of abuse and accusation.

Blaze and Joshua read the reports in the local papers and watched the share price tumble in horror. Like everyone else, they couldn't understand what was happening.

'Was Ayesha on to something?' Blaze asked.

Joshua shrugged. The thought that they might have done something to help the Whaleys made the situation worse.

Later that night Sir John Whaley CBE looked at the photographs of his grandfather, Old John, and Amelia Earhart and thought about the perilous journey his forebear had undergone back and forward across the Atlantic and the sacrifices he'd made to start the family business. Then he looked at pictures of his own father, known as Baby John, who'd driven himself mad with overwork and died of a heart attack aged sixty.

John felt wholly responsible. Taking a picture of Old John, his wife and daughter, he went to his garden shed and hanged himself. He left a note apologising to his workforce and the wider community for letting them down. He professed his innocence and absolute lack of knowledge and understanding about what had happened to his beloved company.

He wrote a love letter to his wife. 'My dear dear Susan, not a single day of our marriage has passed without gratitude. You have been the most wonderful wife, helpmeet, friend, mother and source of strength. Every ounce of my success was due to you and every drop of failure is my fault alone. The shame of failure is stronger than my desire to live. All I want is for you to find a more worthy husband and Lily a more suitable role model. Your devoted and loving John.'

*

A week later, a newspaper ran the tragic story, recounting how a series of (unfounded) rumours had led to the collapse of the company's share price. Whaley Precision Engineering had never failed a safety test. Their graphite blades were not just safe but, as Sir John had promised, revolutionary. Now his dream and the hopes of a whole community lay in tatters. The journalist didn't stint on personal stories; he interviewed the former workforce, had been to the school-yard where Lily Whaley once played with her friends (she and her mother had relocated to Susan's sister's house in Worthing). There were photographs of the deserted factory floor and dormant machin-ery. The story ended with a note of optimism. An American-born businessman, Thomlinson Sleet, had stepped in to buy the company. Though he declined to comment, a spokesman said: 'Sir Thomlinson is committed to promoting the Best of British and in his opinion Whaley Precision Engineering is the perfect example of home-grown manufacturing safeguarding British jobs for British people.'

Perrin, unable to understand where her best friend had gone, was inconsolable. Blaze and Joshua, remembering their conversation with Ayesha, were racked with guilt; should they have listened? Could they have done anything? Few slept well in the Wolfe household.

*

Ayesha and Sleet were having breakfast in the Carolinian morning room. He was on a high-protein diet and the sideboard and hotplates were covered with silver salvers and dishes piled with bacon, eggs and cream sauces.

Taking a copy of *The Times* Ayesha looked at the headlines. There was a photograph of her and Sleet leaving a charity dinner last spring; she took no comfort in looking beautiful and was embarrassed to be linked to the article about her husband stepping in to buy Whaley Precision Engineering.

'This very flattering profile makes you out to be a white knight,' she said, hoping that Sleet would either expose or exonerate himself. Ayesha still didn't have enough information or the technical insight to connect Sleet's activities to Whaley's collapse. She could link (through her MySpy hacks) Kerkyra Capital to TLG in Taiwan but couldn't yet prove that Sleet had deliberately shorted the stock or spread damaging rumours about the company.

'I am a white knight.' Sleet piled his plate high with scrambled eggs, slices of bacon, smoked salmon, hollandaise sauce and muffins. Zamora had called to congratulate him on the deal. 'This kind of thing turns me on,' she'd said. For Sleet her approbation was almost as good as the money he'd made.

Ayesha got up and took some home-grown berries from the sideboard. She was proud of the garden and wished Sleet would try the produce made at Trelawney; that week the head gardener and farmer had brought up fresh goat's-milk cheeses, ricotta, strawberries, beans, tomatoes and peppery wild rocket. She'd been to the local market and bought freshly caught wild trout and brown crabs but Sleet only wanted to eat red meat. He got up and helped himself to seconds of everything.

'Do you need all that?' She found his gluttony disgusting.

'Because it's there. And I can,' he replied, taking an extra piece of bacon and putting it into his mouth. 'By having everything, I don't have to make choices.'

'But you never have the pleasure of one thing, an exquisite experience.'

Sleet rolled his eyes. 'And never know the pain of missing out or making a mistake.'

Ayesha played with the fruit on her plate, trying to think how to move the conversation from food back to propellers without arousing suspicion. 'Whaley seems an unusual kind of investment for you,' she said, forcing her lips into a smile. 'You prefer dealing at arm's length, not getting involved in factory-floor stuff.'

'I am confused by your sudden interest in my business.' He looked at her closely.

'I am trying to be supportive,' she said. 'Perhaps you could help me understand what you're working on. I might even be able to help.'

Sleet appeared unconvinced. 'You stick to your area. Mani-pedis and a bit of art.'

Ayesha put his innuendoes to one side: she had to try and prove her suspicions. 'It's a terrible story – that poor family.' She was watching for any change of expression. 'Sir John's sense of mortification must have been huge to take his own life.'

Sleet's face was impassive. 'He couldn't take the heat so he got out of the kitchen.' He helped himself to a third round of scrambled eggs and bacon.

'I feel for the wife and child.'

'Don't. They still have forty per cent of the company. I'll make them rich again.'

'Thomlinson, is it always about money?'

He looked at her in astonishment. 'What else matters?'

9

August 2016

In the Mistresses' Wing at Trelawney Castle, Clarissa, watched by her daughter Blaze and granddaughter Arabella, was preparing for her wedding which was due to take place later that day. It was 10 a.m., and already warm outside, but the castle's walls were so thick that the heat never penetrated.

'It's wonderful to be back home,' Arabella said. She hadn't been to the castle since their eviction eight years earlier. 'Are you looking forward to living in Italy?'

'Wherever Rodolfo is, I will be happy.' Clarissa wore a pale pink dressing gown and her hair, set earlier that morning, sat in perfect neat curls around her face. The film company had provided a beautician and a masseuse, and while one attended to her fingernails, the other rubbed her feet. Damian Dobbs, behind the camera, captured every stroke of nail polish and every sigh of happiness.

Blaze squirmed in her chair, unable to decide if she should tell her mother about the centre pages of the *Daily Blast* that morning. The paper had sent an investigative journalist to the so-called Castello di Prugnole and found that it, like the family's fortune, had long since passed to others.

'Rodolfo says I must look my absolute best at all times,' Clarissa said, sighing with pleasure as the masseuse released years of tension from her Achilles tendon. 'Italians believe a woman should be a duchess in the drawing room, a chef in the kitchen and a tiger in the bedroom.'

Blaze shrank with embarrassment, thankful that she was positioned out of shot and the camera couldn't capture her expressions or reactions.

Clarissa was deliriously excited – her first marriage had been a deal. She provided two children and a well-run household; Enyon Trelawney gave her a lifestyle and a title. He had been pathologically unfaithful; she was emotionally unavailable. Now, in her eighties, she had fallen in love, like a teenager, giddy, silly and utterly deaf to any misgivings – her own or others'. Banished from view were pictures of Enyon Trelawney or any progeny. Positioned instead on the mantelpiece and side tables were framed photographs of the Duke of Prugnole at polo matches, at the races, on speedboats and yachts in Mediterranean haunts. Not on display were the photos of his four previous wives: a Marchesa from a grand Italian family, a B-movie starlet, the daughter of an industrialist and, most latterly, a blonde half his age.

'Granny?' Arabella asked.

'Never Granny! Do you want people to think I am old?'

Arabella hit herself on the side of her head. 'Sorry. Keep forgetting. So how do you find Mr Right?'

Clarissa harrumphed. 'You don't find Mr Right, you make him! Men are like dogs: they need training. Sometimes with a treat, sometimes a smack. It takes patience and perseverance.'

'Is that what you did with Grandad – sorry, Enyon?'

Clarissa groaned. 'Unfortunately he was the most unbiddable of men. A true Trelawney; as feral as a lion.'

'Could I have a few moments with my mother?' Blaze asked. She had had enough of Clarissa's musings on life.

'Don't leave me alone with her,' Clarissa said. 'She'll want to rain on my parade.'

'I need two minutes.' Blaze was firm.

When the others had left, she sat down in front of Clarissa and took her hands in her own.

'Careful of my nails. They'll smudge.'

'The papers are full of stories about Castello di Prugnole,' Blaze said.

'It's so beautiful, isn't it?' Clarissa said. 'We looked at it on Google Earth the other day.'

'It's owned by some Norwegians. Rodolfo sold it in the fifties. There is no family house, no fortune.'

Clarissa pursed her lips. 'You've always been a vengeful and nasty person, Blaze. Truth be told, I hated you from the moment you were born. That disgusting birthmark on your face made me feel sick every time I looked at you.'

Blaze gasped. How could a mother speak to a child in this way?

'Now you're trying to get revenge.' Clarissa blew on her nails.

'You're mistaken. I want to help you. I don't want you thrown out of your home with nowhere to live.' She paused, remembering her eighteen-year-old self evicted from the castle.

Clarissa rolled her eyes. 'I know you're thinking about that day. It was a custom, darling. When can you accept that? And it made you.'

'It was nothing to do with customs. You hated that I knew about them.'

'I've no idea what you're on about.'

Blaze shook her head in amazement. 'They're both dead. Does it still matter? Are you still keeping up the pretence?'

'La la la la la la,' Clarissa hummed.

Blaze, unable to control herself, started to shout. 'Your husband got my underage friend pregnant in your bed.'

Clarissa put her fingers in her ears. 'La la la, it's my wedding day.'

'And their offspring, Ayesha, has returned to haunt you. Maybe it's a good thing that you're being evicted.' Blaze lowered her voice. 'You'll know what it feels like.'

Clarissa whipped around in her chair. 'Get out and stay out. I never ever want to see you again,' she snarled. 'You are trying to take away my shot at happiness. You nasty person.' She got to her feet and crossed the room to open the door. Outside, Arabella, Damian Dobbs and the beauticians were waiting.

'My daughter is leaving. Sadly, she has an unmissable appointment and won't be attending the wedding. *Quelle domage.*' She turned back to the mirror and looked stone-faced at her reflection.

Blaze stumbled out and across the courtyard. Breathing hard, she rested her head against the castle walls, finding comfort in their coolness. Then she walked through one of the side doors and down a passage. The familiar smell – cold stone topped with the aroma of rush-matting floor runner and a musky dampness rising from the cellar – catapulted her back to her childhood: the little Blaze, excluded from male pursuits, derided by her mother. She continued down the corridor and up the stairs to the library, where the smell of leather and parchment, the mustiness of books, sharpened her sense of desolation.

143

Sitting down on an old chesterfield sofa and looking at the grand fire-place, she remembered many evenings spent in this room – laughter, gossip, arguments, old bores, young blades, and her mother as brittle and sparkly as a Christmas decoration, always holding court. Blaze closed her eyes and imagined the other parts of the castle – all the nooks and crannies, staircases, hidden rooms, attics, even the servants' quarters, were etched in her memory. Which taps spurted water side-ways, which exploded when you turned the faucet, the singing pipes and each creaking floorboard. Now, she suspected, thanks to Barty, Tony and Ayesha, it would all look and smell quite different, but nothing could erase every childhood memory gained, every emotion felt. She loved Joshua's farm – their home – but Trelawney was the core of her foundation, the bedrock of her memories and not even Clarissa or Sleet could detonate those building blocks. Concentrating hard, she tried to gather all the happiest memories. Then she lit a fire and slowly and deliberately tossed all the negative thoughts into its midst. She imagined each dark episode and bundled them into a piece of kindling or a lump of coal which she tossed into the roaring hearth, one by one. The heat of the fire licked her face, turning it red, making her birthmark burn.

'I've been trying to find you,' Joshua stood in the doorway. 'A fire on a day like today?' he asked, looking from the grate to his wife.

'A bonfire of inanities.' She walked over to him and leaned her hot face against his shoulder. 'I'm longing to go home.'

Stepping backwards, Joshua took her by the shoulders. 'Promise we never have to come here again.'

She smiled and nodded her head and crossed her fingers behind her back. 'Never.'

Arabella returned to her grandmother's boudoir and, draping herself over the sofa, let out a huge sigh. 'Granny, you are so lucky to be in love.'

'Don't call me Granny!' Clarissa snapped.

'What shall I call you, then?'

'Rodolfo calls me "honey".'

'That's so sweet,' Arabella said. 'You are lucky.' Picking up a faded green cushion, she hugged it tightly. 'Are you nervous?' she asked.

Her grandmother didn't reply immediately. When she did, her eyes were full of tears. 'I can't imagine what such a good, handsome man is doing marrying me. All I want is to make him proud and happy. I'm frightened of letting him down.'

Damian Dobbs, who'd been filming the Dowager Countess for eight years, felt his heart contract. He had not, until that moment, realised how much Clarissa loved her fiancé and that, for her, the wedding was not a charade or an attempt to boost their ratings. Not for the first time, Damian felt apprehensive; if the Duke was, as he and others suspected, a scoundrel, how would Clarissa cope with humiliation and rejection? Unable to decide if a sad or happy ending was better for viewing figures, he kept filming.

'Dobbs? Dobbs?' Clarissa asked.

Damian's attention snapped back to the present.

'Are you getting these shots?' Examining herself in the mirror, Clarissa pulled the loose skin back on her face and neck. Perhaps it was time to get another lift? She hoped that Rodolfo would agree to pay.

Damian refocused his camera. 'You are fabulous.' Looking at the Dowager Countess through the lens, one of his mother's favourite sayings came back to him. 'It's better to have loved and lost than never to have loved at all.' His sentimental feelings evaporated. Moving his camera down to her hands, he captured a close-up of the dark liver spots on Clarissa's wrists and fingers. Then he filmed the scraggy old neck and bony cleavage, the sparrow-like legs and bunioned feet, the false eyelashes and the skin hanging in folds from her shoulders to her elbows.

Damian Dobbs saw himself as part anthropologist, part naturalist; this was not fly-on-the-wall television, it was a study in humanity. Clarissa's body, like others in their eighties, was withering. Facelifts, cosmetic treatments and expensive clothes could only hide so much. Damian admired Clarissa for being up to the emotional challenge of love, even at her age. Perhaps the Duke was for real: if he wasn't, Damian thought, Clarissa would have sky-high ratings and national sympathy with which to console herself.

It was an unusually warm day. The organisers had set up an open-sided marquee in the newly restored formal gardens which led down to the estuary. Lined in pink silk, the wings of the tent emanated from an exquisite Baroque temple built by the architect Nicholas Hawksmoor to commemorate the birth of the 12th Earl. The austere white marble columns topped with a ziggurat architrave had been polished to their gleaming original best. The back of the temple was lined with pink roses rising from the floor to the ceiling and the same flowers were looped around the chairs, all four hundred, splayed in an arc for for the audience to get the best view. Damian had a five-camera team and another on a cherry picker – he didn't want to miss 'the money shot', the defining but as yet unidentified moment. The Countess might have a heart attack or the Duke might trip over a D-list celebrity.

Rodolfo had been born into privilege. His father, the Duke of Prugnole, was a bridge-playing bon viveur who divided his time between his castle in Tuscany, the South of France and Gstaad. His mother, an American heiress, was known for her pretty ankles and penchant for vodka. On account of his parents' peripatetic lifestyle, Rodolfo never attended school but what he lacked in formal education he substituted with expertise in the art of fine living: he knew the best hotels; how to tell the difference between a Brunello and a Bordeaux. He could make love in seven languages; was a crack shot and a legendary dancer. He had never made a penny. Married four times, with seven children scattered over three continents, Rodolfo was nearly seventy-two years old and down to his last €10,000. Truth to tell, Rodolfo was tired. Tired of being the life and soul of the party, tired of kissing ladies' hands and tired of scraping together monthly bills. He saw a kind of kindred spirit in Clarissa – her husband sounded like a brute, but he admired her fidelity and her adherence to standards of a time past. Nothing more than a chaste kiss would be expected from his new bride and he thought he could make her happy; if they didn't get on, there was more than enough space to lose each other in the castle. Most of all, with one wedding band, Rodolfo knew he could restore the dignity of the House of Prugnole.

It was, of course, the castle that Rodolfo was marrying. The moment he saw it, he fell in love. There were more beautiful buildings in the world – he was familiar with most – but it was Trelawney's setting and in particular the formal gardens that bewitched him (and so many others). No other estate could match the sixty acres of landscaped perfection leading down to the estuary. Over generations, the family had tamed and reshaped the terrain, creating walks and waterways, avenues, terraces, sunken gardens, raised beds, topiary, wild-flower meadows, exotic palmeries, carpet bedding and a 24-acre walled kitchen garden. Wending through the pleasure grounds were streams, waterfalls and, to the south, a vast rhododendron and azalea forest surrounded by ancient laurels. Vistas and views were punctuated with Doric temples and triumphal arches. There were secret grottoes and fierce fountains that, by an ingenious natural system of displacement, shot jets of water more than fifty feet into the air. The combination of the manicured and the wild, the conflagration of man's determined hand and nature's attributes, created an unforgettable experience. Rodolfo imagined spending his mornings with the head gardener planning summer vegetables and autumn borders. He'd pick his wife a bouquet of roses in May and chrysanthemums in the fall. He planned on entertaining his old friends in style and teaching the chef how to make their favourites. Having lived for so long on pasta and Valpolicella, he could almost taste *quenelles de brochet* and the vintage Bordeaux as it massaged his parched taste buds back into life. Rodolfo was not a cynic or a scoundrel: he was a pragmatist. He was too old and too dim to start a new career; he had made love to enough beautiful women and fathered enough children already. His great skill, knowing how to spend money in a measured and cultured way, might as well be put to good use even if it meant eschewing carnal pleasures. As he put his carnation in his top right lapel and looked at his handsome craggy face in the mirror, Rodolfo knew he had made the right decision to ask for Clarissa's hand in marriage. For the rest of her life (and he hoped that wasn't too long), he would make her happy. For the rest of his, he would live in this spectacularly beautiful castle. It wasn't a bad deal.

Clarissa was looking forward to life in the Italian countryside. Neither had lied about their circumstances; neither had been entirely truthful. They spoke in innuendoes about their respective situations and dropped references which would have been accurate more than one hundred years earlier during their families' heydays, not in the dregs of the present day.

*

That morning, Ayesha got the news that her dissertation on Isabella d'Este had won the top prize, the Gettina, at the Courtauld and that she'd been awarded a first-class master's degree. She ran through the corridors of Trelawney to find and tell Tony.

'That, dear girl, is something no one can ever take away from you.'

Yasmin had been gracious as runner-up. 'You deserve it,' she told Ayesha. 'It's a brilliant thesis, written with verve and astonishing depth of research.' Not knowing who else to tell, Ayesha had gone for a celebratory run through the woods, making it back to the castle at 3.30 p.m. with just enough time to shower and change for the wedding. If only, she thought, bounding up the main stairs, she could be as successful in other areas. Thanks to markups on household items and another picture purchase, her nest egg had grown another £100,000 to £325,000 but was still way short of her target.

Standing at the top of the stairs, waiting with her arms crossed, looking hot and very bothered, was Stella and her nanny. Ayesha's heart skipped a beat at the sight of her adorable child, with her dark-auburn curly hair, sleepy almond-shaped eyes and round body squeezed into a pink bridesmaid dress.

'You are the most ravishing and enchanting creature on earth.' Ayesha kissed her tiny nose.

'Where have you been, Mummy? I have waited for nearly one hundred million hours.' Stella pulled at the hem of her dress. 'It's scratchy.'

'Show me what happens when you spin around.'

Stella did a few twirls before tripping over the white tulle petticoat and falling with a howl of frustration in the centre of the landing.

Ayesha bent down and lifted her daughter to her feet. 'You look like a fairy.' She smoothed down her dress.

'Nanny Janet says I am as pretty as you,' Stella said, puffing up her chest, tears stopping as quickly as they'd started.

'Much prettier than Mummy,' Ayesha said.

She looked at her watch. The wedding was due to start in twenty-five minutes. Her natural beauty didn't need much enhancement beyond a swipe of lipstick and a dab of blusher.

Through the open window came the sound of raised voices; guests were mingling and trying to find their places. Ayesha, making sure she couldn't be seen, looked out from her bedroom window. Heat shimmered on the horizon. In the gardens plants were wilting, the heavy heads of dahlias and chrysanthemums turned to the ground. A lot of people had come early to enjoy the grounds and free champagne. They fanned themselves with the service sheets or hats. She spotted several B-list celebrities, some known for cooking or lifestyle shows on television, some famous for being famous. In a far corner were the Trelawney family friends who Ayesha had met briefly at Enyon's funeral. Most of the aristocracy were so broke that they'd drive a long way for a free cucumber sandwich. In one huddle she saw the Duke of Swindon, whose own fortune had been denuded by a series of court cases with impregnated housemaids; His Grace must have sired at least nine children out of wedlock. Windy's breath was as famous as his libido – fourteen-day-old Stilton had nothing on his halitosis; few blamed his wife for outsourcing her conjugal duty. Talking to him was Earl Beachendon, masquerading as a friend of the bride but there mainly as an envoy for Monachorum and Sons, the auction house. Ayesha knew that Beachendon wanted to sell them another work of art and her suspicions were vindicated by the sight of a briefcase at his feet – full, no doubt, of catalogues of expensive masterpieces. The Earl was attended by his still unmarried, now middle-aged daughters, all called something Shakespearean: Olivia, Ophelia and Desdemona. Nearby there were the Wellington d'Aresbys, the Smith-Gore-Browns and the Plantagenet-Parkers. The only thing they shared were their exhausted-looking wardrobes, bad haircuts, and haughtiness. All might be in penury but each and every one of them, based on hundreds of years of inbred self-importance, believed they were grander and more aristocratic than the next person.

'Do you want to go downstairs and show everyone your pretty dress?' Ayesha asked her daughter.

Stella was about to object but, hearing her father's heavy footsteps in the corridor, she took her nanny's hand and walked to the door.

Sleet strode into his wife's boudoir, ignoring his daughter and her nanny. 'Why aren't you ready?' he asked. 'It starts in twenty minutes.'

Ayesha smiled sweetly. 'It won't take long.'

'That's what all women say,' Sleet grumbled.

'Not all your wives have been twenty-six.' Ayesha got up slowly and went to her bathroom. Sleet followed her in and watched as she took off her clothes. It had been some time since he'd seen her naked.

'You're too thin. It's all that running,' he said.

Ayesha turned the shower on and waited until the temperature rose.

'I got a first in my master's degree and a prize for my dissertation,' she told him.

'Who wrote it for you?' Sleet asked.

'I wrote it.' Ayesha looked at him in confusion. Was he making a joke?

'You've never said anything intelligent.' He paused. 'I can't think of one memorable or interesting comment you've made in eight years.'

For once Ayesha answered back. 'We respect different things.'

Walking towards her, Sleet placed his hands over her cheeks and pinched them hard. 'The creation of wealth is a more useful way of spending life than the pursuit of knowledge. I make money for other people, I fill their pension funds, I provide for their families, enable their old age. You stuff your brain with useless facts. When you've got something to boast about, something that matters, shout about it. For now, shut your pretty little mouth.' He gave her cheeks a last painful squeeze and let go.

Ayesha's eyes filled but, not wanting him to see, she tilted her head downwards and turned on the hairdryer, reflecting on her solicitor's advice: make a list of all the unpleasant, abusive or defamatory things your husband says or does to you, your daughter or your staff. She had remarkably little evidence. How would Sleet's kind of abuse count in court, if at all? Your Honour, my husband gives me a generous allowance, I want for nothing. I am allowed to study, to see my friends occasionally. He has other lovers; he doesn't rape or hit me. He takes me to wonderful places, I meet interesting people. No, he doesn't hit or sexually abuse me. But, Your Honour, not a day or an opportunity passes where he doesn't belittle or put me down. I am a nobody in his eyes, an animated doll on his arm. My opinions don't count, my feelings and interior life are ignored. Many wouldn't sympathise with my plight: is my evisceration as a woman, as a sexual being, as an individual, considered? Is everyday endemic abuse a factor? The daily chip chip of abuse rather than raining blows. Are broken promises, lies and subterfuge to be taken into account? No? Your Honour, but why? Because there aren't physical bruises? Because I am not lying sobbing in a ditch? I must try harder to be downtrodden and pathetic. Thank you, Your Honour. I will do my best.

Looking at her cheeks in the mirror, she saw two pink marks but, as yet, no bruises. Surreptitiously, she photographed her face. Then, dabbing some lipstick on her mouth and blush on her cheeks, she shook out her hair and let it fall over her shoulders. 'Shall we go down?' she asked.

He looked at her scornfully. 'Can't you dress like a sophisticated woman rather than a gypsy hobo? Wear heels not sandals. I give you a proper clothes allowance – why can't you look nice for once?'

Most of the Trelawneys were there. Jane Trelawney stayed away, sending best wishes from her studio in Italy. Ambrose, her and Kitto's eldest son, was also absent. Kitto, who was giving his mother away, wore his last good suit, made by Huntsman & Sons, a thirtieth birthday present, now too big. Toby, dressed in the robes of a trainee Buddhist monk, came with his girlfriend Araminta Fogg, the daughter of the local preacher. Arabella looked furious in a frou-frou peach maid-of-honour gown. Aunt Tuffy had left her laboratory and her vast collection of living fleas to attend but refused to change from her normal summer attire: trainers and a shapeless cotton suit. Joshua agreed to look after Perrin while the excommunicated Blaze waited in a nearby pub.

The family and friends were outnumbered 8 to 1 by guests invited by *Hi!* magazine or the television company.

'Who are these frightful people?' Tuffy asked, looking at one couple wearing bright yellow matching suits.

'That one's got more feathers than all the pheasants at one of Enyon's shoots,' Tony said as a woman with a vast headdress walked past. 'And she doesn't have the legs for a short skirt. Someone should tell her.'

Barty was dressed as Liam Gallagher in leather with greasy black hair. The heat seemed to poach his face, and make-up dripped and bubbled. Then he spotted the pop star himself. 'Where's the photographer?' he shouted. 'Hold the front page!' He needed to pee badly but, concerned he'd lose the Oasis frontman in the crowd, decided to hold on.

A band struck up and four hundred guests went to find their seats. Family was in the first row and then celebrities in an ascending order of importance. Barty managed to secure a place next to his doppelgänger: Liam did not look amused. The older man, still desperate to relieve himself, decided the pain of withholding was outweighed by the pleasure of proximity.

No one had foreseen the weather. Cornwall was not known for heatwaves, but today at 4 p.m. the thermometer registered nearly thirty-seven degrees. Make-up ran down faces, sweat patches extended from armpits to waists, underwear cut into soft flesh, feet burst over tight shoes. Barbara Windsor fainted. John McKittrick was taken to lie down. Kevin Bacon and Ruby Wax meditated in the fountain. Only Ayesha, who made a late entrance, looked cool and comfortable in a figure-skimming silk slip dress, her auburn hair, still slightly damp, tied in a loose ponytail, and sandalled feet. The groom could not take his eyes off the young Lady Sleet until Uncle Tony kicked him in the shin.

Joshua and Sleet, intent on avoiding each other, failed and found themselves walking side by side up the aisle towards their seats.

'I hear your business isn't doing well,' Sleet smirked. 'Neither you nor your wife can raise the necessary funds. Agritech? The environment! What a joke.'

Joshua wanted to punch the other man but held his temper in check. 'Short term, it'll be harder to persuade investors. Long term, the environment is the single most important issue that we and our children face. There'll be great returns.' Joshua faced towards him. 'Unlike you, we don't destroy the environment or other people's lives.'

Sleet's face turned from pink to a mottled purple. His temples bulged. He stabbed a finger at Joshua. 'Who are you to judge me? Aren't we all alley cats grubbing around in the back streets of life? Trying to scratch a living? Who says your dustbin is better than mine? That your rubbish is more fragrant? We all shit and eat and shag. We're all driven by the same human urges. Your motives aren't different than mine – they're just dressed up in finer clothes.'

Joshua looked piteously at Sleet's finger. 'Only the weak and ineffectual have to succeed at other people's expense.'

Sleet adopted a condescending expression. 'My job is to make money for my clients now, not at some vague point in the future. I am doing well. Very well. Wish people could say the same about you and your wife. I hear you're haemorrhaging money and punters. That your wife can't even close her fund.'

Joshua clenched his fists. Sleet noticed and grinned. 'Not so Teflon-coated after all, are you? It's hard to sink from the top of your game to nothing more than a piece of detritus.'

Unclenching his fists and taking a long breath, Joshua arranged his face in a smile. 'Blaze and I have something you'll never have.'

'Yeah, what's that?' Sleet's tone was derisory.

'We have enough.' Without waiting for a response, Joshua went down the aisle to his seat.

Sleet stood for a moment, watching his nemesis's back. What an elliptical statement. Was 'Enough' a company? A new kind of AI? Sleet felt a rush of panic – he might be missing out on an investment opportunity. He sent a message to one of his analysts. *Investigate 'Enough' urgently. We need to take a position.*

Clarissa made her way slowly up the rose-lined aisle. The grass under her feet had turned yellow and the flowers wilted. Her face was heavily veiled and, for a minute, with the combination of lace and harsh sunlight in his eyes, the groom thought his bride to be lovely. Behind Clarissa, Arabella, boiling in her dress, was trying to persuade Perrin and Stella, both hot to the point of melting, not to take their clothes off.

'Just half an hour more,' she said to the little bridesmaids, whose cheeks were pinker than their strawberry sashes, 'and this will be over.' Turning towards the entrance, she saw her grandmother wobble a little unsteadily on her high heels. Leaving the girls, Arabella darted backwards and held out a supporting arm.

'Do you want everyone to think I'm old?' Clarissa asked. Straightening her posture, she looked towards her groom.

Arabella went back to her charges.

In the third row, Barty sat next to the man from Oasis. They'd been papped several times and Barty could hardly sit still as he tried to control his bladder.

'Here comes the bride …' He nudged his neighbour as Clarissa walked past them.

'She doesn't look a day over seventy,' Liam said.

Barty, trying to be more like Liam, affected a Mancunian accent. 'Part of the reason we humans love being in love is due to its ability to blur reality in a most reassuring way.'

Liam didn't answer. He couldn't understand a word the man was saying.

Barty read the silence as interest. 'Nowhere is this self-delusion more apparent than in our nuptials. Both are failing to recognise what's happening.'

'Yeah, right,' Liam said, wondering if he could switch seats to get away from this strange creature. Barty couldn't contain himself any more. Getting up, he walked slowly towards the catering tent, hoping to find a bathroom. The waiters and waitresses stood outside watching the wedding. In the distance Barty saw some Portaloos – about four hundred steps too far. His bladder was bursting. In the corner was a large container of Pimm's with pieces of fruit, borage and mint leaves. Barty couldn't hold it any longer. He couldn't help himself and peed into the cocktail. He took the long route back to his seat to find that Liam was still there.

The wedding passed in a warm blur. A local choir did their best with some hymns – the congregation were far too hot to add much lustre to the rendition of 'Mine Eyes Have Seen the Glory'. The aroma of sweat mixed with the scent of lightly toasting roses was overpowering. The moment the service finished, there was a stampede to the bar – many not even waiting for the bride and groom to walk back up the makeshift aisle. Joshua, bundling Perrin into her car seat, left immediately to pick up Blaze: every mile further away from Trelawney his spirits rose. Stella tore off her dress and jumped into the fountain to cool off. Her father, seeing the photographers, pretended to be interested in his daughter's welfare and stood with his arms outstretched and a look of concern on his face (the picture would make the front page of the *Daily Snail* the following day). A big band led by national heart-throb Jools Holland struck up and those who weren't too old or inebriated danced into the cooling night. Sleet went to his air-conditioned cinema to watch football. Using Stella as an excuse, Ayesha left early, put her daughter to bed and climbed in next to her with a book on Renaissance altarpieces.

For many years following, the wedding party of Clarissa to Rodolfo was written up as utterly memorable. The real star was not the happy couple or the celebrities, it was Trelawney Castle. Guests wandered open-mouthed through the rooms, marvelling at the exquisite damasks, furniture and artworks. Lit only by candlelight, the architectural features including cornices, frames and architraves glowed. Velvets and silks shimmered. Oak floorboards and mahogany doors shone. Each painting, many minor masterpieces, was perfectly placed. It was opulent and tasteful: magnificence contained. Of the forty photographers and three TV crews working that night, most soon gave up papping the guests and concentrated on the castle. None were prouder than Clarissa and Rodolfo. To her it was and would always be home. To him it was the apotheosis of a lifetime dream. The Duke of Prugnole had arrived.

Later, the newlyweds appeared on the front steps of the castle to wave to the remaining guests. Someone had tied cans and plastic bottles to the bumper of the white Rolls-Royce hired to take Clarissa and Rodolfo to their hotel. Those members of the Trelawney family and their friends who could still stand up threw confetti at the bride and groom. Damian Dobbs sat in the front seat of the car filming the happy couple. Clarissa had changed into a white tweed Chanel suit whose skirt ended above her knees. Rodolfo wore a sports jacket and chinos.

'You are by far the most handsome groom I've ever seen,' Clarissa cooed.

Rodolfo acknowledged the compliment with a little pat on his new wife's arm.

'I'm looking forward to us being alone,' Clarissa said. She was exhausted by the preparations and celebrations. Her feet hurt and her back ached. She hoped that their suite had a large bath and that her husband would understand if she spent a long time soaking her tired muscles.

'So, Your Grace,' Damian said, 'you've both opted for a short honeymoon – where will you take your bride next?'

Rodolfo picked up his wife's hand and kissed it. 'To paradise, of course.'

Clarissa smiled indulgently. It was as well that her husband was Italian – those kind of remarks with any other accent, she knew, would be awfully oleaginous.

'I hope her new wardrobes will be big enough.' Damian readjusted his camera's focus and zoomed in on a white van following the Rolls-Royce.

Rodolfo turned around in his seat to look.

'What is that?' he asked.

'All my clothes and a few mementoes,' Clarissa said.

'You need all those things for your wedding night?' Rodolfo was confused.

Clarissa laughed merrily. 'He's such a man,' she confided to the camera. 'Like all men, he thinks we women have only a few needs and even fewer changes of outfits.'

'I don't understand.' Rodolfo loosened his tie and wiped his forehead with a silk handkerchief.

Damian turned the camera to the groom. 'The question we all want the answer to is where you and the Countess will be living now that she's vacated Trelawney Castle.'

'What is vacated?' Rodolfo's almost perfect English vanished. 'Tomorrow we return to castle.' He smiled at Clarissa.

'No, darling, tomorrow we go to Castello di Prugnole.'

'Eh?' Rodolfo said, the colour draining from his face.

Damian knelt up in his seat. He finally had the shot. As Blaze had warned and others had suspected, Rodolfo had no castle or fortune or enough brains to understand that he and his new wife were living in a fool's paradise. Clarissa's own compass had been set to the wrong coordinates by a combination of love and wishful thinking. She believed that the sexes were equal – a man's role was to provide, and she assumed Rodolfo was up to the task. The husband and wife had a simultaneous epiphany: they had married a fantasy. Worse still, they had both lost Trelawney. Clarissa had agreed to move out, Rodolfo would never move in. Rodolfo thought the stabbing pain was his heart breaking; he put his hand to his chest and tried to breathe. The pains worsened. The next thing he heard was his wife screaming. After that Rodolfo, Duke of Prugnole remembered nothing.

10

September 2016

The sudden, tragic death of her new husband, the Duke of Prugnole, sent Clarissa's reality show to the top of the television ratings in Great Britain and abroad. Nineteen million people worldwide tuned into each update delivered in twice-daily ten-minute segments. News channels produced edited highlights. She was filmed on her wedding night in a prepaid suite. She was too tired to mourn or even do her make-up. The cameras caught her sobbing, still in her white Chanel suit, splayed on the nylon carpet. The following day she went, followed by news crews, to a dilapidated guesthouse paid for by the production company on the outskirts of Bodmin. Damian Dobbs had selected it carefully – it was called 'Sweet Dreams', a misnomer: the place was small, dingy, dank and, most importantly, certain to maintain public interest. Clarissa was filmed trying to boil an egg in a kettle and make her own bed.

She achieved worldwide fame but this didn't solve her major problem: she had nowhere to live. Spare rooms were offered, including one from an American TV reality family, with others from a bookie, a rapper, a former flame and an illegitimate grandchild of her husband's. She turned all these down. When someone suggested she started a crowdfunding site to raise money for her situation, Clarissa looked aghast. 'One is not part of any crowd. One is an aristocrat.' Words that made some laugh but didn't help.

The family watched with growing consternation.

'We are a laughing stock,' Tony lamented. 'Eight hundred years of hegemony wiped out.' Arabella was relieved her surname was Scott rather than Trelawney. Toby gave an interview to *The Times* saying that his grandmother should become a Buddhist and consciously uncouple from capitalism and unlearn the mindset of materialism. Only Tuffy, who never watched television, escaped the brouhaha. Blaze, despite her mother's previous behaviour, was racked with guilt.

'She has nowhere to go,' she told her husband. 'We have a spare room.'

'No way.' The love Joshua felt for his wife was immense; however, those feelings didn't extend to a single member of her family, all of whom he considered vain and worthless. Blaze's mother got an extra adjective: vile.

'I can't leave her destitute.' She hesitated. 'We missed the chance to help John, let's not make the same mistake.'

Joshua could hardly believe what he was hearing. 'Your mother is spoilt not suicidal.' Overall he kept his feelings about Blaze's family to himself, but on this occasion his anger spilt. 'Would you send our daughter aged twenty on a train to London, with fifty pounds in her pocket, with nowhere to stay and no job?'

Blaze winced. 'Of course not, but my mother is nearly ninety.'

'Have you forgotten what she said and how she spoke to you at the wedding?' Joshua paced around the room. 'Why do you want to help her? To satisfy some ancient Trelawney by-law? For sentimentality? Or has your mother changed from being a selfish, self-obsessed celebrity to a loving parent?'

'Maybe it's the pull of DNA, a need to protect one's own, but I have to help her.'

Joshua shook his head. 'She was a 99 per cent terrible mother.'

'It's the 1 per cent that matters,' Blaze countered.

Joshua looked out of the window. In recent months, their lives had been rocked by guilt and confusion. When they weren't trying to console Perrin over the sudden departure of her best friend Lily, they berated themselves for not having done more to help John Whaley. Ayesha had given the clue – both had ignored it. Nothing, he reminded himself, mattered more than family. Squaring his shoulders, he knelt in front of his wife.

'I'd do anything for you, darling. Anything. And if having your mother to stay will make you happy, then let's do it.'

As the words left his mouth, his heart sank. Could he really do it? Taking Blaze's hands in his, he gave it one more try. 'Before you answer me, can you please decide how much is down to loyalty and pride? Are you trying to protect the Trelawney name from ridicule?'

'It's not that.'

They both knew that part of it was.

'I have an idea – we could try and find her a cottage or an apartment locally. Somewhere super-comfortable with a housekeeper.' He did his best to keep the hope out of his eyes.

Blaze felt a wash of gratitude. This was a far better solution for everyone. 'Thank you,' she whispered.

The callous behaviour of Sir Thomlinson and Lady Sleet, now known as 'The Terminators' or 'The Evictors', kept telephone wires and red-top newspapers humming. While Ayesha was mortified, her husband saw it as free PR – 'shows the world that I mean business'. He had the unflattering cartoons and newspaper articles framed for his bathroom.

Tony and Barty were instructed to redecorate the Mistresses' Wing and expunge any traces of its former occupant. Both men felt uncomfortable about this, particularly as Clarissa was still living in the squalid bedsit near Bodmin. They took care packages over to the Sweet Dreams guesthouse but these made little difference to Clarissa who was inconsolable about the loss of her home and husband. She loathed her new quarters: 'The loo is in the same room as the bath. It's too common for words,' she wailed.

Each time they saw her, Tony and Barty drove away feeling depressed.

'I can't bear the old goat, but to see her reduced to such a pathetic state. Is the term hubert?'

'Hubris,' Tony said.

'I thought Hubris was a breakfast cereal?'

'Perhaps you're right.' Tony couldn't remember. His mental capacity was fading. He could recall every member of staff at Trelawney in 1939 (there'd been fifty-seven) but fought to name one of Jane and Kitto's children. Most of his relations and acquaintances had become 'thingamajig'. He'd leave a room only to forget the purpose of the journey. Worst of all, he felt weary to his soul. Although he was making good money from the Sleets, he thought back wistfully to a life of baked beans on toast: it had been so much simpler.

'I don't know how much longer I can take Sleet's grandiosity,' he said to Barty, who was driving extremely slowly along a twisty Cornish lane. 'I find his world of conspicuous excess soul-destroying.'

'I love spending other people's money,' Barty said. 'I read in the *Daily Snail* that he makes several million pounds a second.'

'He has to sleep sometimes.'

'Money is a bacterial culture which keeps on replicating even with your eyes closed.'

'It can't be that easy.' Tony looked out of the car window. 'His run of good luck can't last forever.'

'Let's hope it sees us out,' Barty said. 'I hate being poor.'

It was a beautiful evening, and the sky had a violet tinge. In the far distance, beyond a patchwork of green fields, the sea sparkled. The car was now going at less than twenty miles per hour.

'If you drive any slower, we'll be overtaken by a sheep,' Tony said.

'Better safe than sorry.'

'What on earth are we being careful for? It's not like we have years to look forward to.'

'Who's a gloomy girl?' Barty looked at his friend tenderly. Then he put his foot on the pedal and increased his speed to about thirty m.p.h. 'Sir Tom and Lady Sleet aren't rubbing along too well. He's not even bothering to be discreet about sleeping with the trainer.'

'Belowstairs gossip is that there's an Albanian.'

'I hope the marriage lasts long enough for Ayesha to get what she needs.' Tony was worried about his great-niece, who had lost weight and much of her natural elan. She spent all day on her phone and carried a little notebook in which she transcribed details in tiny mirror writing.

'What's she jotting down?'

'Who knows – it must be several volumes.' Tony hesitated. 'With any luck, it's for her lecture on Isabella at the Louvre.'

'That sounds fancy pancy.'

'Her dissertation won first prize. I'm so proud of her.'

'I think she's plotting something else,' Barty said. 'Let's hope it's Sleet's downfall. That man gets more and more ghastly by the second. Yesterday he went through all the staff wages and tried to cut them by 10 per cent, saying that costs were out of control.'

'He wouldn't give the skin off his rice pudding.'

The two men sat in silence.

'If you had all that money, darling boy, what would you do with it?' Tony asked.

Barty didn't hesitate. 'I'd have a facelift.'

'Bit late for that, isn't it?'

'It's never too late to look neat. Besides, I might bag a duke.'

'Didn't do Clarissa much good.'

'The only cure for love is to love more, Mummy used to say.'

*

After a few weeks Blaze, heavily incognito in a headscarf and dark glasses, turned up at Sweet Dreams and, without waiting for her mother's assent, she bundled Clarissa into the car and drove her away to her new home on the outskirts of Thame, only a few miles from the Wolfes' house. The cottage was clean, functional, pretty, with its own small garden: Clarissa hated everything about it.

*

When Ayesha woke up at 6 a.m. she turned on her phone and logged into the MySpy app. She read the text from Rodita to Sleet three times to believe it. *Cornish asset disposed £145 million. Exchange fixed for August 1st, 2017.* Ayesha trembled uncontrollably, the phone slipped from her hands and blood throbbed through her temples. She lay on the floor and tried to breathe her heart back to a normal rhythm. Stella was still fast asleep in the bed opposite. Ayesha went to the bathroom next door where she continued to access Sleet's personal emails and scrolled through looking for references to the sale.

From RdC to ST. Medieval Illusions' confirmed bid for £145 million 10 per cent deposit paid. Enjoy property until August 2017. Planning applied for.

Ayesha dabbed at her face with the corner of her pyjamas. Then she looked up the new owner's name online. The more she read, the deeper her heart sank. Medieval Illusions specialised in turning stately homes into theme parks. Its flagship property was a French chateau in the Loire Valley: the main house was a hotel and the parkland had been transformed into a playground with different activities: in one area there were jousters, in another peasants tending animals; there

161

were washerwomen, jugglers, mud wrestlers, spit roasters and animal tenders. Paying, staying guests slept in tents and during the day could live, according to the blurb, like 'a genuine yokel'. It took little imagination to transform Trelawney into an immersive visitor attraction. Perhaps they'd offer a 'serfdom' experience or, for a premium, the chance to sleep in her bed and live like an earl and countess.

It was all her own fault. With Tony and Barty, they'd transformed Trelawney, rescuing it from dilapidation and obscurity and turning it into a valuable commodity. Any hope of a reconciliation or rapprochement with her family was finally over. She had occupied their home and nothing would ever persuade them, divorce or no divorce, that she hadn't planned the whole venture for personal profit.

Little by little she was making some money and recorded every pound in the notebook she kept with her at all times. Over the last month her nest egg had increased to £400,000. She was also accruing more information about her husband's activities. Waking in the middle of the night, she thought about different strategies and ways to hurt him: disabling his huge collection of cars; tipping off the press about his affairs; even warning Zamora Lala. None of these would deliver the killer blow needed.

She waited until Stella was awake, gave her breakfast and, leaving her with the nanny, ran to the station to catch the next train to London. On the way she texted Yasmin. *Emergency. Please can I come and see you.* The taxi ride to Yasmin's digs in the East End took more than an hour from Paddington. The driver, after several valiant but unreciprocated attempts, gave up trying to engage her in conversation. For Ayesha, the journey passed in a blur as she tried to work out what to do next. She hoped visiting Yasmin would offer a brief respite from her own mind.

The cab turned into a side street off Roman Road and, halfway down, Ayesha saw number 34. Outside there were a jumble of bicycles and an overflowing dustbin. Heavy dub music came from an upstairs window. Ayesha rapped hard on the door. Yasmin answered. Her beautiful eyes were smudged with kohl, her dark hair was wrapped in a towel, and she wore a small white dressing gown and fluffy slippers. Next to Ayesha, who was clad in high-heeled suede boots, a matching long suede coat, a Gucci miniskirt and crop top, Yasmin, though tired, looked fresh and young.

'I was in the shower. You been here long?' she asked, leaning forward to kiss her friend.

Ayesha looked around the room; the mess was at the same time slightly disgusting and exciting. There were plates piled high in the sink, an old leather jacket draped over the back of a chair and the smell of old dope and wine.

'Don't live with boys,' Yasmin said, following her stare. 'Are you going to take your glasses off?'

Slowly Ayesha removed her shades to reveal her puffy tear-stained eyes.

Yasmin nodded. 'I'll make the tea. My room's at the top on the left.' She steered Ayesha towards the staircase.

Ayesha let herself into Yasmin's room. It was just large enough for a single bed and a small desk. Unlike the rest of the house, it was scrupulously clean. On the desk there was a family photograph – possibly grandparents, holding the hands of two children aged around nine and ten, several books and a laptop. Minutes later Yasmin appeared and set two cups down.

'It's hard to tell anything about you from your surroundings,' Ayesha said.

Yasmin laughed. 'I don't need much.' She wondered how long it would take her friend to talk about what was happening.

'Family?' Ayesha said, pointing to the photograph.

'My grandparents with my dad and aunty. Taken in Tehran in 1978.' She reached up on to the shelf and took down a large hand-bound book. Flipping it open, Ayesha saw page after page of black and white reproductions of works by Monet, Rothko, Klimt, Bacon and Picasso. 'I've never seen any of these.'

'My grandfather bought them for the Shah and his wife. He was their chief curator and built up the Empress of Persia's personal collection.'

'The quality is incredible,' Ayesha said, turning over pages. 'Why did they buy this stuff?'

'The same reason that many wealthy people always have. Amassing a great collection is the best way to make a silk purse out of a sow's ear. Owning and collecting art confers class. It's like a cleansing system for dirty water: put the ill-gotten gains in one end, buy beautiful things and your money becomes tainted with beauty.'

Ayesha laughed. 'Isabella d'Este did something slightly different. She was born into and married money. She used art as a tool of power and one-upmanship: having the best showed she was stronger than her rivals.' Ayesha took a sip of tea. 'You've given me a great idea for a book: to look at the history of art, money and power. It could span time from Athens to Persia and up to the present day.' She felt a flicker of excitement, imagining a direction for herself which needn't include Sleet but would draw on her love of art and her experience of life amongst the super-rich. For the first time she envisioned a career, a project that she could call her own. Turning back to Yasmin's book, she asked, 'Where is the Shah's collection now?'

'In a secured vault underground in Tehran.' The bitterness in Yasmin's voice was palpable.

'Have these been exhibited or published?' Ayesha asked. 'If not, they should be.'

Yasmin grimaced. 'This is one of the few records. The regime don't like to publicise ownership. They keep the most salacious works out of the country, in a Geneva free port.'

'What happened to your grandfather?' Ayesha asked.

'If he's alive, he's in an underground vault otherwise known as the national prison.' Yasmin's face pinched. Neither her grandmother, now in her eighties, nor her father, aunt, brothers and sisters would ever give up trying to find Omer. She and her brother Reza had made several official requests but without a significant bribe – more money than they had – no information would be forthcoming. Yasmin looked at her friend, filled her cheeks and then blew out harshly. 'One Thursday my grandfather was fully employed in a job he loved, living in a beautiful house with his family.' She clapped her hands together. 'Boom. The Shah is deposed. A *coup d'état*. Omer got his family on the last flights out, promising to join them in a matter of days. That was nearly forty years ago.' She motioned around the room. 'There are 37,000 Persians in this country, scratching a livelihood, dreaming of going home. My family isn't so unusual.'

'Why didn't I know this?' Ayesha questioned.

'You never asked.'

'I'm sorry,' Ayesha said, chastened by her own self-absorption.

'Are you ready to tell me what happened?' Yasmin asked, filling up her friend's cup.

'Hearing your story puts mine into perspective.' She blew gently on the surface of the scalding water to cool it. 'I was a trusting foolish idiot who took a promise at face value. It turns out we were never legally married. There is no binding prenup. All his assets are hidden in offshore accounts. He's sold Trelawney, which was never even mine, without telling me.' Tears dripped down her face. She wiped her nose with the back of her hand. 'How could I be so stupid?'

'You stupid or him duplicitous?' Yasmin passed her a roll of loo paper and then, leaning over, stroked her friend's hair. 'You had no idea? No inkling?'

Ayesha shook her head.

'What are you going to do about it?'

'There's nothing I can do.' Ayesha twisted the edge of her suede coat in her fingers. 'He has all the power.'

Yasmin ran her hands through her hair, buying time before responding. 'I thought you were an intelligent woman?'

Ayesha looked up in surprise.

'What real power does he have? Money, yes, but he can't control your thoughts, your actions. Can he make you turn left when you want to turn right? Tell you how to feel? No. You are projecting authority on to a blank canvas, imbuing him with non-existent qualities.' Taking her friend's hands in her own, Yasmin shook them gently. 'Get in touch with your anger. Use your brain, your imagination, your resources. Don't sit there in your three-thousand-pound Gucci skirt feeling sorry for yourself.'

Ayesha winced; she'd been hoping for sympathy.

'You were eighteen when he married you – a child with breasts and monthly flowers. Three years younger, he'd have been done for underage molestation.'

'I was willing. To an extent I targeted him.' Ayesha remembered turning up to a party wearing nothing but body paint and wisps of fabric to captivate the older man. For many months, she'd refused to sleep with him – partly because she didn't particularly want to but mainly to tease and titillate.

Yasmin laughed. 'You ensnared a thrice-married man more than twice your age using feminine wiles? Give me a break. To him you were another acquisition, one who was young and naive enough for him to mould and manipulate. And now that he's bored of you and has identified the next victim – you're being discarded. With nothing. And that, my dear friend, is what he thinks of you: nothing.'

'We have a child.' Ayesha's voice came out as a whisper.

'How often does he see his other children?' Yasmin already knew the answer.

Ayesha hesitated before her next admission. Looking at her friend's humble surroundings, knowing about her family circumstances, what she was about to admit was so spoilt. 'I am so inept at life. I don't know how I'll survive.'

Yasmin laughed again, not unkindly. 'You'll adapt.'

'What can I do?' Ayesha looked at her friend imploringly.

Yasmin put her arms around her friend. 'The good news is you're in a strong position.'

'I am?' Ayesha's eyes lit up.

'You have nothing to lose.'

Ayesha sank back in the chair. It didn't sound like an advantage.

'If your husband can come up with dastardly schemes, so can you. Set traps, unnerve him, make trouble, expose him, use blackmail, extortion. Do everything he does and has done.'

'It's not how my—'

Yasmin took her by the shoulders and shook her hard.

'What the fuck!' Ayesha was upset and angry.

'That's the feeling you must build on. Get out there. If not for you, then for your daughter. Do you want her to think of you as a power-less woman or a role model?' Yasmin's tone was fierce but loving. She took Ayesha in her arms and held her close. 'You can do this; you are better, braver and more resourceful than Sleet.'

Leaving Yasmin's digs, Ayesha caught a taxi to Paddington and finally remembered to turn on her phone. There were seventy-five messages. She scrolled through quickly to check that there was nothing from or about Stella. To her relief, all the calls were from members of staff looking for domestic direction.

In normal circumstances a driver dropped her in plenty of time at the station, handed her a pre-booked ticket and told her which platform the train was leaving from. Tonight, she purchased her own ticket and ran to make the train. She bought a cup of tea and settled in an almost empty carriage. It was a pitch-dark moonless night and, leaning her face against the headrest, all Ayesha saw was her own rather ghostly reflection strobing in the neon-lit window. The train passed empty-platformed stations and glided through towns, then cities and finally villages as it made its way from London to the West Country. Her friend was right – it was time to stop playing victim. As the miles were eaten up, feelings of gloom were replaced by hope and even glimmers of exhilaration: she had spent far too long buffeted around on others' whims. She would never again be a footnote in someone else's story; a fading figure in a photograph tucked in an album of other forgotten faces and distant memories. She had a sudden over-whelming desire to make a mark, however faint, on the gift of life. She would not waste another second. The ticket collector came towards her and stood, as so many had done before, transfixed by the exquisite young woman. In her past life Ayesha had found this kind of attention embarrassing; their frank admiration had little, she thought, to do with her: her beauty was accidental. But in her new life, which started that day, she saw that her looks were an attribute to be used. She decided to practise on the bulbous-nosed, middle-aged man swaying slightly in the passageway.

'Would you like to see my ticket?' she said, lowering and then rais-ing her eyes.

He nodded soundlessly, opening and closing his mouth, his gaze fixed on the apparition before him.

It was, Ayesha thought, a start.

*

As Sleet's Chief Operating Officer, Rodita's job was to keep Kerkyra Capital out of trouble. She took enormous pride in translating bold ideas into practice. She ignored the moral implications of certain deci-sions; her cut of profits went to her offspring and a country many of whose inhabitants lived below the poverty line. Nor did she have any sympathy for Sleet's investors – they had a choice where they put their money and choosing a company that gave them high returns meant taking high risks. If they lost their stake, it was their own fault.

However, cryptocurrency, and in particular Queen of Coins, tested the limits of Rodita's rectitude. It was their job to put their clients' money into vehicles they could explain and understand. To her, QoC was a scam, a currency unpegged to any national institution, unrec-ognised by any country or official body. Only a few, such as bitcoin, could be publicly traded. Looking at the Queen of Coins website,

Rodita saw that it set its own rules and value, there were no checks or balances, and each coin could only be exchanged for its own products: bogus educational material, T-shirts, sun cream, biscuits and tracksuits. It operated like many other pyramid schemes, with a highly motivated sales force paid on commission. These teams were scattered across Europe, Africa and South America. Anyone who bought a coin was incentivised to sell to others in their address book, creating a large pyramid of unregulated, untrained self-starters.

That morning another email had arrived from Sleet ordering the transfer of a significant sum of Kerkyra Capital's balance sheet into Queen of Coins. The more Rodita found out about Dr Zamora Lala, the more concerned she became. Sitting at her computer, she tried to understand the business model behind Lala's cryptocurrency. There were no listed company accounts or any trace of a holding company; it was a business without records, although there were offices in Tirana and Bangkok. After eleven hours of investigation, she reached the conclusion that QoC was a giant scam with Zamora at the top.

When Rodita raised concerns, Sleet waved them away – £50 million was money he'd made the week before, following a short on crude oil. Zamora said Rodita was too old-fashioned to understand cryptocurrency. Sleet said she should retire; he needed someone modern, not a has-been Filipino.

Rodita tried a different tack. 'If she wasn't so beautiful, would you be investing?'

Sleet turned pink and then red. 'How dare you! You are accusing me of being some moonstruck dumbass?' He pointed at the door. 'Your problem, Rodita, is that you're not clever enough to know your extreme limitations. Buy twenty-five million more in QoCs,' he ordered.

'It'll take your total holding to over seventy-five million,' Rodita said. 'This time I'll transfer it from your personal account.'

'Why?'

'We need that money to leverage your debt. The creditors are jumpy.' Rodita had fielded two calls from their banker that morning.

Sleet looked at his associate. 'Who gives a fuck about them? When I bought my first car I stayed awake every night for a month worrying about how to repay the two hundred and fifty pounds. Now that I've borrowed more than a few billion, I sleep like a baby. You know why?'

'Why?' Rodita had heard the story many times but indulged her boss.

'Now it's the banks who shouldn't sleep – it's their money.' Sleet laughed. He loved this story. 'Take the money from the Junior Trust,' he instructed.

'That's your children's fund.'

Sleet shrugged 'They're fucking spongers. Let them make their own money. In any case, it's all mine. Everything is mine.'

'If it's yours, why did you put it in a separate trust?'

'I was having a weak moment. One gets over these things.'

Rodita was profoundly shocked. Who would take money from their own children, even if it was money you'd given? Sleet had crossed a line. 'A gift is a gift.'

Sleet felt a sliver of doubt. Wives came and went, deals succeeded or failed, but his two stalwarts, Donna and Rodita, were always by his side. 'What's eating you, Rodita? You've been off with me recently.'

Rodita shuffled in her chair. 'I don't understand the decisions you're making. I get propellers and dollars. I can hold gold in my hand. I know why a share goes up and down or a stock fluctuates. This Queen of Coins makes no sense at all. It seems to me like one giant Ponzi scheme.'

Sleet, though he couldn't admit it, had doubts about crypto, but his business acumen, his feel for a deal, was obscured by his obsession with Zamora and he couldn't admit that he was wrong. For all his worldly success, he lacked the self-awareness or patience to accept that no external forces, object or person, however valuable, beautiful or shiny, would ever fill or compensate for the gaping hole at the core of his being. Sleet's need to be loved and admired was a bottomless pit.

Reaching for a box of pencils, he began to snap them in half. 'I'm not interested in your opinions or your amateur sleuthing. This woman is the real deal. Now get the fuck out.'

It was the first time that Rodita had left the office before 8 p.m. in twenty-three years. Wilfredo was at home and rushed to his wife's side.

'Are you ill? Your heart?'

'Beating strongly.'

'What's happened?' Looking at Rodita, he was shocked. His normally sanguine wife, who never raised her voice or overreacted, looked flustered. Taking her arm, he led her to a chair, then hurried to the sideboard and poured her a glass of sherry (the couple never drank – alcohol was kept for very occasional visitors).

Rodita took a quick swig and grimaced.

'It's an issue of respect,' she explained. 'I know my limitations: I will never equal his chutzpah or bravery, I am too timid to be an entrepreneur, but I have been there, day by day, step by step, as we built Kerkyra Capital. I don't deserve to be treated like this.'

'He wants you to sort out another divorce?' Wilfredo asked. The present wife had lasted eight years – five was Sleet's average.

Rodita shrugged. 'There's always a new woman.' She barely ever met the wives, so could hardly feel invested in any of their lives. After the first one, she had devised a system to ensure that no outgoing Mrs or Lady Sleet made much money from her divorce. All assets were hidden in shell companies. The unsuspecting women were lulled into a false sense of security by their husband's supposed generosity, only to be ejected into the real world with comparatively small alimonies and no way of exacting revenge. Rodita felt no pity – they really should have known better and, apart from the first wife, she didn't imagine any of them had married Sleet for love.

'He questioned your judgement?'

'He dismissed my opinion.' She raised both hands skywards. 'Dismissed and belittled personally.'

Wilfredo came around the chair and faced his wife. For the first time in thirty years of marriage, he took control. 'You are leaving.'

'Leaving?'

Wilfredo nodded. 'We are going home to set up a business. Something for our future and for the next generation. We have done well from this country, and they from us, but it's time to help our own. I don't believe you're not an entrepreneur – you are a beautiful, capable tree who hasn't been able to grow because a larger one has been blocking out your light, stealing your water. You are the finest, most wonderful and talented person I know.' He took her hands in his. 'There is nothing you can't do.'

Rodita raised her head and smiled gratefully. 'I know you are right, dear husband, but I have things to put in place before I walk away.'

*

The following week Sleet and Zamora met in the Polo Lounge in New York. It had been her idea. *Taste and Refinement* said Eleven Madison was the only place for dinner. He'd taken the precaution of reserving Sant Ambroeus for breakfast the following morning. He'd flown from Cornwall in his private jet at only eight hours' notice and arrived breathless and befuddled from the long transatlantic flight. He noted that Zamora had the best table in the centre, one where people paid to see and be seen. Many came up to greet her. Sleet, who'd flown across the world to see her and was not used to being treated as a sideshow, wriggled uncomfortably.

'I made a killing on the referendum,' he told her. 'And I'll do very well from an aeronautical company.'

Zamora dipped the cherry into her cocktail, popped it into her mouth and sucked hard.

Sleet quivered with excitement.

Zamora turned her slanted eyes in his direction. 'By 2022 the world will be dominated by the FANGS and cryptocurrency. You should stick your money in them and retire.'

'Will you retire with me?' Sleet asked. 'We could sail around the world together.'

Zamora said nothing.

'When are you going to let me kiss you?'

'I don't kiss married men.'

'I am not married. It's a pretence.'

'You live together.'

'Not for much longer.'

Zamora smiled but gave no commitment. 'My QoC results for this month came in today – another hundred thousand subscribers. Your holding's worth 35 per cent more than when you bought it – why not double up?'

'What would another 25-million-pound investment be worth to you?' Sleet said suggestively and took hold of her hand.

'Think about what it would be worth to you.' Her mouth formed a smile, but her eyes remained cold.

Sleet leaned back in his chair. 'You're driving me mad.'

Rather than answer, Zamora took her lipstick out of her bag and added another layer of red to her perfectly painted mouth. Then she nodded at the waiter and within seconds a bill was produced.

'On my account,' she instructed.

'Hang on. I asked you here,' Sleet said.

'You paid last time.'

'And I'll pay next time and the one after that too.'

Zamora got to her feet and, from a nearby table, her two body-guards sprang up.

'Where are you going?' Sleet asked, pushing his chair back.

'I am going to Albania to see my father – he's not well.'

'I'd like to meet him.' Sleet wanted to eke out as much time as possible with her.

'He wouldn't like you.' She nodded curtly and walked out of the restaurant, her bodyguards forming an orderly wake on either side of her. Sleet had travelled for ten hours in return for forty-five minutes in her presence.

11

October 2016

In the last month, scrimping, saving and adding commissions to bills, Ayesha added to her nest egg, which now stood at £490,000. It was a lot of money but far short of the £145 million she needed to buy Trelawney from Medieval Illusions. Taking Yasmin's advice to heart, there was no time for self-pity or reflection. She had to make the most of every occasion and every hour.

The day the new winter collections dropped, she went to every designer store in London and, using her husband's credit card, spent over £100,000 on new clothes. The following day she took everything back in exchange for cash. Going through her capacious wardrobes, she picked out her favourite pieces and consigned all the rest to an upmarket vintage store in Chelsea. The astonished shop owner made a down payment of £75,000 and promised that Ayesha would see three times that amount even after the 50 per cent commission. Then she took her large collection of handbags to a leading auction house where she was given a reserve of £80,000 for just one Kelly bag; the Birkins, Gucci and Pradas combined were guaranteed to net over £150,000. She stared at the auctioneer in amazement. Sleet had bought them to boost his wife's social standing; she'd never imagined these objects (which she'd never particularly liked) would become crucial building blocks in her future. Next she put the allowance of £1,000 a week that Sleet gave her for beauty treatments (her hair and other fripperies) into 'the future' account. Within a couple of weeks, her fighting fund rose to nearly £925,000.

As a non-regulated private investor unable to place large or complicated bets on the market, she opened a Swiss bank account and employed a broker called Herr Brunner who could help her copy

Sleet's moves by buying or shorting the same stocks. Not everything went up but, following his lead, she increased her portfolio by 25 per cent in one month, taking it to more than a £1 million. Rather than feel pleased with her progress, Ayesha was increasingly despondent: Medieval Illusions were due to take possession of Trelawney in ten months' time.

Potentially, the most lucrative activity was buying art. Dealers made at least 40 per cent from selling works to her husband; from now on, she'd take a cut. Walking around their homes, she chided herself for not thinking of this earlier. At their London residence, Ayesha had, over the last five years, replaced her husband's collection of dull minor impressionists with more exciting Modern British Masters. Had she added a percentage to these, she'd have made several million pounds. Sleet hadn't even noticed when one cloudy haystack was replaced with a bold abstract – for him, art was just wall covering. Once she'd loved looking at the works she'd bought; now she saw them as squandered opportunities. She combed the catalogues, auction rooms and galleries for new works for her husband to buy and for her to mark up. Sleet, thinking only of Zamora, dismissed her suggestions. Ayesha was becoming more desperate. She thought about commissioning a gang to steal the works from their own home, or faking a burglary and doing it herself, but knowing the security system and the permanent guards decided that the risks were too great.

All the time she put on a brave public face: neither her husband nor any of his associates would be given any hint of subterfuge. When Sleet decided to throw open their London home for a work-related cocktail party, she threw herself into the role of perfect consort. This time, Ayesha did her homework and delighted each of their guests with points relevant to their businesses. The following day, three of the guests, all highly successful entrepreneurs, telephoned. Sleet assumed it was about business; they only wanted to talk about art.

The first caller was Ricky O'Fell, the legendary Irish property dealer, responsible for nine out of the twelve tallest buildings in New York and owner of a chunk of most major capital cities. Galling for others in the UHNW bracket were O'Fell's looks – he was so handsome that most assumed he'd strayed off a movie set.

'I see you have a late Bacon,' O'Fell said. 'It must have taken years to find it.'

'Yeah,' Sleet concurred, although he had no idea who or what a Bacon was.

'I bought mine from Bunny Mellon's niece,' O'Fell continued.

'That's cool,' Sleet said and later when he googled Bacon and Mellon, his eyes nearly popped when he saw the price tag: $30 million for two men having sex? Until then he'd thought O'Fell was smart, but the guy was crazy. What was he thinking, spending that kind of money on two homosexuals getting cute with each other? O'Fell segued into a discussion about a joint deal – one that Sleet had been longing to take part in. He checked with his office: Ayesha had bought theirs for less than £5 million; still an eye-watering amount but, by comparison, something of a bargain.

The same day Noah Lane, currently number one in distressed credit, telephoned for the first time, opening the conversation with a compliment on the Sleets' Basquiat.

'It was at the Pompidou retrospective, wasn't it?' Lane asked. Sleet had no idea what the man was talking about.

'I always trust a man who has fine taste in women and art – your wife is best in class, your pictures ain't bad,' Lane continued. Sleet swallowed hard – one more question and he'd be exposed as a fraud. Luckily Lane segued on to a deal the two men might collaborate on. Replacing the phone, Sleet sat back in his chair. Until now he'd thought of buying art as an expensive hobby and a peccadillo to keep Ayesha quiet. Not any more: ownership of these inanimate objects opened doors into an exclusive club. For these financial titans, art chatter was a kind of verbal foreplay leading to deeper conversations about deals and money. He had a sudden revelation: it was art rather than money and success that would give him an entry to a world he longed to join.

It wasn't long before three of the guests telephoned. 'I'll see you at Frieze,' George Solos, the world's biggest arbitrage billionaire, said to him.

'Sure,' Sleet said.

'Freeze or Frieze?' he asked Donna, who suggested he ask Ayesha – she'd know all about that kind of thing.

Sleet didn't want to ask Ayesha or display any kind of ignorance.

'Get me all the books on art,' he instructed.

'Are you sure you mean all?' Donna asked.

'If I say all, I mean all.'

With a front-row seat at the Sleet marriage, Donna decided not to involve Ayesha. She had nothing against her but, knowing the younger woman was on the way out, she thought it simpler to avoid all but necessary contact.

Four days later an articulated lorry full of books turned up at the castle.

'Who knew there was so much to art.' Realising he didn't have the patience to read even one book, Sleet had the whole lot sent to an outhouse.

Ayesha was surprised when Sleet said he wanted to attend the opening of the Frieze art fair in London the following week. Seeing an opportunity to add more money to her fighting fund, she phoned around her dealer acquaintances and had several paintings put on hold, settling in advance her own commission against them. Securing super-VIP tickets, they arrived at 9 a.m., two hours before the next strata of important people. The exhibition was in a huge specially built structure in a corner of Regent's Park. Inside, five hundred gallerists from every part of the world showed their best or most commercial contemporary artists. The lighting was neon white, as disconcerting and dazzling as being trapped in a film star's mouth. Nine long corridors were lined by identical tiny temples of artistic 'excellence'. Sleet spent the first hour charging up and down the stands looking for familiar faces; his prey wasn't art but its ultra-high-net-worth admirers. When he wasn't greeting those he either knew or wanted to know, he took pleasure in denigrating artworks.

'Like, who buys this shit?'

'It turns over hundreds of millions a year,' Ayesha replied. 'It's a showcase for great talent.' For Sleet, moving at great speed, the tent became a visual blur, a ratatouille of colours and shapes. Each time they reached one of Ayesha's chosen dealers, he picked up pace. Her plan was failing and she felt increasingly desperate.

'This is Parastephanos's favourite dealer,' she said, pointing to the well-respected gallerist Stevie Mett's stand.

Sleet finally stopped and started to look around. 'Jeeesus H Christ,' he said, pointing at a large abstract oil. 'Looks like someone mixed shit and vomit and threw it at the wall.' His voice was so loud that people turned to stare at him.

Stevie Mett, sensing trouble, stepped forward, hoping to avoid a scene. 'It's by Douglas Ongogo, a young upcoming artist. He's been chosen to represent his country at the next Venice Biennale.'

'Those guys must be short on options. Tell him to stick to his day job.' Sleet was about to leave when he spotted Aristotle Parastephanos, founder and CEO of the private equity company GreenRock, coming towards them. The Greek was one of the people Sleet admired. Under his aegis, in only fifteen years, GreenRock's AUM had grown from $2 billion to $245 billion. As usual he was flanked by the posse of well-dressed and attractive women who ran different departments in the company. Sleet made a note to copy the configuration; it was kind of cool, like Gaddafi and his all-female Amazonian guards. Unfortunately, Donna and Rodita, his closest aides, wouldn't look the part. Zamora could help choose them. He imagined *Taste and Refinement*'s comment: 'The must-have accessories for all top businessmen – a phalanx of cool ladies.'

Sleet had wanted to meet Parastephanos for several years, but the captain of industry was elusive, transactional, detested short sellers and rarely went out. Married for thirty years, his wife Melitizia Katzantoulis came from the same Greek island; they had seven children and thirty grandchildren and lived in a modest house in North London or on their island. And yet here he was – in flesh and blood – standing right before him.

'Aristotle, hi – Sir Thomlinson Sleet, Kerkyra Capital.' Sleet held out his hand, hoping that it wasn't too sweaty.

Parastephanos shook it, smiled thinly and turned back to look at a work on art on the wall.

'What do you think of the Douglas Ongogo?' he asked one of his entourage, pointing to a vivid, brightly coloured mass of swirls with the slogan 'Fuck the Rich' emblazoned across it.

'It's a load of absolute—' Sleet started.

Ayesha, guessing correctly that Parastephanos was interested in buying the work, interrupted before her husband could go any further. 'The progression of Ongogo's work is fascinating. To think he was in a small township only three years ago and has made this transition both physically and artistically. I love the tension this piece shows between where he's come from and the situation he finds himself in now.' She hoped her paean of praise would encourage Sleet to get his chequebook out.

Sleet wanted to curl up with embarrassment. How could his own partner spout such cock and bull crap? He decided to pretend to Parastephanos that he'd never met this woman before in his life. His heart sank further when the billionaire asked Ayesha, 'What did you say your name is?'

Before she had a moment to respond, Sleet cut in. 'She's called Ms Scott.'

Parastephanos smiled at Ayesha. 'Nice to meet you.' Then he turned back to the painting.

Sleet decided to save him from buying the piece and jumped in front of the work, his arms outstretched. 'Guys like us know things,' he said. 'We don't need labels. We don't need so-called experts telling us what's cool or hip. We see this kind of work for what it is: a total mess. Some guy in a shed takes a few brushes and slaps it on a canvas.'

Ayesha, mortified, was grateful Sleet had introduced her by her maiden name. A few other people joined the group to see what the ruddy-faced gesticulating man was on about.

Stevie Mett, a consummate diplomat, wondered how to try and stop this rant. Controversy was acceptable but flagrant racism on his property could be damaging. He wondered if it was his duty to protect the integrity of the artist or just sell his work, and lamented that the role of the dealer was becoming ever more complicated.

Sleet went up to Parastephanos and clapped him on the shoulder.

'We know better, don't we, Aristotle?' He turned to face the large group of people gathered around the stand.

Parastephanos ignored him and spoke to Ayesha. 'I liked the way you described this. I'd never thought of his journey in that way – it humanises and contextualises what he's trying to do. If you were me, would you buy this?'

'Of course she wouldn't,' Sleet blurted out.

'I think it's wonderful,' Ayesha said.

Looking at her, Parastephanos moved away from Sleet and towards Mett. 'Can you reserve this piece for me?'

Sleet's mouth fell open. He could hardly believe what he was seeing. Parastephanos, one of the great investors, was honestly thinking of buying it?

'Are you his art adviser?' Parastephanos asked Ayesha, nodding in Sleet's direction.

'No,' Ayesha said firmly.

Parastephanos gestured to one of his assistants. 'Give the lady my details.' He smiled at Ayesha. 'It would be great to continue our conversation.'

Ayesha's spirits, dashed by losing out on a commission, rose slightly as she wondered if she could earn a living as a consultant.

Sleet watched in stunned silence as the silvery-haired figure, flanked by six women, headed away from the stand. Stevie Mett gave Sleet a short condescending smile.

'I'll buy that one,' Sleet told the dealer, pointing to another work by the same artist.

'There is a long waiting list. You are not on it,' Mett said, before turning to talk to another client.

After that, Sleet, apart from the odd expostulation, kept quiet. He was surprised how respectfully dealers and fellow collectors treated Ayesha. Sure, they were trying to sell her things, but he could see that they valued her opinion. What's more, from the way she bandied terms and names, she knew the subject. Sleet wondered how he could monetise her knowledge. Art, he saw as he looked around him, was an asset class as well as a calling card.

He soon tired of the long white cubicles and the art-world chat.

'Let's go,' he told Ayesha. Remembering the Buckingham Palace debacle, she followed him out past long queues of exotically dressed people waiting to get in: a couple in matching neon-orange frock coats and top hats; a butch man dressed as a woman in a multi-hooped ball-gown who was posing for photographs. There were women dressed in men's suits and men who might be women wearing suits.

'Who are all these people?' Sleet asked.

'Art tribe,' Ayesha said.

'Why do they dress so weirdly?'

'Every world has its own uniforms and language. Take yours: suits at meetings, chinos at weekends and an awful lot of hypo-babble in the meantime.'

'In my world, we dress blandly so as not to detract from the facts. In yours, people dress outlandishly to distract from the hot air bellowing from their mouths.'

'At least there's something fun to look at!' she said, pointing to a man and woman resplendent in matching luminous-coloured feathered coats and another person of indeterminate sex displaying more facial piercing than skin.

Sleet laughed. 'You can say that again.'

Ayesha pretended to laugh with him. It's a game, she told herself, play along. She and Sleet had put two pictures on hold. Her commission would amount to £125k. Not bad for a morning's work.

Sanjay was waiting outside the front entrance. He opened the door for Sleet. The boss paid the bills and he liked going first. Ayesha knew the drill and waited for the chauffeur to open her door. Settling into the soft white leather seat, Sleet turned to Ayesha. 'So what would it cost to get an art collection? A proper fuck-off one.'

'It's not only about money, it's the time,' Ayesha started to explain. 'A collection isn't an assembly of objects; the best ones are thoughtful juxtapositions of ideas, the interplay between different schools or periods of an artist's work.'

'Don't get pretentious. Let's put it simply. I'll put the money down, you get the goods. But I want to make a blow-their-minds kind of statement. I want the big boys to bow down in reverence.'

'It doesn't work like that. It's not like going to the Paris couture and getting the top dress or taking part in an IPO. Great works have been fought over for decades. Dealers have waiting lists – scores of people wanting the latest Peter Doig or Anselm Kiefer.'

'So get me some of the dead guys.'

'They're even rarer. Their supply is limited.'

Sleet banged his hand on the back of the car seat. 'I don't like the word "no".'

'None of us do,' Ayesha said.

'How much do these things cost?' he asked.

Ayesha thought of the works she longed to buy. For a few million she could build a stunning collection. For a few hundred million he could open his own museum.

'A Giacometti recently sold for eighty million pounds.'

Sleet let out a low whistle. 'Who is this guy Jack O'Metty? Can I meet him?'

'He died decades ago.'

'That was a bad career move – he should have hung on.'

Ayesha didn't laugh – partly as she was unsure if he was making a joke. The two sat in silence as the car made its way through the busy streets of London.

'Does all art go up in value?' Sleet asked.

'Some of the pieces I bought, like the Bacon, have risen by 500 per cent.'

Sleet turned to face her. 'No shit?' Even for him, that was an excellent return. He picked up his tablet and looked at the stock market. 'Few of my shares have made that kind of money. If I'd known how profitable art was, I'd have paid it more attention.'

'Never too late.' Ayesha looked at Sleet's tablet and her heart froze. His screensaver was a photograph of Zamora Lala in a skin-tight white column dress. She was laughing, her head slightly back showing a row of perfect teeth. In one hand she held a champagne flute; in the other a bottle of 1947 Cristal, Sleet's favourite vintage. The detail that shocked Ayesha most was the location: Zamora was on the terrace of their home in the Boltons. Ayesha's body contracted in horror.

Sleet saw her watching the screen. He made no attempt to hide it. He put a hand on her leg and squeezed. It hurt and Ayesha wriggled.

'Do something useful, sweetheart. Go and find me a collection to buy. At the right price, everything's for sale. I want instant. None of this five-year waiting game. I want to be one of the big boys.'

He released his fingers and Ayesha looked down at the red marks on her thigh.

'Can you pull over,' Ayesha asked Sanjay. 'I want to get some air.'

'Get as much as you need. It's free.' Sleet laughed at his own joke. He watched his wife walk away from the car; Ayesha, knowing that he was watching, swung her hips and held her back straight. Sleet and Sanjay saw her go up Portland Place and turn into a side street.

'Beautiful woman, sir,' Sanjay said.

Sleet shrugged. He wasn't looking at Ayesha, he was thinking whether to short copper. The stock had risen dramatically in the last few weeks. His reverie was broken by a call on his private phone. The name 'Zamora' flashed up. The line was so bad that he could hardly hear what she was saying.

'What? Speak up!'

'Meet?' Zamora said – she never bothered with hello or goodbye.

Sleet found the combination of the crackle and her heavy Albanian accent hard to decipher. 'Did you say meat?'

'Meet.'

'What kind of meat?' He was truly confused.

'Cannes meet.'

'Canned meat. Is that healthy?' Sleet wondered if Spam was fashionable in Tirana.

'I going to Cannes,' Zamora said very slowly. 'Now on boat in Sardinia.'

On the other end of the telephone, Sleet blushed and tried to collect his scattered thoughts. 'I can be there in two hours,' he said. Since their first meeting in June, Zamora had led him a merry dance; they met occasionally but she was often a country and occasionally a continent away from him.

Zamora let out a small sad sigh – not totally convincingly. 'Tonight, I fly to New York.'

'I'll pick you up in the jet. We can go together.'

'Another time.'

Sleet tried to contain his frustration. 'How long are you going to make me wait, Zamora?'

'It is my birthday next week.'

'What would you like?'

Zamora didn't hesitate. 'Something very hard …'

Sleet struggled to breathe.

'Something pink or red or blue.'

Sleet breathed in and out several times. She was teasing him but he liked it. With Zamora he saw something entirely new, a true partnership. The Albanian was beautiful and she was tough, bright and similarly obsessed by money. Like him, she'd had a difficult start in life. Morals were luxuries neither of them rated; conscience was a muscle that neither had developed. Sleet imagined a life where he could be himself – without filters, without judgement.

Zamora flipped her phone to video mode. No wonder the reception was bad: she was lying on the deck of a massive speedboat dressed in a small bikini, her body shining with oil, her hair wet. The waves were large, and the boat flew over the water and, as it landed, parts of Zamora's body shook and trembled. 'Where would you like to be, Mr Sleet?' she asked.

Sleet, overcome by excitement, couldn't speak.

The call disconnected. 'Are you there?' Sleet shouted into the phone. 'Call me back.'

On the other end of the line, Zamora laughed and lay back on the boat deck.

Lying next to her, out of shot, clad in a white bikini, Tahira smiled. 'Careful, he'll have a heart attack and we need to make a lot more money out of him.'

'Don't worry. This fish is on the line.'

'Fish can come off lines,' Tahira warned.

She and Zamora had met at business school fifteen years ago and bonded immediately. Unlike the other students, both had no friends, but what they lacked in contacts was compensated with ambition. Their goal was money and power and neither had any qualms about how they achieved these ends. Tahira had the technical skill to set up a digital currency; Zamora and her husband, Nanos, had money to launder crypto, untraceable and unregulated. Together they founded Queen of Coins.

On day one they employed six salespeople and set up a pyramid scheme. Within six months they'd sold several hundred million pounds' worth of QoC and were employing eight hundred people, known as 'miners', in eighteen locations. The highly incentivised sales force, each paid on commission, doubled in size each week. They had started with an initial investment of £100,000. The week before, more than £1 billion had been exchanged for Queen of Coins. Sleet, in their grand scheme, was a bit-part player but important – as a world-renowned financier, his investment in their cryptocurrency gave them credibility. He was also a useful money launderer. His so-called investments were translated into dollars. Anyone who looked closely at their company's structure would see that every dollar spent on a coin went straight into Tahira and Zamora's pockets. The certificates were worthless. Sooner or later they'd get found out but in the short term they needed to transfer as much of their cryptocurrency as possible into legitimate currency which they secreted in untraceable offshore companies.

'How much more money from Sleet we get?' Zamora asked, squirting suncream on to her belly and holding the bottle out so that Tahira could spread more on her back.

'A few more million? It depends how you play him,' Tahira said, rubbing cream into her friend's beautiful alabaster shoulders.

Sexual tension fizzled. If Zamora wasn't married to Nanos, one of Albania's most jealous and vicious gangsters, she would have succumbed to Tahira's many advances, but she had too much to lose – including her life.

'I won't sleep with him,' Zamora said.

Tahira shuddered at the thought.

'If only we could substitute the wife. She's pretty.'

'Threesome?' Tahira liked that idea.

Zamora turned on to her tummy. 'She likes men. Why don't we have a bit of fun with her?'

'Like what?'

'A little bit of torture?'

'We have more important fish to fry.'

Zamora rolled on to her side and bit her friend hard on the arm.

Tahira shouted in pain. 'What did you do that for?'

'Because you are mine. All mine. And don't forget it.'

*

Ayesha stood by the lake in Regent's Park watching the birds, her body awash with fury. Sleet's attempt to humiliate and belittle her in the art world, in front of people whose respect she'd worked so hard to gain, was unconscionable. Turning away, she walked down the avenue of beech trees whose leaves lay like golden tickets on the ground and kicked her way through the clumps, making a whooshing sound as they scattered in her path. Think, she told herself, think. Turning into Avenue Gardens, she meandered past the resplendent carpet bedding and statuary, the pale stone and wild colours in perfect harmony. In ten months' time the contractors would move into Trelawney and by then, if not before, Sleet would leave her with almost nothing.

At the end of one of the avenues she came across a sculpture by Louise Bourgeois, a giant spider made from bronze and granite, large enough for a substantial family to stand under and shelter from the rain. A tiny spider made its way under the legs of its giant bronze imitator. Ayesha watched it scuttle along the ground. Of course, she realised, it's a question of scale. She had been thinking too small. Little percentages here and there were never going to get her what she wanted. A plan, which seemed ludicrous at first, began to crystallise.

Her first decision was to copy Sleet's next bet and to risk all the money she'd made to date. Sleet was convinced that the outsider Donald Trump would confound sceptics and become the next President of the United States and his hunch was supported by polling data made available by Alabaster Analytics. If the Republican triumphed, the stock market would leap upwards in response to his promised tax cuts and free-market policies. She made the decision to put 90 per cent of all her available money on the bet: £1,120,000.

Feeling empowered, she walked on through the park. Her plan B was far more audacious: it would make her rich, seriously rich: it would make enough to buy Trelawney and ensure her and Stella's freedom.

12

November 2016

'Cancelled? What do you mean, cancelled?' Clarissa fixed Damian Dobbs with her most penetrating stare.

Damian, though he'd worked with the Dowager Countess for more than seven years, producing her series *The Last of the Trelawneys*, still found the old lady terrifying. Clarissa was a paper-thin, five-foot-two-inches-tall block of solid imperiousness honed by years of being the chatelaine of her husband's castle.

'The ratings have been falling steadily.'

'I am mobbed in the local town. I can hardly get down the high street without signing twenty autographs.'

'Channel Four saw the numbers have fallen from a peak of three million to less than twenty-five thousand a week.'

'The subject is not lacking.'

'You continue to be magnificent,' Damian agreed with unctuousness and tact.

'Then the fault is yours!' Clarissa was triumphant. 'Find me a more with-it co-producer.'

'We have tried to introduce a few people into our mix.' Damian thought back to the unsuccessful attempts to integrate others into the production team. 'You didn't like Lee-Ann Fong, Henry Conrad, Bee Smith …' There were others he could mention but decided not to.

Clarissa held up her hand. 'They were born below the salt. How could they understand the subtleties of class and breeding? There must be some talented aristocrat looking for a job. I hear most are desperate.'

'We tried William Cator-Bones.'

'His family were on the wrong side in the war.'

'In Iraq?'

'Don't be silly. The Civil War. He was Roundhead.'

'That was a few centuries ago.'

'It's the kind of thing people like us don't forget.'

They sat facing each other on two chintz-covered sofas in Clarissa's cottage. Rented by Blaze for her mother, it had a thatched roof and a small garden with a picket fence. On one side there was a river and on the other a beech wood. Through the window Damian watched undulating branches of the beech which were ablaze with oranges and yellows. A weak November sun pierced etiolated lime leaves, making them seem like parchment. Falling sweet chestnut leaves fluttered to the ground. Two jays screeched at each other from nearby branches, then one flew off, a flash of iridescent blue. A few days earlier, sitting in the same spot, he'd seen a kingfisher dart into a hole on the river-bank. Why, he thought for the five hundredth time, am I shackled to this elderly tyrant when I could be making wonderful programmes about nature and the planet?

'Are you listening?' Clarissa asked, tapping her finger on the side table. She hated her bijoux cottage and the vulgarity of genteel poverty. There were only three rooms downstairs – a sitting room, small dining room and kitchen – and the two bedrooms upstairs had been hastily redone by Barty and Tony to resemble 'Trelawney' style on a much smaller scale. The two men had hung prints of hunting scenes and placed some pieces of dark furniture to break the monotony of modern. The only thing Clarissa liked, although she'd never admit it, was underfloor heating and gallons of hot water. Blaze had found a housekeeper, Mrs Bowley, who used to work for a duke and was slow on her feet but deferential. Clarissa straightened her shoulders. She was a fighter. Upwards and onwards, as Daddy used to say.

Damian summoned up all his courage. 'I have pitched another idea that the channel likes.'

Clarissa turned away to hide her smile. The idiots weren't going to ditch their greatest star.

'It's a comment show. You would be asked to opine on things.'

'What kind of things?'

'Anything from a general election, to what people wore at an event, or a programme on television.'

'Isn't that what I do now?' Clarissa was never slow to offer thoughts on any given subject.

'They want to introduce other voices.'

'Dilution.'

'Augmentation.'

'One will not share the spotlight.' Clarissa crossed her arms defiantly.

Damian shifted on the sofa before delivering the final blow. 'The company has already chosen two co-presenters and they are auditioning others at the moment. They've asked if you'd like to be considered.'

Clarissa took a deep breath. 'And who have they cast?'

'A woman called Winnie Nkosi.'

'Let me guess where she's from.' Clarissa affected a bored tone of voice and stared pointedly out of the window.

'She's a distinguished anthropologist.'

'What's she apologising for?'

'Anthropologist not apologist.'

'You should speak more clearly. I told you to lose that frightful Plymouth twang. You'll get further in life.'

'Winnie Nkosi wrote the seminal book on tribal life. It starts in Borneo and ends up in the Upper East Side. She believes there are similarities to be found in human behaviour all over the world.'

'And who might the other person be?'

'They are called ZHt6.'

'I told you to speak up. Anyone would think you just called someone by a random series of letters and the number 6,' Clarissa laughed.

'I did, actually. They were born a she or a he but became a they and then to avoid any further stereotyping they adopted a moniker.'

Clarissa looked at her hands. 'And what sub-sect, what peccadillo, what extreme form of political representation do they expect me to fulfil? Am I the biting gerontophile? Part of a dying breed of aristocrat? Do they hope I'll die mid-season and boost their ratings?'

Damian didn't answer. She was completely correct.

'You may go now, Dobbs.'

Damian hesitated. 'I'm sorry if—'

Clarissa pointed to the door. 'Go.'

After he'd left, Clarissa took a small gold compact from her bag and patted some foundation on the end of her nose. Then she ran a lipstick over her mouth, checking in a mirror that none had stained her teeth. Finally, she plumped up her hair and straightened her silk shirt, hoping that the 'freshen up' would restore her spirits. But the deep feeling of gloom was unshakeable. She'd been cancelled, found wanting. Her true love was dead. Without her show there was nothing to look forward to apart from death itself. She wondered if it was possible to will oneself to die? But in the next breath she remembered her place on earth – to teach others how to face life with standards and with courage. Clarissa gathered, squaring her shoulders and arranging her mouth in a shallow smile, then rang a little bell on the table before her.

Mrs Bowley poked her head around the kitchen door.

'Your Ladyship?'

'I'll take tea, Bowley.'

'Very good, madam.'

*

'It is the most ridiculous idea I have ever heard,' Tony said, sucking his cheeks in and puffing up his scrawny old chest.

'*Au contraire, mon oncle*. It will work.' Ayesha smiled at him condescendingly. They were sitting in their favourite meeting place, tucked in behind London's National Gallery. The interior, all brass and red velvet, was supposed to look like a *fin-de-siècle* Parisian café, but all the details, from the Formica tabletops to the fluorescent lighting and the fake wooden floor, were wrong. A frieze of poorly painted cancan dancers covered one wall and on the other, for no apparent reason, was a poster of the Eiffel Tower in the snow. Spray-painted gold lettering on the window announced that this was Chou Chou, La Maison de Thé.

Tony took a large spoon of whipped cream topped with hundreds and thousands sprinkles and put it in his mouth.

'I thought you made a tonne from a bet on that ghastly Donald Trump.'

'I doubled my nest egg: I now have two million pounds.' Looking at Tony's disapproving expression, Ayesha added, 'Morality is for those who can afford it. I am in the desperation game.'

'You're sounding like that ghastly Sleet,' Tony said, slurping some chocolate. 'It appears that you're good at making money. I hope you don't give up on studying art – you have a talent.'

Ayesha leaned across the table. 'This is about principles, about not letting Sleet get away with it.'

Tony felt a deep weariness. 'Take me through your new plan again.'

'We are going to sell Sleet some key pieces from the Iranian collection of modern art.'

'But it's locked in a vault in the Ayatollah Khomeini's palace in Tehran!' Tony said. 'How on earth are you going to persuade the Iranians to sell it and get it over here for Sleet to buy?'

'We're not going to sell him the actual art.' Ayesha folded her napkin. 'I am going to commission perfect copies of three paintings which you and I are going to show him.'

'Little old me?' Tony's heart sank. He wanted nothing to do with this scheme.

'Sleet will buy the fakes thinking they are the real thing. The paintings will never leave their vaults.'

'He might not know a Van Gogh if it bit him, but Sleet isn't stupid.'

'It's well documented that the regime keeps some of the risqué works in a free port in Geneva. The Ayatollahs don't want their people to have exposure to naked women. Sleet will check and read about this. He'll think he's seeing and buying the originals.' Ayesha pushed aside her own confection, a triple-chocolate milkshake topped with cream, and pulled a sheaf of press cuttings and black and white reproductions of paintings from her bag. She laid them out in front of Tony like a deck of cards. 'This is the collection built by the last Empress, Farah Diba Pahlavi, in the seventies.'

Tony clapped his hands together. 'I loved Farah. I went to her wedding in 1959 – she wore a dress made by darling Yves and a tiara and necklace of diamonds that made our own royal family's collection look like Smarties. Reza, her husband, was fond of a few sparkly things too. He wore epaulettes and medals like decorations on a Christmas tree. We used to call Tehran the Beverly Hills of the Middle East. It was such a blast.' He paused. 'Then their luck ran out.'

Ayesha needed to keep Tony on track and out of Memory Lane.

Tony spotted a picture of the Empress with the artist Andy Warhol. 'She was as stylish as Jackie Kennedy,' he said, his eyes going misty. 'It's too sad that the world doesn't make women like that anymore.'

'If you knew her so well,' Ayesha said, 'didn't you know she was buying art?'

'I wasn't in my "art" phase then.' Tony looked out of the café window. 'I was a film producer living in Los Angeles.'

'What did you make?' Ayesha hadn't heard about this phase of Tony's illustrious but rather unsuccessful career.

'Like most of Hollywood, I was in a perpetual state of development. Everyone has a project, some have a slate, but only a couple do anything. I only had eyes for Errol.'

'Errol?'

'Errol Flynn!' Tony let out a deep sigh. 'The young are so ignorant. He was the greatest movie star of all time.'

Ayesha wanted to get back to her plan. 'Farah Diba bought masterpieces by Giacometti, Bacon, Martine, Renoir, Pollock, Rothko, to name a few.'

'I don't believe it.' Tony crossed his arms.

'It's all here.' Ayesha flicked through some press cuttings. The first showed a woman in a hijab standing in front of a beautiful Rothko abstract, the colours of a bleeding sunset. On the next piece of paper there were two veiled women next to a Lichtenstein. Tony looked at the black and white reproductions, staring in wonder at a Gaugin and then a Jackson Pollock.

'Where did you get all these?' he asked.

'My friend Yasmin's dad was their chief curator.'

'Is she part of this escapade?'

'I promised her a commission.' Ayesha smiled, remembering Yasmin's delight.

Tony picked up pictures – one by Renoir of a young woman with bare breasts and another by Picasso of a woman in a contorted pose. The third, by Manet, was of a naked woman in a glade overlooked by a man and his dog.

'No wonder the Ayatollahs hide these away. Far too degenerate for them.'

'Exactly! Don't you see? You'll tell Sleet that the pictures are an embarrassment, and the Ayatollah wants a quiet deal.'

'*Moi?* Tell a lie?' Tony looked at her in horror. 'Sleet will never believe me.'

'Darling uncle, I need your help.' She dropped her voice to a whisper. 'He's sold Trelawney to a company that will turn it into a theme park. They will destroy all your and Barty's hard work, everything we've done to restore the place to its former glory.'

'How dare they!' Tony huffed.

'It's not long before the bulldozers arrive.'

Tony's bravura soon evaporated. 'I am an 85-year-old art dealer with gout and rheumatoid Arthur something or other. You need a younger partner in crime.'

'I don't trust anyone else.' She didn't add that she didn't have anyone else to turn to ... they both knew it.

'What if Sleet calls the Iranians himself? Why does he need us?'

'There's an embargo, and sanctions against Americans and Iranians doing business. He would be banned from any activity in the States indefinitely if they found out.'

'Why do the Iranians want to sell now?' Tony was desperate to think of any reason not to go ahead.

'It's the best moment: the price of oil has collapsed, and sanctions are biting. The regime is desperately short of money. It makes sense they'd need to sell their pictures.'

'Sleet's not that stupid. He only has to ask around.'

'He wants instant gratification. There is nothing so corrupting, so instinct blunting, than greed: it makes morons of men and women.'

'Why doesn't he wait – things come up from time to time.'

'You know that. I know that. Sleet won't accept it. That's why you are going to tell him that the best collection in the world has come up and he can get it for a fraction of its real value. The fact that he'll get a market discount will be an incentive.'

'Why will he believe me?'

'You are the only person he knows apart from me who knows about art.'

'He'll never take my word for it.' Tony laughed, nerves making his voice sound high-pitched and squeaky. 'This is ridiculous. It can't be done, and I won't do it.'

Ayesha leaned back in her chair. 'Uncle Tony. I got you out of the hospital when you jumped off the cliff. I set you up with a job and a place to live. I even employed Barty to keep you company. I have dignified your old age.'

'You did and I have thanked you.'

'So this is payback time.'

'This is illegal, immoral and downright bloody dangerous.'

'You will earn one million pounds.'

'What can I do with that kind of money at my age? Gold-plate my coffin?' Tony's guts twisted; he felt quite sick.

Ayesha leaned over the table and put her hand on his. Using her mother's trick, she let one pearl-shaped tear roll down her cheek. Her beautiful almond-shaped eyes widened. 'I have no one else to ask. Think of this as a favour for little Stella.'

Tony was determined not to succumb to her charm or manipulation.

'It's a terrible thing to ask. Forgive me.' She dabbed at the corner of her eyes with a handkerchief. A second pearl-shaped tear ran down her cheek. 'My longing to create a wonderful and secure life for my daughter overrides all sense. After Stella, you are the most important person in the world to me. My one true friend. Thank goodness Stella and I can come and live with you in Earls Court when Sleet throws us out.'

Tony squirmed. The thought of living with two women was more than he could bear. He must think quickly but dredging up thoughts from his old, addled mind was proving hard. 'How will this crazy scheme work?'

'There's a man in Poland, a brilliant forger, who makes such perfect copies that even experts are duped. I will commission counterfeits of three paintings and bring them to a Swiss free port. You, I and Sleet will go and look at them. Sleet will buy them, transfer a hundred and eighty million into an untraceable offshore account and take possession of the works.'

'Which are fakes.' Tony looked at his niece. He was no longer frightened for himself; he was terrified for her. 'Darling girl. I am an old man at the end of my life. You are very young. You have every opportunity to press restart, have another life, ten other lives if you want them. This is an insanely dangerous idea. You'll be caught like a nut in a cracker between two fanatics: your husband stops at nothing; the Iranians don't care about Westerners.'

'The Iranians have nothing to lose or gain. They're not selling.'

'They are proud people who wouldn't want the world to know they own such degenerate art or that they've been used in this kind of sting. There'll be consequences. For you, even for Stella. It's fraud. It's theft. It's probably a lot of other offences.'

Ayesha flashed a disingenuous smile. 'I have been robbed many times in my short life. Before I was even born they took away my father. As a child growing up in India, I was denied equal opportunities because of my illegitimacy. Coming to England, I was ostracised by my own family for the second time. I married, only to discover that my husband has falsified everything that was supposed to guarantee my independence. I don't care about jail. I don't care if I am vilified. I don't even care if this fucks my future. More than revenge, I want to show that no one can treat me like this. I am not a chattel, a nobody, a hopeless little illegitimate bastard.' She got to her feet. 'You know where to find me, darling Tony. If you can't help me, someone will.'

Ayesha stood up slowly, pushed her chair away from the table, left a twenty pound note to cover their bill and left the café.

For a long time after she'd left, Tony sat thinking about their conversation. From the moment he'd seen Ayesha's mother, Anastasia, at a dinner at Trelawney Castle nearly thirty years earlier, he'd had a premonition of trouble. She had been sixteen and already radiating sexual power. Even Tony, who'd never looked at a woman with lust, could feel her presence and was aware that every male eye and most of the women were mesmerised by the slender blonde girl, with the palest of blue eyes, wearing a red silk dress framed by the doorway. The young Anastasia was fully in control of her attributes; she knew the impression she made. Tony had watched his brother and his nephew's faces and felt afraid for the House of Trelawney. Two men falling for the same woman was one thing, but a father and son meant certain trouble. He wasn't the only person to spot the danger. Clarissa and Blaze exchanged worried glances. Jane, who had been hopelessly in love with Kitto, the son and heir of Trelawney, shrank against the wall – certain that her prize was forever lost. When Anastasia went to India, Tony felt relieved. Clarissa had won her husband back and saved her family. Anastasia's exile was supposed to be the end of it. Her revenge was unexpected and came years later: a living, breathing daughter.

Tony was fond of Ayesha – she was determined, clever, damaged and beautiful. She'd been kind to him and had, as she said, dignified his old age. Her kindness came at a price, and she was calling in her debt. She couldn't force him to take part in her Iranian plot but Tony didn't feel he had much choice. At least, he thought, using the table to drag himself up to his shaky old feet, I won't mind being bumped off – it'd been a long life, a rather exhausting one, sometimes fun, occasionally downright miserable and lonely. Tony's only regret was that his life didn't merit an obituary in *The Times*. He would have loved one of those.

*

Ayesha walked from the café to the London Library in St James's Square. The private establishment, created in 1841, was a warren of bookshelves built over five floors. At its heart, there was a magnificent reading room. Spotting a vacant desk in one corner, she picked her way past elderly gentlemen sleeping off lunch in leather armchairs and set up her computer. She'd pre-ordered several books relevant to her forthcoming Gettina lecture: 'Isabella d'Este and the Power of Art'. She was only the third woman chosen to give it and the youngest by some margin. She was pleased to be building her career but her main motivation was ensuring that Isabella might, four centuries on, claim her rightful place amongst history's great patrons. She flicked through several tomes on Renaissance power play but found it difficult to concentrate. After an hour she gave in and opening her laptop, punched the name 'Zamora Lala' into the search engine.

The previous week there had been email traffic between Zamora and Sleet concerning a multimillion-dollar investment in a crypto-mining plant in Tirana. Ayesha put the name of the company in to see who else was involved – one man, Nanos Copje, had come up before. She typed his name into the web and sat back while the computer loaded reference after reference: 77,000 in a matter of minutes. Clicking on the first entry, she read that Copje was the leader of the Bregu clan, one of the fifteen Albanian families involved in organised crime. Active in Europe, the Middle East, South America and Asia, he topped Interpol's list of most wanted criminals and had evaded capture for two decades. For the next two hours, Ayesha read everything she could find on Copje – he was linked to drugs, arms, pimping, prostitution, murder, bribery, money laundering, human and human-organ trafficking. The gang's estimated annual turnover was $2 billion. It seemed the vital ingredient in Copje's success was his reliance on strict family codes: only near relations were allowed to work in the upper echelons of the business. The Copje family married relations to keep secrets close.

Switching to Google Earth, she input the address of Copje's hometown. The name of the place was familiar. Then, staring at the barren land dotted with high-rise blocks of flats, she remembered. Nanos Copje and Zamora Lala had grown up in the same neighbourhood. They must know each other: the question was how well and if her husband had any idea. At first, she wondered why they needed Sleet. Then it dawned on her – their cryptocurrency was simply another form of money laundering. She felt a flash of anger: her daughter's inheritance was being washed away in a swill of illegal activities and drug money. What she couldn't understand was why Sleet hadn't cottoned on.

Her telephone beeped; her train was due to depart in twenty minutes. Leaving the books on the desk, she grabbed her bag and ran out into St James's Square. A taxi was passing and by some fluke the traffic was light. Ayesha ran down the ramp into Paddington Station. The barrier was open and she sprinted along the platform as the whistle was blowing. She found her seat in first class and, settling back into the comfortable chair, closed her eyes. The carriage was nearly empty and, lulled by the steady rock of the train, she fell asleep. At Taunton, three hours later, she woke up and went to the buffet car to get a cup of boiling water. Reaching into her bag, she looked for her sachets of green tea. To her surprise, she found a piece of A4 paper. She unfolded it and there, in neat handwriting, were some words in an unknown language which she carefully copied into her search engine and pressed Translate: 'An Albanian will kill to protect his honour.' Horrified, Ayesha looked around her and then tore the paper into tiny shreds. Peering up and down the carriage, she saw the only other occupants were a mother and her small child and a sleeping middle-aged man. Taking her bag, she walked along the next three compartments looking for anyone likely to have played this horrible joke. She retraced her journey through the library's stacks, trying to remember if anyone had followed her. Was it possible that all the time she'd been spying on Sleet, someone had been spying on her? Then another, more frightening thought occurred. What if the note was left by Zamora or Copje?

She tried to concentrate on the landscape outside the train. The sky was darkening and she could just make out the landscape. Tiny villages sat in folds of hills, steeples peeping over copses, smallholdings hugging hedgerows, and then the sea – a great grey, endless stretch of water. The train hugged the coastline, dipping in and out of tunnels and rocks. At Plymouth it was too dark to see anything outside. Each mile closer to home made Ayesha feel safer.

Arriving at Trelawney Station, she walked quickly through the village back streets. Declan danced around inside her head, nagging, taunting, prodding. She tried to drive him away with thoughts of Isabella d'Este. The great patron had coped with a philandering husband: many of the children in the village of Mantua looked like him. If this hadn't been humiliating enough, she'd then had to cope with Francesco and her sister-in-law Lucrezia's very public affair and pregnancy. Following the death of her husband, Isabella continued to rule Mantua as regent for her young son. She even coped with little Federico's kidnap by the French for three years. Ayesha shivered. The thought of being even three days without Stella was too much to bear. At least, she consoled herself, Stella and I will never be separated and, comforted by that certainty, she ran the last half mile to the castle.

13

January 2017

That Christmas, Sleet left his wife and daughter at Trelawney and disappeared to the Caribbean on to his boat. Ayesha was relieved not to have to pretend to play Happy Families. She asked her whole family to join her: Tony and Barty accepted. The three adults played card games and took it in turns to read to and play with Stella.

At the start of the New Year, Ayesha took an early-morning flight to Gdańsk and a taxi to an industrial estate on the outskirts of the city. It was her third visit to the master copier and, like the earlier two, took place before the commuters hit the morning trail. She wore a blonde wig, dark glasses, a shapeless woollen suit, a big puffy coat and pulled a large nearly empty suitcase. On each occasion she'd travelled by a different airline, buying tickets using a temporary credit card and her mother's old (Indian) passport; the two women looked similar and she'd never got around to registering Anastasia's death. There was little to link her to Secatchin's workshop. The cost of making perfect reproductions of the Iranian works was extortionate – enough to buy a Rolls-Royce – but grandiosity was infectious and years of living with Sleet encouraged a high roll of the dice.

It was bitterly cold in Gdańsk; a continental wind had picked up speed from the coast and whistled down the empty streets. Arriving at 8 a.m., Ayesha rang a bell on an unmarked door where she was met by Lech Secatchin. A failed artist in his own right, Lech, instead of becoming embittered and disillusioned, started a legitimate business realising the seemingly impossible fantasies of artists: he was a brilliant translator and creator of complicated projects. He was also the world's greatest forger.

Walking through the cavernous workshops, Ayesha saw a giant convex mirror made from thousands of tiny scales, designed by a famous artist but manufactured by Lech. In another corner a tapestry depicting a modern family scene in the style of an iconic eighteenth-century Old Master. Both pieces would sell as original works of two famous artists; they might have had the idea but the execution was Lech's.

Looking around, Ayesha spotted complicated reflectography machines as well as more traditional easels and paints. In one corner, pieces of canvas of different hues and thickness hung like sheets. In another there were stacks of frames. Ayesha longed to spend hours there exploring the different methods and skills, but that morning she was focused. She had to be sure that the reproductions were perfect. In three hours' time she'd be taking a train to Geneva and, by the evening after next, everything must be ready.

Lech led the way up a short flight of stairs to a back room. The door was triple-locked and there were four padlocks in place. Taking a large bunch of keys from his belt, Lech let them in. Once inside, he turned the lock. The blinds were drawn, and the only light came from a small lamp on a side table. Flicking a switch on the wall, Lech flooded the room with harsh neon. On three easels in the centre were the pictures Ayesha had commissioned: a Renoir, a Manet and a Picasso. Taking a torch out of her pocket, Ayesha ran it over the surface of the Picasso. It was a small nude of Marie-Thérèse, one of the master's mistresses and mother of his daughter Maya. Marie-Thérèse, creamy-skinned and voluptuous, was running down a beach. Her stripy costume had slipped down, revealing two pendulous breasts; her hair flew behind her. It was a joyous, provocative scene. Ayesha saw the woman as her lover had painted her, capturing the spirit of youthful abandon. Her story, like so many of Picasso's mistresses, would end badly. Marie-Thérèse committed suicide, unable to cope with the rejection by the father of her child, the love of her life. If only, Ayesha thought, she'd been able to hang on to the *joie de vivre* captured in this painting.

As she ran her torch over the surface of the canvas, Ayesha saw how perfectly Lech had copied the original, even though he only had the black and white reproduction to work from.

'How did you match the colours?'

'I found a second-rate painting from exactly the same period, made in France, almost certainly from the same paint supplier that Picasso used. I scraped off the old varnish and used the canvas as my base. The only thing I saved was an embalmed fly which I have added to the top-right corner. In an old catalogue from Maison du Peinture, where Picasso bought his oils, I recreated exactly the combinations he used. Every pigment is a perfect match. The glaze is his recipe.'

Ayesha was relieved by the amount of detail. Forgeries were, with the aid of science, increasingly easy to spot. Minute samples of paint were cross-referenced with original works. Canvases, like trees, could be age-tested. Infrared X-rays could pick out underdrawings, and these could be checked against original drawings. Lech handed Ayesha a magnifying glass and, putting her face close to the surface, she saw tiny bumps of paint and even the artist's smeared fingerprint in the sand.

The forger cleared his throat. 'Once the paint was dry, I put the canvas in my ageing machine.'

'Your what?' she asked.

Lech led her to the back of the room and proudly showed her a small 1950s cooker. 'It belonged to my grandmother. One hour in here at a very low temperature gives the same effect as fifty years hanging on a wall. It's important that these works don't look too pristine.' He opened the door into the next room where forty hairdryers, each on their own stands, were trained on a small Renaissance-style painting. 'This one was supposed to have been smuggled by Napoleon over the Alps on a donkey. I spent hours trying to recreate the effects of wind, rain and snow on a canvas.'

They went back to the Picasso. Lech turned the picture over. 'The back of the canvas is as important as the front,' he explained, show-ing Ayesha various stamps and pieces of paper stuck to the rear. The biggest bore the name of Kahnweiler, Picasso's dealer for many years. Then there were two others, one from an auction house in the 1950s and another from a major museum where the painting had been shown in the 1960s. The most impressive was postcard-size and bore the crest and waxed seal of His Imperial Majesty, the Shah of Iran of the House of Pahlavi, the Shahanshah and the Aryamehr composed of the Lion and the Sun symbol in the first quarter, the Faravahar in the second quarter, the two-pointed sword of Ali (Zulfiqar) in the third quarter and the Simurgh in the fourth quarter. Overall, in the centre, was a circle depicting Mount Damavand with a rising sun, the symbol of the Pahlavi dynasty. The shield was topped by the Pahlavi crown and surrounded by the chain of the Order of Pahlavi.

'What does this mean?' Ayesha asked.

'Shahanshah is "King of Kings", Aryamehr "Light of Aryans" and the last bit is "He gave me power",' Lech explained. 'Little wonder that the new regime in Iran wanted him out.'

'Are you sure that every painting in their collection had this stamp?'

Lech nodded. 'It's documented in your friend's book.'

Ayesha looked closely at the Renoir and the Manet while Lech explained the exacting techniques to make these exact replicas of their originals.

'Are you sure no one could tell the difference?' she asked.

'Even if the original and these were side by side, most would be fooled.' He hesitated. 'Of course I can't account for any electronic tags or damage done since the pictures entered Tehran.'

Satisfied that the risk was worth taking, Ayesha unzipped her suitcase and took out a large velvet bag. Inside was £150,000 in £50 notes.

'Do you want to count it?' she asked.

Lech smiled. 'It's not in your interest to con me!'

One hour later, another taxi dropped Ayesha at Gdańsk airport. In the Ladies' she changed her outfit, this time putting on a red wig and a tight blue dress. The suitcase was considerably heavier for this part of the journey, and she watched nervously as the steward checked it and it rolled away from her on a long conveyor belt. After a short flight, she landed in Geneva. Checking the contents of the case in the washroom, she saw that the three carefully wrapped paintings were intact. She changed once more, this time into black jeans, a white silk shirt, a thick puffy jacket and a curly blonde wig. At the free port, no one paid her much attention. They took the money, assigned her a safety deposit box, and confirmed the request for a viewing room the following day. At 7 p.m. Ayesha boarded a flight to London. She sat in 24C, a window seat, and didn't talk to her neighbours or take any refreshments. This time she had no luggage and walked off the plane, through customs and on to the Paddington Express. When the train pulled into London, she felt her muscles relax. She'd done it. It was going to work. Every second of the journey had gone exactly to plan. She decided to take a taxi back to the Boltons. There wasn't much of a queue. Sitting in the back seat, she pulled off the wig and ran her hands through her sweaty hair.

*

The following morning, Ayesha and Tony met at Northolt and a Special Services car took them across the tarmac to Sleet's plane. Ayesha had not seen or heard from her husband for a fortnight – he'd been away 'on business'. Hacking his phone, she'd watched his progress around the world in pursuit of Zamora.

'Good morning, Lady Sleet.' The pilot came out to greet her.

'Hello, Johannes. Is my husband here?'

'He'll be here in ten minutes. He's asked that you buckle up and we'll take off as soon as he arrives.'

Quarter of an hour later, Sleet arrived with an independent dealer. 'I don't believe we've ever been introduced.' Dame Rebecca Winkleman held out her hand to Tony. She was a respected doyenne of the art world and could spot a fake at two hundred yards.

Oh my god, Tony thought. We are going to be exposed. I am going to end up in prison.

'I thought all dealers knew each other,' Sleet said.

'There are dealers and there are dealers,' Rebecca said, implying that Tony was a lower breed.

Tony and Ayesha exchanged worried glances.

The flight passed in total silence. Sleet was glued to his tablet, Rebecca read a book about Picasso by John Richardson, while Ayesha and Tony pretended to leaf through magazines. Tony suspected they'd be met by Interpol at Geneva, and he would see out his remaining years in a Swiss jail. Exposure was a matter of time. Just as well he was almost dead. He was sorry for his niece who'd meet an ignominious end. He hoped the conditions in her jail would be acceptable. In some ways he thought the confinement might be rather relaxing. He was awfully tired of running around after the Sleets. He racked his old brain, trying to remember the whiff of scandal surrounding Rebecca's father. Somewhere near Nice, it came back to him. Her father, Memling Winkleman, had pretended to be Jewish, going as far as having a concentration camp number tattooed on his arm. He'd built up one of the great collections of Old Masters and impressionist works and had a particular genius for unearthing hidden masterpieces. But one work of art, by Watteau, linked him to the Nazis and it transpired that far from being a Holocaust survivor, Memling had worked as Göring's personal art thief, using extortion and theft to force Jews to give up their masterpieces. His ill-gotten gains were restituted to the descendants of victims but his business was passed to his daughter, Rebecca, who whitewashed her own reputation with judicious and generous donations to large institutions. Tony caught Rebecca's eye and then touched his nose twice and nodded slowly: she needed to know he remembered everything. Two spots of red appeared on her cheeks. Everyone has a dirty little secret, Tony thought and, feeling a bit more confident, closed his eyes and slept soundly for the last part of the journey.

Ayesha was silently panicking. Sleet had never said he was bringing an expert: in better times, Donna might have told Lady Sleet that an extra person was expected on the flight but it was a reflection on her standing that even the PAs didn't bother with her any more. Rebecca Winkleman had a fearsome reputation and, as the authenticator of the estate of both Renoir and Manet, knew more about these works than anyone else. She was ruthless at demoting pictures from 'by' an artist to 'school of'. Ayesha feared the game was up. Lech was brilliant at making fakes but a real work of art exuded magic beyond the composition or provenance. A copy, however perfect, couldn't recreate the invisible energy made by the process of creation or the connection between an artist and his intended audience. Rebecca, Ayesha knew, would spot this immediately. How crazy to think she could pull off this sting? Her thoughts went to her beloved Stella. If Ayesha went to prison, Sleet would win custody. She hoped the judge would be understanding.

The free port was about thirty minutes by car from the airport. The monumental warehouses were surrounded by a high barbed-wire fence. There were two checkpoints before the car pulled up in front of a doorway. Tony handed over the password (delivered the day before by motorcycle messenger) and they were shown to a small side room.

'What is this place?' Sleet asked.

'I am surprised you don't know about it,' Ayesha said. 'Free ports are neutral territories, free of tax or governmental intrusion, where people keep billions of euros of paintings, sculptures, archaeological finds, together with vintage wines, cigars, gold bars, luxury cars, wads of cash and data banks. There are others in Luxembourg, Singapore, Shanghai, Monaco and Delaware.'

'Could be useful,' Sleet said, wondering if Zamora knew about places like this.

Tony rang the bell on the side of the wall and, moments later, a uniformed guard wearing white gloves entered. He carried a crate that was padlocked, and another guard appeared with a small gadget.

'Put your finger on the sensor and it will generate a special passcode. This lasts for less than five minutes,' Tony instructed.

The guard left and Sleet's thumb generated a long series of digits. Ayesha, the only person with good enough eyes, punched the number into the lock and the crate's padlocks sprang open.

Tony stepped forward and slowly lifted the lid to reveal a beautiful, frameless Renoir nude, set in a protective red velvet cushion. Even he, who'd seen the greatest works by that master, mainly in museums or top private collections, gasped. It was impossible to believe it was a copy; the colours shimmered and danced. Many of Renoir's nudes tended towards the chocolate box – slightly rounded, winsome creatures staring coyly at the viewer – but not this one. The young woman was neither provocative nor coquettish – she owned her naked body, she had nothing to prove, no one to impress or entice. She lay on a sofa, her long limbs outstretched and one arm behind her head as if she'd recently awakened from a delicious sleep. A deep-pink blanket the same tone as her nipples had slipped on to the floor. Her pubic hair was partially hidden behind one hand. The tones of her skin and her hair were echoed in a bunch of spring flowers on the table behind.

'I wouldn't say no,' Sleet said, leering over Tony's shoulder.

Ayesha didn't react, although her stomach contracted with fear as Rebecca took out her torch and leaned in.

'What do you think?' Sleet turned to Rebecca. She went close to the painting and shone the beam over the surface. Then she gently lifted it from its red velvet resting place and turned it over, scrutinising the back of the canvas with almost as much care as the front.

Ayesha watched her closely. She'd heard about but had never met the legendary Dame Rebecca, former chair of the Courtauld Museum and one of the most respected art experts. She wondered how Sleet had happened upon her – it was an unusual but brilliant choice of adviser.

Rebecca opened her mouth to speak but, before the words formulated, Tony cleared his throat.

'Didn't your father have a few wonderful Renoirs?' His voice was honeyed but his gaze gimlet clear. 'And a great Watteau?' He'd fired the warning shot across her bows.

Rebecca sent him a venomous glance.

Ayesha intercepted both looks but didn't understand the context.

Rebecca smoothed her skirt, flushing red as she struggled with her conscience. Tony held his breath: what happened next would seal his and Ayesha's fate.

'It's a great Renoir,' Rebecca said. 'The colours, the handling of the paint, the delicacy of the impasto, the elan of the brushwork.'

Ayesha's sense of relief was so enormous that she thought her legs might give way.

Tony sat down on the one available chair. 'You are a woman of impeccable judgement,' he told Rebecca, who ignored him.

'How much is it worth?' Sleet asked.

Rebecca, used to dealing with boorish clients, didn't miss a beat. 'I'd put a conservative value of seventy million pounds, but at auction, if the right buyers were competing against each other, it would fetch considerably more.'

Sleet let out a low whistle. 'How long did it take the guy to paint something like this?'

'In his early life he couldn't afford paint. Then, just as his career was getting going, the Franco-Prussian War broke out and brought the art market to a close. As you know'– Sleet didn't – 'the whole point of the impressionists was to paint quickly and outside. This was clearly painted indoors – I suspect the subject was a mistress.'

'I was just thinking about the time I made eight hundred million dollars in one night out of Brexit,' said Sleet. 'So, if this guy makes the same after a few weeks dabbing colour on an old sheet, I am a kind of genius.'

Tony thought he was making a joke and laughed.

'What's so fucking funny?' Sleet said, his eyes narrowing. 'What have you ever done apart from sponge off other people? I suppose you could call that an art form?'

Ayesha interceded. 'Where are the other works?'

Tony rang a bell. The uniformed gloved handler arrived and started to pack the Renoir away.

'Hang on a minute, I want that. It's mine.' Sleet stepped forward and, turning to the attendant, said 'Wrap it to go. I'll take it now.'

'Darling, there's a deal to be done.' Ayesha put on her most sooth-ing voice. The second painting was brought in. This was by Edouard Manet, a contemporary of Renoir. It measured twenty-four inches by twenty and showed a naked woman lying by a stream.

'They liked their girls butt-naked – like me,' Sleet said. He looked at Rebecca. 'If these are so good, why don't the Iranians hang on to them?'

'Nakedness is an affront to their beliefs,' Ayesha explained. 'More importantly, there's a cash-flow issue.'

'Yeah, oil prices – not something you'd understand.'

Ayesha bit her tongue.

'How much is this one?' he asked Rebecca.

'Around twenty-five million pounds, possibly a bit more, depend-ing on its provenance before it went into the Shah's collection.'

'I want it.'

Rebecca hesitated. She was hoping for a reprieve, a way out of this compromising situation. 'These pictures were bought in the seventies – we'll need to check their provenance.'

'They might have been stolen by Nazis,' Tony interrupted, looking at Rebecca.

He was cut off by Sleet.

'Yeah, yeah – I read about that in one of the Sunday colour supple-ments. But it's only a problem if you lend it to a museum and some member of the public sees it. I want this stuff for my private walls. Have they been in any catalogues?'

'Not to the best of my knowledge.'

'But you're the expert, right?' He leaned close into Rebecca's face.

She turned away, frightened of showing her feelings. 'I authenticate works by Renoir and Manet.'

'And you say these are the real deal?'

Tony gave three short sharp coughs.

Rebecca looked at him and then at the ceiling. Finally she answered, 'Definitely.'

'Without a doubt?' Tony looked at her.

'Without a doubt,' she repeated.

'So do the deal with the Iranians. Get me the merch,' Sleet instructed.

'That is Mr Scott's department,' Rebecca said crisply.

'Get on the next plane, Tony my boy.' Sleet took Tony's chin and tweaked it between his fingers.

Tony swallowed hard. 'There is another picture, a beautiful Picasso.'

Sleet looked at his watch. 'You stay and see it. I need to get going.' He turned to Ayesha. 'You can find your own way back.'

After he'd left, Rebecca took her bag and made for the door. She rang the bell and waited for the guard to let her out. Turning at the last minute, she said to Tony, 'May you rot in hell.'

Tony smiled sweetly. 'I look forward to seeing you there.'

The door closed and Ayesha turned to look at her uncle. 'What was that about?'

Not wanting to dampen his great niece's spirits, Tony offered as much assurance as he could muster. 'Nothing to worry about.'

'We deserve a glass of champagne. We did it!' Ayesha jumped up and down. Adding together the Renoir (£50 million), Picasso (£45 million) and Manet (£22 million), plus the other pieces in the 'collection', she had made enough money to give Yasmin a hefty bonus, and so long as a bank guaranteed a hefty mortgage, she could secure Trelawney's future. Tony looked at her with avuncular fondness. He did not, for one second, think the deal was in the bag.

*

The following day Blaze and Tony met at their favourite restaurant, the Wolseley on Piccadilly.

'Darling, you look awful,' Tony said, holding his niece's hands and looking her up and down. 'Like a praying mantis.'

Blaze had dressed from head to foot in black.

'I came to you to feel better, not worse.' Uncharacteristically, Blaze burst into tears.

Tony looked around the busy restaurant hoping no one was watching. 'Darling. I have a reputation as a life enhancer to uphold. You are threatening my USP.' He beckoned to the waiter. 'Mario, for goodness' sake find me the most discreet table, behind a plant if possible.'

'I'm sorry,' Blaze sniffled, searching for a tissue in her bag.

'I'm appalled,' Tony said and whipped his silk handkerchief out of his breast pocket. 'It's Hermès, given to me by Gary Cooper in 1957. Your bogies will stain it.'

Blaze took it and blew her nose loudly and deeply.

'Quelle horreur,' Tony said and Blaze couldn't help laughing.

'I'm so sorry.'

'You should be. Frightful behaviour.'

Mario led them to the back of the restaurant and up some stairs to a balcony. It took Tony some time to pull himself up to the top.

'It might kill me getting up but at least no one can see us.'

'Don't be mean,' Blaze said, already feeling transformed by Tony. Humour rather than sympathy was the Trelawney family's method of dealing with crisis.

'First things first. Mario, bring us two Bloody Marys.'

'It's not even midday!' Blaze protested.

'In that case, Mario, make them doubles.'

'I'll be under the table.'

'That would be a blessing.' Without looking at the menu or consulting Blaze he placed their order.

'Mario, please bring two full English breakfasts. I'd like caviar on my eggs as my niece is paying.' Sitting back in his chair, he looked at his niece. 'Affairs of the heart?'

Blaze dabbed at her eyes with a napkin.

'I can't imagine why anyone would submit themselves to that awful institution of marriage in the first place. Such a ghastly idea that you'd willingly commit to one person, lose your independence, privacy and opportunities, and then, if it goes wrong, have to give up up most of your worldly possessions. What idiot came up with that?' Tony, considering his niece, took a drink from Mario and sucked enthusiastically through a straw. For years her life had been defined by a lack of love. She'd been so frightened of getting hurt, so determined not to open up to any random opportunity, that she pollarded her life, cutting off the limbs of opportunities to meet others or take personal risks. Her routine had been fixed and frenetic: appointments, deadlines, diets, exercise. Everything had been transactional and focused. Occasionally Tony had lifted the curtain and seen what lay behind the perfectly composed facade. Then Joshua had come as if from nowhere and his certainty about his feelings for Blaze, along with his quiet self-confidence, cut through her fears. Slowly but surely, mainly by turning up, by not letting her down, he'd convinced her into marriage.

'It's nothing to do with Joshua – we're happier than ever.'

'The child?' Tony tried to remember what it was called.

'She's fine too.'

Stumped, Tony sat back in his chair. 'So what are you blubbing about?'

'In July last year, Ayesha gave us a chance to save someone's life. We ignored her. Our friend killed himself.'

'That was six months ago. Have you been in touch with her since?'

Blaze shook her head.

Tony took another large suck, enjoying the bite of Tabasco and Worcester sauce on the back of his throat. 'If anyone else had told you, would you have listened?' he asked.

Miserably, Blaze assented. 'We've got so used to hating her, putting all our problems at her door, that we dismissed her warnings.'

Tony paused, gathering his thoughts. 'It's so convenient to have someone to blame. Maybe that's why you're crying – the loss of the communal scapegoat.'

Blaze nodded. Her resentment had calcified and, like a barnacle stuck to a rock, it had been easier to cling on to it than prise it away.

'Poor Ayesha,' Tony said. 'You have no idea what she is going through.'

'Don't make me feel guilty about her too.'

Suddenly, Tony turned the colour of parchment and tried to hide behind the plant. 'He's here.'

'Who's here?' Blaze looked down into the well of the restaurant and saw Sleet bound in.

Tony took three slurps of his Bloody Mary. 'Could you ask for some water, darling? Tonykins is not feeling too good.'

Blaze gesticulated to the waiter and, while she was waiting, fanned her uncle with her hands. 'Do you have any pills I should give you? Is it your heart? Shall I call an ambulance?'

Tony flapped his face with his napkin. 'Oh Blaze, Tony has done something not so clever. Or too clever by half. When my part is discovered, I will either be bumped off or put in the slammer.'

Blaze couldn't imagine what crime her ancient old uncle might have committed. Bank robbery? Arson? Murder? Looking at his decrepit frame, it was hard to visualise Tony having the strength to do more than swing a feather duster at a cloud. She made him drink a glass of water before asking him to explain.

'Oh darling. I dipped my little toe into the water of dishonesty and now I'm up to my neck.' The glass shook in his hand and Blaze gently took it from him and placed it on the table. She leaned over the balustrade and saw Sleet sit down in the centre of the room. A few minutes later a tall blonde woman flanked by two bodyguards came and sat next to him. Blaze noticed Sleet blushing with pleasure. She turned her attention back to her uncle.

'Start from the beginning.'

Tony spoke in a whisper, terrified that Sleet might overhear. 'I can't tell you – there's too much at stake. It's not just me – there's Ayesha and Stella and Yasmin the art student.' His voice rose to a low wail. He took the handkerchief, tried to stuff it into his mouth and, remembering Blaze's bogies, dropped it on the floor.

'Art student?' Blaze asked.

'She and Ayesha are pretending to be acting on behalf of the Ayatollah.'

Blaze, nonplussed, tried to find a thread in the narrative. And failed.

'Have you seen a doctor recently?'

'I am not suffering from dementia, if that's what you're suggesting,' Tony said testily. 'I have a hundred per cent of my mental fatalities.'

'Mental faculties?' Blaze put her hand on her uncle's shoulder. 'Please tell me what's going on. I swear on Perrin's head that I won't repeat a word you say.'

Over the course of the next half an hour, Tony told Blaze about the Iranian deal. He'd never thought for a minute that it would come off, but Sleet had that morning agreed to pay £117 million into a nameless Swiss bank account.

'How did you persuade him to buy a collection he hadn't seen?' Sleet was greedy but she never thought him stupid.

'He's decided that "art is cool" and wants to impress some big hedge cutters.'

'Hedge funders?'

'Same thing.'

'Not quite. He paid that kind of money sight unseen?'

'Three of the star paintings were put on view.'

'Were they legit?'

'The originals are tip-top works.'

Blaze could hardly believe what she was hearing. 'You're selling forgeries? Tony, what were you thinking?'

'That's the problem. I wasn't thinking. I never thought it would get this far.'

'And those paintings are now hanging on Sleet's wall?'

'They are being collected from Geneva later today. I am to install them this evening.'

'What happens when the rest of the shipment fails to arrive?'

'They will but not quite the originals.'

'Not quite?'

'Their twins are being made in Gdańsk. There's a chappie who uses extraordinary thermal and infrared imaging – he has a machine to copy every bump, every nook and cranny. It's hard to tell the difference, even if you're an expert.'

'And if Sleet gets an expert or realises what's happened?'

'He'll have to call the Iranian Embassy and ask for his merchandise.'

'And they will profess absolute ignorance.' Blaze blew out her cheeks. 'It's kind of brilliant. But bloody dangerous. Who's the forger?'

'He's our weakest link,' Tony admitted.

'Didn't Sleet get an independent art adviser?'

'She's incriminated in something else, so unlikely to say anything.'

Blaze looked at her uncle. 'Your best insurance policy is the embargo between the US and Iran: Sleet can't admit that he was involved in any covert financial activity with the Iranians. If he does, he'll have every American law enforcement outfit – the IRS, the FBI, the CIA and the rest – on his back, forever.'

'But he can still come back to Tonykins and skin me alive.' Tony gesticulated over the balcony. 'What happens if "she" finds out?'

Blaze followed his gaze to the blonde woman sitting with Sleet. 'Who is it?'

'Zamora Lala. Sleet's mistress. She does something in something – I am in such a fluster I can't remember what it is.'

Blaze's head was reeling. 'Mistress?'

'Part and parcel of how Ayesha persuaded poor old Tony to get involved.'

Blaze stared over the balcony to get a closer look at the woman. 'She reminds me of Anastasia. Older, less fine-boned but remarkably similar.'

'That's what Ayesha said.'

Blaze tried to collect her thoughts. 'Can your name be linked to any bank accounts?'

'I have nothing to do with that.'

'Can you be blamed for authenticating the works?'

'I made the right noises.'

'Oh, Tony. The whole plan is so brilliant and barmy that you'll almost certainly get away with it.'

Tony's face brightened. 'You sure?'

'Of course I am not sure.'

Tony's face fell again. 'At least it's the end of my life. It's been a fine innings.' Then he started to laugh.

'What?'

'I might get an obituary after all. "Aristocratic thief. *The Tony Scott Affair*." I see Brad Pitt playing me, or George Clooney. I so wish I could tell Barty – the jealousy would kill him.' Taking a sausage, he stabbed it into the middle of an egg and took a big bite.

Blaze, busy with meetings in London, had got home late: Joshua and Perrin were already asleep. She'd climbed into bed next to her husband and slipped her hand around his waist. Feeling her next to him, Joshua pushed his back into her and kissed her hand tenderly before falling asleep again. She woke a few hours later to find his space empty, the sheets cold. She got out of bed and looked in the bathroom. And then in Perrin's room, and then ran downstairs. There was no sign. Slipping her bare feet into some wellington boots, she pulled on an overcoat and hat. Opening the door, a blast of cold air and flurries of snow hit her face. She stumbled across the courtyard to his office but the room was locked and in darkness. Then, looking around, she saw faded foot-steps in the grass and followed them up the path towards the river. In the far distance she saw a familiar figure bent into the wind. Stumbling slightly on the boggy ground, she started to run towards him.

'Joshua! Joshua!' she called.

He turned and looked down the hill towards her. Then he started to run too.

'What are you doing?' he said, taking her in his arms.

'What are *you* doing?' she asked.

Holding her close, he sent his hot breath into her hair.

'I am so ashamed,' he said. They were not responsible for what had happened, but both felt implicated. In the months since John's death, the local community had been badly affected. Once the major employer in the area, Whaley Precision Engineering had been run as a paternalistic company where employees were well rewarded and their families were looked after. Now that Sleet had taken control, he'd sacked half the workforce, cut all benefits and reduced the remaining staff's wages by 20 per cent. The perceived 'problem' with the new graphite blade was quickly resolved. Its manufacture was moved from Buckinghamshire to a more 'cost-effective' factory in Taiwan.

'We must stop tearing ourselves to pieces. At least we can harness our misery. Do something positive. We must nail Sleet. Expose him for who he is,' Blaze said.

'And help Ayesha?' Joshua added.

Blaze surprised herself. 'Yes, and help Ayesha and Stella.'

For the next few days, while their daughter was at school, Blaze and Joshua abandoned all other commitments and spent every hour on the Whaley–Sleet axis. They pinned large pieces of paper to the wall of Joshua's office and wrote the names of different companies and key individuals, trying to make connections between apparently disparate facts and figures. Ayesha had mentioned a company called TLG. It was Blaze who identified an aeronautical business, a runner-up to the Boeing contract, based in Taiwan. Together they traced the owner-ship to a company based in Panama called Austell1972, a subsidiary of another firm called Fowey1972 based in the British Virgin Islands. That one, in turn, was a subsidiary of another in Liechtenstein which had affiliations with one in Delaware and another in the Cayman Islands. It was classic Moneyland, that borderless, stateless place where the super-rich and the super-shady lived without scrutiny, hiding their assets from the taxman and prying governments. In Moneyland, it was literally impossible to establish ownership and prove Sleet's involvement.

It was Blaze's idea to contact Ayesha.

'Are you sure?' Joshua asked, knowing too well the enmity his wife felt towards the younger woman.

'For John's sake,' Blaze replied. And then added, 'And I won't have to offer our daughter any more daft excuses.' Perrin's campaign to meet her cousin was unabated.

14

February 2017

Sleet wanted to use Kerkyra Capital's assets to subsidise the payment of the pictures but on this occasion Rodita's stubbornness prevailed.

'I'm buying assets at a knockdown price that will triple in value every year,' Sleet argued.

'All the more reason to use your own money.'

'You are robbing our clients of a great opportunity.' Sleet, enraged by his subordinate's behaviour, threw a telephone in her direction. Rodita sidestepped the projectile: she'd had years of practice.

'If it's that fail-safe, then why not disclose what you're buying and from whom?'

'It's a secret deal.' Sleet didn't dare admit to anyone: the consequences of being known to deal with the Iranians would be catastrophic. With strict embargoes in place, no legitimate businessman with dual US citizenship would be stupid enough to risk their reputation and future. But covetousness overcame caution. That week's *Taste and Refinement* was all about art and how a great collection conferred the fairy dust of class on its owner. Later, when sanctions were lifted, he'd show his pictures in public and imagined his own wing at a major institution or possibly his own museum – he'd call it 'The Sleet'. No one would ever forget him. He hoped his biological and adoptive parents who'd both tossed him aside, and all those condescending naysayers who'd written him off as the Vulgarian, would have to pay to enter. Most of all he imagined Zamora at the opening. She was his real masterpiece, the one he'd been waiting for. Finally, he'd met someone who was on his level, with whom he saw eye to eye, who shared the same values.

Rodita cleared her throat.

'What?' Sleet asked.

'We can only use company assets if you show us the deal sheet,' Rodita insisted. 'What is it you're buying?'

Sleet slammed his hand so hard on the table that it shuddered. 'I'm getting bored of you. Without me you'd have been nothing, no one, still grubbing around in that shitty little garret in Hendon. I made you. I created you.'

'I live in Finchley.'

'Who gives a fuck where you live!'

Rodita stood up slowly – inside she was boiling with rage but determined not to give Sleet the satisfaction of seeing his words mattered.

'Is that all?' she asked.

'No, it fucking isn't. Go to your office. Call J.P. Morgan and Credit Suisse. Raise the down payment of a hundred and seventeen million pounds in cash, transfer it to this account in Switzerland. If they need collateral, secure it against my houses, that Trelawney deal and personal assets. Do what you're told. Now.'

Even Rodita, who was used to Sleet's temper, was shocked. She went back to her office and waited for the phone to ring. In the past, Sleet would get angry but would call to apologise (like all bullies, he lacked courage). Rodita sat there watching the seconds tick by. And then the minutes. After one hour she picked up the phone to the bankers and secured the loan against Sleet's personal assets, to be transferred within twenty-eight days. At the last minute she switched the payment from cash to Sleet's Queen of Coins holding and transferred the cryptocurrency into the anonymous-sounding Swiss account. Let others take responsibility. Rodita was only sorry she wouldn't be around to witness the battles.

Her final act of revenge was to open her computer, go into their brokers' account and take away the safety valve that stopped clients from removing all their money. Until then, redemptions were limited to 10 per cent. Now, if anything untoward happened, there'd be no protection. Assets under Kerkyra Capital's control could slip from £48 billion to zero in a matter of hours. She'd spent too many years helping to build the company to want to destroy it but she could no longer justify propping up an institution pegged to an increasingly erratic principal.

She packed her things into a large carrier bag and a cardboard box and left her office for the last time.

Seeing Rodita laden with stuff, Donna ran after her and asked, 'Where are you going?'

Rodita smiled. 'Home.'

Donna followed her to the lift. 'Don't do anything rash. We need you.'

Rodita stopped and looked at her. 'We?' she said in amazement. 'We? It's never been about we or us, Donna. It's only ever been about him.' She clutched the cardboard box to her chest. 'I can't understand why it's taken me so long to see it.'

'What are you talking about?' Donna asked.

Rodita shrugged.

'You need a rest, Rodita. Go home and take some time off. You'll feel differently tomorrow.' A knot of panic was audible in Donna's throat. Rodita could not, must not be right. If she was, then what were the last two decades of her professional life about? A life of 24/7 on call, the abuse, the loss of friendships, strained relationships with her family because 'he' always came first. 'We are part of a team, Rodita,' she said, putting a consoling hand on her shoulder. 'In our own way, we helped build this great company. He couldn't have done it without us.'

'Great company?' Rodita laughed, a short, mirthless bark. 'We trade on misery.' She pressed the button for the lift. 'I'll be replaced by another – someone probably less talented but definitely more malleable. We're useful, Donna, but not essential.' Then Rodita looked at her colleague kindly. 'You probably are the nearest he's ever got to a decent relationship … you're closer to him than any of his wives.'

The lift arrived and, getting in, Rodita manoeuvred the box, freed her right hand and pressed the ground-floor button.

Donna watched the steel doors close and saw herself reflected in them. A neat middle-aged woman with a clipboard. She tried to imagine herself in another life – a secretary to a council or a regional business. A sales rep or a teacher.

'Donna! Donna!' Sleet's familiar shout rang out. 'Where are you?'

Donna smiled at herself in the reflection and, tucking a stray hair behind her ear, hurried towards his office.

*

The Gettina Prize lecture took place at the Musée du Louvre. It was held every other year and awarded to the best dissertation in Europe.

More than thirty universities submitted applicants. The honour came with a small amount of prize money and enormous kudos. The Courtauld had put forward two candidates – Yasmin and Ayesha – both supremely qualified, both for different reasons desperate to win. Ayesha knew that it would give her the imprimatur to be taken seriously. Yasmin needed the prize money and the professional affidavit. Yasmin was gracious in defeat. 'You are doing this for both of us. Don't get it wrong.' In the weeks leading up to the lecture, she helped her friend finesse every line of her presentation.

On the night, there were a hundred people in the audience, including leading art historians and several eminent cultural critics. The room was deep in the bowels of the museum, an oval wood-lined auditorium where the great European art historians and curators had presented their papers, elaborated on theories honed over long lives. Ayesha had spent most of the last few weeks adapting her dissertation; the lecture was, she hoped, the ship to launch her career as an author, curator and collector. Many in the audience assumed (wrongly) that she'd won because of her wealthy husband: museums, even the Louvre, were desperate for cash and there were twelve directors of development hovering anxiously, hoping to catch the financier. All were disappointed to find out that he wasn't attending: no reason given.

The title of the lecture was 'Love and Agony: Triumphs and Tribulations in the Life of Isabella d'Este, a Renaissance Woman'. The evening would end with a spectacular reveal: with Tony's help, Ayesha had discovered a 'sleeper', an unidentified masterpiece, in the vaults of the Louvre. Through dogged research and cross-referencing in Isabella's archive, she'd identified that a certain picture labelled 'Venetian Woman c.1569' was in fact a lost masterpiece, a portrait of Isabella by the great artist Titian. It had been sitting under the experts' noses for over a century.

The revelation would be even sweeter as the artistic community treated her with scepticism and in some cases hostility. In their opinion she was a dilettante, another of those privileged women who took courses to make themselves look better and upgrade their dinner-party chatter. A curator at the Louvre in charge of Renaissance questioned loftily if a woman of twenty-six had any right to opine on such an important subject as art history. His colleague questioned if she'd chosen Isabella as just another rich pampered woman who liked shopping. Knowing that both men were likely to be in the audience, Ayesha had prepared carefully for the evening: revenge, as her mother used to say, was a dish best served cold. Her lecture was peppered with new research, meticulously checked.

For the evening she had dressed down, scraping her long hair back into a chignon, wearing scant make-up and a well-cut black suit. At first her voice shook with fear but, as she continued talking about a subject she knew so well, Ayesha grew in confidence.

'We know from Isabella's letters – there are twelve thousand in the archive – that she was exacting and specific about her commissions. Painters were left in no doubt about what she wanted, including small details such as what the gods or goddesses should wear, which direction birds should fly, the placing of animals and the allegories themselves. Some have suggested that she longed to paint or create and this attention to detail came from personal frustration. Others claim that Isabella liked to delight her guests with detailed descriptions of what each symbol or juxtaposition meant. A third option is that she was a woman who liked to control. As we know, her husband was frequently away, fighting or carousing, leaving Isabella to run the court and the country. Given her intimate involvement in affairs of state, the hundreds of decisions she had to make, instructing an artist would have been an extension of her daily practice. Her reputation preceded her. Although Leonardo da Vinci drew her portrait, he refused all her commissions. Another contemporary, Giovanni Bellini, refused to paint a particular allegory, turning down her request in 1496. Isabella, not a woman to give up, kept writing to him until, in 1502, she agreed to settle for a Nativity if it included Joseph, John the Baptist and "the beasts". Bellini again refused, saying that his Nativity must be his own composition. Eventually she gave way – the painting arrived in 1504. She must have been pleased, for she asked for more works. Bellini, however, had had enough.'

To her surprise, Ayesha was enjoying herself. The hours of preparation and detailed research gave her confidence in her subject and a fluency of speech. She paused deliberately and shuffled her papers with a dash of theatricality. For the next section of her lecture, she needed their attention.

'I am about to tell you something shocking and possibly painful for certain members of this audience. You will remember the criticism I received from the Louvre's esteemed curators for suggesting that another portrait of Isabella by the great master Titian might still exist. "Only a fantasist would think that," one wrote. Another accused me of being an opportunist who would use money I had not earned to unearth a so-called sleeper and then pay experts to authenticate it. I feel for those who poured such scorn on my efforts, who rubbished my research, who called my motives into doubt. If only they had put as much energy into finding the "lost" portrait, they might have realised that the original is right here, at the Louvre.'

Her words were greeted by the harrumphing of sceptics in one quarter and interested chatter elsewhere. Then, slowly, painstakingly and forensically, Ayesha outlined her research. She didn't care that some might be bored or that the detail was exhaustive. Her hunch was correct and backed up with facts. 'For those who might have missed what I was saying, *Apollo* magazine will publish my article in full next month. In the meantime,' she said, turning to the director and his head of collections, 'I am delighted that France's premier museum and the French people can now claim to have discovered an additional painting by Titian in their collection. This important and revelatory work, showing Isabella as she really was at the age of fifty, has been overlooked for one and a half centuries. I saw it myself this morning on a visit to your stacks. She is a little dusty, but once cleaned of three hundred years of varnish and effluvium, I am convinced that she will hang alongside the best of the rest – both artist and his subject matter rightfully reclaiming their fitting place in the pantheon of great artists and their patrons.'

Ayesha hesitated and turned to an attendant standing nearby. 'Please bring out the work.'

With some pomp and ceremony, two museum guards approached the stage holding a painting between them. It was covered with a dark cloth. Ayesha got down from the dais and walked towards it. Standing behind the painting, she slowly peeled away the cloth to reveal the Titian.

There was a hushed silence followed by a general murmur. Ayesha waited until the room was quiet. Then she clicked on the next slide in her presentation.

'You'll see from the X-rays taken from this painting that there are ghosts of other images under the one you see. By all accounts – and you'll find the footnotes and research notes in my article – Isabella was a difficult subject. Far less beautiful than her sister Beatrice, the Duchess of Milan, or her rival in love, Lucrezia Borgia, Isabella detested her own appearance. One of the reasons few images survive is that she destroyed nearly all of them. You can see here' – she clicked through some more slides – 'how even the great Titian struggled. Another painter, Leonardo da Vinci, made this drawing of Isabella' – another slide – 'which, though painted when she was sixty, portrays a much younger woman. And here is Titian's portrait of her now in the Gemäldegalerie in Berlin.'

Ayesha turned to the audience. 'One of the reasons the painting before you went missing is that Titian was ordered by Isabella to dispose of it. While it's not one of his best works, even he couldn't bring himself to paint over the image.'

Out of the corner of her eye, Ayesha saw one or two of the older curators leave the room. They couldn't bear their ignorance to be exposed, especially by a young woman. 'How did the painting end up here in Paris? As many know, after Isabella's death her rooms and her legacy were neglected, her belongings were scattered over the palace. In 1627 Charles I of Nevers gifted many of the paintings she'd commissioned to Cardinal Richelieu who added them to Louis XIV's collection. And, as we all know, the royal paintings became the basis of the Louvre.'

At the end of her presentation there was thunderous applause from some and deafening silence from others. The audience split into those who were impressed by her thesis and reveal and others who found it fanciful or impertinent. At the drinks reception, many academics gave her a wide berth; few could understand how a mere student had uncovered one of the Renaissance's great mysteries on their watch.

Ayesha slipped away early and walked away from the Louvre down the Seine to St-Germain. She'd expected to feel triumphant or at least vindicated but instead felt sad that there was no one to share the moment with. Yasmin was working and even Tony couldn't be persuaded to make the trip to Paris. She took a quieter route, crossing the Pont des Arts, but saw immediately that was a mistake. It was a beautiful evening and the bridge was thronged with couples taking selfies or clipping padlocks to the railings as a sign of never-ending love. Ayesha knew she should be feeling happier. Any moment £117 million would land in her newly created Swiss bank account, payment for the Iranian works. This added to the £2 million she'd made on side deals gave her a feeling of security and hope. The lecture had been a success: a publisher had suggested a two-book deal. Yet, with nothing but a string of betrayals behind her, it wasn't surprising that she didn't trust anyone or anything.

She took a circuitous route through the Left Bank along Rue Jacob and through tiny streets before finding a table in the Café de Flore. Ordering a croque-monsieur and a glass of red wine, she imagined, like so many others, tables of yesteryear where the artistic luminaries Hemingway, de Beauvoir, Sartre, Picasso and others had once sat.

A young man sidled up to her and asked if the seat next to her was free. Was she waiting for someone? He was handsome, with short dark hair and pale brown eyes. He slid into the banquette next to her and for the next forty minutes they flirted, Ayesha entertaining thoughts of a night of passion. Isn't that what Paris was meant for? She could hardly be unfaithful to a man who'd never married her. But for all her new companion's easy charm, she couldn't summon up the energy and soon rose, bidding him goodnight. Donna had booked her a night at the Ritz, not in the Presidential Suite where she and Sleet normally stayed but in a small double on the wrong side of the building, yet another sign of her loss of status. At least, she thought, I will soon have money of my own.

Before turning down the bed, she checked the Swiss account. Nothing had come in although it had been expected for more than a fortnight and her nervousness increased each day. She'd promised a sum of money to Yasmin to help her find her grandfather. There was the debt to the free-port storage unit of €125,000. On Raymond Mishra's advice, she'd employed a property lawyer to draw up papers to open negotiations with Medieval Illusions. Her nest egg was getting smaller, not bigger.

The following morning, she rang Herr Brunner, the Swiss banker and broker. He was courteous but guarded. He confirmed they had received a transfer. Ayesha could hardly believe it: Stella and she were free. Tears of relief rushed to her eyes and spilled down her cheeks. Herr Brunner hesitated and cleared his throat. There was, he told her, an irregularity. The entire amount was in an unrecognised and unregulated currency. It was, he said, most peculiar. Its name was Queen of Coins. Ayesha's heart contracted. She struggled to breathe.

'Don't accept it,' she begged.

'There's nowhere and no way to return it,' the apologetic banker admitted. 'It has no SWIFT code, it doesn't conform to any forex regulations.'

In a panic, Ayesha went to the Queen of Coins site and tried to exchange the cryptocurrency into dollars or pounds but the only items the company had on offer were T-shirts, educational material and sun cream. Nor was it tradable on any platforms. She called Brunner again. He suggested that she revert to the vendor. *How can I?* Ayesha wanted to scream. The most frightening aspect was who had done this? Her husband? His inamorata? The Albanians? Meanwhile she was fielding calls from Yasmin and Lech who wanted to know when they'd get paid. Her credibility with her friend and associate was fading. She spent the morning at the Ritz checking the Queen of Coins website repeatedly. There were no telephone numbers, only emails. Creating anonymous accounts, she sent messages, varying between polite and abusive, asking why her currency couldn't be exchanged. Every single one had an automatic bounce-back. *Due to technical issues, we are unable to respond today. We are working hard to correct the situation.* She had been well and truly out-scammed.

*

Clarissa, desperate to remain on television and remain in control of her output, had come up with her own idea for a series. Much to Damian Dobbs's surprise, it was to feature two other people: Barty St George and Princess Amelia. Damian knew that she detested Barty but, given the sparsity of her social circle (most were long deceased), she had few options. Furthermore, few were prepared to sacrifice themselves on the altar of political incorrectness. Like her, Amelia and Barty loved the oxygen of publicity and would say anything for a headline or a laugh.

'We will call ourselves "The Three Old Gits",' she told the Princess, Barty and Damian.

'The three *what*?' Amelia's hearing had deteriorated in the last year. She held a large brass trumpet, the very same used by her grandfather, George VII. It didn't help much but she liked the look.

'It's a word that means—'

'Distinguished,' Barty cut in, not wanting Amelia to disagree with any part of the proposal. All he'd ever wanted was his own series on television. 'I'd sky-dive naked strapped to a boa constrictor if they asked,' he'd told Tony.

'Why old?' Amelia asked. 'I don't consider myself old.'

'You're ninety-two!' Clarissa said.

'I refuse to discuss years – frightfully infra dig. Anyway, who says things have to go up? It was probably a Chinese idea – it's always the Communists' fault.'

'What are you talking about, Amelia?' Clarissa asked.

Amelia drew herself up. 'When "help" asks if their pay packet can go up, it's Chinese infiltration.'

'Is that what you told them?' Barty asked.

'No! I just said what goes up can come down. I always suggest paying less.'

'I bet that went down a bomb,' Barty said.

'In the good old days, "help" had nowhere else to go. Born into service; die in service. Now they have such highfalutin ideas. I blame the Chinese.' Amelia tapped her hand on the table to make her point.

When Damian had first heard Clarissa's idea, he'd been unsure, but as the conversation between the three principals progressed, he became increasingly excited. Clarissa noticed his reddening face and couldn't resist asking.

'What happened to the other proposal you wanted me to audition for?'

'It came to nothing.' Damian had heard that Ms Nkosi and the person who identified as ZHt6 agreed deferentially on every single topic; rampant political correctness had turned out to be bad television.

'It was bad because I refused to take part!' Clarissa said, turning to the other gits. 'Can you imagine having the temerity to ask me to audition? The Countess of Trelawney coming up in front of a panel?'

'I'd have done it,' Barty said. 'Might have been fun.'

'You'd go to the opening of a crisp packet,' Clarissa snapped.

'Or a barn door,' the Princess added.

Damian wished he was filming already.

'Why aren't you filming?' Clarissa was having the same thoughts. 'Honestly, Dobbs, it's a wonder you got anywhere before me.' She hesitated. 'Come to think of it, you didn't.'

Damian scrambled for his camera and turned it on.

'We're going to do warts and all,' Clarissa said. 'We might be elderly but we're cutting edge.'

'Elderly is such a common word,' Barty said. 'Like sushi or serviettes, scented candles, Ibiza.'

'And loving your mother,' Amelia and Clarissa said in unison. For nearly forty-five years they'd heard Barty complain about common things.

'Common is quite a good starting point for our first discussion,' Clarissa said. 'Let's talk about Theresa May.'

Her suggestion was met by howls.

'Do we have to? Those leopard-skin kitten-heeled shoes.'

'We should defend women,' Barty said. 'She's brave to call a general election.'

'She has as much charisma as a teabag.'

'What is a teabag?' Amelia asked.

'I have no idea,' Clarissa admitted.

'You can't imagine that Jeremy Crowbar is going to win.'

'Corbyn!'

'Cor, he's frightful,' Barty said.

'Barty! We can't have jokes of that calibre,' Clarissa remonstrated.

'I found it funny.'

'Well, it wasn't.'

Damian caught Barty's crestfallen look and the slight wobble of his lower lip. 'Who do you think will win the election?' he asked, trying to change the direction of the conversation.

'No one,' Clarissa said. 'They're equally revolting. It'll be a dead heat.'

'Poppycock. Someone must win,' Amelia said.

'It's not like Wimbledon. You don't keep going till the light fades.'

'We'll have a hung parliament.'

'Hang them all! What a wonderful idea.' Amelia clapped her hands. 'It all went wrong when they took away the death penalty.'

'You should be given a deaf penalty,' Clarissa said. 'Death and deaf; hang and hung have different meanings.'

'My education stopped with the Romans,' Amelia said.

'You're not that old,' Barty teased.

'I remember our governess saying, "Julius Caesar was misunderstood," then she closed the book and that was that. Do you know, the whole of my life I've wondered about that statement?'

'Was Julius Caesar misunderstood?'

'Who was he anyway?'

Clarissa and Barty looked at each other and burst out laughing. Damian's camera shook.

'What?' Amelia said. 'Did I miss something?' She put her trumpet to her ear. 'Tell me.'

15

March 2017

MARCH 3RD

Sleet was feeling pleased; life without Rodita was going surprisingly well. Her successor, Felix Manningford-Tripplestone, never disagreed with a word. Felix had been to Eton and Sandhurst, served a tour of Iraq and several in Afghanistan. He left the army with a couple of stripes, a medal and a gammy leg before reinventing himself as a 'chief of staff'. What he knew about private equity could be written on the back of a postage stamp but what he lacked in experience was compensated by eagerness. Sleet was delighted to have found someone who did his bidding without asking questions.

'What you have to understand, Felix,' he told the younger man, 'is that success is a delicate matrix of opportunity, graft and acumen. I am one of the few people who has all three.'

'Quite so,' Felix said.

Sleet felt invincible. Every area of his life was improving. His campaign to make love to and marry Zamora was inching forward and, as a bonus, her cryptocurrency had increased in value. On paper, the £150 million Queen of Coins he'd bought had gone up by 75 per cent. The week before, George Solos and Ricky O'Fell had come to dinner. Conversation was dominated not by market movements but the extraordinary quality of Sleet's art collection. O'Fell offered him twice what he'd paid for the Picasso. It was a novelty having a soon-to-be-ex kind of wife who made rather than cost him money.

He considered, briefly, keeping Ayesha around but that would be too easy. He could buy in art consultants without the bother of having to eat breakfast with them. For a man used to getting anything at any time, and for whom challenges were increasingly hard to find, Zamora made him feel alive. While his wealthy contemporaries spent money trying to fly to outer space, erect museums or solve world health issues, Sleet decided that the wooing of Zamora Lala, while exceedingly expensive, was far more enjoyable than endless discussions about malarial swamps, donor recognition or space walking. She was his personal meteor shower, a cosmic explosion blowing off his outer layers.

There were tiny cracks in Zamora's facade that gave hope of eventual conquest. The week before, she'd let him kiss her – fleetingly, admittedly, but still mouth on mouth, tips of tongues engaging. On a few occasions she let her guard slip revealing a lack of sophistication. He teased her when he put three ice cubes in the glass of vintage Cristal. She didn't understand the importance of tipping concierges and maître d's. Her handbags were chosen for their price rather than their design (a mistake Ayesha would never make). The colour of her nails matched her lipstick. When he pointed out these peccadilloes, he caught a rare moment of fear and vulnerability.

'Show me, teach me,' she asked.

He never admitted that his own sophistication was learned recently. 'It's all about *Taste and Refinement*,' Sleet had said.

'Is that a company?'

'No, but it should be. Good idea to try and make money out of it.'

Felix cleared his throat noisily. For the last few minutes, Sleet had been mentally absent.

'Is that all, sir?' Felix asked.

Sleet looked at his chief of staff. 'One last thing. Tahira thinks the Prime Minister will call an election, probably in June. I intend to stand.'

At this disclosure, Felix's normally impenetrable expression slipped to one of surprise. 'Stand, sir?'

'Run as a candidate. Whatever the stupid terminology you Brits use.'

'Which party will you be "standing for"?' Felix kept his tone even. He couldn't imagine why his boss would want to lay himself open to the scrutiny which came with public office for such meagre returns. Backbench MPs have little power; ministers get flack, followed by a reshuffle. The best a British politician could hope for is obscurity.

'I'm going with Nigel. A safe seat near Trelawney. Tahira has done the polling. Cornwall is strictly Brexit. Those wet-wad Tories have no hope of winning. I have done my time in local pubs. I know what people want.'

Felix felt a deep sense of unease not shared by his boss who continued with his instructions.

'Talk to Tahira. She knows what you must do next and how much it costs. I've made her my senior campaign manager. She has a team ready to go.'

'When will they make the announcement?'

'I'm told next month.'

'How do you see my role, sir?'

'To make sure everything goes well.' Sleet beamed. 'There's one other thing,' he continued. 'I want to organise the greatest ever party. It'll take place the night after the election.'

'Hard to plan without an actual date.'

'You'll manage. It'll be an almighty celebration.'

'Of your election to Parliament?'

'Obviously, and to introduce the world to Zamora.'

'Should I involve your wife in the arrangements?' Felix asked.

Sleet snorted. 'My so-called wife will not be invited.'

*

The text came, a tiny ray of hope in a bleak outlook. *Please will you and Stella come to lunch on Sunday? Blaze.* Since Paris, Ayesha had gone into a slough of despondency. Her big idea to save Trelawney had failed and it had cost her, in expenses, much of her nest egg. In the last month she had hustled where possible for work, sending out scores of ideas for articles to highbrow publications like the *Burlington* ('The Use of Pigments in the Quattrocento') and also to less salubrious publications like the *Daily Blast* ('Best Places to Eat in the Caribbean'). She had signed up to an elite model agency. So far, the only job on offer was in Bali – too far and too long away from Stella. There were meetings with her publishing house to discuss the forthcoming book on Isabella d'Este (the advance was less money than a single couture dress). Her endeavours and almost certain failure to save the castle were matched in velocity by a growing determination to bring Sleet to justice. Her sense of outrage was increased when she worked out that, after costs and price of purchase, he'd made more than £50 million profit from the sale of Trelawney; excluding the contents, most of which she had chosen and bought for a reasonable sum. She could and would not let him walk away, profit, rob and humiliate her without consequences.

Still following Sleet's activities on MySpy, she read exchanges between him and another short seller, Willy Perkins. For some time they'd been planning to cause a share plummet in LighterYou by spreading negative stories about carcinogenic contents in a new product. Ayesha read their exchange closely. She didn't entirely understand the mechanism of what they were proposing but was frustrated that her nest egg, after the Iranian fiasco, wasn't growing and she had no other big ideas. Her sense of desperation increasing by the day, she decided to make a major punt and bet her whole net worth by copying one of Sleet's moves. She instructed her broker in Geneva, Herr Brunner, to borrow £2 million pounds of LighterYou shares and sell them immediately for £6. According to Sleet's exchanges, she would be able to buy these back later at a much lower price; he predicted they'd fall to £3. Ayesha predicted making a tidy profit and doubling her fighting fund.

The invitation to see Blaze and Joshua came out of the blue. Blaze hadn't been in touch since Café Romeo. Ayesha suspected that lunch was a sop to her half-sister's conscience. She considered refusing the invitation but accepted for Stella's sake, so her daughter could meet her cousin. She spent the next couple of days deciding what to bring as a present. She must strike the right balance between grandiosity and familiarity. Something to eat? A delicious bottle of wine? In the end she decided on a toy for Perrin. Sleet was away – she didn't know where nor did Donna disclose. After breakfast, she scooped up Stella, packed some snacks and children's books in a bag and, strapping her daughter into the car seat, headed east. Unused to driving, she stalled twice on the journey. It was a cold, icy morning. Once or twice she felt the car skid on the twisty side roads and it was a relief to turn on to the salted main carriageway. Ayesha skirted alongside Dartmoor and saw the tors dusted with snow and the wild ponies huddled together with their backs set against a harsh wind.

To keep Stella amused, they sang and played games.

'I-spy, with my little eye, "m" for Mummy smiling.' Stella had not mastered the rules.

Glancing in the mirror, Ayesha saw the reflection of a happy face, a welcome change from the last weeks.

Stella slept for an hour and woke up hungry and disorientated. Ayesha found a motorway service station where they ate chips and ice cream, and she bought her daughter and her niece matching huge pink fluffy bears.

'Get the bears ready,' she told her daughter as they bumped up the track to the Wolfes' farm. Pulling up outside the house, Ayesha got up and unstrapped Stella and placed a bear in each arm. Blaze came out holding Perrin's hand. Stella handed over the gift and the two little girls looked at each other. Perrin was pale and dark-haired. She was a year older but looked younger. Stella, brimming with confidence, hugged her cousin.

'Your bear is Jemmy. Mine is Charlie.' Then she took Perrin's hand. 'Where is your playroom?' Perrin, partly from surprise, turned and led Stella inside to a small room off the kitchen.

Ayesha stepped forward to kiss her half-sister. Blaze sidestepped. Joshua adored his wife but there were times, such as now, when he found her social awkwardness bewildering. To compensate, he gave Ayesha a hug.

'Welcome! Coffee? Tea?'

Ayesha nodded gratefully. The three stood around the kitchen table. Blaze knew it was up to her to say something but found it wasn't easy to overcome her long-held feelings of resentment. Although she loved Joshua's farm and considered it her home, Trelawney was and always would be where her heart resided. She'd lived away from the castle longer than she'd lived there but still felt umbilically, irrationally linked to the place of her birth and where she'd spent her formative years.

After a few minutes, Ayesha broke the silence. 'I am not asking for forgiveness or friendship: I'd like both but don't expect either. Whatever you think, I love Trelawney and want to secure its future.'

'Why do you care so much?' Blaze asked. 'You weren't even born there.'

Ayesha recoiled from the accusation. Here was another member of the family, her own family, doubting her right to be part of the clan.

Was this how her mother felt? Didn't Blaze remember what it was like to be ostracised? She kept a check on her feelings – she needed Blaze and Joshua. 'I was born on the outside looking in; I've always wanted to be on the inside looking out.'

Blaze listened but didn't react. Ayesha changed tack. 'I have done absolutely everything in my power to raise enough money but sadly my best efforts have come to little.' She wanted to let them know she had tried and not sat around waiting to be rescued.

Blaze and Joshua exchanged glances. Tony had told Blaze about the Iranian deal but neither knew quite what to believe. Ayesha, intercepting their looks, thought they were heaping condescension on rejection and was hit by a wave of anger.

'Why should Sleet get away with this? His only justification is that he thinks he's better and more deserving. Superior. He should not be allowed to cheat and denude whoever he feels like.' Then she looked her half-sister in the eyes. 'The Blaze I remember wouldn't have walked away from justice and fairness.'

Blaze, not wanting to betray emotion, looked away and out of the window down the river snaking through their valley. She longed to pull up a drawbridge with Ayesha firmly on the other side and wished she hadn't got involved again with her and Sleet. Out of the corner of her eye she watched Ayesha gather her things and walk to the door of the playroom. Joshua didn't move; it had to be Blaze's decision.

'Wait!' Blaze called out. Ayesha froze but didn't turn around. 'Joshua and I have been doing some investigative work. There are things that don't make sense to us. Perhaps they will to you.'

She stood up and, bypassing Ayesha, called to the children, 'We're going to Daddy's office. Will you be OK?'

Two happy voices called, 'Yes,' in unison.

Blaze and Joshua led the way across the courtyard. Ayesha looked around the room. One wall of the barn was hi-tech, covered with computer screens showing fluctuations in the world's financial markets. But the rest of the building was made for comfort – a large chintz-covered sofa, a box of Perrin's toys, framed photographs of the three of them on holiday. The old Turkish carpet was worn away, possibly by the former inhabitant of a dog basket still under Joshua's desk. It was markedly different to how she and Sleet lived, in a place kept constantly cleaned and tidied by a large retinue of staff.

For the next hour, Ayesha, Blaze and Joshua cross-referenced on big white sheets of paper the information they'd gathered. Ayesha added the detail she'd learned from MySpy and overheard conversations. Together they drew maps, diagrams, stock-market results and information relevant to their mission: to investigate if Sleet had played any part in Whaley Precision Engineering's stock crash and, if so, to hold him to account. Still racked with remorse that he hadn't listened to Ayesha's warnings months earlier, Joshua was determined to uncover the truth: if Sleet had knowingly and deliberately caused the collapse of Whaley's then he was implicated in John's suicide. Worse still was the thought of Sleet taking advantage of the share-price collapse to buy the company at a knock-down price. For Blaze, nailing Sleet was about trying to save Trelawney, but with overlays from the past. During the crash of 2008, Sleet had deliberately destroyed her company and her reputation.

The three of them sat side by side in front of a map full of interconnecting circles.

'You've done some amazing detective work,' Joshua observed. 'How did you find out all this stuff?'

Ayesha was too frightened to tell anyone about MySpy. Whatever Digby had said, she was sure it was illegal. She was certain, too, that Blaze and Joshua would think less of her if they knew the depths she'd sunk to.

'I picked up stuff from dinners and phone conversations. I made notes and then tried to work out what it meant later.' She hesitated. 'I don't understand a lot of it.' Then, to change the subject, she pointed to Joshua's wall charts. 'So the red ones are Cayman Islands, the blue are Channel Islands?'

'Black are Panama, yellow are the Bahamas,' Blaze added.

'Between twenty-one to thirty-two trillion dollars are hidden in offshore companies,' Joshua explained. 'They're economic equivalents of astrophysical black holes.'

'Why are they legal?'

'There's no interest group more rich and powerful than the rich and powerful.'

Blaze cleared her throat. 'There is some positive news. We can trace Sleet through three offshore companies to TLG, the underbidders in the Boeing propeller contract.'

'Is that enough to put him in prison?' Ayesha's spirits rose.

Joshua shook his head. 'It smells nasty but he can argue that any businessman would have done the same. Susan Whaley's share options and financial worth have increased dramatically even since the IPO. Sleet has made her richer.'

'Slim consolation for losing your beloved husband and life.' Blaze looked at Joshua; she'd forfeit every penny and any possession before giving him up.

'Are you cold, darling?' Joshua asked and put some more logs into the stove. Blaze smiled at him and he put his arms around her and kissed the top of her head. For Ayesha, the proximity to such a loving relationship highlighted the sterility of her own. Joshua and Blaze took every opportunity to show each other kindness.

While Ayesha noticed their tenderness, Blaze saw how thin the younger woman had become, her wedding ring slipping up and down her finger, her collarbones jutting out behind a T-shirt. Ayesha's hands trembled when she held a cup or a pencil. Her hair, once a thick, shining mass of auburn locks, hung lankly over her shoulders.

'Can we expose his practices of targeting shareholders of other companies with misinformation?' Ayesha asked.

'It's called short and distort. People are rarely charged but occasionally someone is done for market manipulation and intentionally spreading false rumours,' Joshua said.

Ayesha, feeling guilty about her bet on LighterYou, didn't say anything.

'So for people like Sleet, rules don't apply: he can use and manipulate any company or even a country for his own ends without retribution,' Joshua continued.

After a few moments' silence Blaze spoke. 'He or his cronies will make a mistake. We must be there, on alert waiting for it to happen.'

'We'll work assiduously.' Joshua got to his feet and, tapping his watch, said to his wife, 'Let's make the girls some supper.'

'Your turn!' Blaze laughed. Then, turning to Ayesha, she admitted, 'He's a much better cook than I am.'

'I should go. It's a long drive.' Ayesha didn't want to leave.

'Stay for tea.' Blaze smiled at her. 'I'm happy the children are getting on.' Then she hesitated and, without looking directly at her half-sister, said, 'We will help you.'

Ayesha drove home in high spirits. With Blaze and Joshua's help, she could salvage her self-esteem and start to rebuild a new life for herself and Stella. It almost certainly wouldn't be at Trelawney but she imagined a small flat in London close to a good local school. Perhaps she'd train as a teacher and have the holidays to spend with her daughter. After putting Stella to bed, she spent a pleasant evening perusing flats in different parts of the capital. Her sense of optimism was so buoyant that she decided to turn her phone off for a few days so as not to let Sleet or his activities infect her mood.

When she finally reconnected to life, she saw sixty-four missed calls from Herr Brunner. There were texts too. *Urgent. I need to speak to you.* Before returning his messages she looked up LighterYou's share price, expecting it to have fallen. Her fingers froze over the keyboard. Instead of going down, LighterYou's stock had risen from £6 to £11. She called her banker. The news was far worse than she feared.

'Lady Sleet, I tried again and again to reach you. The bank had no option but to close your position.'

'What?'

'There were margin calls to meet,' he explained. 'You borrowed shares at £6. As the price rose, you had to pay the owners back considerably more. It went the wrong way.'

'I don't understand,' Ayesha whispered.

'Your losses were exceeding your net worth. We took a decision.'

'What do I have left?'

Herr Brunner cleared his throat. 'Your assets under our management have decreased.' He cleared his throat. 'Unfortunately you have lost everything.'

'Everything?' Ayesha said.

'From the two million pounds we have retained a hundred and seventy-five thousand. I am so sorry.'

Devastated, Ayesha sat back in her chair. Dreams of a London flat evaporated. She'd be lucky to afford a bedsit. Nor could she blame Sleet – this time the mistakes were all her own.

16

April 2017

Easter was late that year. Sleet fretted where to go: the only certainty was that Ayesha wouldn't be invited. The snow was melting in Aspen and St Moritz; Europe was still too cold for yachting. He rang around his newly made alpha-male friends in the hope of casually solving the problem. Ricky O'Fell was going to his country estate in County Cork; Aristotle Parastephanos to his island in Greece; George Solos and twenty friends were driving across the desert to raise money for starving children.

'That sounds super-worthy,' Sleet said, wondering if he should suggest coming – maybe with one of his Aston Martins or Ferraris.

'We take Citroën deux chevaux and spend five nights in tented camps.'

To Sleet this sounded like utter hell. He messaged Zamora. *Tell me anywhere, anywhere in the world you'd like to go, and I'll meet you there.* To his delight she responded with a voicemail. Sleet listened to it twenty times to make sure – she was on her plane and, mixed with her accent, it was hard to decipher. He played it to Donna. After some consultation they decided she'd said the Aman hotel in Bhutan on April 15th.

'Of course, she'd want to visit another almost Communist country.'

'I think it's a monarchy with a parliament,' Donna said.

'So why would she want to go there?'

Donna shrugged. Although used to her boss's obsessions, this one was exhausting. Zamora, if she took his calls, often hung up mid-sentence or put him on hold for several minutes without any explanation. Tentative meetings were changed several times and, if they happened (which was rare), the locations were switched at the eleventh hour. It was left to Donna to seek impossible last-minute landing or docking permissions (plane and boat), to organise visas and get the best tables at various restaurants. Sometimes she put holds on places in four different countries. Donna was beginning to value Ayesha who, except for a couple of annoying requests for pizza and other sundries, had been reasonably easy to manage.

Sleet couldn't cope with loss of control. Each time Zamora stood him up, and this was far more often than when she consented to see him, he ranted, raged, wept and shook. The floor was covered with shards of pencils; he got through four or five shirts a day. In the process of finding 'true love' he was on the verge of losing his mind.

Bhutan presented additional challenges. Donna, working with Sleet's pilots, had read up about the logistical issues. Its one airport, Paro, was 1.5 miles above sea level and surrounded by sharp peaks of up to 18,000 feet. Planes could only enter from one direction before sharply banking to avoid crashing into high mountains.

'I am postcommercial,' Sleet thundered when Donna suggested he change flights in Bangkok and pick up a national carrier, the country's own airline.

'It's the most dangerous airport in the world,' Donna reasoned. 'Only eight pilots are qualified to land there.'

'How's Zamora doing it?' Sleet asked.

Donna shrugged. In spite of repeated attempts to establish contact with Zamora, the Albanian had no office and never answered her phone or email.

'Send the guys on a training course,' Sleet instructed and his team of pilots were duly dispatched to Kathmandu for intensive instruction in how to navigate Bhutanese peaks.

Donna's next issue was securing the best suite at the Aman hotel and at the five lodges spread through the country. A rock star and a Saudi sheik had booked all the rooms except for one small double. Donna was not perturbed: she had encountered worse problems; it was a question of money. In this case, it was a very considerable amount. Sleet had a sliding scale to describe costs of holidays. A 'scratch' holiday was not worth taking – if something cost less than several hundred thousand then it was too widely available. It must be an 'ouch' (between £250 and £500k) to be worthwhile. When Donna told him the total price (without extras) of the Bhutanese jaunt, Sleet bellowed that it was 'a WTF cut my balls off' kind but it was worth it for Zamora.

The preparations for the adventure took up a lot of Donna's time. April was the beginning of Bhutan's rainy season and, to make sure that her boss and his inamorata had the right clothes, she invested in his and hers outdoor gear. The country's hospitals were hardly Sloan Kettering, so she took the precaution of paying for a leading specialist and his family to have a fully paid holiday in a nearby hotel. She arranged for a chef from Bangkok and another from Singapore (both world renowned) to supplement the Aman team. Sleet's own housekeeper, who understood her boss's peccadilloes, would be flown out from London to oversee preparations. If Sleet knew how thorough his PA was, he'd never acknowledge it – that was her job, she was well remunerated.

He arrived in Paro two days before Zamora, to make sure that every detail was perfect. The airport was quaint and the suite at the hotel breathtaking. He went through the menus, the kitchen, the laundry and discussed the excursions. Zamora had not given him her flight times and, as no other private jet was registered to land, on the day of her arrival he met every incoming plane. She didn't appear on any. Trying to play it cool, he decided not to call. The following two days there was still no sign. Sleet was increasingly anxious. He was finding it hard to sleep and the internet and phone connection were lousy. The holiday was costing him a fortune and he was missing out on market fluctuations.

On day five, Easter Monday he called her. 'Where are you?' he said. 'I here.'

Sleet's heart leapt. 'Why didn't you say? I've been meeting every fucking plane. Did you walk over the border?'

Zamora yawned. 'Course not walk. PJ. I go tomorrow. Tonight dinner with Petr and Oleg at Vlad's house. You come?'

'Petr? Oleg?' What was she talking about?

'I have yacht outside hotel. We go by sea.'

Sleet looked out of his window. There was no sea, not even a lake, just a stream. 'Where did you say you were?'

Again she mumbled. He could swear it was Bhutan. 'Can you text me your exact location? I will be with you in ten minutes.'

His phone pinged seconds later. The red pin on the map was in a place called Budva. Budva was in Montenegro. It didn't even sound like Bhutan. He punched the distance into his phone: 6,438 miles. He checked his watch. It was 6 p.m.

'When did you say you were going?' he asked.

'Seven hours.'

The panic attack hit him like a truck. When Sleet came to he had a nasty gash on the side of his face, and his arm hurt. The doctor was there in fifteen minutes. In his report, sent to Donna, he noted that the wound needed four stitches. The arm wasn't broken but the shoulder was dislocated. Otherwise, the patient would heal quickly. There was a postscript, something the doctor couldn't explain and had never seen before: the floor of the suite was covered with broken pencils.

*

For Ayesha, Sleet's absence was a relief. It left her more time with Stella at Trelawney. When she wasn't with her daughter, she obsessively tracked and traced all aspects of Sleet's life. One whole wall of her study was now covered with Post-it notes and figures. She double-locked the door and had a padlock attached so that no staff or family member could pry on her research. Directly after Easter Sunday, she drove back to the Wolfes' farm. As she turned on to the track she marvelled at the landscape's transformation. Bare and frosty on her last visit, it was now a green oasis. The trees were coming into leaf. The larches were unfurling and the leaves of limes hung like delicate medallions. The hedgerows were foaming white seas of blackthorn flowers and the banks were covered with cow parsley and wild strawberries. Through the thicket of hedge and trunk, carpets of bluebells were beginning to open, interspersed with the bell-shaped flowers of snake's-head fritillaries. The track ended and the valley opened: four huge horse chestnuts were in full bloom, with great white candles of flowers standing proud at the end of every branch. The fields were scattered with daisies and dandelions creating swathes of white and yellow amidst the green pasture. Ayesha was so overcome by the beauty of the place that she stopped the car, rolled down the window and drank in the smells. It was the first time she admitted that there might be another place as romantic as her beloved Trelawney.

This time, Ayesha left Stella at home with her nanny. Though she still couldn't admit to MySpying, she hoped Blaze and Joshua would

240

be able to help her interpret some of the more arcane information neatly filed in boxes in the boot of her car. To date, there'd been frustratingly little; Sleet, with Rodita's help, had navigated a careful, untraceable course.

Joshua and Blaze led her to the barn where tea, cake and biscuits were laid out. Blaze insisted Ayesha ate something before they started.

'You've learned how to bake,' Ayesha said, biting into the delicious walnut and coffee sponge.

'I made it!' Joshua laughed.

'I still can't cook,' Blaze admitted.

Joshua put his arm around his wife. 'It's a relief to be better at one thing.'

'One thing?' Ayesha said with mock incredulity.

'How are things at home?' Blaze asked.

Ayesha hesitated. 'You heard about his obsession with an Albanian?' She couldn't bear to mention Zamora by name.

Blaze looked sympathetically at Ayesha. 'I'm sorry – it must be painful.'

'And humiliating. Everyone who works for us, all our social set know that he's about to leave me for her. Sometimes I get piteous looks but mostly I am seen as the discarded wife and no use to anyone. I don't go out any more.'

Ayesha hesitated, knowing that the next piece of information would horrify Blaze. 'He's going to stand as a UKIP candidate in the next election, representing Austell.'

Blaze jumped back as if scalded. 'How dare he! Politics is serious. It's about people and principles.'

'He'll hate the red tape,' Joshua said, trying to soothe his wife.

'He doesn't have any morals – we know that – nor does he care about Cornwall or its inhabitants. He spends more time in London now, when he isn't ...' Ayesha tried to swallow away a lump in her throat. She knew from tracking his flight plan where he was and had a fairly solid guess at why. Wiping the last crumbs of cake from her mouth, she said, 'My hunch is that Medieval Illusions is more likely to get planning if the application is backed by the local MP. Sleet expects to stand, win, get the proposal through and then he'll probably resign.'

'The cynical son of a bitch,' Joshua said. 'Isn't he American?'

'He has dual nationality.'

'He can't just rock up on polling day and expect to win,' Blaze said.

'You remember I mentioned Tahira Khan from Alabaster Analytics? She's running his campaign and has persuaded him it's a dead cert. They're aggressively targeting the undecided; those who've yet to work out who they support. She says they need a 9 per cent swing to win.'

Blaze paced up and down the barn. 'Aren't there rules about what you can spend on elections? It's a small amount and highly regulated. One helicopter trip to Cornwall would blow his budget.'

'We can demand an audit when it's over.' Ayesha had done her research.

'That will be too late. Those things take months, sometimes years,' Joshua said.

The three of them stood despondently, staring into their cups of tea. Nearby a murder of magpies chattered noisily.

'We mustn't lose hope,' Joshua said. 'He will make a mistake.'

'Rodita's successor is unlikely to be as careful or clever.' Blaze tried to sound reassuring.

'Maybe his mistress will be his undoing. Obsessions make men careless.' Joshua pulled a large piece of paper into the centre of the table. 'Did either of you hear about the Albanian Ponzi scandals in the nineties?'

Blaze and Ayesha looked at him blankly.

'There were eight or nine pyramid schemes. At one point these involved two thirds of all inhabitants and half of the country's GDP. Many lost everything. There was nothing they or their government could do. Inflation went up by 28 per cent and the Albanian currency collapsed. At least two thousand people were killed in riots. Government buildings were set on fire. Schools were closed for three years.' Joshua had written down the names of the different schemes and traced the losses.

'I don't understand the connection,' Ayesha said. 'Zamora was only a young girl at the time.'

Joshua nodded but continued. 'There are similarities between some cryptocurrencies and pyramid schemes. Both are unregulated and promise get-rich-quick fixes. Both systems take newly invested money to pay the interest to the earlier investors.'

'Can we prove a connection between Zamora and the pyramid schemes?' Blaze asked.

Joshua shook his head. 'Not yet, but it's a strange coincidence.'

Something pricked the back of Ayesha's mind. Something she'd read. 'Was one of the schemes connected with a family named Copje?' she asked.

Joshua snorted. 'Scratch a rotten deal and you'll find that family.' He'd heard about Nanos and his people.

Ayesha took some paperwork from one of her boxes. 'I traced Zamora back to a village called Seranda. The Copjes are another local family.' She flicked over the page. 'There's a report of Nanos marrying a local girl called Dita Lala.' She showed them the smudgy picture of Dita being crowned as Miss Seranda.

'Wow, is that the same person?' Blaze asked.

Ayesha nodded.

'This was in 1998?' Joshua pointed out. The original text was in Albanian but, using Google Translate, Ayesha had transcribed the passages.

'The same girl appears in the capital, Tirana, a few years later and then at different universities. She was only thirteen when they got married.'

'So it's official, she is his wife,' Blaze said.

'Married to a gangster?' Joshua leaned on the back of his chair, not sure whether to laugh or feel very frightened for his wife's half-sister.

'It's hard to check records in Albania; little is digitised,' Ayesha continued. 'After trawling a lot of websites, I found this. It's taken from Cannes *Yachting News*.' She passed a photocopy over the table. Blaze and Joshua looked at it closely. It showed a picture of a man in sunglasses and a woman with cropped hair holding hands on the back of a boat. The name of the vessel was clear: *La Zamora*.

'Does Sleet know any of this?'

'I don't think so,' Ayesha said. 'He's dumbstruck with admiration for her.' Her voice cracked. 'She's beautiful and successful.' She hesitated. 'And she looks more like Anastasia than I do.'

Blaze put her hand on Ayesha's arm. 'Sleet's the ultimate capitalist, always trying to upgrade. Nothing's ever enough. It must be bigger, better, shinier, newer.' She looked at the younger woman. 'He was obsessed by your mother. Everyone was. Anastasia didn't give him time to get over it, she was off to the next one; so, for Sleet, she's the one that got away, and that's given her mythical but entirely unearned powers.'

'I wish I'd known her then,' Ayesha said, thinking of the mother she knew, so twisted by resentment that her beauty was mired by bitterness at the way her life had turned out. Taking a breath, she asked, 'Was she as attractive as everyone says?'

'Yes, probably. But remember, beauty is only a canvas on which to project our fantasies. A landscape for our dreams. We were so dazzled by her looks that we never thought about who your mother was or what she wanted.'

Ayesha smiled at her half-sister gratefully.

Joshua watched the rapprochement between the two women with relief but was still concerned about the Albanians. 'We need to be extremely careful. These guys don't value life, particularly if it's a life which gets between them and profit.'

Ayesha nodded. She didn't tell them about the note in her bag.

For the rest of the afternoon, they worked their way methodically through Ayesha's files. Listening to Blaze and Joshua talk about investing and the markets, Ayesha understood that it was possible to create wealth, build businesses and contribute to an economy in a sustainable and inclusive way. Finance was the engine that powered every aspect of people's lives. It was the blood that kept the body of the country working. The bricks for the future. For a few like Sleet, it was just an opportunity for personal gain; he didn't care about negative consequences.

To be more efficient, they decided to split their roles into three areas. Joshua would concentrate on the Taiwanese angle, interview the previous CEO of TLG and see what he could find out about the business. Blaze would see if there were any loopholes in the sales contract with Medieval Illusions. Both were loath to give Ayesha too much to do: the younger woman looked so fragile. Her hands shook; there was a permanent tic in her right eye; the skin on her face was sallow and sank into her cheekbones; her clothes, now several sizes too big, hung like weeds off her shoulders and hips.

The light was fading and Ayesha wanted to get back to Cornwall to put Stella to bed. Blaze waved at the taillights of the departing car. 'She is completely out of her depth,' she said to Joshua as they walked back into the house.

By the time Ayesha arrived home, it was dark. She was surprised to see two large delivery lorries parked at the front of the castle and workmen running in and out. Entering the hall, she saw that it had been dressed to resemble a huge fairy grotto. Hundreds of thousands of tiny fairy lights twinkled in a bed of tulle and velvet. Open-mouthed, she went into the next room to find it transformed into a magical arbour with a velvet dais and fronds of material studded with sequins. At first, she thought that Tony and Barty were having an elaborate joke. In the Great Hall she saw James, the estate manager, and asked what was happening.

'A party, My Lady. For Miss Stella.' He jerked his head towards a far door. 'Sir Thomlinson's back. He's in his office.'

Ayesha ran along the corridor and found her husband with three colleagues. 'Can I see you alone?' she asked.

'Hello, dear wife,' Sleet said with an exaggerated smile. He stood up and held out his arms. Ayesha was confused by this rare display of emotion. She could not bring herself to touch him and stood back while his associates gathered their papers and made for the door.

'Sorry, guys, but you know that her ladyship never wants to see me solo, so I have to make the most of any opportunity,' Sleet called after them. Then he sat down in his chair, leaned back and linked his hands behind his head. 'What do you want?'

'What's this about a party?' The sound of men's voices and clanking poles was audible.

'I'm throwing my beloved daughter a birthday she'll never forget.' He beamed from ear to ear.

'Her birthday is in September.'

'Is it?' Sleet shrugged. 'She can be like the Queen and have two dates.'

'Who've you invited?' Ayesha asked.

'No one yet. Spur-of-the-moment decision. We'll ask her whole class.' Sleet waved his arms. 'The whole year.'

Ayesha leaned against the wall. Nothing was making sense. 'She doesn't go to school. She's at nursery, two days a week, with two other children. She's only four.'

'What does she do all day?' Sleet asked.

'She hangs out with me or, if I'm busy, with Jan the nanny. We go riding, paint pictures, bake. Normal stuff.'

Sleet looked surprised. 'I thought you were always in London.'

'I go to London once a fortnight. This is my home.' It was only then that Ayesha saw the cut on his face. 'What happened?'

'An altercation with a table leg.'

She came round in front of the desk. 'Why are you giving this party? Why now?'

'I want the world to see what a perfect father I am.'

Ayesha snorted derisively. 'Recording a "happy moment" is not fatherhood. Being a parent is about wiping away tears, picking up toys, spending hours doing the same puzzle, teaching them how to read.'

Sleet looked at her, a slow smile creeping across his face. 'When we met I found your naivety so cute.'

Ayesha wondered what he meant. Brushing the comment aside, she asked, 'So where will you find children?'

'We'll find some local brats. I'll get Donna to talk to the village. It'll look even better. "Devoted father throws party for daughter and impoverished kids."' He waved his right hand in the air. 'The press are coming.'

A dark shadow flitted across her heart. Ayesha bent over the desk, putting her face close to his. 'Why?'

He leaned forward and scrutinised her. 'You've lost your looks – you're skin and bone.'

Lost for an answer she walked out of the room with as much dignity as she could muster but once outside, leaned against the wall for stability. Something about her husband's behaviour wasn't making sense: in normal circumstances he did everything possible to avoid the press. Sleet had no interest in children. He'd outsourced the care of his elder four and hardly saw them. He couldn't, wouldn't have changed his views on parenthood. Could he? Her heart started to beat fast and her body shook.

Waiting until he went downstairs to dinner, Ayesha let herself into his office and opened the desk drawers. One was full of folders. In the first she saw lists of codes and numbers, almost certainly relating to Sleet's bank accounts and took a photograph of each page on her phone. One day these could be useful. The next file had 'Stella' emblazoned across the front. It was heavy and full of photographs. Ayesha put it on the desk and started to flick through the contents. There were scores of images of Sleet with Stella – some moments she recognised, like the helicopter ride or snaps taken at Clarissa's wedding. There were others she didn't recognise at all, of Sleet and Stella cooking, riding, painting.

The contents of the next folder overrode all other thoughts. It contained many pictures of herself. She recognised all as innocent moments but the angles made them appear compromising. In one it appeared that Yasmin and she were kissing. In another she and a group of students sat in a bar. She hadn't drunk a thing but was carrying a round bought for her friends. The clock on the wall said 4 p.m. The inference was clear: one of them was the better parent and that person wasn't her.

She wondered whether to take and destroy the folders but knew that there'd be copies. Perhaps her most powerful card was that Sleet didn't suspect subterfuge: to him she was still naive, silly little Ayesha. Declan rampaged through every cell in her body, gyrating around her veins. Trembling from head to foot, she had to chase the demons away.

A workman saw the young woman leave the castle and run across the park. 'What nutter takes exercise at this time of night?' he asked his mate.

Two hours later, when the runner hadn't reappeared, a search party was organised. Ayesha was found unconscious at the foot of Guto's Gulley. An ambulance was called. The diagnosis was exhaustion and malnutrition. She woke the following morning on a drip in the local hospital. Stella's party went ahead without her. Sleet stayed long enough for the photo opportunity. Stella, missing her mother and not knowing any of the other children, ran and hid in her room and refused to come out.

17

May 2017

For the last 200 of their 800-year history, the Trelawney family hadn't won prizes except at their own garden fete. So it was with amazement and great pride that the present generation learned that their own Tuffy Scott had won the Charleson Award for a lifetime achievement in science. Only a handful of women had ever been recognised: the first was Marie Curie in 1903. Winners had to have made a significant sustained impact in their chosen field, published at least thirty papers and be at the helm of an authorised laboratory or institute. In the past, Tuffy had turned down other awards, seeing them as a distraction or about the donor over the recipient, but she relented on the Charleson because the prize money, £10 million, would future-proof her research faculty and students for the next five years. She stipulated that the ceremony would take place in London or Oxford without press, a celebratory dinner or any 'of that guff'.

All the Trelawneys were asked.

'Frightful relief to be known for something which isn't embarrassing,' Tony said to his great-niece, Arabella, on the telephone. 'Finally we're in the papers for something commendable.'

'She doesn't want press,' Arabella reminded him.

'I might have to ring that fellow at the *Daily Snail*,' Tony said. He used to supplement his income by planting the odd society story.

'She'll hate it,' Arabella said.

'She won't read it.' Tony loved leaking the odd story; he didn't do it for money anymore, but liked being in the 'know'. 'Darling, I meant to ask. What is a hexapod?' Tony said, reading the invitation to Tuffy's lecture. 'The Effect of Climate Change on Hexapod Invertebrates' had made the link between the rise in temperatures and the loss of 24 per cent of the world's insects species.

'Anything with six legs.'

'Don't spiders have eight legs?' Tony said, feeling frightfully clever.

In the back of a black cab, barrelling their way towards Tuffy's ceremony at the Guildhall, were the stars of *The Three Old Gits*: Clarissa, Barty and Princess Amelia. Since its first airing in March, the series had been a ratings and tabloid sensation. THE ANTIDOTE WE'VE ALL BEEN WAITING FOR was the banner headline in the *Sun*. PURE PLEASURE echoed the *Mail*. More than seven million viewers tuned in each week; Clarissa was, once again, a national heroine. The trio's words and gestures were right now being captured by documentary film-maker Damian Dobbs who was crouched on the floor with his small camera.

Barty wriggled uncomfortably. To celebrate scientific pioneers, he was dressed as an eighteenth-century explorer in a white suit several sizes too small, a pith helmet and brown lace-up shoes. He could hardly breathe and tried to fan himself with a butterfly net. 'It's rather marvellous of Tuffy. I have never won anything. Not even an egg and spoon race,' he said.

'I'm always on the winning side.' Clarissa smoothed out an imaginary wrinkle on her Chanel suit skirt. Thanks to her figure and notoriety, she didn't have to recycle old clothes – fashion designers and couturiers sent her new ones.

'Name one success!' Barty challenged.

Clarissa detested her co-presenter's newfound confidence. She preferred the old, highly obsequious Barty. The uppity little man was beginning to get on her nerves. 'The best flower arrangement at the Trelawney fete fifty-seven years in a row,' she said.

'Not impressive! They must give it to you. *Droit de seigneur* and all that,' Barty countered.

'The gardener grew the flowers and made the arrangements! He should have got it,' Princess Amelia pointed out. 'One so misses having a gardener,' she added.

'I commissioned the displays. I paid his wages. He was my gardener.' For Clarissa, staff were extensions of herself. She trained, paid and suffered them. Without her, they wouldn't exist.

'Poppycock and piffle,' Barty said. 'If that was the case, all Renaissance paintings would be signed Medici and Sforza not Raphael and Leonardo.'

'You can't compare *The Last Supper* with my roses,' Clarissa snapped. She turned to Princess Amelia. 'When did you win anything?'

Amelia thought long and hard but, in the process, forgot the question.

'I do hate London,' Clarissa observed as the taxi sped through the City.

'I used to think the streets were paved with gold and diamonds,' Barty said, remembering his arrival in the capital sixty years earlier.

'Where did you go to school, Bartholomew?' Clarissa asked.

'I forget,' Barty said quickly. The last thing he wanted was anyone prying into his past.

Seeing a flicker of insecurity race across his face, Clarissa kept going. 'Bet it was an MPSIA.'

'What does that mean?' Amelia asked.

'Minor public school, I'm afraid,' Clarissa said.

Barty wriggled in his seat. All he had to do was repeat the name of a private school, but he was so hot and uncomfortable that he couldn't remember one.

'We're waiting, Bartholomey.' A sixth sense told Clarissa that the man was hiding something. He'd become much too big for his boots since joining the Old Gits and his public approval ratings, while not as high as hers, were climbing. She couldn't stand any competition.

Barty felt his lip wobble as he tried to keep a lid on his emotions.

'Spit it out,' Clarissa taunted.

Barty burst into tears. Tiny rivulets of black mascara mixed with rouge and orange eyeshadow then meandered through white foundation and dripped on to white lapels. Damian could hardly believe his luck.

'So attention-seeking!' Clarissa said, convinced that Barty was trying to upstage her.

'I'm not who you think I am,' Barty sobbed.

'Who the devil are you, then?' Princess Amelia leaned over Clarissa and took a closer look at her co-presenter.

After sixty years, Barty was no longer able to maintain the pretence. 'I am not Barthomley Chesterfield Fitzroy St George.'

'You look awfully like him,' Princess Amelia said.

Between sobs, Barty explained. 'I was born in Stoke on March 14th, 1946. My parents were Ethel and Barry Dunn. I was the third of seven children; they christened me Reg.'

'God, how ghastly.' Clarissa rolled her eyes. 'Ethel, Barry and Reg!'

'I know!' Barty wiped his face with a silk cravat. 'I was born mortified.'

Clarissa tried to move further away from him but there was little space on the back seat.

'There was no future for "queers" in Stoke.'

'Where is Stoke?' Clarissa asked.

'North of Watford,' Amelia said. 'I stood in for Lilibet once and opened a porcelain factory. They were frightfully disappointed it was me.' She remembered the occasions when the appearance of a minor royal meant major dissatisfaction.

Barty, hiccuping through his tears, continued. 'So I left. Hitch-hiked to London. Shed my old persona like an unwanted skin.'

'Build a bridge and get over yourself,' Clarissa whispered.

'I don't understand,' Amelia said. She took out her hearing aid and gave it a good shake.

'I met a person who recommended the gentlemen's lavatories in Piccadilly station.'

'If only you'd taken the train to oblivion.' Clarissa crossed her arms and looked out of the window.

'My first night I was picked up by a Tory minister who took me to "the house". From there I graduated to the stately homes. It didn't take very long.'

'This is prime-time television. Be careful, please,' Damian Dobbs said.

'We should cut this whole section,' Clarissa said. Turning to Barty she hissed, 'Put down the shovel and step away from the hole. You'll regret this.'

Barty ignored her. 'The ladies loved me – I was fun and naughty and safe. Whether you were stuck in a shooting butt on a Scottish moor, on a royal train in Rajasthan, or at a dowager duchess's tea party, I made things amusing. Soon I became known as "darling Barty" – society's fixtures and fittings were planned around my availability.'

'I never planned anything around you,' Clarissa said.

'You've always been a prize bitch, Clarissa.' Barty started to cry again. 'A total absolute 100 per cent bitch.'

'I must admit I agree,' Amelia said. 'I could never stand you, Clarissa. Class is not all about breeding; it's as much to do with behaviour. You might have the title of Countess but you have the demeanour of a peasant.'

'If I'm invited to your funeral,' Barty added, 'I'll accept only because you won't be there.'

Clarissa's mouth opened and closed. She couldn't believe what she was hearing. Recruiting Barty and Amelia had been a terrible mistake.

'You're fired,' she said to them both. 'From now on, it's One Old Git. Me. Stop the cab. Now!' Clarissa knocked hard on the glass partition. 'Stop here, my good man.'

'Where are you going?' Damian asked.

'None of your business.'

Clarissa got out of the taxi. 'None of you are invited to my sister-in-law's prize-giving any more. Including you, Dobbs.' Without bothering to shut the door, she walked down the street and into an alley. She had no idea where she was. All the roads were dirty and looked the same. Holding her handbag close to her side, she marched purposefully and kept her back straight in case Dobbs was still filming. Only when out of sight did she allow herself a little cry, the first for seventy years since Daddy had been declared missing in action.

'Rally, Clarissa, rally,' she told herself. 'Don't let the hoi polloi win. Remember, you are one of the Big People. You have a duty of care and obligation to lead the population.' Taking a small compact out of her bag, she checked her make-up. It was still perfect. Then she walked on and, seeing a black cab, stuck out her hand. The cabbie jumped out to help her in and then asked for her autograph. He'd had George and Amal in the back last week – they'd all been talking about her. Clarissa had no idea who the Clooneys were but felt somewhat better. Her dignity was nearly restored.

*

The next group of Trelawneys to make their way to the Guildhall were the Cornish contingent. Observers saw a strange-looking bunch all on foot. A father and son, dressed in cargo pants, sweatshirts and sou'westers, were carrying camping equipment – a tent, stove, kettle and two sleeping bags (they were preparing to sit in at St Paul's for a week of active disruption). There was an elegant woman in shorts and gold sandals with straps that wrapped around her legs from the ankle to the knee. Holding her hand was a middle-aged woman in an A-line dress and lace-up shoes. As they walked towards the great building, Jane looked at their shadows reflected on the pavement. Kitto and Toby made amorphous shapes – part one-man band, part ectoplasm. Morawase was like a blade of grass: thin, elegant and moving sinuously. Since returning from Italy, the three of them had been sharing the former marital home, Garroway Cottage. The arrangement, though unconventional, suited them. Jane and Morawase treated Kitto like their young adult child, the only role he was suited for.

Kitto adored Morawase. 'My wife has upgraded,' he was fond of telling people. 'She's found someone so much better than me.'

Rounding the corner was the Wolfe family. 'Jane, Morawase!' Blaze called out. She wore a claret velvet suit and white silk shirt. Her hair hung loosely around her face. Joshua, never at ease with a group of Trelawneys, stood to one side while Perrin let herself be hugged.

'Isn't this fantastic?' Blaze enthused. 'Finally something to celebrate.'

'There was Arabella's degree,' Jane said, remembering the proudest moment of her life.

'Of course,' Blaze said. 'I meant one where we were all present.'

'The last time was Perrin's christening. That was special.' Kitto laughed. 'The first time we met Joshua.' Turning to his brother-in-law, he reverted to the old English tradition of clapping the man hard on the shoulder. Joshua smiled with as much enthusiasm he could muster; his wife's family were to be endured.

'I hear Tuffy's refusing to change from her corduroy suit,' Blaze said.

'Come on, Mummy!' Perrin pulled at her mother's hand. She'd been promised the place they were going to was something like Hogwarts, the school from her favourite book. Her friendship with Stella, who she now saw regularly, was transforming Perrin into a confident little girl. 'So let's go!' she insisted.

'She reminds me of the younger Blaze,' Kitto said, looking at his niece.

The motley crew walked along the side streets, chatting amiably: Kitto and Toby telling Joshua about their plans to disrupt London; Jane, Blaze and Morawase discussing the forthcoming election.

'The thought of Sleet winning is unbearable,' Jane said. 'You can't move in Cornwall without seeing his ugly mug. His posters are everywhere.'

'Worse are his slogans,' Morawase butted in. '"Take back control". "Make Cornwall great again". "Drain the Westminster swamp". He's stolen the Trump campaign and transported it to the West Country.'

'Don't people see through it?' Blaze asked. The following day Joshua was flying to Taiwan to meet the former CEO of TLG. They must do everything, anything, to stop the Vulgarian.

'Aunty Blaze,' Toby interrupted. 'Are you still doing that green stuff?'

Blaze noticed he smelt slightly – not unpleasant but a whiff of grass mixed with unwashed hair. She wondered if her nephew would ever reach emotional maturity. 'My VC invests in clean energy and environmentally friendly supplies.'

'Cool,' Toby said. 'Would it like to support our new movement? It's called Rise Up. It's going to save the planet. Dad and I are members.'

'I am very pleased someone is going to,' Blaze said, wondering if her nephew and brother were the right people for the job.

'We're going to disrupt everything, everyone, everywhere, to bring attention to what's going on.' His voice, full of passion and commitment, rose in tone.

'Sounds a bit like anarchy?' Blaze said.

'Exactly! We want to put power back in the hands of the people.'

Kitto had caught up with his son. 'The human race is completely unprepared for what's happening: floods, wildfire, extremes of weather, breakdown of society.'

'Crop failure,' Toby added.

'Conventional approaches and politics have failed utterly because those in power are compromised by economic self-interest.'

'The fat cats are fucking us.'

'What are the cats doing?' Perrin asked.

'They are ducking,' Joshua said quickly.

'Why would cats duck?' Perrin was perplexed. Her question was drowned out by Kitto.

'The time for denial is over, the time to act is now!' He punched the air.

'But why protest and disrupt? Won't that lose you millions of supporters? Ordinary people whose lives will be turned upside down?' Blaze asked.

'We don't care about the masses,' Toby said.

'Then who are you doing this for?'

'The cats?' Perrin asked.

Their attention was distracted by the sight of Arabella and Tony on the other side of the road. Tony was beautifully dressed in an elegant 1940s tweed suit. Poking out of his breast pocket was a splash of emerald-green handkerchief. Seen from afar, Blaze realised how old he'd become, walking slowly with one arm on Arabella's, the other on a silver-topped cane. She felt a sudden deep pang – the thought of life without her beloved uncle, the man who'd brought so much light and humour into all their lives.

'Tony, Arabella,' she called out. Tony stopped and very slowly turned to look for her. Blaze ran across the road to give him a hug. She bent down and saw a thin film obscuring his merry blue irises, something she'd never noticed before. When she put her arm around his back, his bones, obscured by the material of his suit, were the first thing she felt.

*

Ayesha was determined not to miss the event. Since her discharge from hospital she had hardly left the castle and wouldn't let Stella out of her sight. The fear of losing her daughter was overwhelming. Memories flooded back. She remembered the first foetal flutter, like a butterfly trapped in her stomach. Then the hearty punch and kick. The mewling of a newborn. The greedy suckle. The smell of her baby's head. A tiny hand wrapped fiercely around her finger. The red-faced fury. The sleeping smile. The dimpled legs. The triumphant first crawl. Words emerging from babble. The wobbly walk. The belly laugh. An almost inconsolable nightmare. The grazed knee. The tantrum. Painting a pony. Her first ice cream. Together, these tiny moments unfurling made a necklace of memories that had become Ayesha's most treasured possession. And for all this time, four years of Stella's life, she'd thought she was protecting her daughter; but now that she faced losing her, she thought it might be the other way around. Stella was her guide star, had shown her how to love and what mattered. Without her, what was the point?

All daily tasks were exhausting. She forced herself to eat, to wash her hair and get dressed, but most of the time felt that she was dragging her body and spirits through an almost unbearably heavy fog. The Charleson prize represented a faint light breaking through the gloom: in case anything happened to her, in case she lost custody, she wanted Stella to meet her extended family, to know where she came from and that there was an alternative life.

Strapping her daughter into her car seat, Ayesha set off. On the drive, she hardly noticed the landscape change, keeping her eyes fixed ahead on the dark grey river of the road. Lorries the size of ocean liners whooshed past, sucking her sports car into their wake. Ayesha concentrated on the white stripes in the middle of the road, trying to count them as they passed. After 700 or 800 she lost the thread and started again. Numbers kept the desolation at bay. She had not, since arriving in England nine years ago, intent on finding her real father, felt so absent of hope. Everything she'd worked so hard to achieve hung in the balance; she had no idea what to do next or how to live. She'd been reduced to petty thievery, had bet her ill-gotten gains and lost. Like blotting paper in water, her being was dissolving.

The family had reserved seats in the front two rows of the Guildhall. The building was already full of students, fellow academics and members of the public, about two thousand in total.

'She knows an awful lot of people,' Jane said, astonished by the turnout.

'Hard to find a more badly dressed bunch.' Tony looked around at the fellow guests.

'Academics don't care about clothes,' Arabella said defensively. 'They have other things to worry about.'

'I was thinking more about personal hygiene,' Tony countered. 'Is growing mould under the armpits an experiment?'

'Where's the party food?' Perrin asked.

'Grown-ups don't have jelly and cake,' Joshua told her.

'Then I don't ever want to get older.' Perrin's lip wobbled.

'Eat as much as you can now; being an adult is defined by trying to avoid cake.' Tony fished in his pocket and found a small bar of fruit and nut chocolate which he passed surreptitiously to his great-niece.

'I have a reserved seat.' Clarissa's unmistakable voice rang out from the entrance. The Guildhall was long and the floor was tiled. Clarissa's heart contracted – what if she slipped and fell? She imagined being stuck in bed while Barty hogged the limelight.

'Watch out! Here comes the real star of the show,' Tony said. 'Don't put her near me.'

'Tobias!' Clarissa spotted her grandson at the front. 'Come here. Now.'

Toby made his way towards the main door.

'Hurry up, I might grow old,' she hissed.

'Wait till she smells Toby,' Jane said to Blaze. 'He hasn't washed his clothes for a long time.'

They watched Toby hold out a rather grubby arm to his grandmother. She took it and they walked on for a few paces before her nose began to twitch suspiciously. She looked around and then, turning her face towards her grandson, let out a little scream.

'You smell like a compost heap. Go away.' She took a handkerchief from her pocket and covered her nose.

Toby sniffed his armpits. 'They are a bit whiffy but if I keep my elbows by my side?' he suggested.

'I will walk alone.' Clarissa, back straight and eyes fixed ahead, made her way towards the stage.

Perrin caught sight of Ayesha and her daughter. 'Stella, Stella, here!' she called out, waving to her cousin. Stella, cooped up in a car for nearly four hours, let go of her mother's hand and charged down the centre aisle. She was wearing red tights, a white dress, and her curls bounced around her face. Behind her, walking very slowly, came Ayesha. She wore a grey silk dress and looked as pale and slight as a wisp of smoke. Her lips were the same tone as her skin, her hair was pulled back in a tight bun and the only splash of colour were the dark rims under her eyes. Blaze stood up and ushered her half-sister into a chair next to her. Ayesha smiled wanly as if the display of any more emotion would have finished her. The two little girls, Stella and Perrin, shared a seat and whispered to each other.

There was a sudden silence as the lights onstage were turned up. The Vice Chancellor of Oxford appeared on the platform and started to give a long and effusive eulogy about Tuffy, detailing her life's work, her awards, papers and research. She was abruptly cut off by the prize recipient herself who stormed out from the wings.

'Thanks, but no one's interested in all that stuff,' Tuffy said gruffly. 'And I can't wait for this thing to be over. Work to do.'

'She could have brushed her eyebrows,' Clarissa said in a stage whisper. Tuffy's were naturally bushy but this evening they seemed particularly hirsute and each time she spoke they moved independently of her face, like two large animated caterpillars.

Tuffy cleared her throat. 'Every person in this room is a murderer.' She looked around and her eyes fixed on her family. 'We are slowly but surely, bit by bit, destroying our planet with our eyes open. Some of you recycle your rubbish, perhaps you even drive an electric car, maybe you've given up red meat, but it's not enough. The climate crisis is serious, it is urgent, and it is growing.'

'What are those bushy things on her eyes?' Perrin asked.

'In the last four years, 70 per cent of all North American moose have been killed by winter tick infection. Rising sea levels threaten our coastlines. Pollinators like bees are decimated by insecticides and loss of natural habitats. Human lives depend on functioning ecosystems. Insect collapse will lead to ecological disaster.' Tuffy strode to the front of the stage. Her voice rose. 'Bird populations dependent on bugs for food have fallen by between 15 per cent and 28 per cent in the last twenty years. The number of butterflies in the Netherlands has fallen by 84 per cent in the last 130 years.' Tuffy shouted her frustration at the audience.

Perrin burst into tears. 'I never killed a butterfly.'

'She didn't mean that,' Blaze comforted her daughter.

But before Tuffy could continue there was a commotion at the back of the hall, followed by loud footsteps. The audience turned to look. Up the centre of the main aisle strode Sleet with a film crew in his wake. He clapped his hands above his head. 'Well put, well put!' He ran around the side of the stage and up on to the dais. 'Good afternoon, everybody.'

'Who the hell are you?' Tuffy asked.

'Someone call security!' Clarissa shouted. 'There's a vulgarian in our midst.'

'Dear Aunt Taffy,' Sleet said, turning to the cameras. He tried to plant a kiss on her cheek but Tuffy sidestepped his move.

Sleet, unperturbed by the slight, turned back to his film crew. 'I am pleased to be taking a short break from electioneering in Cornwall to highlight the importance of the environment, a key subject in my campaign.'

'Tell that to his helicopter, yacht and ninety-nine vintage gas-guzzling cars,' Toby huffed.

If Sleet heard, he ignored the heckle. 'We are the UK Independence Party and we care about climate change.'

At the mention of UKIP, boos went up in the audience.

'Who are you?' Tuffy asked again.

'Congratulations on your prize, Aunt Taffy.'

'She's called *Tuffy*!' Toby yelled.

'I stand shoulder to shoulder with my people,' Sleet said, sidling up to Tuffy and beckoning to his press team. There was an explosion of flashes as he sneaked a quick embrace. Picture taken, he strode off the stage. Tuffy, for the first time in her professional life, lost the power of speech. She looked around the room and then exited. Arabella ran backstage to find her aunt. The Vice Chancellor reappeared to try and quell the crowd but, seeing it was a hopeless mission, disappeared again. Only Tony seemed genuinely delighted. 'That was fun! Much more fun than a rant about woodlice and sexy pod things.'

Ayesha, mortified by Sleet's behaviour, decided to slip outside to get some air. As she climbed to her feet, the room went out of focus, and she slumped to the floor. She heard something crack and then felt shooting pains in her head. Regaining consciousness, she thought she might be at the bottom of a swimming pool. The surface was ripply; she could see vague outlines of faces and disembodied voices were all melting into one amorphous sound.

'Can you hear me, miss?' someone asked, shining a torch into her eye. She tried to reply but her tongue wouldn't move. 'Does anyone know this woman?' the same person called out. Ayesha was aware of footsteps and murmuring.

'Yes, I do,' Kitto said.

'How do you know her, sir?'

260

'She's my sister. I am her next of kin.'

Ayesha wondered if she was dreaming. Kitto was acknowledging her.

'No, she's not!' Clarissa's voice rang out. 'We have never seen her before.'

'Shut up, Mum,' Blaze said.

Ayesha squinted into the light to see Blaze and Kitto's anxious faces. Blaze gently stroked her forehead.

'Your fall sounded like a pistol shot,' Kitto said. 'You'll have one hell of a bump.' Putting his hand behind her back he helped her sit up.

'She might have concussion. She should go to hospital,' someone suggested.

'Thank you,' Blaze said. 'You don't have to worry – we'll look after her.'

Hearing these words, ones she'd longed for her whole life, Ayesha started to cry.

'Are you in pain?' Kitto said, his voice soaked with anxiety.

Ayesha wanted to shake her head but it hurt too much to move.

'She must have concussion,' Toby said, leaning in. Ayesha's head ached but she was smiling.

Clarissa looked. 'She's gone squiffy.'

'Shut up!' three Trelawneys said in unison.

*

Sleet, pleased with his intervention at the prize-giving, sat in the back of his car heading for Northolt where his jet would take him to Paris to meet Zamora. Since the debacle of Bhutan/Budva, he hadn't seen her and was determined not to lose any time in securing their engagement.

Felix sat in the front seat and, together, he and Sleet were going through the last-minute canvassing. The polls were not looking positive but Tahira assured him that Alabaster Analytics had done their job – the persuadables were for turning and, in a little over a month's time, victory was his.

'I want leaflets distributed to every single person in the county. Why not give everyone who votes for me a hundred pounds cash? That would get them out.'

Felix shifted in his seat. 'As I explained, sir, there's a cap on spending of eight thousand and seven hundred pounds – or nine pence per registered parliamentary elector.'

'Ridiculous. Why would they do that?'

'To make it a fair and level playing field.'

'But life isn't like that!'

Felix squirmed. To date, the electoral offences committed by his employer included undue influence, bribery and false statements. People were talking. There had been complaints from rival candidates. Felix had been placed in the uncomfortable position of explaining that use of personal means of transport, including a private plane and helicopter, was exempt. He tried another tack. 'It would be disappointing to win the seat and then be disqualified for flouting the rules.'

Sleet stabbed his finger at his chief of staff. 'You're wrong. Not winning would be catastrophic. Losers are condemned to the dustbin of history. Who remembers the runners-up in the hundred-metre Olympic final? Or at Wimbledon? Who cares about the person who just missed the contract? Or the second son who didn't inherit? Coming first is the only thing that matters.' He slapped his hand on his thigh. 'Spend more money. OK?'

Felix nodded. Instead of trying to bribe minor officials, he decided to make a sizeable donation to the local old people's home – that was putting money into constituents' hands.

Sleet turned up the radio. There was no good news, least of all for the government. Two terrorist attacks in quick succession – one in Manchester, the other at London Bridge – reflected badly on the Tories' claim to be the party of law and order. Meanwhile Jeremy Corbyn was alienating traditional Labour voters. A safe seat, Sleet thought, I am going to decimate the opposition.

'What people need is some light relief. Find me six cows,' he told Felix.

'A herd?' Felix asked.

'I don't know how many cows make a herd but get me more than Boris.'

'Boris has cows?' Felix tried to imagine a Johnson farmyard in Islington.

'Boris got headlines for auctioneering a dairy cow during the Leave campaign. He called it a "beautiful milker".'

Felix vaguely remembered the stunt.

'Life is a numbers game, Felix. Get me lots of cows.'

Felix smiled wanly. 'Certainly, sir.'

Sleet was feeling confident. Polls showed that Tory support was 'dropping off a cliff'. 'Let's go through arrangements for my engagement party.'

'We have thirty food stations serving dishes from every corner of the earth. Tom Jones is the warm-up act for Beyoncé who'll come on at midnight. We will have continuous replay of your victory speech on all the monitors.' Felix was enjoying organising this party; there was no budget and minimal interference.

Sleet stretched his legs and, opening the car's mini-fridge, took out an ice-cold Coke Zero. 'Tell me who else has accepted?' The guest list and yeses had hardly changed in three weeks but going through the names gave him a kick. If only his loser parents could see him now. It was tempting to contact them and reveal what they were missing out on. He might even send them a few hundred dollars as a consolation prize.

Felix had repeated the names so often that he didn't need to refer to the list. 'So far, three British and eleven foreign royals. The chairman of the Bank of England, seventeen of the top fifty CEOs, eighty A-list celebrities, two hundred B-listers. Seven editors of major newspapers.'

'The Prime Minister?'

'You said you didn't want Theresa May!'

'Just checking you listened.'

'We have Nigel, Boris, Emmanuel and Brigitte.'

'What about Donald?'

'He's sending Ivanka and Jared.'

Sleet was pleased with the list and the arrangements. It was going to be the party of the century. 'And where's the present?'

Felix tapped his pocket.

'Give it to me.' Sleet flipped open the box and stared at the magnificent stone. 'She will like it, won't she?' he asked.

Three hours later, Sleet and Zamora came face to face in the presidential suite at the Ritz. She wore a white silk trouser suit the same colour as her nails, her shoes and her bleached blonde hair. Her mouth was painted scarlet, and the only other flash of colour were her iridescent pale-blue eyes. She moved sinuously, like a cat, crossing the room to look out of the window down on to the Place Vendôme and then stalking back to the door and then lowering herself into a nearby chair. Sleet, mesmerised, was rooted in place, a small blue sofa. Frightened of having a panic attack brought on by her presence and the importance of his mission, he breathed slowly, inhaling deeply and loudly exhaling with a long whistle between his teeth. He looked at her, imagining their future triumphs in business, their status and superiority. For him, Zamora the person hardly existed – she was a composite of his fantasies.

On Donna's instructions, a florist had covered the damask walls from floor to ceiling with pink and white roses. Sleet, who suffered from hayfever, felt his nose itching. Taking one of the large linen napkins, he blew loudly.

'You ill?' Zamora said, leaning back in her chair. She'd grown up in a place with so little access to medicine that even minor illnesses were dangerous.

'Pollen,' Sleet said.

Zamora had never heard of this disease and hoped it wasn't contagious.

Two waiters hovered: one with vintage Cristal; the other, though Sleet didn't know it, was one of Zamora's personal guards masquerading as a member of staff. Sleet was so intent on the proposal that he couldn't concentrate on conversation. Zamora didn't want to be there but, following a successful cocaine trade between Colombia and the Netherlands, the Copjes had surplus cash to launder, and Sleet, by investing more in QoC, could help.

Glancing at her watch, Zamora wondered how quickly she could excuse herself.

Sleet was impatient, wanting to proceed with his mission, but knew that a bit of preliminary conversation was part of the package. 'How's crypto?' he asked, leaning towards her.

Zamora shifted to the far edge of her chair, wanting to keep a fair distance. 'Making so much money. You should put in more. Queen of Coins up by 70 per cent.'

'That's great. Do you invest in anything else? Spread your bets?' Sleet asked, letting out a long, calming whistle.

Zamora, hearing 'spread your breasts', recoiled.

Seeing her concerned expression, Sleet added, 'We could open our kimonos and share our positions.'

Kimonos? Zamora's English was excellent but there were still pockets of confusion, particularly with financial colloquialisms. She cast a glance at one of the waiters.

Assuming she was hungry, Sleet snapped his fingers. 'Bring the first course,' he told the attendants. A large pot of caviar was produced.

Seeing her favourite food, Zamora smiled.

Sleet, pleased to have pleased her, started to explain. 'This is the best. Off the scale. It's called Almas and only comes from an Iranian beluga fish.'

'Black gold. Around thirty-four thousand dollars for one kilogram,' Zamora said. 'I know. Better than beluga or Ossetra.'

'You know your caviar,' Sleet said. Ayesha annoyed him by taking so little interest in these badges of luxury which were for him the outward manifestation of his success. Two weeks earlier he'd brought home a vintage Aston Martin DB2 – her only comment was 'Does it go fast?' When he upgraded his plane from a G4 to a G600, she had the temerity to question its environmental credentials. A wife should praise her husband's choices.

Zamora took a large spoonful of caviar and, without bothering with the blinis, chopped eggs and onions, put it straight into her mouth.

Sleet found the movement so erotic that he nearly fainted. 'Do that again, will you?'

Zamora shrugged. She was beginning to enjoy herself.

'Vodka?' she asked. A waiter immediately produced two small shot glasses and a bottle of frozen Billionaire Vodka.

'*Gëzuar,*' she said, knocking back the shot.

'*Gëzuar?*' he asked.

'"Cheers" in Albanian.'

'*Gëzuar,*' he shouted and downed his in one.

Zamora held out her glass and, when it had been refilled, tipped it down her throat. Sleet copied her. Five shots later, he forgot about the deep breathing.

'*Gëzuar!* You are the most beautiful woman I've ever seen,' he told her, nearly meaning it.

Zamora smiled and took another spoon of caviar followed by more vodka; the more he drank, the more relaxed she felt. She could drink a bottle and remain sober. Judging from his sweaty brow, his slightly slurred words, Sleet was already tipsy.

'We are doing special edition of my coins,' she said. 'I want you as my close partner.' She ran her tongue over her scarlet mouth to remove a few tiny eggs.

Sleet swallowed hard. 'How much?'

'Two hundred million.'

'What do I get in return?'

'Close partnership.'

Emboldened by drink and her remarks, Sleet slid off the sofa on to one knee before her and took the velvet box from his pocket. Zamora looked down at his rust-coloured hair and slightly sweaty neck. She glanced at her bodyguard who tapped the gun in his pocket.

'This won't come as a surprise, Miss Lala—' Sleet started.

'Dr Lala. I am Doctor of Economics.'

'Zamora. I love you. I have loved you from the first moment I saw you.' He looked up at his inamorata's face – she seemed a little bored but, deciding this was her resting face, Sleet continued. 'You and I are meant for each other. We are like Fred and Ginger, cheese and biscuits, yin and yang.' He hesitated, to try to think of other great partnerships.

Zamora leaned past him and took another spoonful of caviar: she'd probably have to leave soon and it was a pity to waste it. Sleet flipped open the lid of the small box. Zamora's eyes widened. Sitting on a velvet cushion was an enormous, flawless diamond … She loved diamonds even more than caviar.

Sleet caught her expression and smiled. 'It's a perfect, 22-carat pink diamond – "the Gwalior", after a maharaja who once owned it.'

'It is beautiful.' Zamora had never seen anything so lovely.

'Give me your finger.' Sleet held out the ring.

Without thinking, she held out her hand and Sleet slipped the ring on to her engagement finger. 'You've made me the happiest man alive.' Tears sprang to his eyes. Zamora's eyes also moistened – devastated that she'd have to give it back. The situation was getting out of hand, a potential 'kompromat'.

She stood up rather abruptly, accidentally catching Sleet's chin with her knee. Then she took off the ring and dropped it on the floor.

'What are you doing?' he asked, rubbing his cheek.

'Need time.'

'We've got lots of time,' he said, getting to his feet.

'Thinking time.'

'I've done all the thinking I need.'

'Buy more coins and we discuss.' She took off across the room. Her suitor lurched after her. He didn't know what happened next.

There was a sharp pain in his neck and he fell face down on the floor. The rhythm of his breathing shattered and the familiar signs of an attack started. Within seconds his suit and shirt were drenched. His heart clattered. Looking at the white-clad figure, followed by a waiter, disappearing through the door was a relief. She wouldn't see him at his most vulnerable. The remaining attendant called management. Donna was nearby, in a small single room in a three-star hotel, a short taxi ride away. Twenty minutes later, she appeared with pencils and medication. She opened the window and loosened his shirt collar and waited while he broke pencils and struggled to contain his breathing. Within half an hour, Sleet was sitting in a fluffy white gown.

'I'd say things are going pretty well and it's all down to me,' he told Donna. 'I'm exactly what this country needs – a man of action. I might even go for the top job. That'd be a good story. Abandoned orphan becomes Prime Minister. My Zamora will make a great First Lady: Melania's a good-looking broad but nothing comes close to my girl.'

18

June 2017

With Medieval Illusions due to take possession on August 1st and Sleet relocated to London, Ayesha asked the family to return for a last hurrah at the castle. Only Arabella, who had moved to the West Coast of America and Tony, who didn't want to leave his home or Barty, declined. Clarissa moved straight back into the state rooms. Jane, Morawase and Kitto chose the Georgian wing. Toby pitched his tent on the south lawn and Blaze, Perrin and Joshua, wanting a bit of autonomy, camped in the Mistresses' Wing. Tuffy, taking a rare break from her Oxford lab, moved into the furthest, plainest bedroom in the servants' quarters. The family had, each in their own way, been devastated to hear that the castle would pass from one of their own to a company after eight hundred years of uninterrupted ownership. However, these feelings were completely superseded by the news that Sleet was fighting for custody of his daughter.

'Bricks and mortar is one thing but blood and bones is completely other,' Kitto said in a rousing speech.

'Sleet might be taking our inheritance, but he will not succeed in taking kin,' Blaze echoed.

It was the first time since the Great War that all Trelawneys had been united in purpose: Ayesha must keep Stella. The Carolinian dining room was turned into the HQ for 'Operation C' (for Custody) and the focus of their attention was discrediting the Vulgarian.

'Our best defence,' Blaze reminded everyone at their Monday morning meeting, 'is to prove that he is untrustworthy, dishonest and an unsuitable parent.'

'I thought we wanted him in prison,' Toby countered.

'He deserves nothing less,' agreed Jane.

'They should lock him up and throw away the key,' Kitto added.

Ayesha, in attendance, sat motionless at one end of the table. Any talk of the loss of custody of her daughter sent her into a catatonic state. She was also exhausted. Every night after her family went to bed she spent hours trying to crack the passwords on Sleet's private bank accounts. By a process of deduction, using their SWIFT and other identifying codes, she matched the numbers to the entities, uncovering a web of accounts stretching from Panama to Shanghai. She wrote down memorable names, places and dates from Sleet's life that he might have used as passwords – his birthplace in Texas, anagrams of his children's names, former addresses and a childhood dog. None worked. It reminded her of mining Isabella d'Este's archive, but was far less rewarding. Her eyes kept closing and while she tried to listen to what others were saying, their voices melded into a single wall of sound.

Joshua raised his hands for quiet. 'Let me remind you what we have so far.' Spread along the thirty-foot-long oak table were neat piles of papers, documents and photographs, each relating to aspects of Sleet's empire or activities. 'Medieval Illusions is a legitimate solvent concern, and the transaction was a normal exchange between two offshore companies.'

'Is there any legal way of dissolving the deal?' Morawase asked.

'Only if the place turns out to be condemned or contaminated,' Blaze explained.

'Contaminated by vulgarians,' Clarissa sniped.

Joshua ignored his mother-in-law. 'On Whaley Precision Engineering we have some positive steps. As you know, I went to Taiwan to interview Ray Tanaka, the former CEO of TLG.'

'What is TLG?' Jane asked.

'The runner-up to Whaley in the Boeing contract,' Toby reminded his mother.

Joshua continued. 'Tanaka reported that Sleet used threatening and coercive language to him and his colleagues.'

Blaze picked up her husband's story. 'We're trying to connect Alabaster Analytics to the discrediting of Whaley's graphite blade.'

'What's the link between Sleet and Alabaster?' Morawase asked.

'There is a spider's web with a woman called Tahira Khan in the middle,' Blaze explained.

'She's also managing his election campaign.' Joshua hesitated. 'We can't prove it, but we suspect that there are connections with Zamora Lala's cryptocurrency.'

'What a snakepit.'

'Sounds like a slam dunk,' Toby said. 'You must be relieved.' He smiled at Ayesha who was rocking side to side with her eyes closed.

Blaze cleared her throat. 'None of these deliver the killer blow. Custody cases are relatively quick, but this stuff –' she waved her hand up and down the piles of paper '– can take years to reach court. We need to find something urgently.'

Through the open window came the sound of two happy children, Perrin and Stella, playing in the garden.

'What about electoral fraud?' Morawase asked. 'He's spending hundreds of thousands on his campaign.'

'Electoral commissions also take ages to settle,' said Blaze.

'You can't move for the Tory battle buses. Clogging up the whole of Cornwall.' Toby and Kitto had done some tyre slashing the day before, acts which gave them pleasure but only added to more misery for local drivers.

Toby reached over to the pile relating to Zamora and picked up a heavily embossed invitation asking guests to celebrate the new Member of Parliament and the guest of honour, Dr Zamora Lala.

'I don't want to add more misery, but this Albanian woman seems like the most unsuitable stepmother.'

Ayesha, unable to stand it a minute longer, got up and ran out of the room.

'I should go.' Blaze started after her.

To everyone's surprise, Clarissa stood up. 'I shall deal with it.'

Blaze and Jane exchanged doubtful looks. The antipathy between Clarissa and Ayesha was palpable.

Clarissa found her husband's daughter in the Grinling Gibbons room, curled up under the large carved oak tree. Ayesha flinched when she saw the older woman but didn't say anything.

Clarissa, brushing an imaginary piece of fluff from her skirt, cleared her throat. 'Your mother, Blaze and Jane used this room as a den,' she said.

'Their initials are over there.' Ayesha pointed to the far corner. Clarissa walked over, her black court shoes clack-clacking on the floor. Opening her small clutch bag, she took out a torch, kept handy to supplement her fading eyesight, and shone its beam over the three sets of initials.

Ayesha hugged her knees to her chest. The darkness made her brave. 'Why did you try to destroy my mother?' she asked.

Clarissa gave a snort of mirthless laughter but kept her composure. 'You can tell a story a million different ways; even hard facts are open to wildly different interpretations.' She traced the torch beam over the carvings.

'Give me your version,' Ayesha said.

Clicking off the torch, Clarissa turned to look at the younger woman. 'Your grandparents were killed when your mother was eight. Orphaned, she had no known relations. I took her in and adopted her. This house became her home. She was treated as an equal with my children. Sounds awful, but I liked her more than my own daughter. Blaze was the wrong side of pretty – that hideous birthmark – and so angry. Your mother was fun, ravishing; everyone loved her.'

'Including your husband.'

Clarissa held up her hands and then lowered them along with her voice. 'What my husband did was unforgivable. But your mother was dangerous. Even as a little girl she didn't play by any known rules. She was mesmerising and amoral. She had no boundaries. We called her "the child with a gypsy heart".' Clarissa spoke in clipped, even tones.

'Are you trying to blame her?' Ayesha's voice rose in amazement.

'Of course not. She was only sixteen; my husband was in his sixties,' Clarissa said. 'I did not and will not forgive him.' She placed a hand against the wall to steady herself. She should have carried a stick but vanity overcame practicality.

Clarissa continued. 'My husband – your father – had had other affairs. Many. For decades I turned a blind eye, knowing that he'd come home, that these extramarital dalliances reflected his libido and his ego. I was his rock, his foundation – no one else came close to my role. But Anastasia threatened everything. His feelings for her were in a different league. It was pathetic to witness a man – once powerful, in command – felled by emotion. He was prepared to give everything up for her – not just me, but our life, our children, our home.'

'They were in love,' Ayesha said, repeating her mother's well-told story.

Clarissa shook her head. 'Enyon loved her. Your mother made it clear that he was just a short chapter in her life.'

'You expelled her. She was pregnant with me; you left her high and dry.'

Clarissa's voice turned fierce. 'Rubbish. I offered to move out of the main house into the dower house in the grounds.'

'Why would you do that?'

Clarissa paused and thought for a while. 'I didn't want to leave Trelawney; rather be a spurned woman within the ramparts.' She hesitated. 'Enyon and I had a partnership; we had roles and commitments. Odd as it seemed, it worked.'

'Hardly romantic.'

'Women fall in love when they get to know a man. For men it's the opposite. That's love's great tragedy.'

'My mother was in love with Enyon.'

'Your mother was in love with being loved. At sixteen she discovered her enormous power to captivate and seduce. Enyon was her first conquest. He wasn't her last.'

'That's not what she told me.' As Ayesha spoke, her certainty wavered. There were too many holes in her mother's version of events, including the major one: Anastasia told her that Kitto, not Enyon, was her real father. Ayesha found out the truth from a newspaper article. Since then, she'd questioned other aspects of her mother's narrative. But nothing had prepared her for the next twist in the story.

'Around the time of your conception, your mother was also having an affair with a famous pop star, a tycoon and an Indian prince, the Maharaja of Balakphur.'

'No, that can't be true!' Ayesha cried out, but as the words left her mouth, pieces of a jigsaw suddenly fitted together, and the gossip and tittle-tattle that had dogged her childhood at Balakphur made sense: Anastasia had tricked the Maharaja into marriage. Ayesha didn't want to believe this version of events, but it explained certain things. Why else would a heavily pregnant young woman opt to live in another country and why did the deeply conservative Maharaja agree to marry if he hadn't thought the child was his? It explained, too, her stepfather's antipathy towards her and his family's hostility to her mother. Finally the whispers at court made sense, as did her and Anastasia's eventual brutal expulsion from the palace.

'Why are you telling me this?'

Clarissa looked up at the fronds of a delicately carved tree and saw a tiny field mouse peeking out from behind a leaf. She cleared her throat. 'To my surprise, I find that I like you; and the greatest compliment you can give someone is honesty.'

'And if I told you that everyone, including me, loathes you?'

Clarissa laughed. 'Being liked has never interested me. Not in the slightest. Even by my own family. They mock my attempts to get on the TV, to be famous, but I don't give a tuppenny fuck.'

'What do you care about?'

'I'm not given to self-reflection or navel gazing. Frightful waste of time. Nor do I believe in God or an afterlife. If there was a divine, kind being, he wouldn't have taken Fa and my beloved brothers. I am eighty-six, nearly eighty-seven, and I intend to squeeze every drop out of my remaining days. Not for me the dribble dribble in an old people's home. I wake up every single morning and decide to live each moment as if it's my last. And that, young lady, is what you're going to do. I only have a few years, if that, but you have decades.'

'Why do you bother?'

'I want to go in a blaze of publicity, wearing a Chanel suit and my best pearls.'

Despite her anger, Ayesha smiled, imagining Clarissa lying rigid, back straight, arms crossed, make-up perfect, in her coffin.

The older woman walked over to Ayesha and held out her hand. 'Get up.' When Ayesha didn't move, Clarissa fluttered her fingers. 'Sitting around feeling sorry for yourself is not going to win you custody of your daughter. If you want revenge, then you'll have to fight for it. Right now, you're handing that dreadful Vulgarian victory on a plate.'

Ayesha looked at the outstretched hand and hesitated. 'I feel so desperately unhappy.'

Clarissa put her hands on her hips and looked down at the younger woman. 'People are under a frightful misapprehension that life is supposed to be "nice" and "fun" and that they deserve love. Absolute poppycock and piffle. Life is to be endured. The naive imagine that life is made of seasons and that spring will follow winter and lead to summer. Make no mistake, my girl, whatever the weather you must make the most of it. Now come on.' She held out her hand again.

Ayesha took it and got to her feet.

'That's better.' Clarissa's voice was crisp but gentle. 'I'm going to do something for you I've never done for anyone. I am going to make you breakfast. They say I can't even boil an egg. Well, let's see. You'll be my first victim. And then we're going to wash and set your hair.' Together they walked out into the sunlit Georgian ballroom towards the kitchen.

*

On June 7th, the morning before election day, the staff at Sleet's London residence debated whether to lay out the daily newspapers on the breakfast side table. They decided to go ahead and lined one hundred boxes of pencils along the wall. When Sleet came downstairs at 7 a.m., his butler, the two footmen and six other members of the household hid behind the green baize door listening to the sound of china and silver flying around the room, smashing against windows and radiators, punctuated by bellows of rage. Felix waited for fifteen minutes before going in. His employer was sitting on the floor snapping pencils in half, his face mottled with rage.

'I have today's itinerary, sir,' Felix said, stepping over smashed crockery and rashers of bacon.

'She's already married,' Sleet said, holding up a copy of the *Daily Blast*. On the front page there was a picture of Zamora coming out of the Ritz in Paris with a swarthy dark-haired man identified as Nanos Copje. The photograph, apparently, had been taken the previous week.

'Never believe what you read in the press,' Felix said soothingly. 'They are trying to put you off your stride.'

'Are you sure?' Sleet's voice was so soft, so pathetic, that Felix (almost) felt sorry for him.

'It's a big day. Important to have some breakfast.' Felix held out his hand. He'd been trained to comfort troops suffering from extreme PTSD. To him, Sleet, slumped in the debris of a temper tantrum, reminded him of a wounded veteran. He steered his employer through the shards of broken china to the table. Then, taking a silver salver, he found scattered pieces of bacon and a vaguely intact fried egg (thrown earlier at the wall). He set the plate in front of Sleet and coaxed him to eat something, as if talking to a little child.

Later that morning, they flew by helicopter to Cornwall to attend the last hustings. Felix had, as Sleet requested, arranged a photo shoot with six cattle. Trying to repeat Boris Johnson's bonhomie, Sleet pointed to one of their udders.

'I love a pair of juicy titties.'

No one laughed. When one of the cows squirted the contents of her breakfast over his shoes, the photograph went viral with the headline SIR THOMLINSON SPLAT.

Outside his campaign headquarters in St Austell, he came face to face with an actual voter.

'And what's your name, lovely lady?'

'Milly. What's your ticket?' the woman asked.

'"Take back control". "Drain the Westminster swamp". "Stop immigrants".' Sleet repeated his mantra.

'There was a referendum,' Milly pointed out.

'Of course.' The prospective candidate beamed.

'You and your lot are too dim to recognise that you've had your day. It's over, Rover. Go home, back to your fancy ways and your out-of-date slogans. You're not wanted here.'

The same evening, the reinvigorated Ayesha, with Clarissa by her side, called in all former members of staff who'd worked for the Sleets and witnessed her being a mother. Each interview was filmed by Damian Dobbs, Clarissa's producer. One by one they gave a clear and unequivocal account of her devotion and Sleet's unique brand of absentee parenting. Damian drove to London to record a session with the midwife who'd delivered Stella, who confirmed that Sleet had not been at the birth. Nor, according to the maternity nurse and nannies, had he taken the slightest interest in Stella or any of her childhood illnesses.

Under Clarissa's wing Ayesha's transformation was extraordinary. The two women were inseparable. Clarissa made Ayesha eat and take care of herself. While she wasn't the type to heap praise, she would give her young protégée a nod of approval. Ayesha often looked to her for confirmation.

Blaze found it unsettling. 'If only my mother had been in touch with parenting skills when I was a child,' she lamented late one night to Joshua.

'You are a walking miracle, my darling,' he said. 'How anyone could have survived such fierce emotional neglect is beyond me. And you've turned out to be a wonderful wife and mother.'

Blaze was only partially mollified; in truth, she was a little bit jealous.

On June 8th, the whole Trelawney family went to vote. The paparazzi were there waiting for Clarissa and Ayesha, the two local celebrities.

'It's like the good old days,' Clarissa said, posing for the camera. 'When I was first married, people used to doff their caps when a Trelawney walked past.'

'No one wears caps any more,' Toby pointed out.

'Another drop in standards.'

Returning home, they tried to live a normal day. All were on tenter-hooks; the soul of Cornwall was at stake. At 10 p.m. the final votes were cast and counting began. None of the family had much of an appetite. The two little girls were put to bed, while the grown-ups sat disconsolately around the television in the Georgian sitting room.

Anticipating the final announcement, Sleet waited at the local town hall practising his victory speech. It had been commissioned from a leading journalist, a respected economist and a well-known historian. It spoke about the history of Cornish independence, the county taking back control, and how he would restore businesses in the area – the big reveal being that his own home would soon be made over to a new tourist attraction. His first decree as MP would be to relax local planning laws.

When the results came through, the family leapt off their sofas and punched the air. Even Tuffy did a little jig.

In the town hall, Sleet seemed not to understand. He asked for the result to be repeated, not once but twice. He'd done disastrously, only just keeping his deposit. The Conservatives had won the seat by a comfortable majority, followed by the Liberal Democrats, Labour and the Free Cornwall Party. The only candidate that did worse than Sleet was 'Mr Badger's Tea Party', headed by a gerontophile who believed that the British cuppa was under threat from cappuccinos. Sleet still wouldn't accept the count. Assuming there'd been a mistake, he confronted the chief accounting officer. All this was caught on film by

TV crews who, following the day's revelations, were poised to capture the businessman's success or failure.

In the Georgian drawing room at Trelawney Castle, Kitto cracked open a bottle of champagne. The family made a toast.

'To the right person winning.'

'And the wrong one losing.'

Sleet looked around the election hall, hoping to see Tahira, but she was absent. Zamora's phone was turned off. Only Sanjay, the chauffeur, and Felix waited in the wings, both looking embarrassed.

'They made a mistake,' Sleet thundered at his chief of staff.

'Undoubtedly, sir. We have asked for a further recount.'

Sleet's self-confidence, honed by years of success, briefly overrode the reality of what was happening. 'Imagine tomorrow's headlines. And the photographs. We'll knock all that tittle-tattle off the front pages,' he said bullishly. Then, catching his chief of staff's concerned look, he asked, 'You know something?'

Felix shook his head vigorously. He must stay employed until tomorrow when his pay cheque was due. 'Let's leave now. No point hanging around any longer.'

They flew in silence to London. Once home, Sleet dismissed his staff and ate alone. That night he broke four hundred boxes of pencils. A record.

By the following morning, Sleet had retrofitted the previous night's narrative. Zamora hadn't taken his calls because she, the romantic, was preparing for her big night. Her so-called marriage was a myth put out by people wishing to hurt him. The recount would go his way. He instructed Felix to change the design of the party. He wanted a central pyramid whose sides would drop, revealing the future Lady Sleet dripping in diamonds and glamour. The A-listers, he told Felix, would line up to cheer.

As the day wore on, Sleet's nervousness grew. He sat in the office, with all four screens turned to the major TV channels, waiting for good news. The fourth recount delivered the same result. A few stations showed reruns of the cow incident and him berating the accounting officer. The hours ticked past and neither he nor any of his team could raise his nearly fiancée on any platform: phone, email, WhatsApp or Facebook.

'Turn up Channel Two,' Sleet said, spotting one of the TV monitors. '*The Three Old Gits* is on.'

Felix adjusted the volume. The camera closed in on Clarissa. 'We called him the Vulgarian. I've never met a more louche, unrefined, ghastly human being,' she said. 'And he is the most appalling father – could not recognise any of his own children in a line-up.'

'Money can't buy taste or style,' Princess Amelia added.

Sleet threw an iPad at the television but couldn't tear his eyes away.

Only Barty was quiet. He was dressed as King Henry VIII, a reference to the much-married Sir Thomlinson Sleet. The costume was hot and uncomfortable. He was finding it difficult to breathe under the layers of velvet, the whalebone stays and ruff collar.

'Lady Sleet has been noticeably absent from the campaign trail. There are rumours circulating that she's unwell,' the presenter asked Clarissa. 'Can you confirm her health and whereabouts?'

Clarissa did not hesitate. 'She's in dazzling shape. Unlike her husband, Ayesha loves Cornwall. She's been at our house, Trelawney, for some time. Her main concern is and always has been her daughter's wellbeing. One has never met a more devoted, loving mother.'

'Would you describe yourself as maternal?'

Princess Amelia laughed. 'Clarissa prefers dogs.'

'They're more intelligent than your chosen beast, the horse,' Clarissa snapped. 'And their riders.'

Amelia had been one of Enyon's many mistresses and their dalliances often took place on the hunting field. The princess pursed her lips but was way beyond the age of embarrassment. She agreed with her old friend, John Betjeman – her only regret was not having had more sex.

'Barty – do you have anything to add?' the presenter asked, wanting to bring the third guest in. Barty had been unusually silent for the whole show.

'Could I have some water?' Barty clutched his chest. It hurt awfully. His head began to spin. The room seemed dreadfully hot. He clawed at his doublet, trying to loosen the pearl buttons. His heavy gold necklace slipped, and his doublet was cutting off the blood supply to his nether regions. Seeing stars, he reached up with his hands, tried to grab one and lost consciousness.

Clarissa looked down at him sprawled on the floor. 'He'll do anything to upstage me. Throw some water on him. He won't want his make-up to drip.'

'Someone call a doctor!' The presenter got to his knees to loosen Barty's velvet doublet.

Clarissa gave him a kick on his shin. 'Get up now. You're not in some awful public house.'

It began to occur to Sleet that things weren't going his way. He read and reread the reports circulating online and in the tabloids. Another photograph of Zamora and Nanos Copje emerged. There was even a child. Turning his attention to Ayesha, some stories said she was colluding with Blaze and Joshua. His confidence wobbled. Was he, as one paper suggested, the victim of a Trelawney curse placed eight hundred years earlier on any non-family member who tried to live in the castle?

Calling Felix into the room, he asked, 'Have you found her yet?'

'She's not answering messages or taking calls.' Felix wondered how a man as sophisticated as Sleet could be so naive.

'What about Tahira?'

'Also a little absent.' Felix hesitated – he wasn't sure whether to tell his employer that Zamora and Tahira had boarded a private plane at Northolt that afternoon bound for Albania. He'd garnered the information from one of his former officers, a steady chap called Lloyd who ran the base.

'The party must go on,' Sleet said, thinking about the evening ahead. 'She'll be there.'

Felix shuffled from foot to foot. 'The thing is —'

Sleet whipped round. 'Come on, out with it.'

'Rather a lot of people have cancelled.'

'Cancelled?'

'Have said that they are not available.' Felix smiled ruefully.

'How many?'

Felix hesitated: every single bigwig and A-lister had chucked. 'A lot of people will turn up,' he said, not believing his own words.

'Where's Lady Sleet?'

'She's still at Trelawney.'

'With my daughter?'

Felix nodded.

'Zamora will reappear. She's probably keeping a low profile to protect me. She's a wonderful woman. There are those who are born to rule and be great, those who are born to serve and follow. I am one of the former.' He shrugged. 'It's something those Cornish hillbillies couldn't understand. Thousands of years of subjugation, serfdom and inbreeding have not served them well. Too bad. They had a chance to change and failed to take it. I feel kinda sorry for them.'

'Yes, sir.' Felix couldn't think of anything else to say.

'Now, you unctuous prick,' Sleet said, 'go and make sure the party's perfect.' He looked at his watch. 'I'll have a nap now and we'll leave in two hours.'

As Felix predicted, the party was a desultory affair. Of the 1,000 invited, only 250 turned up and Sleet didn't recognise any of them. Beyoncé cancelled at the last moment, and though Tom Jones did his best, the old showman couldn't get a single person on the dance floor. Sleet waited for Zamora to turn up. He had the Gwalior diamond ring in his pocket. He would give it to her on arrival and together they'd descend in the silver pyramid. Sir Thomlinson and Dr Zamora Lala.

It was only after midnight, when she hadn't responded to any of his texts, he decided to go home.

Outside there were banks of photographers eager to photograph him and his new 'partner'. The shouts and barrage of flashes were bewildering. Then the paps jumped their barrier and surrounded him.

'Where's Miss Lala? Some say she's done a bunk?'

'We photographed her in Tirana about an hour ago.'

'How does it feel being cuckolded by a mobster's wife?'

'Been ditched before, Sir Thom?'

'Where's your wife? Has she left you too?'

The more intense the flashes, the louder the voices, the more discombobulated Sleet became. He looked around for his security people and Sanjay but could see none of them.

'People are saying that you make money from other people's misery.'

'That you funded Brexit only to make a killing.'

'Are you involved with the Albanian mafia?'

'Why didn't Donald or Nigel come tonight?'

'Where was Boris?'

The noises became insufferably loud, the flashes so vivid that Sleet clawed at his black tie. Struggling for breath, he fell to his knees, and then his nose and cheek hit the pavement. His last memory was eyeballing another man's trainer.

*

The call came in late. Tony had gone to bed and was asleep when the telephone rang. He hurried to it as quickly as he could without risking injury.

'I see. How awful. I will be there as soon as possible,' he said.

His arthritis was so bad that his socks took twenty minutes to put on. The key was to get the right angle so his hands could reach his toes. He was in such a fluster that, for the first time in eighty-five years, he didn't bother with either socks or clean underpants.

'Oh, hurry up, you old fool. Hurry up,' he scolded himself, trying to button his shirt. Then he grabbed a silk scarf – once the colour of violets, now mottled pinks – slung it around his neck and hobbled out of the flat.

Fifteen minutes later, he was standing on the Earls Court Road looking for a taxi. It was a balmy night, at least, but for some reason no cabs passed. He started walking west, glancing over his shoulder for a comforting orange light in the distance. Soon his shoes, though well worn in, began to rub the papery skin on his ankles. He wished he'd worn socks – at his age, blisters took months to heal; he knew he should stop and wait but was desperate to get there in time.

A taxi finally came. Tony waved his arms frantically and the cabbie pulled over. 'Oh, thank you. Oh, goodness. I thought you'd never come,' he said. The door was so heavy that the driver jumped out to help Tony climb into the back.

'St Mary's, Paddington, please. As quickly as you can.' In his hand he had a small scrap of paper, but hard as he tried, he couldn't make out the words or letters. In his hurry to leave, he'd forgotten his spectacles. The journey passed in a blur of lights and sounds. The hospital was unmissable, a large red-brick Victorian block next to the train station he knew so well.

The driver dropped him by the correct entrance and even offered to help find the right ward. He didn't think the old boy should be left on his own. His shirt was buttoned up wrong and egg-stained. He'd forgotten to brush his hair and, although there wasn't much left, it stuck out in various directions.

Tony longed to accept the offer of help but declined: the cabbie probably had children and other dependants, while he … a sob caught in his throat. He only had one real friend in the world. Inside St Mary's, the staircases and hallways were endless. At three in the morning there were few people around. Without his glasses, Tony couldn't read any of the signs. Becoming increasingly anxious, he managed to find a kindly porter who took him in a groaning lift to the third floor, then along two corridors to a ward. The room was dimly lit and there were ten beds filled with sleeping humps.

'Here's your friend,' the porter said, pulling up a chair for Tony to sit on.

Tony sat down and peered into the gloom. 'Hello, dear Barty,' he whispered.

Barty slowly turned his head. 'You made it. Thank you.' His voice was soft and raspy and his irises, normally a rich brown, were strangely colourless. 'Poor old heart's given up.'

Tony took Barty's hand. 'It's the bravest, merriest heart I ever met.'

Barty smiled. 'What a nice thing to say.'

Tony squeezed his friend's hand gently.

'Did you know the average heart beats forty million times a year?'

Tony shook his head. He couldn't speak; his throat had closed.

'Has the cat got your tongue?' Barty asked.

Tony nodded.

'I'm sorry to leave you. Always thought you'd go first.'

'I was depending on it,' Tony croaked. 'Do you have to go, old bean? I'm awfully fond of you. Can't imagine life without our jokes.' Tears were running down his face and a deep, dark desolation coursed through his body.

'You'll just have to act as if I'm still there. I've left you Greta Garbo's coat. Put it on the end of your bed and talk to me every night.' Barty gripped Tony's hand. 'You've been such a dear in my life. Our time at Trelawney made the last years a jolly jape. I'm so annoyed that I won't be able to see what happens next. Let's hope that ghastly Vulgarian gets his comeuppance. Is he still in hospital?'

'Yes, but recovering.'

'Bother.' Barty wheezed and struggled to catch his breath. Through deep rasps he managed to ask, 'And Ayesha?'

'Barricaded in the castle with the family, working their way through the last dregs of Sleet's cellar.'

The machine by Barty's bed let out a squeak. Tony waved his arms about in alarm. 'Should I call a nurse?'

'Too late, old boy.' Barty smiled weakly. 'What about Clarissa? I am so annoyed I never got to boil her head.'

'She and Ayesha are as thick as thieves,' Tony said, keeping an eye on the digital readings flashing on a screen above him. He was certain the peaks were becoming less high.

Barty squeezed his hand again. 'You have to admire the old girl's spirit.' He was staring up at the ceiling.

Thinking he might have died, Tony shook his arm gently.

'I'm still here. Do you know what I was thinking about? That, for all my hard work, effort, opportunities and luck, life never matched up to my dreams.'

'Dreams are the shock absorbers between hope and reality. They make the business of living less painful,' Tony said.

Barty opened his eyes wide. 'Did you read that somewhere?'

'I presume so. Doesn't sound very me.'

'Back of a cornflakes box?' Barty cleared his throat, a terrible sound like gravel on glass. Fighting for breath, he said, 'Tell me something normal.'

'Arabella called today. Did you know that you can make free long-distance calls now on the internet?'

'You're the only person I telephone short or long distance.'

Tony's tears had stopped flowing but the deep ache inside remained. 'Can't they do anything? Sleet must have a man somewhere. The rich always have a miracle-worker.'

Barty shook his head. 'I'm a goner. Massive attack this morning. I hung on to say goodbye to you.'

'Don't. I'm going to cry again.' Tony lowered his head and kissed Barty's hand.

'I have a last favour to ask,' Barty said.

'Anything, darling.'

'Would you organise a fancy funeral? Use my last Trelawney money. It would be nice to have a bit of a do. I want my ashes to be taken back to Stoke in a white Rolls-Royce and scattered from the car window in the street where I was born.'

Tony recoiled. It sounded like a ghastly idea. 'What will people say?'

'The dead don't care! All those years worrying what people think – gone. Please hire ten Rolls-Royces – only the white variety. I want Frank and Bing blaring at full blast. Maybe one of those glass carriages pulled by horses with plumes.'

'Awfully Kray brothers.'

'No, darling: Disney Princess.' Barty smiled.

'I never knew about the Cinderella complex.' Tony's heart sank. He hated going north of Watford. 'Why don't we bury you at Trelawney? There's no one there to say we can't. We had such fun there. You have as much right as any of us to claim a patch of ground. We could lie side by side and gossip forever.'

Barty shook his head. 'I'm a northerner, born and bred. It's where I belong.'

The two men sat in silence for a while. Both their hearts were hurting – for different reasons.

'Are you frightened, darling?' Tony asked after a bit.

Barty nodded. 'Terrified. What if there are no celestial parties, no welcoming cocktails, no burning pits, no angels, no devils? What if it's just me?'

Tony was sure that death was a great big nothingness but couldn't bear his friend's sadness. 'Don't worry, it'll be a riot. Imagine all the great musicians waiting to serenade you. Fats Domino and Ella, Billie and Duke?'

'Frank and Bing?'

'You'll dance with Grace Kelly and Ginger Rogers.' Tony tried to remember all Barty's heroes and all the characters from history that he'd emulated. 'Marie Antoinette will bake you a cake. Antoine Watteau will do your portrait. Anne Boleyn will sing a lullaby. Genghis Khan will chase away your nightmares.' He paused, trying to remember others.

Tony looked down at his friend. Barty had a slight smile on his face and his eyes were closed. Tony squeezed his hand but this time the pressure wasn't returned.

'Barty,' he said, leaning over him. 'Barty, are you there?' Placing his ear near Barty's mouth, he listened for a breath. There was nothing.

285

'Oh, darling, don't go yet. Please, I'm not ready,' Tony sobbed. 'Please wait for me.' He pumped Barty's hand, hoping for a response: nothing. He stroked Barty's face, which in death looked far smoother and less lined. He noticed that the eyeliner and mascara were still intact. Trust Barty to put his face on before a heart attack.

'Oh, dear dear boy. I never told you I loved you,' Tony said.

An hour later, during her rounds, the young ward nurse found Tony fast asleep, still holding his dead friend's hand. She made him a cup of tea and put him in a taxi.

'Is there anyone at home I can call?' she asked.

'I've got Greta Garbo,' Tony said, thinking about the old fur coat.

'It's nice to have company,' she said. 'I'm so glad you have someone.'

Tony straightened his shoulders, smiled courteously, and walked out of the hospital towards the station. He had just enough money to get to Trelawney. Look out, Clarissa, he thought, I'm coming home.

*

On the morning after Sleet's party Ayesha was first down to the breakfast room. A man dressed as a butler who she didn't recognise was standing near the side table. Glancing in his direction, she was surprised to see him step towards her. He held a large envelope in his hand. Without thinking, she took it and the butler turned and left. Ayesha ripped open the envelope. A quick scan of the documents confirmed that Sleet had served her divorce papers. Racing through the pages, she gasped: Sleet was, as she feared, seeking full custody of Stella; seeing it in black and white knocked the wind out of her lungs. Bracing herself with outstretched arms, she took five deep breaths. The feelings of panic passed quickly: her family was beside her; she was not alone. Together they'd win. At worst, she'd have to share Stella with Sleet and she could at least make sure that Janet accompanied her daughter on every visit.

Leaving the legal documents where they lay, she looked at the newspaper headlines. All led with a version of the same photograph – Sleet lying unconscious on the pavement. Her only disappointment was that he was not dead; that would have solved a lot of her problems. The reports said that he'd been taken to the Princess Grace

Hospital where he'd spent a comfortable night and was undergoing tests. Flicking through the newspapers, Ayesha saw a new narrative emerging: one where she was a harridan and Sleet was a cuckold. Even Zamora came over as a serious person trying to democratise money through her cryptocurrency. She should have expected a spirited defence from Sleet and his PR team, but she was still shocked by seeing herself depicted as an evil witch in print.

When Stella traipsed into the room, rubbing sleep from her tiny eyes, Ayesha pushed the worst newspaper articles and the custody papers to the bottom of the pile.

'Is that Daddy?' Stella asked, picking up the *Daily Blast*.

'Yes, darling. He's having a nap.' Ayesha swept the rest of the papers off the table. 'Have some cereal. We have chocolate Krispies today.'

'Why isn't he in bed?' Stella climbed on to a chair, her feet dangling over the side.

'You know Daddy – he owns everything so one night he thought he'd try one of his outside beds.'

Stella looked at her mother sceptically. 'Well, tell him that I don't like it.'

Ayesha kissed her daughter. 'What are we going to do today?' she said, changing the subject. She didn't know if she'd win the case, but she did know that she'd put every single ounce of her being into trying.

'Perrin and I want to ride Mickey,' Stella said.

'Let's go and see him, then.' Ayesha took her daughter's hand and led her through the house. Was it her imagination or were the staff looking at her strangely? The head butler was his normal professional self but the two housemaids turned as she walked past. Crossing the herbaceous borders, the gardeners who usually smiled and straightened their backs when she approached now gave no sign of having seen her. In the stables, the groom greeted Stella warmly but ignored her mother. They believed what they read: she was a duplicitous, amoral woman.

Later the same day, the estate manager James came to see Ayesha. 'Sir Thomlinson has given us notice. Says the house is to be vacated.'

'That's what I understand.' Ayesha looked at him. 'Please can you pass on my sincere thanks and apologies to everyone?'

She broke the news to the family at teatime. 'The staff have been fired. We're on our own.'

'We'll manage.' Jane smiled sweetly. 'I did before,' she said, remembering how she'd single-handedly cooked and cleaned for her family.

Ayesha turned to her sister-in-law. 'This time you're not doing it alone. We'll have a rota. Even Clarissa will help.'

'One does not help,' Clarissa said firmly.

'Then one does not eat,' Kitto said.

*

Sleet's room at the Princess Grace Hospital reminded him of his first apartment: white and beige and functional. He thought back to those early years with Marion, wife number one. She'd been supportive, given him a couple of kids, but ultimately was too parochial to help his career. Kelly, wife number two, had been too avaricious. Wife number three, Liora, left him for the cook. He was looking forward to Ayesha being relegated to the back bench.

Felix knocked and came into the room. His salary had been doubled since the general election. Sleet couldn't afford to lose another ally.

The chief of staff shifted from foot to foot.

'Out with it,' Sleet said.

'Sir, there have been a lot of redemptions from Kerkyra Capital today.'

'I expected that. It's happened before and they'll regret it. I'll discharge myself today, go back to work and show the world I'm still number one. What are we looking at? Around 5 per cent, 10 per cent?'

Felix consulted a piece of paper. 'In the last thirty-six hours, investors have withdrawn 55 per cent of the company's funds.'

Sleet leaned back in the bed, gripping the metal sides. 'Have you got the decimal point in the right place?'

Seeing his employer's face, Felix asked, 'Can I get you a glass of water?'

'We have an override to stop withdrawals. Why isn't it working?'

Felix looked uncomfortable.

'What's that face for? Just close the fund.'

'Rodita cancelled the override before she left.'

'So un-fucking-do it.'

'It will take a few days. We must get a court order.'

Sleet's pink face had turned purple. He rose from his hospital bed and took two steps towards Felix, who didn't flinch – he had killed men in the past and could dispatch Sleet easily. One quick chop to the side of his neck and the man would be paralysed for life.

'Step back, please, sir.'

Unnerved by Felix's tone, Sleet stopped. Sweat was pouring down his pyjamas. Had someone turned up the heating?

Felix assumed that he was about to witness a panic attack and braced himself.

Sleet's heart thumped. He waited, but nothing happened. He swallowed and sat down on the edge of his bed.

Then Sleet started to laugh. There was no rushing of blood to his head, no palpitations. Even his father's mocking voice had disappeared.

He took his pyjama top off and then let the bottoms slide to the floor. Felix averted his gaze.

'Pass me my clothes.' Sleet pointed to the cupboard.

'It's pouring with rain outside. I'll get you an umbrella.'

Sleet looked out of the window at the rain bouncing off the pavement. 'It's frigging June. What's wrong with this country?' He pulled on his boxers and shook out his trousers. 'Assemble the team at HQ. We're going to murder the market.'

Felix thought about one of his mother's sayings: 'Planet Rich is different; they do things differently there.'

Sleet's problems were just beginning. With so many investors withdrawing their capital and the assets under management diminishing by the day, meeting the interest payments on the loans was increasingly difficult. Felix was loyal but lacked any of Rodita's skills. The new chief of staff didn't know the difference between a put option or a call note. He got the APR and the escrow holdbacks confused with collateral, and the MOP and MLPs merged into one. Sleet had no option but to sell assets quickly. The first objects to go were the works of art Ayesha had bought. Stevie Mett could smell a distressed debtor from a distance. Sleet kept the Iranian paintings but accepted £25 million for the rest: less than half of its market value. His most valuable remaining asset was Trelawney and his children's and ex-wives' trusts. On August 1st, the day that Medieval Illusions completed, he'd be paid the last 80 per cent of the purchase price: his only hope of staving off bankruptcy. If that didn't work, then he'd liquidate his dependants' portfolios.

19

July 2017

Perhaps it was time passing, the days dripping like grains of sand through an hourglass, but the last few weeks at the castle were highly productive for each member of the family. Clarissa and her producer, Damian Dobbs, worked on a pilot for a series called *The Countess Investigates* – the premise was Clarissa, acting as a detective, would look into a cause or try and solve a crime. The first programme would take up the plight of gullible individuals who invested in what Clarissa called 'fake cryptothingamabobs'. Jane, finally able to get a perspective on Trelawney memories, happy and painful, started a new set of designs. Tuffy, who'd been absent from Cornwall for nine years, now caught up on the effects of climate change on a native insect population she'd documented in the castle grounds for many decades. Blaze and Joshua worked tirelessly on their investigation into Sleet's malpractices. Tony was inconsolable: not even his beloved childhood home compensated for the loss of Barty.

When Ayesha wasn't with Stella, she spent hours trying to crack Sleet's bank codes. Her family tried to interest her in walks or other pursuits, but she shrugged off their suggestions with a faint smile. The court case to decide who got custody of Stella was set for July 30th, the same day that Trelawney passed to its new owners. After that, Ayesha would be homeless. Clarissa was adamant: her home (even though she hated the cottage in Thame) would be their home. Stella would attend the same school as Perrin. Without her family's support, Ayesha would not have made it through those last weeks. It took every ounce of strength and self-control for her not to think about the future and to concentrate instead on creating happy memories for her daughter.

In the middle of the month, the Wolfes had to return to their Buckinghamshire farm for the harvest. To say thank you Ayesha decided to prepare an unforgettable last supper in their honour. Sleet's chefs had left a larder stocked with every imaginable herb and spice and she assembled her favourites on the kitchen counter: cayenne pepper, coriander and cumin seeds, cardamom pods, fenugreek, cinnamon sticks and even asafoetida which she would use to give the dal and green beans a smoky garlicky flavour. Grinding the spices with the pestle and mortar brought back the happier memories of her childhood. In Balakphur palace Ayesha had been one of many displaced people. Their foreignness made her feel less lonely, and she'd been glad to spend every free hour (there were many) in the kitchen.

The tantalising smell of herbs and spices wafted under doorways and along passages of the castle. Clarissa, who 'didn't do foreign food', admitted her taste buds were titillated. The scent reminded Tony of an affair with a wildly handsome and charming polo player, a memory so exquisite and sensual that he forgot about Barty for twenty whole minutes. Jane was so inspired by the aroma that she decided to spend the winter in Jaipur, a place known for its printing presses and craft. Kitto wept for the trips he'd never taken, for the adventures he'd forgone in his attempt to save Trelawney. Joshua and Blaze lay in bed watching their daughter Perrin sleep, her arm thrown back over her head and her lips slightly apart. Both knew that, for all their efforts, they'd failed Ayesha and Trelawney. Sleet might gain custody of Stella and would, no doubt, rebuild his business.

Stella, still in her pyjamas, came into the kitchen.

'I hope Daddy isn't on the ground. He'll be wet.'

Wiping her hands on a towel, Ayesha poured some cereal into a bowl and topped it with milk.

'You smell funny,' Stella said, wrinkling her nose. 'Why are your hands orange?'

Ayesha looked at her fingers stained yellow by the turmeric and cayenne. 'I'm making a special supper for all the family.'

'Can I stay up?' Stella's face puckered in expectation of the answer.

'Tonight you can.'

'Can I ride after breakfast?' Stella decided to make the most of her mother's munificence.

'Of course!'

Stella ate her cereal while Ayesha washed and cleared away the bowls and put the dishes to marinate in the fridge. Taking Stella's hand in hers, she led her through the herbaceous borders, all ablaze with colour, to the paddock where the pony lived.

'Do a cartwheel, Mummy,' Stella implored.

Ayesha tried but ended up in a heap on the grass.

'What happened?' Stella ran over to her.

'Things are a bit too upside down for now.'

'Why are you crying, Mummy?'

Tears poured down Ayesha's face. 'Because I love you so so so much.'

Stella shrugged and ran ahead to find Mickey. Ayesha lay crumpled in the grass, her body heaving. The weeks of being brave, of putting on a false happy face, evaporated. Declan was camped permanently on her chest – if he got any heavier, she realised her heart might break.

'Get up. Now.'

Ayesha opened her eyes to see Tony's diminutive figure looking down at her.

'The grass is still damp,' he said. 'I'd hold out my hand to help you up but it might fall off.' He held a silver-topped walking stick. 'If you stand up, I have a magic cure.' He unscrewed the top and took a little sniff. 'This belonged to Barty. It works.'

Ayesha struggled to her feet, wiping her tears and bits of grass from her face. She sniffed at the stick. 'It's whisky!'

'Purely medicinal. Emergencies only.' He pushed the stick towards her.

Ayesha took a swig. It burned the back of her throat and she nearly coughed it out. Liking the short route to oblivion, she swallowed more of Barty's cure-all.

'Steady on, old girl. You might get squiffy,' Tony said, and then remembering that those were the words his beloved friend had used on Paddington station, he too started to weep.

Tuffy spotted them an hour later, pickled but jollier for it, sitting on a garden bench. Hating all forms of human emotion (a waste of time, in her opinion), she gave them a wide berth and walked down Guto's Gulley to collect more specimens.

*

That evening, Ayesha set the table in the grand dining room. She got out all the silver candlesticks and the best damask napkins. The service was Hanoverian, made for George V and bought from the estate of a famous New York hostess. She, Perrin and Stella picked bunches of flowers from the herbaceous borders and arranged them in silver bowls down the centre of the table. They put out the children's favourite toys and hand-drew name cards for the seating plan. Sleet had the rest of his cellar back to London, but she'd found some champagne and an excellent Riesling in the local supermarket to pair with Indian food. Stella and Perrin delivered handmade invitations that specified 'fancy dress'. Ayesha wore one of her mother's embroidered saris and the gold bangles she'd brought from India eight years earlier. She'd made Stella and Perrin matching saris from a piece of discarded curtain fabric and the three of them had ringed their eyes with kohl and painted bindis on their foreheads. Tony and Kitto had found some dusty old Nehru jackets in the dressing-up box. Morawase had wrapped several pieces of tulle, left over from Clarissa's wedding decorations, around her body and bound it with tassels borrowed from a pair of curtains. Jane had hand-painted a white shirt and trousers with vines and roses. Blaze and Joshua made turbans from bed covers. Toby and Tuffy wore matching costumes from old pieces of material tacked together. Clarissa stole the show by wearing her first wedding dress; the lace was a little torn and age-stained but under her heavy lace veil she didn't look a day over seventy.

The family, whose palates were rarely titillated by exotic ingredients, could hardly cope with layer upon layer of delicately spiced food. The massive sideboard was covered with different dishes: chicken, beef, fourteen types of vegetables, breads, condiments and chutneys. Clarissa admitted that it was 'perfectly bearable'.

'Is this how you ate as a child?' Tony asked, taking a second helping of bharwan bhindi, okra stuffed with ground herbs.

'I didn't eat with the family,' Ayesha told them. 'In the servants' hall we lived on dal, rice and beans.'

'Why didn't you eat with them?' Toby asked.

'As an illegitimate child, not even related to the family, I was lucky, apparently, not to be thrown to the dogs.' Ayesha concentrated on mopping up her chicken with a piece of naan bread. Jane and Blaze exchanged guilty looks.

'Who were your friends, Mummy?' Stella asked.

Frightened she might cry, Ayesha changed the subject and, raising her glass, proposed a toast. 'Here's to our family.'

Everyone – even Perrin and Stella, who drank a mixture of water and apple juice – drank and repeated, 'To our family.' Only Joshua mumbled the words and glanced surreptitiously at his watch; only a few hours before freedom.

Kitto stood up and recited Wordsworth, substituting forgotten lines with de-dum de-dahs. Toby sang. Stella and Perrin took off their scratchy saris and ran around the table. A summer storm broke and rain thrummed against the castle's panes of glass while flashes of lightning strobed. The family took their places again for pudding – kulfi, an ice cream made using evaporated milk, sugar, nuts and cardamom.

'Look what I found today,' Tuffy said, producing a box of dead insects.

'Not now, Tuffy!' Clarissa remonstrated.

Tuffy ignored her. 'They are all deformed.' She held up an earwig between her fingers and pointed to its distended thorax. Then she picked up a spider with nine legs.

'This one has a big head.' Stella pointed to another insect.

'I collected them all from Guto's Gulley,' Tuffy explained. 'It shows the lingering effect of arsenic on the landscape. I found many more examples within a seventy-five-metre radius.'

'What are you talking about?' Jane asked.

'Until the nineteenth century there were tin and arsenic mines all around the castle grounds. This area is littered with their remains. The family got rich off the thousands of tons of poisons dug out of the soil. The workforce had no safety equipment – they stopped up their mouths and noses with old rags. Many died.'

'I remember the miners' children having health issues years after the last shafts were closed at the end of the war,' Clarissa said.

'Did our children play in the gulley?' Joshua asked Blaze, his face twisted with worry.

'I don't think so.' She took his hand and squeezed it. 'But Kitto and I used to play there as children.'

'It's why you were born deformed,' Clarissa said to Blaze.

Joshua rose and leaned over the table, barely able to contain his fury. 'She has a birthmark, not a deformity.'

Clarissa pursed her lips.

'Don't tell Medieval Illusions,' Toby said, helping himself to another spoonful of ice cream. 'The Environment Act has a national priorities list. Landowners have a duty to clean up – whatever the cost. Guto's Gulley must be a mile long. It'll cost them more than they're paying for the property.'

There was silence around the table as the news sank in. Then Blaze stood up and kissed her malodorous nephew on the cheek. Joshua and Ayesha jumped up and down and hugged each other. Jane and Morawase kissed. Only Toby and Tuffy looked bemused.

'What do we do now?' Blaze asked. 'Send Sleet a legal letter? Inform Medieval Illusions?'

'Write to the Environment Agency?'

To everyone's surprise, Kitto got to his feet. 'I am going to manage this.'

His relations exchanged nervous glances. Kitto's last visit to London hadn't been a success. All his business or legal transactions had ended in failure.

'We wouldn't be in this mess if it wasn't for my incompetence,' he said firmly.

That night, Jane cut his hair. Kitto ironed his own shirt (badly) and hung his good suit next to the bath to encourage creases away. The whole family put him on the train the following morning. Kitto did his best to look brave as he waved goodbye, but the scene reminded him of being sent to prep school alone aged six and, once out of sight, he turned his head to the window willing the tears to stop.

The receptionist at Kerkyra Capital looked sceptically at the stooped grey-haired man in his ill-fitting suit. She could see the vestiges of good looks and noticed the signet ring on his pinkie finger, but this was not a Captain of Industry or one of her boss's normal kind of visitor.

Donna came to collect him. 'Hello, Lord Trelawney,' she said. 'Sir Thomlinson is very busy today, but I will try and get you in for twenty minutes.'

Kitto smiled outwardly; inwardly his bowels were liquifying – he hoped it wouldn't be too long. 'Ten minutes is ample,' he told her.

She asked him to wait on a beige sofa opposite a huge quotation stencilled on the wall in gold. *Greed is right. Greed works – Gordon*

Gekko. Through the plate-glass window to one side he saw scores of young people glued to computer screens. A constant stream of men and women made their way in and out of Sleet's office. When the door opened and closed, Kitto got a glimpse of the Vulgarian sitting at the desk at the other end of the room. He was on his third water when Donna returned.

'Please follow me.'

Kitto walked across the heavy wool carpet, his shoes making neither noise nor indentation. Sleet didn't look up from his screen as Kitto entered. He stood like a child waiting for attention before a headmaster.

After a few minutes, Sleet flicked him a glance. 'What do you want?'

Kitto clenched his buttocks and took a deep breath. From an inside jacket pocket, he produced a bunch of papers. 'These are some reports, prepared by my Aunt Tuffy, on the toxicity of the parkland at Trelawney.'

Sleet waved him away with his hand. 'The place is sold – didn't you hear? Go talk to the new owners.' His eyes returned to his screen. 'Take your boring little problems somewhere else. The Trelawneys have sponged off me for long enough. I'm sure your state will provide benefits – my turn's over.'

A whoosh of bravura shot through Kitto. 'This country has an Environment Act enshrined with national priorities. Under Section 1154 of the 2016 amendment, it is incumbent on landowners to remove hazardous waste and clean up the landscape they own, whatever the cost.'

Sleet couldn't hide his irritation. 'Stop wasting my time. Unlike some, I have a job.'

Kitto, former head of Pop at Eton, captain of cricket, *Tatler*'s 'Swoon of the Year' and subscriber to the Royal Society for the Protection of Birds, drew himself up to his full six foot two. 'You think you can buy or bribe yourself out of trouble. This time it'll be harder.'

'As I said, I don't own it. How can I be guilty of something I didn't know about?' Sleet, unruffled, waved his hands like a person trying to bat away a fly.

Kitto shuffled through the papers. 'Here is a receipt from the artist Andy Goldsworthy from 2012. He was commissioned to cover the mile-long Guto's Gulley in slate – a place where nothing would grow. You deliberately covered up toxic land.'

'I've never heard of Andy Goldsworthy!' This was true but he did remember vaguely, at his wife's request, signing the piece-of-commission note.

'Here's a report by Tuffy Scott detailing the effect that arsenic mining has had on the insect population.'

'She's an ancient old bat – no one cares what she thinks.' Sleet was beginning to feel a little nervous.

Kitto produced a photostat of the front page of the *Daily Blast*. 'You are quoted saying that your Aunt Tuffy is the most important scientist working today.'

Sleet, leaning back in his chair, beamed. 'I get it! You want to launch a charity to protect earwigs or field mice? You want a donation or something.' He'd finally figured out what the man was after and it was kind of amusing. 'I'll give you fifty pounds.'

Sleet's insouciance irritated Kitto. 'Centuries of mining have left a dangerous residue, making the land unsuitable for public use.' He placed a zoned map of the park on the desk – most of the areas around the house were shaded in red or yellow and stamped on both were internationally recognisable signs for poison. 'You sold Trelawney to Medieval Illusions using a standard contract which gives that company the right to cancel the contract at any point within twenty-four months if there was any significant misrepresentation by the vendor. All the cost for cleaning up the land would fall to you.'

Now he had Sleet's attention: he needed the sale to Medieval Illusions to cover his obligations. Without it, the parachute out of danger might not open. Sleet got to his feet. 'Are you threatening me?' He stabbed his finger in Kitto's direction.

The angrier the financier became, the calmer Kitto felt. 'I think we can come to an agreement.'

Sleet's face had turned a merry red. His eyes bulged. His voice rose an octave. 'I'll ruin you.'

Kitto laughed. 'You already have, old bean. I don't have a pot to piss in.' He took one last piece of paper out of his pocket. 'Sign here and we can lose these reports.' Raising his hands, he fluttered his fingers in the air. 'Gone like a puff of smoke.'

Sleet snatched the paper and read it. 'What the fuck?'

'Think about it.' Kitto looked at his watch. 'There's a train from Paddington in one hour. Either I take it back to Cornwall or I'll keep my appointment with Maxim LeGrand of Medieval Illusions.' He waited for Sleet to react, but the other man just stood there. With no further ideas, Kitto turned and walked out of the office towards the lift. As he pressed the button his legs nearly gave way and he held the wall to steady himself. The lift arrived and the steel doors opened. Yet again he'd failed. His heart broke for Ayesha. He stepped inside and felt the lift hurtle down forty-eight floors. With each number passed, his pride evaporated.

He should have let someone else come – stupid him for thinking he could wrest a deal from anyone. There was no appointment with Medieval Illusions – Sleet must have seen through his bluff. He'd lost his family's fortune, their home; and now, worst of all, his half-sister's custody of her daughter. The weight of shame was so heavy that he had to drag his feet to the Tube station.

'Lord Trelawney! Wait a minute, please.' Behind him, Kitto heard a woman's voice and the clack of heels. He stopped and turned. Donna was running towards him. In her left hand she clutched a piece of paper. Kitto took it from her and his eyes scanned the page. He stood up, two inches taller, and squared his shoulders. Kitto Trelawney had done something good with his life.

*

On July 30th, Ayesha and Sleet met in the Royal Courts of Justice in London. She was represented by Mishra; Sleet by three solicitors. Presiding over the hearing was a judge, Lady Keen. It was a closed session; there were no jury, press or members of the public.

Lady Keen cleared her throat and opened proceedings. Her kindly face, a cloud of white hair and blue eyes belied a fearsome reputation. She looked at Ayesha and Mishra and then at Sleet's team.

'In return for unfettered and unoccupied access to Trelawney Castle, your client, Sir Thomlinson Sleet, is prepared to sign away rights of access or any kind of custody to Miss Stella Sleet until such an age where she is desirous to seek any relationship?'

Sleet's leading solicitor looked at his client to make sure. Sleet nodded. 'He is.'

Then, turning to Mishra, the judge asked, 'Is your client, Ms Ayesha Scott, clear that in signing these papers she gives up any claim to maintenance or child support in perpetuity?'

'She is.' Although Mishra had advised otherwise, Ayesha was adamant about not taking one penny of Sleet's money.

The judge continued. 'Another aspect of this agreement is that Sir Thomlinson Sleet will sign a restraining order preventing any contact either in person or online with Ms Scott or his daughter Miss Stella Sleet. Any communications will be done via lawyers at his expense.'

Sleet's lawyers conferred and nodded.

'Is there anything else either of your clients wishes to add?'

'How do I know she won't renege on the deal?' Sleet burst out. 'That scum family is still there and there's less than forty-eight hours to go before we finally exchange.'

Mishra smiled and steepled his fingers. 'My client has more to lose than money. There is absolutely nothing she would do to jeopardise custody of her daughter. The entire family will vacate and the property will be free and clear for the new occupants as agreed on August 1st. She and her family also guarantee to have no contact whatsoever with Medieval Illusions and have signed an NDA not to talk about or disclose any information regarding the property, its artworks, landscape or history.'

'If the sale doesn't go through, she'll lose a lot more than a child,' Sleet threatened. The sale of the castle would wipe out his debts and give him the chance to start again. He was fond of Stella – she was a delightful, unspoiled and affectionate creature – but he could make more babies if he wanted to. Sleet smirked: he'd come out on top again – no child support, two less mouths to feed. Nevertheless, looking across the table at the mother of his child, he felt, for the first time, some respect. She had fought ferociously for custody of their daughter.

The faithful Donna was standing by his car. It was raining again and she balanced a crumpled newspaper over her head to shield her recently set hair. Sanjay held a large umbrella over his boss to protect him from the deluge.

'What are you doing here?' Sleet asked.

'I came to see if you were OK, or needed anything,' Donna said. 'I imagine that was difficult.'

Sleet looked at her. 'If you were better-looking, I'd marry you.'

Donna, unsure if this was a joke, a compliment or a put-down, summoned a thin smile. 'I am already married.'

'You are?' Sleet was astonished.

'To Rhydian. Thirty years next month. You've met him at the Christmas events.'

'I did?' Sleet had no recollection. The thought that Donna wasn't devoted 24/7 to his cause was perturbing. 'Children?'

'No time.' The corners of Donna's mouth turned down and she gave a sad shrug. 'Working for you is more than a job.'

'You took two weeks' holiday last summer!' Sleet remembered how furious it'd made him.

Sanjay opened the car door and Sleet got into the back. Donna hovered. They were going to the same place; she assumed he'd offer her a lift.

'See you at the office,' he said, before nodding to Sanjay to close the door.

Donna stood for some time watching the car wend its way through traffic along the Strand. Her hairdo got ruined as she walked along the road to the bus stop. Looking down, she saw that her newish pair of Russell and Bromley court shoes were soaked, and the pale tan leather had turned a muddy brown. For the first time, Donna wondered if there wasn't more to life than running around after Sleet. For many years Rhydian had been talking about moving to his hometown of Aberystwyth. Donna wouldn't need to worry about expensive shoes in Wales. A taxi drove past at high speed, sending the watery contents of a pothole splaying across the pavement and splashing Donna's suit: there'd be no need for twinsets, pussy-bow shirts or nylons in Wales either. The week before, she'd received a postcard from Rodita who, with Wilfredo, had bought a beach hotel on an island. Donna's heart lurched when she saw the white sandy beach and palm trees.

She waited for the bus in the lee of a doorway. Her phone beeped. It was Sleet. *Where the fuck are you? There's work to do.* Donna contemplated the quietness of Wales: walks in the mountains, keeping chickens, making marmalade, long afternoons with her husband and his family in the pub. She'd always fancied taking up needlework, learning another language, having longer holidays. The more she thought about these options, the more despondent she felt. She hit Reply on her phone. *Be with you in a jiffy.*

*

On her way back to Trelawney, Ayesha stopped to pick up Stella from Blaze and Joshua's home. She was happy to see Tony in residence. 'I am a useless house guest. Can't boil an egg. Frightened of getting in the way,' he said, looking nervously at Joshua.

'You're no trouble,' Joshua said warmly. 'And it's lovely for Perrin to have an uncle around.'

Ayesha, seeing the extended family unit, felt a sudden pang.

'Will you be all right?' Blaze asked. 'Are you sure you don't want to stay here for a bit? There's lots of room.'

'Are you really moving in with Clarissa?' Joshua asked incredulously.

Ayesha evaded their questions. It was easier. They put her long embraces down to a difficult day. Before leaving, Ayesha gave Blaze a small package. It contained two golden bangles brought from India nine years earlier.

'I had the date of my mother's birth engraved on one and her death on the other,' she explained. 'And your three initials on both – AK, JB and BS.'

'That was sweet,' Blaze said as she, Joshua, Tony and Perrin waved goodbye to the departing car.

Tony said nothing. During his long years, he'd slipped in and out of alternative lives and recognised the signs. 'Good luck, darling girl,' he said in such a low voice that no one else heard.

Ayesha couldn't get a nagging thought out of her head. Like a wasp trapped in a glass jar, it buzzed and bounced around inside her brain. She'd overlooked something vital. It haunted her all the way back to Cornwall, while she was giving her daughter a bath and making her supper. Climbing into the narrow bed next to Stella's, she was exhausted but could not quieten her thoughts. What was it? Outside, rain lashed and drummed against the window. She watched her sleeping daughter's face, trying to push away any lingering fear. The papers were signed, the agreement had been ratified in the presence of a judge, but she was still scared – what parent would ever swap their child for money? Someone so heartless would stop at nothing.

20

August 2017

Just after midnight, unable to sleep, Ayesha slipped out of Stella's bed. She stopped by the kitchen, chose a stubby knife and walked along the corridor to the Grinling Gibbons room. Pushing open the door, she turned on the light and sat cross-legged on the floor opposite her mother's portrait, a large round pendant cast in bronze. When she left India, Ayesha had only enough money to mark her mother's grave with a simple black granite cross inscribed with her name and dates: 1972–2008. The pendant, six inches in diameter, was based on a photograph of the eighteen-year-old Anastasia and, set in the heart of the oak tree, was a far grander and more fitting memorial.

'I brought you home, Mama,' Ayesha whispered. Taking the knife out of her pocket, she etched her and Stella's initials into the wood below Anastasia's image. Turning on her phone torch, she ran the beam of light over the faces of the past Earls of Trelawney. Those men were her forebears, but they were not her people; all they shared was a shadow of a genetic code and a passion for a castle. Had they, like her, found Trelawney inspiring and overwhelming? A bottomless pit of need and demands? There was and always would be something more – a broken window, a sagging pipe, a damaged crenellation. She felt for the eldest sons, burdened by the heavy responsibility of caring for the place, and for their younger siblings, whose lives were defined by the lightness of their inheritance. And now, after eight hundred years, Ayesha was breaking the hereditary chains: she was the last Trelawney; no family members would live there again. Sitting beneath the portraits, she imagined her forebears' recriminations. 'Of course, she let us down – she's a woman, what do you expect?' Ayesha wondered whether to be ashamed or proud. Were traditions the fabric that kept society together or the shackles that prevented progress? With the arrival of Medieval Illusions, Trelawney, a house designed to delight a few, would thrill many hundreds of thousands. What, she wondered, would Anastasia think?

Suddenly the wasp burst out of its jar. Of course! Sleet had, unwittingly, given her his password: Anastasia 22.5.72. She ran to her study and turned on the computer. The machine purred into life. Ayesha typed 'Southern Trust' into the engine. Seconds later, the log-in page appeared. She tapped the first of Sleet's account numbers into the upper line, and then her mother's name and date of birth into the password box, and held her breath. The screen dissolved and there on the monitor were all Sleet's accounts. Clicking through them at speed, she read with surprise that the figures were in hundreds of thousands, not millions, let alone billions. Was there missing money or was Sleet's fortune less capacious than he liked to admit? It was 3 a.m. Sitting back in her chair, she forced herself to take a moment's reflection. With one and a half hours left, she had to focus and prioritise.

She cracked her finger joints one at a time and stretched. Slowly but surely, she started to work her way through the different accounts, hoping the password would give the bearer rights to make alterations. The first couple of financial records were minor. The third was more interesting. Titled 'TS1', it contained the deeds of his first wife, Marion's, house. It was registered to a company at 186 Harley Street and Sleet was the sole beneficiary. Ayesha suspected that Marion had also been promised financial security and a home in her own name. The documents made clear this wasn't the case. She hadn't met any of the previous Lady Sleets but felt a certain sympathy with all three. With no idea if it would work, she deleted Sleet's name and made Marion Sleet the sole beneficiary of TS1. She repeated the exercise in TS2 and TS3 for wives two and three, Kelly and Liora. Then she removed Sleet's name from all documents in which his four other children were cited as beneficiaries and put their mothers in as protectors. Her final act was to put the house in the Boltons in a trust for Stella's benefit, accessible when she turned eighteen.

It was 4.45 a.m.; hardly any time to make further changes. Her last decision was to reset all the passwords. Warning lights flashed on each. *This step is irreversible. No way of retrieval.* Ayesha typed gobbledegook into each: a random list of letters, numbers and signs. She would never remember it – nor would anyone else. She smiled, imagining Sleet's fury when his trusted password failed to work followed by hysterical attempts to crack into his own accounts. It would surely become a record 'pencil' day.

She ran upstairs to her room and, taking two small suitcases out of the cupboard, she packed some papers, essential clothes, and toys. She took one book, an anthology, *Knapsack*, which her father Enyon Trelawney had taken to war. The day before, she'd withdrawn £25,000 in cash and she hid this in the lining of her suitcase; it was enough to keep them going until she found work. She transferred the balance, £150,000, to Yasmin's personal account: the settling of a promise, or part of it, made.

She left her other belongings neatly packed or hung in wardrobes. She wouldn't need the designer clothes, handbags or make-up. Putting the keys to Trelawney, her car and their London abode on Sleet's desk, she topped the pile with her fake diamond ring, her credit cards and chequebooks. She woke and dressed her sleepy daughter. Carrying the two small cases under one arm, she took Stella's hand and guided her down the stairs to the basement. Pulling open the trapdoor, they climbed down into the secret tunnel. Built in the seventeenth century by one of her Cavalier ancestors to escape Roundhead invaders, it led from the centre of the castle all the way to the estuary. When mother and daughter arrived at the water's edge they were covered in dust and cobwebs. A few days earlier, Ayesha had hidden a rowing boat in the reeds. She helped Stella in, loaded the luggage and pushed off. The current was strong and the boat, though old, moved easily through the water. Ayesha only needed the oars to steer. They glided silently downstream past Trelawney. At the estuary's deepest point, in view of the castle, Ayesha unclasped her mother's ruby pendant from her neck and wound the chain around Enyon's *Knapsack*. Tossing the bundle into the water, she watched it sink into murky depths. Picking up the oars again, she rowed to another village further down the estuary where a pre-booked taxi was already waiting.

The driver got out and, looking down into the boat, his heart skipped. Perhaps it was the freshness of the air combined with the golden glow of the early-morning sun, but the young woman's beauty was so unexpected, so luminous, that he wondered if she was an apparition. Transfixed, he stood rooted to the spot.

Ayesha threw the two cases up on to the quay and helped Stella out of the boat. 'Could you take these?' Ayesha pointed to their bags. To the driver, her voice was soft, husky, with a lilt, a trace of an accent he couldn't quite place.

'Hello?' Ayesha said. The driver, his trance broken but still speechless, put the suitcases into the boot of the car. Then, straightening his back, he held open the car door for the little girl.

'Are you going to sit with your sister?' he asked, finally finding some words.

'That's my mummy,' Stella said.

Ayesha got into the car and did up Stella's and then her own belt.

'Where to?' he said, not daring to look in the rear-view mirror in case he was mesmerised once again.

'Bristol airport, please.' Ayesha settled back into the seat and, as the car set off, she turned to look at Trelawney. A fiery sun had risen over the estuary, burning through the mist. The water's surface, ruffled by a slight breeze, glittered and sparkled. The pasture was an emerald green and the sky a bright neon blue. In its midst sat the castle, its facade glowing. Trelawney had never looked more lovely.

Leaning forward in her seat, she addressed the driver. 'Can you pull over?'

He stopped the car in a gateway and Ayesha took one last look at her old home. On impulse, she raised her hand to salute the castle. Perhaps it was a scudding cloud but the windows seemed to wink at her, flashing gold and then dark in the sunlight.

Ten miles before the airport, they stopped at a village post office where Ayesha bought her daughter a banana and a bun. At the counter, she took a thick manila envelope out of her bag. It was addressed to Clarissa, the Dowager Countess of Trelawney, c/o *The Countess Investigates*, and contained enough material for a TV series devoted to the misdemeanours of Sir Thomlinson Sleet. It did not include information that might expose herself or details of the Iranian deal (the latter could be used in case of an emergency only). Nor were there any references to the Environment Act or contamination of Trelawney land. Kitto had struck the deal: she got Stella; Sleet got their silence.

The envelope did contain other incriminating information: emails written (and intercepted on MySpy) over a period of eight weeks from June to the end of August 2016 to senior executives at firms with large holdings of Whaley Precision Engineering questioning the safety of Whaley's new graphite blades; there were copies of messages between Sleet and his senior executives, including Rodita Della Cruz, outlining the strategy to destroy Whaley's reputation and buy the company at a knockdown price. Also included were plans for the merger with the Taiwanese manufacturer TLG made before Whaley's IPO. Thanks to the copious work done by Blaze and Joshua, there were papers exposing links between Kerkyra Capital, Sir Thomlinson Sleet, Alabaster Analytics and the close financial and personal ties between Ms Khan, Dr Lala and a man high on Interpol's most wanted list, Nanos Copje, which included joint ownership of a crypto mining plant in Tirana.

Another folder revealed forty examples of breaches in electoral guidelines by the prospective candidate for Austell. Sir Thomlinson Sleet had overspent his allowable quota on advertising, entertainment and travel by 10,000 per cent.

Before pushing the manila envelope into the post box, Ayesha replayed her motives for wanting to expose Sleet. Revenge? Vindictiveness? Justice? A combination of all those, but mostly she didn't want Sleet to have the opportunity to ruin more lives. Ayesha would recover; John Whaley would not.

The car sped through the countryside. Stella, who'd been playing with her toy pony, looked up at her mother. 'What will happen to Mickey?' she asked.

In her hurry to get everything ready, Ayesha had forgotten what story to tell her daughter about her pony. 'He'll stay at Trelawney.'

'Will we see him soon?' Stella's lip trembled.

'Yes, and there'll be other ponies.'

A large tear rolled down Stella's face. 'When will I see my daddy?'

Remembering the pain of being fatherless, Ayesha's insides twisted and yet here she was inflicting the same destiny on her beloved daughter. Not wanting to lie, she distracted the little girl by pointing out a heron on the side of a river. The ploy would only work a few times. One day they'd return to England to claim her daughter's inheritance: perhaps then, Stella would seek a relationship with Sleet. In the meantime, Ayesha resolved to give her daughter double the reassurance, triple the support and quadruple the love to make up any deficit.

Reaching the airport, she paid the taxi driver and, holding Stella's hand, led her to a ladies' bathroom. From there she sent Clarissa a text. *Mission accomplished.*

High time, Clarissa replied immediately.

Ayesha didn't trust Sleet to abide by his restraining order and, fearful of the consequences of his fury, she decided, for the time being, to sever all ties with her family and her former life. If the price of safety was anonymity and exile, she was prepared to pay. Her next step was to erase all of her telephone's contents. Then she flushed the SIM card down the loo and chucked the handset into a nearby bin. Argentina was one of the few countries that neither she nor Sleet had visited so she bought two single tickets to Buenos Aires with cash. She and Stella boarded the flight using their new Irish passports, supplied at considerable speed and expense by Private Investigator Lawrence Digby. The photograph, taken the previous week, showed a young woman with scraped-back hair and a cautious smile. Her new name, Alwyn Tree, happened to be an anagram of Trelawney. It would take time to finesse this unfamiliar identity. For now, if anyone asked, she was recently widowed and travelling with her only daughter. Her degrees and prizes were registered to another person, but she'd keep her guide stars close: Isabella d'Este, Artemisia Gentileschi and other brilliant mentors who'd carved uncompromising roles in hostile worlds.

Settling Stella into her seat, Ayesha realised that Declan was missing. There was no stone in her heart, his all-pervasive gloom had evaporated. Perhaps, she thought, Mr D. Malregard doesn't like economy travel.

Ayesha was leaving England with fewer possessions than she'd arrived with nine years earlier. Then she'd had three suitcases and a plan based mainly on her mother's wishes: to become part of her father's family, to live in their castle and marry a fabulously wealthy man. She scored the hat-trick and, in the process, nearly lost her sanity. Sleet had beguiled, hoodwinked, and discarded her. Her naive younger self had taken his promises at face value. No one warned her that nightmares lurk in the shadows of dreams.

Her mother's life had been defined by what she'd lost; her husband's determined by what he could gain. Ayesha's future would be inspired by different criteria. Moving abroad wasn't running away, it was galloping full speed ahead on her terms. For all of her short life

Ayesha had been known as someone's daughter or wife. From this day forward, she would be quintessentially and authentically herself. No more compromising, no more trying to live up to others' standards or expectations. She and Stella would make and live by their own rules. Ayesha would teach her daughter how to laugh, love, fail, flail, be angry, sad, proud, humble, and how to face the future head on with grace and fortitude. They'd toast memories in moonbeams and dip experiences in rainbows.

She placed their carry-ons in the overhead locker. Clicking the locker shut, she sat down next to her daughter.

Stella looked up from her book. 'What's happening, Mummy?'

Ayesha smiled and kissed the top of her daughter's head. 'We're going on a great big adventure.'

Acknowledgements

This book was started in lockdown, a period of gloom, confinement and fear – hardly conducive to writing a social satire set in a cosmopolitan, free-wheeling world. Highlights of that period included unexpected time with my three beloved daughters, Nell, Clemency and Rose; a rotation of daily walks with my sister Emmy and friends Milly and Hen; and frequent calls with Fi and Lisa. One of the reasons that Ayesha, the heroine of this book, gets into so much trouble is that she doesn't have the great privilege and support of close female friendships.

My agent, Sarah Chalfant, is always my first reader, and I am indebted to her analysis, encouragement and business acumen. Her team at The Wylie Agency, including Jessica Bullock, Rebecca Nagel and Charles Buchan, have shepherded my books through different technologies and markets with the utmost skill.

This is the third time that Alexandra Pringle, editor supreme, has chosen one of my books for Bloomsbury. Immeasurable thanks are due for her belief in my work and for the guidance and generosity she's shown at every turn. Her decision to pursue new challenges will leave an enormous void in publishing, but her legacy – wave after wave of words by many wonderful writers – will inspire new generations.

Her successor, Emma Herdman, has been a joy to work with. This book has benefitted from two different approaches and skill sets. I'd also like to extend my thanks to the other 'bloomsberries' – Nigel Newton, Paul Baggaley, Elisabeth Denison, Sarah-Jane

Forder, Sarah Bance and Carmen Balit – who have helped transform a baggy manuscript into an object of beauty.

This is my fourth collaboration with Shelley Wanger at PRH. To be published in America by one of the great houses and be part of her illustrious stable is a dizzying accolade.

This book picks up the stories of a family, the subjects of my last novel, *House of Trelawney*. I wanted to see how the same characters had fared since the financial crash of 2008 and to explore the changes wrought in society, finance and politics. Set in 2016, *High Time* touches on many contemporary headwinds including cryptocurrency, Brexit, financial skullduggery, art world shenanigans and the shadowlands of international politics. I am grateful to the following for sharing their intel: my father, Jacob; Francesco Goedhuis, Amy Thompson, Susan Adams, Charity Brandreth and BL. And to those generous readers and dear friends who ploughed through and helped improve early drafts: Mala Goankar, Rosie Boycott and Jenni Russell.

Last but not least, my thanks to Yoav, for his unwavering support, good humour and ability to help find the trees in the woods.

A Note on the Author

Hannah Rothschild is an author, filmmaker, philanthropist and businesswoman. Her first novel, *The Improbability of Love*, was shortlisted for the Baileys Women's Prize for Fiction and won the Bollinger Everyman Wodehouse Prize for Comic Fiction. Her second novel, *House of Trelawney*, was runner-up for the Everyman Wodehouse. The first woman to chair London's National Gallery, she was awarded a CBE for services to literature and philanthropy.

A Note on the Type

The text of this book is set in Linotype Stempel Garamond, a version of Garamond adapted and first used by the Stempel foundry in 1924. It is one of several versions of Garamond based on the designs of Claude Garamond. It is thought that Garamond based his font on Bembo, cut in 1495 by Francesco Griffo in collaboration with the Italian printer Aldus Manutius. Garamond types were first used in books printed in Paris around 1532. Many of the present-day versions of this type are based on the *Typi Academiae* of Jean Jannon cut in Sedan in 1615.

Claude Garamond was born in Paris in 1480. He learned how to cut type from his father and by the age of fifteen he was able to fashion steel punches the size of a pica with great precision. At the age of sixty he was commissioned by King Francis I to design a Greek alphabet, and for this he was given the honourable title of royal type founder. He died in 1561.